THE SIGN OF THE GRANDMASTER

Zharkov saw Gilead only twice during the twenty-five years after their first match.

On both occasions, Zharkov had killed him. On both occasions, the Grandmaster had returned.

And now the medallion had surfaced, and Alexander Zharkov knew what it meant. He knew it as surely as he knew the sun would rise in the morning. He had feared it for years.

Justin Gilead—the Grandmaster—was alive.

Unconsciously, Zharkov's hands lifted to the high Russian military collar he wore.

He tore open the collar. Beneath it, burned into his flesh and scarred into ugly permanence, was the mark of the coiled snake.

GRANDMASTER

WARREN MURPHY
& MOLLY COCHRAN

PINNACLE BOOKS **NEW YORK**

*For Sondra O. and the
folks who live on the hill*

This novel is a work of fiction. Names, characters, places, and
incidents are either the product of the author's imagination or
are used fictitiously. Any resemblance to actual events or places
or persons, living or dead, is entirely coincidental.

GRANDMASTER

Copyright © 1984 by Warren Murphy and Molly Cochran

All rights reserved, including the right to reproduce this book
or portions thereof in any form.

An original Pinnacle Books edition, published for the first time
anywhere.

First printing/October 1984

ISBN: 0-523-42205-9

Can. ISBN: 0-523-43195-3

Cover art by Stephanie and Mark Gerber

Printed in the United States of America

PINNACLE BOOKS, INC.
1430 Broadway
New York, New York 10018

9 8 7 6 5 4 3 2 1

Somewhere a bell faintly tinkled. The room was as large as a castle courtyard, lit by clusters of tall scented candles in each of the four corners, but the ceilings were so high that no light reached there, and looking up gave him the feeling of staring up at a dead sky, on a night without stars.

Figures scurried by along the base of the walls. Their movements were soft, and although he could see only shadows, he knew that they were women.

Three feather-filled cushions, each of them eight feet square, were piled atop each other in the center of the room. A woman lay on the cushions, and he knew, without knowing, that she was the one he had been summoned to see.

He hesitated, but the woman beckoned him forward with a slow movement of her graceful arm. She was naked but for a golden chain wrapped three times around her waist. As he drew closer he could see that her hair was black and long, pulled forward over her left shoulder so that it draped across her breasts. Even in the dim candlelight, her hair glistened like oiled glass and her eyes seemed made up of thousands of individual amber crystals, each of them reflecting the light from the candles in the room. Closer to her, the scent of incense was stronger, almost overpowering. He drew it deep into his lungs and felt warmth radiate from inside him.

He stood now in front of the cushions, his knees almost touching them, looking down at the woman. Her body was as artfully arranged as an old master's composition; though she

1

was naked, the placement of her hair and the shadows that darkened her made it impossible for him to see her clearly.

"Do you know why I have had you brought here?" she asked him in Russian. Her voice was musical, its pitch exactly the same as that of the bell that still tinged softly from one of the far corners of the room. He breathed deeply again; his body felt as if it were losing its muscles; he wondered if she had spoken or if he had merely imagined the bell was speaking to him.

She was looking at him, waiting for an answer. He tried to speak, but no words came. He shook his head.

"Because you belong to me," she said softly. Her eyes never left his face.

Belong to her? No. No one belonged to anyone else. He summoned up his will and again tried to speak. This time, with effort, he forced the words out. "Madam, I . . ."

She ignored him. "From the day of your birth, you have belonged to me."

"And if I do not so choose?" he said thickly. He was surprised that he had been able to speak the words; speaking was such an effort.

"The choice is not yours," she said, a hint of annoyance tingeing the smooth, throaty sounds. "You are only a man. Do not forget that. You are limited by your senses, your mortality. But I will make you more than a man."

She paused as if awaiting an answer, but he could no longer speak. The very presence of the woman seemed to obliterate his sensibility and reason. He wanted only to be invited to lie down with her on the soft cushions, to rest his body and his aching, confused mind.

"You are my chosen one," she said. "I have searched the earth for you."

He stared at her, unable to tear his eyes away from her shadowy face. "Why?" he asked softly, feeling cold. "Who am I to you?"

A smile flickered around the edge of her mouth. "In all things there is opposition, reversal. Yin and yang, light and darkness, good and evil. In those beings of power, there are also two sides. Do you understand?"

He drew a deep breath to try to clear his mind, but instead his lungs were filled again with the sinuous fire of the incense. This place was somehow infused with magic, he knew, power-

ful magic. Lapping around the borders of his consciousness
was fear. The woman was soft and dark and smooth and rich
as dreams, but there was no comfort in her for him.

"Is there someone who will come to this place?" he asked.
"Someone to challenge me, perhaps? An evil man . . ."

The woman's smile broadened into a coarse, harsh laugh
that resounded through the room.

The man did not understand. He waited for her to explain,
but instead she rolled over onto her back without speaking.
Suddenly her body came alive, breasts thrust forward, the
dark curled hair between her legs sharply visible in the
candlelight. She was holding something in her hands. It was a
snake fashioned out of gold, long and curved into an *S*. Its
scales were meticulously carved, its mouth open with its
tongue darting out as if it sensed danger.

She placed it between her legs and drew it slowly between
her thighs. Her eyes deigned to meet his. "Come to me," she
commanded.

He came.

She held the gold snake up to him. Its luster seemed to
grow in intensity, hurting his eyes. He feared the snake.

"Take it," she said.

Trembling, he accepted the carved serpent. It burned his
hands. His very soul seemed to gasp at the contact.

"An evil man has already come," she purred. Her voice
licked him with promise. "The Prince of Death has come. *My*
evil man."

He closed his eyes. He understood. "My goddess," he
said.

She placed her silky hands on top of his. At her touch, his
fear of the snake's power vanished. With a sigh, he snapped
the golden serpent in two.

"Yes," she said softly into his ear, filling him with a deep,
perverse lust that he realized he had longed for all his life.
She had been right: He had no choice. His destiny was to
serve her, to drink her magic, to live in spheres high above
the scrambling and rutting of common men.

"My Prince of Death. You have the seeds of greatness in
you. I will make those seeds bloom, my prince. And you will
kill the golden snake for me."

"I will," he promised.

Then she opened to him and wrapped her body around his and, as the bell still faintly tinkled and the air grew heavier with the scents of incense and carnality, she took him into the depths of his own darkness.

Book One

THE COILED SNAKE

The dock on Pihlaja Island was deserted, as it always was in Helsinki's black early mornings. The patrolman yawned and checked the luminous face of his wristwatch. It was an hour before dawn. Just another ninety minutes and he would drag his chilled body home and bury it in the warmth of his wife.

He heard a faint scratching sound behind him and he wheeled, his right hand slapping down toward his heavy leather police holster, but then he relaxed as he saw a solitary wharf rat running down the middle of the wooden dock.

He smiled grimly, faintly embarrassed at his display of nerves. The *punkkarit*, the local hoodlums, had everybody frightened. Each day, the newspapers carried stories of their plundering raids, and all the members of the police's tiny dock squad had been warned to be extra watchful while on duty. Moored ships could be a paradise for vandals and burglars.

The patrolman's footfalls echoed heavily along the bleak wharf. His breath blew out in clouds. Soon all the harbors in the Gulf of Finland would be closed with the first ice. In the distance a sleeping tanker sent tubes of yellow light over the black gulf. Nearer, tied up to the condemned section of wharf where the policeman walked, another vessel rocked silently on the water. It was a fishing boat, sizable but ancient, a black, empty hulk without even an identifying name on its transom. He walked toward it. The boat was obviously abandoned, although he had never seen it before.

7

Suddenly, behind him, the numberless rats housed in the decayed pier house set up an indignant chatter and scattered in all directions. The policeman turned toward the source of the noise, a thin line of sweat rising across his forehead. *Punkkarit?* Here? He pulled his night stick out of his belt as he approached the low stone building.

But it wasn't the kids with their Mohawk haircuts and snapping switchblades. He cursed softly and smiled with relief at the dim figure crouched against the crumbling facade of the pier house. The man was asleep. He was dressed in a ragged sailor's jacket and a pair of filthy trousers. Under his head was a tattered old duffel, which the man used as a pillow.

"Hey, what's this?" the officer said in Finnish, prodding the man with his toe. The vagabond snorted awake and strained to focus his eyes on the policeman. "Get moving. You can't sleep here."

He repeated the command in Swedish. The man stirred slowly. "And take your things. You won't be coming back." He pointed at the duffel with his night stick.

The derelict obeyed. He brought himself to his feet shakily. Then, shivering, he dragged the ragged canvas bag away from the wall. He looked up at the officer with watery eyes.

"Well, go on," the policeman said, gesturing with his head toward the end of the dock. The man padded away softly, his back bent. The officer watched him go, then walked back to the black boat.

He stepped carefully over its mooring lines and scanned the vessel with his flashlight. Over the place where the ship's name normally would have been, a black-painted board hung suspended from two hooks.

That was odd, he thought. It was as if someone had purposely concealed the identity of the old hulk. He leaned over the pier, reached out with his stick, and lifted the board. For a moment the name *Kronen* gleamed in white letters against the black crupper. The policeman straightened and let the board fall back against the vessel with a slap. He moved farther along the pier, the beam from the flashlight moving in a straight line along the length of the craft. He stopped, looked at the boat again, and shook his head in puzzlement. Why would anyone try to conceal the name of a boat? Unless the boat had been stolen.

He reached behind him and pulled his small mobile radio from the leather holder on his belt. Just before he depressed the button, his neck snapped backward and his spine lurched with a painful blow from the rear. The flashlight hurtled out of his hand into the water below, and the radio dropped onto the wooden dock with a muffled thud.

"What . . . what . . .'' the policeman groaned, buckling to his knees.

He twisted his head and saw the hobo standing above him, looking completely different from the boozy tramp he had chased from the dock. The man he saw now was as blankly efficient as a machine, avoiding the policeman's eyes as he yanked him to his feet.

"No, please,'' the policeman began. But by then the knife in the hobo's hands was already singing upward.

The officer gasped once, his eyes bulging in shock as the blade tore into the left side of his throat and sliced up to his right ear. His hands struck out, jerking wildly, as if they had been electrified. His feet skidded. A stream of bubbling blood hissed out from his neck, forming a cloud of vapor in the cold air as it shot forward in an arc. His head fell back on the hobo's shoulder.

Silently, four black-clad men appeared on the deck of the black boat. The *Kronen*'s engine roared to life. Keeping his head down to avoid the stream of blood, the hobo hoisted the body and heaved it into the gulf. The policeman's lifeless face, still bearing an expression of horrified surprise, shimmered near the surface for a moment.

The boat was pulling out. The hobo kicked the policeman's radio into the water, ran back for his duffel, tossed it on deck, and leaped after it. He caught hold of a rail and pulled himself on board as the *Kronen* sped out of the harbor.

His knife and the right side of his face were bathed in blood.

The captain relinquished the wheel to a crewman, then turned and stared without expression at the blood- and sweat-soaked man who stood before him, as if trying to decide whether or not to allow his visitor to remain on board. His face, dark and windburned around intelligent eyes that seemed incapable of surprise, held traces of both contempt and amusement for the man with the duffel who waited silently for his verdict.

"I'm only a smuggler, you know," the captain said finally, his English lilted with Scandinavian cadences. "Killing police is not part of our contract."

The man didn't answer. A heavy drop of perspiration rolled unnoticed down his face, streaking through the caked blood on his cheek. The muscles around his jaw were clenched tightly.

"Ah," the captain said with disgust and jerked his thumb toward the cabin below.

With a ragged sigh, the man hurried down the companionway.

Below deck, he stood in the small main cabin, alone, rubbing his arms to ward off the sudden chill that always came over him after moments of great fear. With some surprise, he noticed that the knife he had used to kill the Finnish policeman, a Bundswehr combat model, was still clenched in his fist. He unclasped the hand with effort, and the Bundswehr clattered to the floor. Its outline was imprinted on his blood-encrusted palm. He stooped over to pick it up, rinsed it off under the saltwater tap of the sink, dried it carefully, and replaced it in his coat pocket.

How long? he thought as he washed the brown film from his hands. He was forty-four years old, the oldest active field agent he knew. How many more border runs could he make before his nerve gave out completely? How much terror could a man stand in his life? He closed his eyes to the salt sting of the water as it ran over his face and head.

He dried himself on a rag remnant of a towel and, still shivering, sat down at the cabin's rough plank table. From his duffel bag he removed a watertight plastic pouch, which he opened and emptied onto the table. He had already checked everything in the pouch three times, but the difference between three times and four times someday might be the difference between living and dying.

He nodded silently as he checked the bag's contents in the dim light of the single oil lamp. There were two well-forged Finnish passports for a husband and wife. There was a Russian identity card with his own photograph on it and a set of Russian work papers. There was a fully loaded Swiss Hammerli eight-shot pistol. Inside a slim manila envelope was two thousand dollars in American money, an unimpressive amount of Russian rubles, and his American passport under his true name of Frank Riesling.

Enough, perhaps, to get him into and out of Russia with his two illegal passengers. Certainly enough to get him killed if he was caught before he reached Moscow.

But all this for a chess player?

He thought momentarily of the dead policeman, and his hands trembled. He bolted from his place at the table and ran to the small ship's head in the rear of the cabin where he vomited into the stained, smelly toilet. A policeman murdered? For a chess player? Was it worth it?

As he sat again at the table and began scooping the contents back into the black plastic pouch, he knew he would have to try to sleep, despite his jangled nerves. He had not slept the night before, and the journey ahead was a long one.

The Finnish fishing boat would take him to Hamina, near the Russian border. Then Saarinen, the captain, would send two of his three crewmen to take Riesling northward, overland, on a route that ran west of the Russian city of Vyborg.

Directly north of Vyborg, they would leave him, and he would be on his own. The trip into Vyborg itself was going to be a bitch without sleep, he knew. On foot all the way, which was rough in October, even with the help of a corrupt old border patrol guard who averted his eyes in return for a healthy bribe and got to secretly stick it to his superiors for busting him from a posh posting in Leningrad to serve out his commission in the frozen provinces.

If he managed to cross the border and *if* he managed to avoid the KGB agents on spy-catching duty in Vyborg, then he would have a train ride into Leningrad and an hour's flight to Moscow. The chess player, whose name was Kutsenko, and his wife were supposed to be ready to leave Moscow immediately. The three of them would go back the way Riesling had come. In Hamina, they would board Captain Saarinen's fishing boat and be on their way to Stockholm.

All right, he thought. It had started out badly with the policeman, but it was manageable. Riesling had made the trip a dozen times.

But never before, he thought bitterly, on such short notice. Never before without first getting advance approval from headquarters. Was he right to go? Was he right to chance it?

Stubbornly, he pushed the questions out of his mind. Two hours to Hamina.

He looked longingly at the small bunk across the cabin as Captain Saarinen entered, a grease-smudged bottle of Koskenkorva vodka in one hand. In his other hand was the remains of a large, toothmarked *makkara* sausage, and he gave off its fumes as well as those of French Gitane cigarettes, which he smoked constantly, insisting that the dark brown tobacco, unlike the "blonde" used in American cigarettes, was healthful for the human organism. Somehow, it seemed not to have done anything healthful for his chronic cough.

As soon as Saarinen walked through the doorway, Riesling rose automatically, and his hand darted toward the pistol inside the plastic pouch. When he saw it was the captain, he peered past him toward the small companionway behind.

"Sit down, sit down," Saarinen said with annoyance. "There's some trouble, but nothing to do with the business back on the wharf." He lit a blackened candle lamp on the table. The light cast huge shadows on the grease-spattered wall.

"What, then?" Riesling asked coldly.

Saarinen gestured to Riesling's empty chair with his chin and pulled a cracked mug from behind the sink. "You," the captain said, his dark eyes now twinkling like a satyr's. "I have brought you on this run for many months, yes? I do not even know your name, and yet I know you like a brother. And like a brother, I worry for you. Always nervous, always expecting the worst. That is your way, but you will drive yourself to sickness, my friend." He splashed some vodka into the mug and took a swig from the bottle himself.

"You agreed to take me to Hamina," Riesling said stubbornly.

Saarinen sighed. "Hamina, yes. But I do not think my men can take you to Vyborg."

Riesling reached into his coat and produced a thick envelope filled with currency. He slid it along the tabletop toward Saarinen. Wordlessly the captain hefted the envelope and stuffed it into his pocket. "Enough for Hamina," he said.

"What trouble?" Riesling asked quietly.

Saarinen poured a long draft into his mouth and exhaled noisily. "The Russians have doubled up on their Finnish border patrols," he said. "Your friend in Vyborg has been removed."

"The old man at the guard station?"

Saarinen nodded. "Shot."

"What about you?"

"The ship's running empty," Saarinen said. The *Kronen* had made a tidy fortune for Saarinen by illegally transporting food and small machinery to Russia and its satellite states. His three crewmen, all experienced smugglers, carried the goods into Soviet bloc countries and sold them at highly inflated prices on the black market. Only one of his band, Saarinen claimed, had ever been stopped by the authorities, and that man had been killed on the spot, leaving Saarinen's lucrative business to thrive undetected.

Riesling, like Saarinen, entered and left the Soviet Union frequently for illicit purposes, but the goods he smuggled were people. Scientists, scholars, the occasional military defector—people who would never be permitted to leave Russia alive—had been guided by Riesling to the West. It was this mutuality of purpose that had brought the American agent and the Finnish criminal sailor together in a symbiotic no-questions relationship that had lasted for the better part of two years.

"Is Vyborg the only place with reinforcements?" Riesling asked, trying to hold down a rising panic.

"Everywhere. All the border entries except in the far north. And that's useless. It has already been snowing heavily for weeks everywhere north of Kuhmo."

Riesling swallowed. "Why do you think . . . ?"

The captain shrugged his meaty shoulders. "There's a new premier in Russia, and I expect the KGB is trying to make an impression so he doesn't fry their asses." He shrugged again. "It'll wear off before long."

"Christ," Riesling said under his breath.

"Even the run to Hamina is a danger now. Gogland is crawling with secret police. You'll see when we pass."

Riesling rose and went to the small porthole on the starboard side of the cabin. Gogland Island, a Russian outpost square in the middle of the Gulf of Finland, was not yet visible in the foggy dawn light.

"They won't stop us," Saarinen explained reassuringly, cutting a thick slice off the sausage with his pocketknife.

"The *Kronen* is a fishing vessel registered in Helsinki. We are permitted in these waters." He stuffed the meat into his mouth and chewed noisily. "If not for you, there would be nothing extraordinary about this trip at all. We would have passed Gogland in any case."

He washed the meat down with a long drink of the Koskenkorva. "But Hamina is too far for an ordinary fishing boat from Helsinki. This time, we will blame the sea for taking us so far off course or the drunkenness of the captain," he said with a laugh. "But we will not make this trip again. Not until the Russians have decided once again that losing a few of their countrymen to the West is not worth the effort at the borders, eh?"

Riesling looked at him sharply. How much did the man know?

"Take it easy," Saarinen said. "I would have to be blind not to notice that the passengers with you on the return route were all Russians. The boots, the clothing. Even their breath is Russian. Russians smell bad. Don't insult my intelligence."

He took another drink and wiped the spillings from his chin on his sleeve. "Anyway, I don't care. I have not led a blameless life myself. But the difference between us, my friend, is that I have no government behind me, as you do."

He waved away Riesling's objections before they could begin. "I do not believe that you are transporting Russians out of Russia for your own enjoyment. So if the KGB catches you, they question you, a little torture, perhaps . . ." He shrugged expressively. "In the end, they trade you for one of their own spies. Not so bad, eh? But if they catch Saarinen, he hangs. So peace, yes?" He held up the bottle in salute.

Riesling drank thoughtfully, his eyes never leaving the Finn. Saarinen smiled. "Well, we're only young once. My men will take you as near to Vyborg as possible—in Finland, that is."

Well, at least that was something, Riesling thought.

But not much. It meant he was apparently going to be deposited near a heavily guarded Russian border station and left to his own devices for getting into the Soviet Union and out again with the premier Russian chess champion and his wife.

"Unless you want us to turn around and go back," Saarinen said, as if reading the American's mind. "As far as the dock authorities are concerned, the *Kronen* has been at sea since yesterday. You won't be linked with that unfortunate policeman.'' He paused. "You didn't have to kill him, you know.''

"Yes, I did,'' Riesling said flatly. "He saw the name of your docked boat, which has supposedly been out to sea since yesterday, and he was radioing his headquarters. A word from him and you might have trouble . . . I might have trouble.''

"If you say so,'' Saarinen said, but Riesling was not listening. Why the hell hadn't he been warned about the border buildup? Were they going to wait until he got caught? The CIA had its head up its ass again. Maybe he should wait. Let that damned chess-playing Kutsenko get out of Russia later, some other way.

No. He couldn't abort now. Kutsenko wasn't just a chess player; he was the champion of the world. His defection would make the Russians crazy. No. Riesling would go into Moscow and from there, play it by ear.

If he could get into Moscow. The Finnish border buildup might mean that his cover had been blown. His mind raced, juggling all the possibilities.

As if reading his thoughts, the dark Finn smiled and pulled out a deck of cards. "To Hamina?'' he asked, shuffling.

Riesling nodded. At least playing cards would break the tension he felt. He placed a twenty dollar bill on the table. Saarinen, he knew, gambled only with American dollars.

"Very well, my friend,'' Saarinen said, digging through his pockets. With a slap, he brought forth a heap of crushed Gitanes, a dirty handkerchief, several matchbooks, a wad of soiled, sea-dampened bills, an assortment of coins of various currencies, and a lumpen piece of yellow metal on a chain.

Riesling gasped involuntarily at the sight of the necklace.

"All my worldly possessions,'' Saarinen said. He straightened out one of the cigarettes and lit it, spitting the loose tobacco onto his lap, then began sifting through the bills with stubby fingers. "I do not wish to lose the money you gave me for this trip at cards. With this new fire under the Russians' arses, I will probably need it.'' He patted his coat over where he had placed Riesling's envelope and laughed. "But of course, if it is an interesting game . . .''

"May I?'' Riesling asked, picking up the gold necklace. It seemed hot to his touch, and with a small exhalation of air, he dropped it back onto the table, where it glinted dully. The chain held a circle medallion the size of an American quarter. The gold was speckled with grime embedded in a thousand small craters. In the center was the figure of a coiled snake with a small droplet of imperfectly poured gold at the base. Riesling's hands shook as he stared at it, unable to tear his gaze away from the ornament. It seemed to glow, and the spot where it had touched Riesling's flesh felt marked somehow, as if he had been stabbed and the shock of it had sent a sudden shot of fear into the pit of his stomach.

"It is a strange thing, that," Saarinen said quietly. "I felt it, too. Almost a power it had. I nearly threw it away." He laughed quickly. "But who throws real gold away, eh? And the snake may be an antique. I thought I would hold it until I get to Stockholm and see what it's worth."

Riesling's heart was thudding. He had seen the medallion before. It had hung then around the neck of a man now dead, a man with extraordinary power, a man who had once saved Riesling's life.

"Where did you get this?" His words came out in a hoarse whisper.

Saarinen tossed a crumpled twenty into the center of the table and dealt the cards. "Podhale. Near the Tatra Mountains, in Poland."

Riesling looked up, his face drained of color. "Where in the Podhale?"

"A village about twenty kilometers north of Zakopane. I forget the name. Cards?"

Riesling picked up his hand slowly. "When?" he asked.

"What? Do you want cards or not?"

The American forced his attention back to the cards and discarded two. "When did you pick it up? The medallion."

"Oh, that." Saarinen laughed as he tossed down a card and dealt more from the deck. "I don't know. Two months. Maybe three." The long ash from his cigarette dropped onto his shoulder and rolled in an untidy trail down the front of his jacket. He sheared off another slice of sausage and offered the rest to Riesling. He shook his head and stared at the amulet.

"There's a story," the captain said, belching. "Some fool runs up to me as I'm driving out of the village in a donkey cart. Of course, I was ready to shoot the bastard—it was dead night and me without any papers and my pockets full of cash—but he didn't act like any kind of military type. Arms flapping, checking behind him every other second. So I figured a family man who'd stolen something in the village for a little food money. I had to laugh." He took another swallow and gestured to his partner to get on with the game.

Riesling breathed deeply. "He stole it from a grave, didn't he?"

The captain cocked his head and looked at him, curious. "How did you know about the grave?"

Riesling shook his head. A grave robber. Of course. There wasn't any other explanation. Even the Grandmaster didn't rise from beneath six feet of earth. He had seen the records himself, the photographs the Russians had gloatingly sent. Death was death, the final victor. For all the Grandmaster's miracles, he couldn't stand up to death.

He threw in another ten dollars. "I knew the man it belonged to," he said simply. "He was killed outside of Zakopane. In the Podhale. He wore that medallion when he was buried. That was four years ago."

Saarinen smiled. "But it couldn't be the same medal," he said indulgently.

"It was the same. The drop of gold on the bottom of the snake. Hand poured, very old. It'll bring you a hundred or more American in Stockholm."

Saarinen stared at him for a moment, then burst into a fit of bellowing laughter, banging the bottle on the tabletop. "Well, I'll be a son of a whore!" he shouted, brimming with mirth. "I'm going to make a dollar or two. Wonderful."

Riesling won the hand and scraped in his winnings. Saarinen handed him the deck. "Fucking Polacks'll tell you anything," the captain said, lighting another cigarette between bursts of wheezing laughter. "You should have heard the maniac. Psst. Psst." He performed an elaborate pantomime of a man whispering secrets as he scanned the horizons for unseen law officers. Riesling smiled. "Been in the family for years, he says. Belongs to the Undead One, he says. Shot by a Russian colonel. Buried in a rock slide. Dug up and buried again. Risen from the dead, yet!" He chortled. "Pretty good, eh? The Polish Jesus Christ."

Riesling dropped the card he was dealing. His fingers froze suspended in midair.

The Grandmaster had been killed in a rock slide.

"Excuse me," Riesling said, pulling the cards back to him.

Scowling, Saarinen picked up the dropped card. It was a deuce. He tossed it back with a grin. "Just checking."

Riesling said slowly. "He didn't happen to mention how he got the medallion, I suppose."

"Oh, he had an answer for everything, that one. Said his son found it buried outside the house where this vampire or whatever, the Undead One, lived. With the village whore, no less!" He guffawed so hard that tears streamed down his cheeks. "On my mother's grave, I swear that's what he said. Mary Magdalene, no doubt. I had to give him the money after that." Hooting, he drained the bottle with a vengeance and rummaged behind the sink for another.

"How long did he have the amulet?" Riesling asked.

"Well, maybe it was four years," Saarinen said. He belched loudly as he returned to the table with a fresh bottle of vodka. "He said he was afraid to sell it because the Russians might find out he had it. But he'd sell it to me because I was leaving the country."

"And the dead man?" Riesling asked.

"You mean the Undead One?" Saarinen said mockingly. "Remember? We're talking about a Polack vampire here."

"What happened to him?" Riesling said as he made a show of looking at his cards.

Saarinen lowered his voice into the hushed tones of a storyteller unfolding a tale of horror and death. "The Russian colonel," he said. "He came looking for the Undead One, and the vampire vanished. The Russian killed the whore in a rage. No one ever saw the Undead One again. The Polack swears the grave was empty."

"You're right," Riesling said lightly. "Another fairy tale."

Saarinen leaped from the bench. "There's Gogland." He pointed to a speck of land ahead, barely visible through the porthole. He ran to the companionway and shouted, "Cast your nets!" to the men on deck. Then he blustered from the cabin as the sailors above threw out the fishing nets.

In a few minutes he returned, bleary from the blast of morning sunlight. "For the sea patrols," he said. "We won't stay here long. No fish." He winked and sat back down heavily in front of his cards. "New deal," he said, shoving them aside.

Riesling gathered up the cards again.

"Not that I don't trust you, my friend," Saarinen said.

"I understand."

"You think it's worth a hundred American? I got it for five hundred zlotys. What's that? Twenty American, I think. That's the first time I ever made a profit on a Polack. You know, my brother married a Polack. That's why I have to go there."

Riesling dealt. With a grunt, Saarinen put his feet up on the table and rested his head on the sink behind him. "Rising from the dead," he muttered. "Speaking English. Playing chess. Must have been drunk out of his mind."

"What's that?" Riesling asked sharply.

Saarinen raised by twenty. "Drunk. Drunk, I said."

"You said chess." Suddenly Riesling was shivering.

Saarinen smacked his lips sleepily and grinned. "Who knows? Maybe in Poland, Jesus Christ is an English-speaking vampire chess player. If you've got your own pope, you can do anything."

Riesling tried to steady his hands. "Saarinen, I want that medallion," he said. With a start, the captain brought himself out of his doze. "I'll give you two hundred dollars for it."

Saarinen took his time answering. He appraised the American slowly, his smiling eyes taking in the clenched jaw and sudden outpouring of sweat. "Sentimental reasons?" he asked.

Riesling worked to keep his face a blank. "The dead man had relatives," he said. "They'd like to have it."

"Ah, yes, for the relatives." The captain stroked the sooty growth on his chin. "Quite a large sum, my friend. The necklace must be a valuable object. To you, at least, eh?"

His smile faded. Riesling's Hammerli pistol was pointed directly at his face.

"Two hundred dollars," Riesling said.

Saarinen spread out his hands in a gesture of helplessness. "My friend," he said soothingly. His satyr's smile returned. "Make it three."

Andrew Starcher ran his hands over his face, vaguely hoping that the gesture would somehow stop the headache pounding in his brain. He read the coded message from the American consulate in Leningrad in front of him for the second time, then reached in his desk drawer for the vial of Aldril.

"Tranquilizers?" Corfus asked, an amused smile softening his blunt Tartar features.

"Blood pressure pills. I'm a rare spy. I'm going to die of old age, I guess." Starcher shook out two of the tablets and washed them down with cold coffee.

At sixty-six, Andrew Starcher was a recruiting poster for the American diplomat—genteel, distinguished, his snow white hair and hawklike nose bespeaking generations of good breeding. Grimacing, he pushed the telex cable toward his assistant.

Outside, the first snowfall was accumulating in the cobalt twilight of the Arbat district of Moscow, its graceful old homes twinkling with warm light. In that snow, Starcher knew, someone was watching.

Someone was always watching. Any number of KGB pavement artists with their cigarette-lighter cameras and miniature radio transceivers invariably lurked around the American embassy at any given time, and the office of the cultural attaché was particularly fascinating to them.

Starcher had known about diplomatic espionage since his first days with the CIA, but it had always seemed like a joke. Even newspapers weren't particularly interested in stories about diplomatic personnel who were chased out of a country for spying.

Now, here he was, after twenty-five years in the field, arranging square-dancing exhibitions and tours of Moscow for American movie stars, and he was vaguely embarrassed about it, even though it was only the cover for his true job as the top CIA man in the city.

Mike Corfus bent over the rumpled cablegram, squinting as he followed Starcher's decoding markings. His bulky appearance belied Corfus's sharp intelligence. The son of Russian immigrants who'd settled on New York's seamy Lower East Side, he had worked his way through Yale and had graduated summa cum laude right into the CIA, without any of the usual family connections.

He had been in Moscow only a month, serving as Starcher's eyes and legs. Where Starcher, locked up by his visibility, could only conjecture about what the Soviets were doing, Corfus could go out on the street and find out. He was Starcher's deputy in dealing with field agents like Riesling.

Corfus's immediate predecessor had died a suicide, hanged in his home. It was the sort of "suicide" the KGB specialized in for annoying diplomatic personnel. Corfus welcomed the risk. He was fluent in Russian, was as tough as a commando, hated the Communists, and Starcher trusted him.

"I don't understand the message," Corfus said honestly.

"It's very simple," Starcher said. "Riesling left a message at one of our drops in Leningrad. He's got a lead on two big Russians who want to defect, and he's on his way here to set it up. Saarinen brought him in."

"Who's Saarinen?"

"Some degenerate Finnish fishing captain whom Riesling always uses. But the message says that Riesling's got some big news for me."

"Hold on," Corfus said. "Two defectors. What two defectors?"

"I don't know. I queried Helsinki, but they didn't even know Riesling took off on this run. He went without authorization."

"Great," Corfus said sarcastically. "He's got big news for you. What news? Did he say?"

Starcher shook his head. "I think this is going to be the last run for Riesling. He's losing his judgment."

He reached for one of the thick Havana cigars he kept on his desk, debated whether or not to heed his doctor's orders, and the doctor lost. He bit the end off the cigar, spitting it out with guilty satisfaction.

Corfus said, "I don't know how the hell he got through the Finnish border. The KGB is crawling up there."

"That's what I'm afraid of," Starcher said. "Maybe he picked up a tail and knows about it. Maybe that's why he left this message so vague, just in case it got into the wrong hands."

"So we wait?" Corfus said.

"We wait," Starcher said as he lit the long black cigar.

As Corfus sprawled on the leather banquette alongside the large desk, he said, "I don't understand about Finland anyway. Why did the Russkies pack the border? They own Finland."

"They own Cuba, too," Starcher said, "and they're sending people in there, too." He blew out a thin stream of white smoke. Cuba was what he didn't understand. Finland was a perennial escape route for Russian defectors. The KGB could always make a case for beefing up personnel there, particularly with a new premier to impress.

But Cuba? Cuba was totally in Russia's pocket. Yet, the island had been getting a slow buildup of KGB agents and troops, and despite Fidel Castro's loud complaints, the new men were neither withdrawn nor explained.

"There's no pattern," Corfus said. "That's what's confusing."

"Oh, there's a pattern," Starcher said. "There's always a pattern. Nichevo." He sighed. It was the only explanation, and it frightened him.

"Nichevo?" Corfus smiled, surprised. "It means 'nothing. Who cares?' It means a lot of things."

"I know. A joke of Joseph Stalin's," Starcher said. He walked over to the window and looked down at the snow-covered street. Beneath a street lamp stood a man, shivering in the cold, surrounded by new snow. He had not moved from his spot in hours.

Starcher laughed bitterly. "Another hero of the cold war," he said, staring at the little man below. But he felt the same twinge of envy he had felt every day since he had been posted in Moscow, consigned to stare out at the world beyond the goldfish bowl that was the embassy.

Starcher missed the field work. He had left his aristocratic southern roots to do battle in three bloody wars and every filthy secret skirmish in between. This world, peopled with misfits—from the shivering little man on the pavement below to the secret masters who pulled the invisible strings that set earthshaking events in motion—this was the world he had chosen to live in, to die in. He had never married, never spawned the offspring from his family's ancient and promising gene pool. Because the work came first. Not the Company— the work.

It was a perversion, he supposed, as sick and senseless as the urge to molest small children. To be in love with secrecy, to relish fear, was more than simple patriotism. A man of Starcher's age ought to have outgrown it, he knew. Most agents burned out quickly and looked forward to working behind a desk.

Riesling, for instance. The man had been a good agent, cautious, experienced, and smart, but his nerve was giving out. During the past few months, Riesling had acquired small mannerisms—grinding his teeth, taking fits of shivering chills— that worried Starcher. And now Riesling's judgment was going, too.

God, he'd love to replace Riesling himself. That'd give a laugh to the administrators at Langley. A sixty-six-year-old man . . . No, he thought, sighing. He belonged right where he was. Standing in a glass house for every first-year KGB agent in Moscow to see. The grand old spymaster, directing the movement of others, while he himself remained helpless, rooted, respectable, impotent.

"I just never thought I'd be the one who was being watched," he said quietly.

"Beg your pardon?" Corfus said.

His voice snapped Starcher back to reality.

"Never mind," he said, drawing the draperies.

"Is Nichevo a branch of the KGB?" Corfus asked.

"No. Nichevo's not a branch of anything anymore, except maybe Stalin's ghost. It started out as one, though. Small work. Blackmailing diplomats with prostitutes, paying ex-CIA men to write exposés of the Company, convincing the state to pump hormones into Soviet athletes, minor things to make the West look bad."

"Kind of a Department of Dirty Tricks," Corfus said with a smile. He had always liked the old man.

"You could say that. After Stalin bullied his way into becoming a Russian legend, though, he didn't want to be associated with the low-life antics of the group anymore, so he put his nephew in charge." He blew a perfect smoke ring toward the ceiling. "The story goes that when the nephew asked Stalin about the name of the organization he was going to run, Stalin answered, 'Who cares?' and sent him away. *Nichevo?*"

Corfus laughed. "Doesn't sound too dangerous to me."

"Ah," Starcher said, holding up a bony finger. "But the nephew turned out to be sharper than Stalin expected. He kept the group small, but over the years he replaced Stalin's thugs with a half-dozen of the best brains in Russia and the satellite states. He chose them himself, from the universities, the military, even from the civil service, but never from Intelligence, never from the KGB. From what I've been able to dig up, he worked with the Soviet spy apparatus, but he distrusted the bastards like poison."

He coughed, and his face registered pain. Cigars had been forbidden to him since a bullet in East Berlin pierced his left lung. That had been Starcher's last field assignment.

A field career ended honorably, according to the boys at headquarters. It was small consolation for the constant pain that signaled the end of his life's work.

"Sit down," Corfus said, as he stepped over to Starcher to lead him to the leather banquette.

Starcher pushed him aside. "Don't patronize me," he said acidly. "I'm not the doddering old fool I look like." Corfus backed off, and, feeling guilty, Starcher harrumphed and sat down anyway. "At any rate, he found these men and women and gave them a chance to grow with Nichevo, dirty tricks and all, while the organization grew. By the time Khrushchev got booted out of office, Nichevo was in charge of planning big stuff. The invasion of neutral countries, the infiltration of propagandists into every undeveloped nation receiving aid from the United States, Soviet subs in enemy waters, the buildup of military bases hidden in a hundred obscure spots around the world, you name it." He spread his arms.

"Where is he now, this nephew of Stalin's?"

"His name was Zharkov. He died four, five years ago. Bleeding ulcers."

Corfus looked up. "Oh. Well, then . . ."

"He had a son during the war," Starcher said, making circles with his cigar in the ashtray. "A very bright boy, brains right off the charts. Alexander Zharkov. Graduated with top honors from Moscow University, made full colonel in the army when he was thirty. Zharkov trained him himself since childhood. Rumor has it that the boy started attending the Nichevo directorate meetings as soon as he was out of short pants. Zharkov wasn't taking any chances about who was going to succeed him. Alexander lived and breathed Nichevo until he joined the army and was sent out on military patrol. He was in Poland when his father died. He came back to head up Nichevo."

"And you think he's behind the men moving into Cuba?"

"It's got the signs. No explanation and no apparent reason. It's got Zharkov's stamp all over it."

"Would he be behind Finland?" Corfus asked.

Starcher stubbed out his cigar with some viciousness. "That I don't know. I don't think so." He looked at his watch. "It's almost six," he said. "I want you to take up a watch."

"Sure," Corfus said, rising. "Here?"

"No, I'll stay here. Riesling will contact me if everything's clear. But if there's trouble, his fallback is always at the Samarkand Hotel. I can't be seen with him, of course. Bad policy."

Corfus smiled. "I understand."

"You've met him?"

"Once. I know his face."

"Good. If he shows up at the Samarkand, he's hot, understand?"

Corfus nodded.

"You'll have to move quickly. Get him to the safe house on Ohkotney as soon as you can. I'll wait here for your call."

"What if he doesn't come?" Corfus asked.

"Wait till nine o'clock at the bar—that's the most visible area—then order dinner. It'll give him a little more time in case he needs it. I'll page you at the Samarkand if he contacts me first."

Corfus hesitated by the door. "And if he doesn't get in touch with either of us?"

But Starcher wasn't listening. He was back at the window, peering out through the drapes at the small man standing, shivering in the snow.

_____CHAPTER THREE

At six o'clock, Riesling was still two hours outside Moscow. He had stolen one car in Leningrad, then switched autos at Kalinin, stealing an old ZIL parked on a busy street.

Punchy. He hadn't slept for days. That was it. The dead policeman in Helsinki, the harrowing sojourn through the Russian border, the long drive from Leningrad. All of it had exhausted him.

And the medallion. He felt for it in his pocket. Even its touch was frightening, ominous. It weighted him with the same feeling he used to get on the football field at school, the dull ache when he was running for the ball during a critical point in the game. As the ball soared overhead, he knew—by the wind, by the awkwardness of his legs, his balance imperceptibly off, by some despairing cry within—that he wasn't going to catch the pass. It was during those moments, as if he had some special insight, beyond reason or the connotation of words, that he knew he was going to lose.

"Just get to Starcher," he said aloud, letting go of the medallion in his pocket.

He searched his rearview mirror. Clean, no gray Fiat. All right. He'd lost the car, with its lone occupant wearing a white stocking cap, somewhere in Kalinin.

More likely, he'd never been followed in the first place. In all probability, the man in the stocking cap was an ordinary Russian, a factory worker, a telephone man, just someone driving into Moscow with no more sense of Riesling's identity than the man in the moon.

27

He shook his head to clear it. When you begin to suspect everyone, when the stink of treachery permeated every corner of your world, you were finished. The suspicion would break you. It distracted you. In time, it killed you.

"Burnout," he muttered. No one was following him. He'd just spent too long on the job.

Once he reached Moscow, he would ask Starcher to recommend an immediate transfer. To anywhere. And a leave. He would go to Monte Carlo or the Aegean and drink himself stuporous and find a woman. And let all the men in all the white stocking caps go back to all their jobs at all the docks and factories or wherever they all worked, and to hell with them. No more. Not for him.

He dumped the ZIL at Kiev station and boarded a crowded metro car ripe with the odors of *tabaka* and *shashlik*. He had made it to Moscow. For the first time in days, he began to feel some semblance of safety.

All for a goddamned chess player, he thought, easing into the luxury of a vacant seat. A hell of a way for a good field man to go, over a two-bit defector who wasn't even in intelligence.

Yet that was how they did go, he knew. An overheard word, a chance sighting, and death blew its whistle and sent you to the bench. No fanfare. No trial by twelve good men and true. Just a bullet in the back while you weren't looking.

He was sweating. From his pocket he pulled out a handkerchief and gasped audibly. The gold medallion was dangling from its chain in the folds of the cloth. He stuffed it quickly back into his pocket and rose, pretending not to notice the stares of the other passengers around him.

He worked his way toward the front of the train. Starcher was going to have to get the chess player out of Russia. Riesling was through. The trip from Finland into Russia had been rough. Trying to go out the same way, with the added baggage of a chess player and a woman, would be suicide. The border was just too tightly sealed. He wasn't taking anyone back through Finland again, ever.

He had three things on his mind. Tell the chess player the deal was off for the time being. Then get to Starcher. *And get rid of the medallion,* he thought, near panic. It was doing something to him, almost as if it had a power of its own that was too strong to harness. Christ, why had it come to him?

Perhaps because he owed a debt. It had been . . . how long, eight years? Riesling had been sent into East Berlin to pick up a defector, but it had been a setup. When he went to meet the defector, there was no defector. Only the KGB waiting for him.

He had gotten out of the trap but, with a shoulder dislocated and a knee injured, had been able to flee only to the third floor of an industrial storage loft in a seamy commercial corner of the city. The KGB had followed and had ringed the building with men. That they hadn't rushed the building was clear indication that they wanted him alive, perhaps as a prime exhibit in some showy for-Western-consumption spy trial. There was no way out, and Riesling had carefully checked his revolver, placed his extra shells on the floor in front of him, and sat down to wait. One bullet would be for him.

He passed out from the pain.

Then someone was shaking him.

He struggled to open his eyes and then to focus them. The first thing he saw was a golden coiled snake close to his face. He squeezed his eyes shut and opened them again. The coiled snake was on a medallion. It hung around the neck of a young man with piercing sky blue eyes.

Riesling had tried to speak, but the man had clapped a hand over his mouth.

"Don't talk," he whispered. "We're getting out of here."

"Who are you?" Riesling said.

"I work for Starcher. They call me the Grandmaster," the young man said.

"I don't know if I can move," Riesling had said. "My shoulder's separated, and my leg's messed up."

"We'll manage."

As the man helped him to his feet, Riesling saw that a section of the corrugated steel wall of the storage loft had been ripped open, as if by a giant can opener. A tear, shaped like the pupil of a cat's eye, four feet long and a foot wide, allowed moonlight to seep into the loft.

The Grandmaster led Riesling to the hole in the steel, slid through himself, and then reached back for the American agent. "Put your good arm around my neck," he whispered, "and hold on for dear life."

Riesling followed the man, threw his right arm around him,

and then they were moving down the side of the building, three stories down into a narrow alley, closed off at both ends, that separated the loft building from the tenement next door.

When they reached the ground, the Grandmaster helped Riesling to the tenement building and they went inside. Before the door closed behind them, though, Riesling looked back. He had thought there was a rope hanging from the ugly gash of ripped steel in the loft building. But there was no rope. How had they climbed down the smooth steel side of a building? He could not ask.

They traveled silently through the cellars of a half-dozen buildings before exiting onto a street.

"Sorry, but you're going to have to get into the trunk," the Grandmaster said as they approached a battered old Ford sedan. Riesling nodded. As the trunk lid closed on him, the last thing he saw was the coiled snake medallion around the young man's neck.

The pain knocked him out, and he did not know how long he was unconscious. When the trunk was opened again, two Americans in dark clothes helped him out and into a boat that moved him across the river and into the free half of Berlin.

The Grandmaster was gone; Riesling never saw him again. And months later when he asked Starcher who he was, Starcher said simply, "He works for me sometimes."

"How did he get me out?"

"I don't know," Starcher said. "He does those things." He would say no more.

Riesling came back to the present as he heard the train conductor's voice crackle over the loudspeaker in his car. He felt as if he were choking, and when the metro stopped at Mayakovsky Square, he roughly shoved his way through the passengers in front of him to get outside to the open air.

The chess player, Ivan Kutsenko, was waiting in the dirty little café off Gorky Street. His rubber-galoshed feet were crossed at the ankles, and he twirled his hat in his hands as he glanced in continuous rotation at the four corners of the room.

He was the chess champion of the world, famed for the subtle, far-reaching brilliance of his play and his total nervelessness at the chessboard. Yet, Riesling thought with disgust, here he sat as twitchy as a drunk driver in a police lockup. It was dark outside, but Kutsenko was still wearing sunglasses. Probably he thought they were a disguise. All he needed was a hand-painted sign on his chest: "Arrest me. I'm trying to defect to the West."

He couldn't look more suspicious if he had a stick of dynamite in his mouth, Riesling thought. The American agent brushed some imaginary lint from the lapel of the East German–made topcoat he wore and removed his homburg. He hung up the clothing, then with a feigned expression of surprise, greeted the chess player like a long-lost acquaintance.

"Do join me," Kutsenko said, rising, his eyes behind the dark glasses darting around the room.

Unobtrusively, Riesling slipped into the chess player's seat at the table. It faced the window, and Riesling was better prepared to spot a tail than was Kutsenko, who looked as if he was about to collapse in a fit of nerves.

Smiling, he ordered a beer as he cased the room. Three other tables were occupied, by old men, mostly. A single man who walked with a limp stood at the counter and sipped coffee. No white stocking cap. It had been a delusion, after all. Burnout.

"Our arrangements are canceled," Riesling said softly.

The chess player's face fell. "But my wife," he protested. "We have prepared everything."

"I'm sorry. It's not possible. My people will be in touch with you about an alternate route."

"When?" Kutsenko was on the verge of tears. "Already they're watching me. My wife was discharged from her post. No reason was given."

Riesling felt his stomach turn a slow revolution. "Recently?"

"Today."

Blown. It was all blown.

Riesling smiled tightly as the waitress placed the stein in front of him. "I understand you will be playing in a chess tournament in Havana later this year," he said, struggling to look as if they were exchanging casual pleasantries.

"Perhaps. One is never sure . . ."

"Be there. With your wife. I'll arrange for one of our men to meet you."

"How will I know him?" Kutsenko said, choking in fear.

Riesling thought for a moment, then said, "He'll talk about

the weather. He'll say, 'In Havana, the sun is hot, but it's good for the sugar crop.' Can you remember that?''

Kutsenko nodded. "Will you excuse me for a moment?" Riesling asked, rising. He made his way toward the rest room at the back at a leisurely pace.

Riesling had selected the café as a meeting place because of its layout. Two crude wooden partitions separated the lavatories from the dining area. Beyond them, the small kitchen led directly to a rear exit. Without doubt, Riesling thought, the café had lost more than one customer through the kitchen door, since it couldn't be spotted from the dining room. Riesling went out silently, leaving the chess player to figure out his departure for himself.

In the café, the man standing at the counter crooked a finger toward the front window.

On Gorky Street, the immense Tchaikovsky Concert Hall glittered in the sunlight, flanked by the Mossovyet and the Sovremennik Youth Theater. To Riesling's right rose the tall tower of the Samarkand Hotel.

It would have to be the Samarkand now, he thought. He was blown, because surely the Russians had someone watching Kutsenko. It was just a matter of time now. Coatless but sweating profusely, he walked down the wide boulevard with what semblance of casualness he could muster, scanning the long lines of workers waiting outside the meat markets, stamping and exhaling clouds like steaming horses.

He didn't know what prompted him to turn around, to search the crowd behind him. The instinct was so ingrained in Riesling that he never questioned it. He was a professional.

So it was that he was not horrified or even terribly surprised at the certain knowledge that he was going to die.

Behind him, less than a block away, was the man in the white stocking cap.

Mike Corfus felt like a connoisseur as he swirled his brandy near the candlelight. The bar of the Samarkand was elevated a few feet off the lobby floor, and from his vantage point at the railing, Corfus could watch both the front and the side doors of the hotel.

He liked the Samarkand, with its Byzantine flourishes and pre-Revolutionary charm. It was part of another Russia, peopled with aristocrats who walked these floors in jewel-buckled shoes, where the silk gowns of ladies wearing tiaras rustled softly as they moved.

Corfus smiled to himself. Sometimes his own naiveté amused him. In czarist Russia, he would have been a serf. He even looked like a serf. Times didn't change that much.

In the lobby below, a German tourist with a camera dangling around his neck posed his squat wife in front of a mural depicting Tamerlane as he led his Mongol archers to victory along the Silk Road.

"Ein Augenblick," the German shouted, waving the other occupants of the lobby toward the corners while he adjusted his camera. *"Gehen Sie heraus!"*

Corfus could tell by the facial features of the people in the lobby that most of them were Russians. They ignored the German's commands to move out of his way.

"Another?" the bar waitress asked indifferently, gesturing to Corfus's half-empty glass.

"No, thanks. I'd like to take my time," he answered in flawless Russian. The waitress sneered and lumbered away.

Russian women, Corfus decided, should all be fitted with mudguards.

A loud crack, like a clap of thunder, sounded from somewhere near the kitchen. Corfus saw the waitress look up and amble slightly faster toward the rear of the hotel. The other patrons hesitated for a moment, then resumed their conversations. In the lobby, the German tourist had handed the camera to his wife and was seated formally in one of the hotel's red upholstered chairs in front of the massive side doors. His sneakers dangled beneath an expanse of exposed white shin. He was shouting orders at her, gesturing angrily as she fiddled with the camera's knobs and buttons. The squat woman was bent over like a snail, peering with great concentration into the viewfinder, when suddenly she straightened up, her face ashen.

"Was is los?" the tourist bellowed. But by then the woman's scream had riveted the attention of everyone in the lobby.

The panic was instantaneous. Behind the German, through the curtained glass double doors, staggered a man covered with blood. Half his shoulder was blown off, and he clutched with agonizing effort at the strands of flesh that remained. Blood spurted out of him like a fountain, splashing into his face in a sickening rhythm. He shielded his eyes from the light with his good hand.

As the passersby veered around the man with expressions of horror on their faces, two red-uniformed hotel clerks strode over to him. With amazing strength, he knocked one of them sprawling on the carpet, then continued his rabid-dog walk toward the bar, where the occupants shouted their objections and backed away. Corfus half rose, feeling nauseated.

"Help him," a woman shrieked in provincial accents. "Why doesn't anyone help him?"

As one of the hotel clerks tackled the bleeding man from behind and forced him to the floor, Corfus recognized his face. "Oh, my God," he whispered.

"Just a moment. We've called an ambulance," the clerk shouted. The man flailed beneath him.

"No!" he screamed. The sound was a cry of betrayal, of agony. His arm shot up and quavered in the air.

Corfus scrambled down the steps on wobbly legs and forced his way through the melee. "Riesling," he said, "Starcher sent me."

It seemed so horribly inadequate. But Riesling's eyes brightened at the words. He groaned as he stretched his violently shaking hand toward Corfus.

"Help me," he said.

Corfus bent over the wounded man. Riesling moaned, pulling himself close. The blood from his shoulder seeped into Corfus's suit. The flesh from his exploded shoulder hung in strips. With a gasp, he grabbed the useless, blood-drenched hand dangling at his side and stuffed it into his pocket.

He reeked of sweat and fear. The hotel clerk looked to Corfus with shock and disgust. "Sir?" he asked meekly.

"It's all right. Hurry up that ambulance."

"In Havana," Riesling sputtered, then was seized with a spasm of pain that shook him the length of his body. "In Havana . . ." he mumbled and Corfus leaned closer to hear.

A burst of blinding white light gave Corfus a jolt. The German tourist was assiduously snapping pictures of the two of them, while his wife tugged, sobbing, at his jacket. *"Bitte,"* she wailed. *"Bitte, nein . . ."* He pushed her aside and snapped another picture.

"Get the hell out of here, you vulture!" Corfus shouted at him in English.

Riesling clutched at him. "No time," he whispered. "Take." He thrust his good hand into his jacket pocket and handed him a blood-soaked bundle of papers. He repeated the action twice more, each time coming up clutching scraps of personal property.

"Please, wait for the ambulance," Corfus said, but Riesling kept turning over his belongings, one pocket after the other. All the while, he kept talking wildly between ragged gasps, while Corfus struggled to hear him. Riesling forced his way into the pocket that contained his other hand. When he brought it back up, the dead left hand was wound around a metal chain to which was attached a gold disc. He screamed with pain as he untangled the hand, suspended in the air like a puppet's, and the medallion fell to the floor.

The German's camera flashed again.

"Take it. Pick it up!" Riesling commanded. Sweat poured into the corners of his mouth. Holding on to the dying man, Corfus stooped to pick up the gold necklace.

Then, inexplicably, Riesling let go of Corfus and kicked him in his side, and Corfus sprawled backward. Before he could regain his footing, hell had opened up and swallowed them all.

In the double doorway stood two men, both carrying heavy pistols. One of the men, scanning the crowd, wore a white stocking cap, his features blunt and menacing. The other was smaller and bareheaded. He took aim.

Corfus caught sight of Riesling as the wounded man struggled to his feet, then lurched a few feet away from him toward the other exit. His throat closed in pity. In less than a second, he knew, the man was going to die in front of his eyes.

The bullet caught the spy square in the back, and Riesling arched convulsively and flipped sideways in midair, his shattered arm flinging outward in a spray of blood.

The next moments were pure madness. Riesling's hand clawed at the floor. Somehow, he was managing, in the extreme of suffering, to move toward a cluster of terrified, shrieking onlookers plastered against the wall. The bareheaded man fired again at Riesling. His body jerked upward and then fell forward with a thump.

Corfus backed away. His stomach wrenched. The man in the stocking cap was standing in firing position again, impervious to the screams of the people in the lobby.

And he was aiming directly at Corfus.

In the next second, a woman, sobbing in panic, lunged in front of Corfus. The bullet took her in the head, exploding it like a melon.

The brutal act was accentuated by a flash of white light.

The photographer, scurrying toward the main doors with his prized camera, suddenly fell backward, a gaping hole torn in the right side of his throat.

It had all happened in a span of seconds. The stampede for the exits began, and Corfus went with the crowd. Outside, a swarm of onlookers had already begun to collect. He didn't see the gunmen leave. He looked back once. All he saw were the splayed bodies of Riesling, the woman with half a head, and the German photographer.

Starcher said nothing for several minutes. He just sat at his desk, the light from the lamp forming a pool of yellow light over the haphazard items that Corfus had placed there. Slowly

Starcher shifted the objects around to form two neat double lines.

He picked up the three passports in the upper left corner and leafed through them. The American passport was Riesling's. The other two were Finnish and had evidently been stolen or were still in the process of preparation, since the stamped photographs of the subjects were missing. They belonged, ostensibly, to a Rickard and Mirja Trojloi. The other items on the desk were Riesling's Russian working papers and identity card and a manila envelope containing some six thousand rubles and several hundred dollars in American bills.

He set them down again. "He gave you all of this?" he asked, gesturing to the collection of papers and oddments.

Corfus nodded. "He emptied his pockets and stuffed everything into my hands."

Starcher squeezed his eyes shut. His headache was back. "Were you spotted?"

Corfus snorted. "Damn right. The bastard had a gun pointed dead at me."

"What happened?"

Corfus lowered his eyes. "Someone—a woman—got in the way." Starcher looked up at the ceiling. "It got pretty bad, Andy."

Starcher nodded, expressionless. An incidental murder. Riesling had tried to save Corfus's life by pulling the gunfire away from him. "What did Riesling say? Try to remember the exact words."

"I don't think he was lucid," Corfus said. "He didn't make a lot of sense."

"Go ahead."

"He said something about Havana, first. The sugar crop or something. Really, it didn't seem to mean anything."

"What did he say exactly?" Starcher pressed.

"All right, all right. He said, 'In Havana, the sun is hot, but it's good for the sugar crop.' That's what he said. Exactly."

Starcher sat back. "Havana?" he whispered. Riesling only traveled between Finland and the Soviet Union. What was in Havana?

"I told you it didn't make sense."

"Are you sure about Havana?" Starcher said slowly. "Could it have been Hamina? They sound alike."

"It was Havana," Corfus said stubbornly. "Anyway, they don't grow sugar in Finland."

Starcher exhaled. "What else? Was that all?"

"No. He said something else when he gave me the necklace."

"The necklace?"

"The guy was cracked, I tell you."

Starcher rummaged through the items on his desk. "What necklace?" he asked, frowning.

Corfus poked around the items. "I know he gave it to me," he mumbled. "It was after he dumped the rest of the stuff into my hands. He acted as if it was important. Maybe it's still in my pocket." He rose and walked to the small divan where he had draped his coat and rummaged through the pockets. "Here it is. It must have gotten stuck in the lining."

He tossed the gold medallion onto the glass desktop with a clatter.

Starcher stared at it for a moment, unmoving. The gold disc with its ancient coiled snake figurine seemed to glow with a terrible power.

Corfus looked from the medallion to Starcher. "What—what's the matter?"

Starcher reached out for the necklace with tentative fingers. He rubbed the gold thoughtfully. It felt warm to his touch.

So long, so long ago . . .

"What did Riesling say?" Starcher asked, pulling off his bifocals with a grimace. The hand that had touched the medallion trembled.

"He said the Grandmaster was alive."

Starcher shot out of his chair. An intense pain coursed down his left arm. "What?"

"It was the last thing he said," Corfus said, confused. "Tell Starcher that the Grandmaster is alive. Are you all right?"

Starcher groaned and gasped for air. His chest tightened as if a steel band were squeezing his lungs together. The corner of his desk shot up to meet his gaze; his chair toppled with a heavy crash. "The medallion," he said softly. But of course that was ridiculous. Even the Grandmaster's coiled snake didn't possess the power to stop a man's heart. With a sigh, he lost consciousness in a sea of pain.

CHAPTER FIVE

Alexander Zharkov filled his lungs with the crisp October air mixed with the smell of new bread from the bakery on Neglimmaya Street. To his left, several blocks away, the twenty towers of the Kremlin's fortress walls pricked the sky. Beyond them, the bright-colored gingerbread domes of St. Basil's Cathedral stood in splendid ancient barbarism.

It was said in the old legends that Ivan the Terrible plucked out the eyes of the cathedral's designers so that its magnificence might never be duplicated. Zharkov's eyes rested for a moment on the structure, as they did each morning. He understood the belligerent, bloody czar of all the Russias, now defiled for his selfish achievements.

He had understood since his days as a student, when he had first set his unworldly eyes on the great cathedral. While his contemporaries set about ensuring the success of their careers by vocally damning the excesses of the corrupt kings and praising the weekly agricultural output of the Ukraine, Zharkov had been silent, listening, planning. Even then he had understood the price of greatness, and respected it.

He turned down a side street lined with modest homes, their shutters open. He nodded to an old grandmother, a *baba*, who swept her steps each morning as Zharkov passed. She smiled toothlessly and watched him walk toward the two-story house that no one on the street spoke of.

The people in the neighborhood knew that it was not a home. It was not a brothel, because no women came or left there. It was not an office, because no office sounds issued from the small house with the tightly closed windows. Only a crew of workmen in a truck came to the dark little house with regularity, letting themselves in before dawn every day with dollies loaded with electronic equipment, and then let themselves out within the hour. Those neighbors who guessed that the equipment was for electronic security sweeps of the premises kept the information to themselves. Such knowledge was not welcome in Moscow.

The house belonged to Nichevo. Sporadically it served as the meeting ground for five or six serious, silent men. Zharkov was the youngest among them. And the most powerful.

A heavy-set man carrying a brown envelope stood at the foot of the steps leading to the front door of the house. They exchanged glances tentatively. Years of secret meetings had inured them both against demonstrative Russian welcomes in full sunlight.

"Comrade," Zharkov said, with the briefest nod toward the brown envelope. He unlocked the front door. It closed behind them with a double click. Zharkov led the heavy-set man through the front parlor and into a small office containing little more than a desk, a few uncomfortable wooden chairs, and a wall of new metal file cabinets on which rested incongruously an ornate chessboard inlaid with ebony and ivory.

"You are well, Sergei?" Zharkov said with more warmth once they were away from the inquisitive eyes of the people on the street.

"Well enough. My son wishes to change his course of study at the university. He wants to take up art," the man with the envelope said with a shrug.

Zharkov smiled at the man's obvious discomfort. General Sergei Ostrakov was KGB in the style of Stalin: a trained bear of a man who obeyed blindly, killed easily, lived automatically, and spared little thought for the inconsequentials of life, which included every activity not directly linked to his personal survival. "Art is a worthwhile study," Zharkov said.

"Not for the son of a fighting man. Disgraceful. You are lucky not to be fettered with the burden of a family, Alyosha." He used the friendly Russian diminutive for Alexander, but the name seemed to come from his mouth only with effort.

"Your coat?" Zharkov said.

The KGB man shook his head. "No. I'll just stay a minute." He tossed the envelope onto Zharkov's desk. "There's something in there that might interest you."

He was fishing for something, Zharkov knew, and he refused to rise to the bait. He sat on the soft leather chair behind his desk and slowly lit a cigarette. The envelope remained untouched on the desk.

After a few seconds of awkward silence, Ostrakov spoke again. "This is something in your field of interest," he said. "Kutsenko is attempting to defect to the Americans. He met with an agent last night."

"Which agent?" Zharkov asked mildly, his hooded eyes still looking down at his cigarette.

"We think it was Frank Riesling. He divested himself of any identification before he died, but our researchers made him from some photographs." He thrust his chin toward the brown envelope. "He worked out of Helsinki, taking defectors out through the northern route."

"And what happened?" Zharkov asked.

"Nothing," Ostrakov said. "It's in the envelope."

Zharkov leaned forward and pulled a sheaf of photographs from the envelope. The first was of a fat woman posing for her portrait in front of a mural. The second showed another woman, arms outstretched, falling as her face exploded into fragments.

"Some of these are inconsequential," Ostrakov said offhandedly. He gestured to the photo of the woman in her moment of death. "An accident," he said.

Angrily, Zharkov slammed the photos down on his desk without looking at the rest.

"What happened to Riesling?"

"He's dead."

"Your men killed him?"

"Yes."

"And Kutsenko?"

"He is being watched. I've had him watched for two weeks now," Ostrakov said, "ever since I learned he was planning to defect. I had his wife fired from her job at the hospital," he said proudly.

"You idiot," Zharkov snapped.

Ostrakov bristled, but Zharkov ignored him and began to look again through the rest of the photos. He blew out a lungful of smoke in disgust. Nichevo had given him a certain power over the KGB, but it would never be enough power to change the mentality of its people. The KGB was cluttered with heavy-handed fools.

"That's the agent," Ostrakov said. The third photograph showed a man reeling to the floor in agony, his shoulder blown away. In the foreground were several shadows hovering around neatly upholstered furniture.

"Where were these taken?" Zharkov asked incredulously.

"At the Samarkand Hotel, around eight o'clock yesterday evening. There was a man taking pictures of the incident, an East German tourist."

"A *tourist?*" Zharkov shouted, throwing the photographs down onto the desk. "You had a man shot to death in the lobby of a busy hotel during peak hours"—he slammed his fist down on the picture of the dying woman—"killing God knows how many innocent bystanders . . ."

"Only two bystanders, comrade," Ostrakov said coldly. "The German tourist was taking incriminating photographs, as you can see. It was unavoidable." He stepped back a pace, his friendly intimacy replaced by the official persona of his rank. "Colonel Zharkov, I wish to remind you that Nichevo's function does not extend to dictating what the KGB will do."

"You do not have to remind me. Every bungled performance by your organization reminds me." With a snap, he picked up the photographs again.

"I am trying to remember that you are my friend, Comrade Colonel," Ostrakov said angrily. He rambled on, but Zharkov didn't hear him. He was transfixed by the last photograph in the series. It showed Riesling, screaming in pain before the bewildered, terrified face of a dark young man, as a shiny metal object glittered in the air on its way to the floor. The carved surface of the object was facing the camera.

Zharkov held his breath as he pulled a magnifying glass from his desk drawer and held it over the black-and-white photograph. Under the lens, the object leaped into prominence.

It was a medallion bearing the figure of a coiled snake in a circle.

Zharkov closed his eyes. He felt dizzy. The Grandmaster had surfaced.

"It is the same, isn't it?" Ostrakov asked.

Zharkov looked up, his eyes alert and suspicious. "I don't know what you mean," he said.

The KGB man spread his arms. "Alyosha," he said in a strained attempt at friendliness. "We have spent many years together. We have marched in the snows of the Caucasus, killed together in the jungles. We have bathed together and shared women. I know the mark you keep beneath your collar."

Zharkov swallowed, trying to focus on the fat man who seemed to sway in front of him. "Why have you come?" he asked quietly.

"The medallion. We wish to know its significance. Before he died, Riesling passed everything in his possession to the man in the photograph. We've identified him as Michael Corfus. He's a liaison officer at the American embassy, but he's Starcher's deputy in the CIA."

"I know who he is," Zharkov said. "You've captured him, too?"

Ostrakov shrugged. "No. With his diplomatic immunity, he could only be expatriated anyway. We're keeping an eye on him."

"In your usual subtle fashion, no doubt," Zharkov said. He stubbed out the cigarette. He allowed himself only a handful every day and never one before lunch. This idiot and the other fools at the KGB had stuck their blundering fat hands into a sensitive Nichevo operation, and it was Zharkov's own fault. He should have taken greater care to keep the KGB out.

The facts were clear. Riesling had passed the medallion to Corfus. He should never have been allowed to leave the premises, but the KGB decided not to capture him at all. Why should they? They were probably still busy celebrating their successful terrorizing of a hotel full of foreign visitors. Two bystanders dead. Riesling killed. Kutsenko alerted.

All a waste.

And worst of all, the medallion was gone.

He looked up and met Ostrakov's eyes. They were the eyes of a beast of burden, trained to see only what they expected, blind to truth. No, Zharkov would not tell the KGB anything.

"The medallion," Ostrakov prompted.

Zharkov dismissed it with a flick of his hand. "Meaningless," he said. He stood up and extracted from a file cabinet a plain green folder. "The green signifies a closed case," he said, slapping the folder into Ostrakov's open hands. Inside were medical reports, a detailed account of the circumstances of death, and a grainy photograph of a dark-haired man lying in a shallow open grave. The face in the photograph, smeared with dirt and lacerated with small cuts, looked vital even in death. The clothes he wore were rough, handmade garments of the style worn by the *goral* of the Polish highlands. Around his neck was a medallion that bore the image of a coiled snake.

"Who was he? He's wearing the same medallion."

Zharkov answered in a monotone. "The one last night was probably a copy. His name was Justin Gilead. He was a chess player, and the CIA ran him around the world. He was killed in an avalanche in Poland four years ago. I was there at the time."

Ostrakov grunted, tossing down the green folder. "The Americans know about this?"

Zharkov nodded. "I saw that they got copies of the file."

"And your neck, Comrade?" Ostrakov asked bluntly.

Zharkov's hooded eyes flashed. "It is an old scar. It means nothing. Not to me and not to you and not to your superiors. Understand?"

The KGB man sputtered in front of Zharkov's vehemence. "I thought the medal might contain some kind of secret message," he said.

"You should have asked Riesling before your thugs pulled the trigger," Zharkov said dryly. "Where is Kutsenko now?"

"My men have him under surveillance," Ostrakov said.

"I want him left alone," Zharkov said.

Ostrakov's face clouded. "But that's impossible. He is the world chess champion, and he is planning to defect. Impossible. My superiors—"

"And I want his wife to be given her job back. She should be made to believe it was all a mistake."

"I will never be permitted to—"

"I will take full authority for this," Zharkov said. "I'll send a report to the directorate today. They'll understand. Kutsenko is very vital to plans that Nichevo is working on."

"What plans?"

"You know better than to ask that," Zharkov said curtly.

He led Ostrakov through the front parlor and to the door. "If you don't believe me, wait for instructions from your superiors. That is the Russian way, I suppose."

"Zharkov, I've told you—"

"Just try not to kill Kutsenko in the meantime. Or this Corfus. I think I will need him as well."

"You are insulting, Alexander Vassilovitch," Ostrakov said, his face red. "There is a new premier. I do not think Nichevo will continue to ride roughshod much longer."

"Until that happens, good day, Comrade," Zharkov said without expression.

Settling down to write his request to Ostrakov's superiors, his hands passed over the green folder. Inside lay the photograph of the dead Justin Gilead. Zharkov took it out and studied it again. In repose, Gilead's face was almost that of a boy, and it was as a boy that Zharkov best remembered him, hunched over a chessboard in a banquet room of the Hôtel de Crillon in Paris.

It had been a match between children, a meeting of two lonely, gifted ten-year-old boys who had drawn themselves into the magic of a strange game where kingdoms were lost and won in the turn of a thought. Alexander Zharkov had played against Justin Gilead then, in the sight of chess masters from all over Europe and the Soviet Union.

Young Alyosha had burned with shame when his father strapped a radio receiver to his forearm before the match. He explained that the American boy, Gilead, was probably the finest child chess player in the world and that Zharkov could not leave the game to chance.

"I play well, too, father," Alyosha had protested, but the receiver remained.

During the match, the Russian grandmasters conferred on each of Alyosha's moves. His instructions were broadcast to him through minute electric shocks on the flesh of the Russian boy's arm. The first set of signals named the piece to move; the second told him which square to occupy. He clenched his teeth to hold back his tears during the sham match. He wanted to play Gilead alone, to match his mind to his opponent's. As it was, Alyosha was little more than a robot mechanically moving pieces on a board. He looked across at the young American with the raven black hair, grateful that Gilead's head was always down, over the board, studying the pieces and the positions.

Alyosha read the signal on his forearm and made another move. For the first time, Justin Gilead looked up, revealing a pair of eyes of the most extraordinary electric blue Zharkov had ever seen. They were old eyes, wise and pained, locked strangely into a child's face and body. Gilead moved a knight and said softly, "Check. Mate in five."

Stunned, Alyosha turned and looked across the room to where the delegation of Russian chess masters were following the moves on a portable chessboard. His father's face was flushed with anger. Alyosha knew there would be no more instructions, no more radio signals.

He resigned. As the two boys stood up to shake hands, Gilead whispered, "Do you speak English?"

"A little," Alyosha said numbly.

"I hope someday I can play against you, and not those men back there." He nodded toward the rear of the room.

"Oh . . ." Alyosha wanted to die of shame.

"Your sleeve," Gilead said.

Zharkov looked at his shirt cuff, where a small wire looped close to the fabric. "You knew."

"It's all right," Gilead said. "Another day. Another place. We will play a real game."

After the match, Justin was surrounded by press photographers and reporters, eager for a story on the young chess genius. He never mentioned Alyosha's radio receiver.

There had not been a rematch. Zharkov was permitted to continue his chess career until he began his military service. He followed his father to Nichevo meetings, said nothing, and listened. Justin Gilead disappeared off the face of the earth that very week.

Zharkov saw Gilead only twice during the twenty-five years that followed.

On both occasions, Zharkov had killed him. On both occasions, the Grandmaster had returned.

The second time had been four years ago in Poland. The Grandmaster had survived and escaped, but then had vanished from the earth. The Americans did not know where he was, in fact believed him dead, and even Zharkov's far-flung network of spies had not been able to find a trace of him. The

Russian eventually had come to believe that Justin Gilead had died of his wounds.

Died. The way a human being would have.

And now the medallion had surfaced, and while Ostrakov did not know what it meant, Alexander Zharkov did. He knew it as surely as he knew the sun would rise in the morning. He had feared it for years.

Justin Gilead—the Grandmaster—was alive.

Unconsciously, Zharkov's hands lifted to the high Russian military collar he wore.

Justin Gilead. The hunter. The hunted. Their destinies were as entwined as their pasts, and Zharkov knew he could never leave Gilead's death to others. That task, he knew, had been assigned to him and him alone since the moment of his birth.

He tore open the collar. Beneath it, burned into his flesh and scarred into ugly permanence, was the mark of the coiled snake.

Book Two

THE WEARER OF THE BLUE HAT

Justin Gilead learned early about death. His mother, a stage actress of remarkable beauty, died before Justin was three years old. His father, a novelist known worldwide by the single name Leviathan, which graced a stream of flashy if embarrassingly illiterate best-sellers, decided during his wife's funeral that the care of a preschool infant would hinder mightily the extensive research in the bars and bordellos of Europe necessary to produce his masterpieces.

As a result, Justin was raised in different cities around the United States by a succession of faceless aunts and uncles and chance associates of his father's who welcomed Leviathan's fat checks in return for sheltering and feeding a small boy who spoke little, had few friends, and amused himself by playing solitary games of chess during the lonely evenings of his childhood. One uncle encouraged him, and soon Justin was playing in, and winning, tournaments. When he was nine, he finished second in the United States junior chess championships.

Donald Gilead learned of his son's ability at the chessboard only when the invitation for Justin to participate in the French tournament reached him while he was in Paris arguing with a whore over the price of an evening. Thinking of the good publicity the boy's victory could generate for Leviathan's book, the elder Gilead had Justin flown over alone like so much baggage.

After Justin's triumphant match with the young Russian prodigy, the boy accompanied his father into the dim bars and illegal gambling houses in the seedy side streets of Courbevoie, where Donald Gilead found comfort. They did not speak much to each other. Gilead had all but forgotten the presence of the quiet boy. Justin, too, kept to his own thoughts. They were of robes.

Yellow robes. The back of the chess hall had been full of small, dark men in yellow robes, watching, concentrating. But their focus was not on the game. He, Justin Gilead, had been the object of their attention. He could feel them; their thoughts were almost palpable to him. And in words that were not words, the men in the yellow robes had said, *Come. You are of us. The man is not your father. This is not your home. We have come to take you home.*

At first he had found the intense stares of the small men to be distracting, but whatever energy—that was the only word he could think of for their strange communication through distance, their language without words—they sent to him shortly had the reverse effect. It concentrated his vision. It tightened his ranging mind until there was nothing for him to see or question or understand except the chess pieces in front of him, the knights and bishops and pawns that moved to his direction. For the length of that extraordinary match with the Russian boy who had not been permitted to control his own pieces, Justin Gilead did not merely play the game. He *was* the game.

He wished he could talk to someone about the old group of men in their yellow robes and the unearthly feeling of power they had sent to him during the match. Slowly he looked around the bar. His father, shirt unbuttoned down to the belly, was fondling the breasts of a dirty-looking blond woman to the encouragement of other bleary-eyed patrons.

No, there was no one who would understand about the men in the yellow robes. He looked the other way and tried to stay awake. At the far end of the bar, a dark man with a sharp nose and thinning hair sat silently, watching Justin's father and the blond woman.

His father shouted something, and the woman shouted back, spewing out a stream of gutter French. Justin turned in time to see his father reel back drunkenly, then smash his fist into the woman's face. She screamed. A small explosion of blood sprayed from her nose.

Swiftly, his face blank, the dark man at the end of the bar

rose. As he walked toward Justin's father, who had collapsed across the bar, he reached into the short cloth jacket he wore and popped open a knife with a six-inch-long blade.

All conversation stopped. The only sound in the bar was the rhythmic chant of a frothy French jazz tune. The bar patrons quickly slinked off their stools and away like unseeing worms. The barman stood stock-still as if to convince the man with the knife of his discretion. The man with the knife jerked his head toward the door.

Donald Gilead, his hands held shakily above his head, staggered wildly toward the exit, the man and the blond woman behind him.

Justin was frozen. He stood up on rubber legs and looked around the bar frantically, searching for someone who would help, but no one paid any attention to the boy. Running, he made his way out the door in time to see the dark man jab the blade into his father's bloated, exposed belly. Donald Gilead stared ahead stupidly for a moment, shuffling on his feet, then crashed backward into the slime of the stone-paved street.

The boy stared at the scene, breathing shallowly, watching his father's open eyes glaze over like those of some huge felled beast. A trickle of filthy water from the street formed a black pool around the dead man's face and mixed with the thread of blood oozing from between his lips. A wave of shock and revulsion rippled up through Justin's insides. For a moment, the man lying dead in the street looked no more human than the carcass of a slaughtered bull.

He looked up uncomprehendingly at the two figures standing over the body, the blond woman with her nose blackened comically with smeared blood, and the dark man holding the switchblade. By the harsh blue-white light of the street lamp, the knife glinted like a moving, living thing as the man walked slowly toward Justin, his breathing audible in the quiet night.

Justin backed away. Slowly at first, his hands shielding his face like a childish mask, he watched the silver gleam of the blade alternately disappear into shadow and shine brightly under the light as the dark man came closer, faster, toward him. His head bumped against the rough surface of a wall. The bump sent one message shooting through his body, and that was that this man, this stranger, was going to kill him.

He ran. Through the street, past heaps of rotting garbage and half-open back doorways reeking of liquor and stale smoke he ran, panting, not daring to look back, trying to keep his footing on the slippery stones of the pavement.

Two men walked out of one of the dingy bars along the street. Justin scurried up to them, clutching one of the men by the leg of his trousers.

"Stop him!" he yelled, pointing. "He's got a knife. He killed my father, and he's going to kill me, too."

Shrugging profusely, the man said something in French that was meant, Justin guessed, to sound comforting. Justin kept pointing, trying to indicate through his gestures that someone was after him. The two men looked at each other, then took a few steps down the street. The running footsteps had stopped. The dark man was gone. There was no one in view except a man and a woman, strolling arm in arm at a leisurely pace.

The Frenchman with Justin gestured to the couple and spoke something that sounded like a question.

"No," Justin said, relief flooding through him.

Then, as the couple passed beneath the street lamp, Justin recognized the blond woman. And beside her, the man with the knife, now hidden from view.

The woman smiled and called a name, holding out her arms.

"Ah," the Frenchman said, lifting Justin off the ground. He laughed and called something to the dark man and the blonde as he offered Justin to them.

Justin screamed, kicking the Frenchman in his side. "Put me down!"

The Frenchman dropped him with a curse and shouted at the couple. They paid him no attention. They were running after the boy.

The two sets of footsteps dropped off to one. The dark man was alone again. The winding street grew darker. Several of the street lamps had been smashed, and the seedy bars had given way to abandoned buildings and vacant lots. There was no one here, and Justin's limbs were trembling from the long exertion.

Still the footsteps came.

Justin forced himself to keep running, searching for a wider cross street, where he could lose himself, find a taxi, a police-

man . . . No. He had learned his lesson with the Frenchman.
Anyone he stopped would smile and shrug, not comprehending his pleas for help. And then turn him over to the dark man
with the shiny knife. There was nowhere for him to go but
straight into the darkness, running as long as he could, until
the dark man caught him, until . . .

His legs buckled. With a groan, Justin hit the pavement on
his knees and slapped forward, skinning his face. He heard
his breath whistling out of him. He closed his eyes. He
couldn't run anymore.

Farther.

He looked up. There was no one. Only the silent night
broken by the sound of the dark man's footsteps, walking
now.

Farther.

It was not a word, exactly, but a command nonetheless,
some unspoken will that was drawing him up, pushing him
forward.

The chess pieces, think only of the chess pieces.

He propelled himself ahead, his knees hurting, the bits of
gravel embedded in his cheek beginning to sting.

I am the game.

The silent force was stronger. It pulled him, enveloped him
like strange music growing louder. It was all around him,
along with the scent of almonds and lush flowers. It was
overpowering, an eerie chorus of voices calling to him, leading him to them.

He picked up speed, traveling as fast as he could, his lungs
bursting, his body wracked. He wished it were all a dream,
and that he would awake in Aunt Jane's house or Uncle Sid's
apartment and he would be safe in Houston or Cincinnati or in
any of the other places he'd been instructed to call home. But
he knew it was no dream. The street was real, the footsteps
behind him were real, the knife the dark man carried was
real.

Still, something peculiar was happening to him, something
like a dream. The music, the flowers, the scent of almonds:
Peculiar yet somehow . . . familiar.

I am the game.

When he saw the darkened alleyway, he knew he could go
no farther. It led to a dead end. There was no light at the end
of the alley. No place to hide. Nowhere to go from there. It

was the end of his journey. Yet this was where the music had called him.

Exhausted, he sat down in the alley and waited for the dark man.

When he arrived, the dark man stood squarely in the middle of the alley entrance, in silhouette. Justin watched him reach into his jacket. Holding his arm aloft, the dark man pressed the switch of the knife, and the blade shot upward, casting a long shadow. He closed in.

With a cry, Justin scrambled to his feet. Once again he heard the man's labored breathing.

"Go away!" he screamed.

The breathing grew louder.

"Please," Justin whispered.

The dark man lunged.

Justin leaped backward. As he did, he felt the brush of something soft against his face. Soft . . . and smelling of almonds.

He gasped at what came next. In a split second the darkened alleyway was filled with billowing forms, graceful as the flapping of birds' wings. *Something* had been waiting in the shadows of the alleyway, something so silent it could not be heard even in dead silence. That something whirled now in formation around the stunned man with the knife. He crouched down, babbling, and still the forms moved, too swiftly to see.

The dark man stabbed viciously into the circle that surrounded him, but the blade cut only through empty air. He arced, thrusting frantically, attacking the floating, unearthly forms like a caged animal.

Justin watched in awed terror. For behind the strange, blurred forms, surrounding them and filling the alley, was the music he had heard, powerful and sweet, as loud as a symphony.

The dark man lunged again. The circle broke, spitting him out like a seed. The moving forms became still. The music stopped.

They were men, Justin noted with astonishment. *The men at the tournament.* Six small men in yellow robes, almost identical with their shaved heads, who could move so fast that his own eyes saw nothing but a blur. They formed a line now, blocking the path between the dark man and the opening of the alley. One of them stepped forward two paces and stopped, silent.

Snarling, the dark man raised his dagger overhead in warning as he backed up toward Justin. With a swat, he grabbed the boy by his collar and yanked him forward, the knife held at his throat, and began inching forward.

Justin shuddered, feeling uncontrollable, noiseless tears streaming hotly down his cheeks. He had been caught, and the six little men in front of him had helped to catch him. The blade against his throat felt cold. He would be killed in minutes, maybe sooner. The music was gone now. It had betrayed him.

Behind him, the dark man gave a little laugh that sounded like a bark as he edged past the yellow-robed man standing in front of the others. There was no other movement. The yellow-robed man in front, older than the rest of his band, was as still as a tree, his lined face expressionless except for something in his eyes, something more felt than seen, a question unasked, a command unspoken.

Is it your will?

As if he had been hit by a hammer, Justin looked up, oblivious to the constricting pain of the knife against his skin. The yellow-robed man was looking straight ahead, not at him. Yet he *was* watching Justin, the boy felt it, knew it, watching from somewhere behind his eyes. And Justin knew this man as well as if he had spent a lifetime with him.

"It is my will," the boy whispered, understanding nothing, yet as sure of his authority over the yellow-robed men as he had been of anything in his life.

Instantly the yellow-robed man was in the air, kicking the knife out of the hands of the killer with what seemed like effortless ease. Justin watched the blade whirl upward like a propeller. With another blow to his back, the dark man shrieked and reeled toward the far end of the alleyway, clutching behind him. Then he looked up, his eyes widened in terror. Before he could scream, the blade of the descending knife struck with a thud and buried itself deep in his throat.

The dark man's arms shook spasmodically. In the moment before he fell, he jerked his head to the side and looked directly at Justin. The dazed expression in his eyes looked to the boy exactly like his father's at the moment of his death.

Justin stared at the dead man, the knife growing out of his

neck. The exhibition he had just witnessed was a more terrifying act than he could ever have imagined. The knife, *alone*, had killed from the air, like some vengeful sword sent by the gods. It had been a display not so much of strength as of—magic.

Who were these men? Justin began to tremble violently. What were they planning to do with him?

At that moment, the yellow-robed man standing apart from the others fell to his knees in the dirty alleyway. The others formed a circle around the boy and followed suit, spreading their fanciful garments on the stone pavement.

"Who are you?" the boy asked as he looked down on the circle centered around him.

"I am Tagore," the man answered. "We have sought you for many years, O Patanjali."

Justin blinked. "But that's not—"

The little man held up his hand, commanding silence. "There is no question now. You do not yet understand, but you have shown yourself to be the one we seek. I welcome you back to your home in the world of men."

He bowed low, his head touching the pavement in front of him. The others bowed as well. Justin Gilead alone remained standing among them. He wanted to tell them that they had made some kind of mistake, that he wasn't who they thought he was, that he didn't know what was going on, didn't understand anything that had gone on since the dark man had stabbed his father on the street. He was tired and hungry and frightened, and all he wanted to do was to rest somewhere.

But he remained where he was, standing inside the circle of men prostrated in obeisance to him, because the music had come back, and the scent of almonds, like a memory, filled the air.

Justin was hungry.

The journey overland had taken more than three months through the European countryside and the vast stretches of wild, uninhabited hill country that had once belonged to the Saracen Empire. Tagore and his band of yellow-robed men paid no heed to modern boundaries, or to the wars that raged along those boundaries. Always, he seemed to have an instinct for the least traveled ways, leading his men and their young charge into the most desolate regions, from the tall pine forests of the west into the arid plains of southern Asia, where even in summer the icy winds from the Himalayas shook the patches of scrub grass and could freeze a man to death.

But not these men, Justin thought as one of them prepared a fire from small sticks. His hands moved with incredible speed as he twirled a stick into the base of a chip of stone. It ignited at once. Justin was no longer amazed at the skills these small men possessed. After the meal was cooked, Justin knew, another of the yellow-robed men would hold his hand directly over the flames and press them into the earth, leaving no mark on either the ground or his flesh.

He had questioned at first. He had complained of the welts and blisters on his feet, despite his shoes, of the constant ache in his legs. At a command from Tagore, the men all removed their sandals and walked barefoot, carrying Justin on their backs. When he objected to the gruel they ate as daily fare, an unpleasant mixture of brick tea, sour milk, salt, rancid butter, fragments of dried white cheese and roasted barley, which they carried with them, one of the men killed a goat and brought it to their camp. To Justin's delight, they roasted the goat and placed a huge shank of meat before him. The man who had brought the dead goat bowed to Justin, then to Tagore, and left.

Justin ate ravenously, barely noticing that the others were not eating at all. He offered some of the meat to Tagore, but the old man refused.

"Aren't you hungry?" Justin asked.

"No," Tagore said simply.

The meal finished, Justin wrapped himself in a blanket, as usual, while the others lay on the bare ground with only scattered shrubs and rocks for shelter against the night winds. He couldn't sleep. Rising, he saw only four of the six men. Some distance away, Tagore knelt on a rocky stretch of ground, facing the mountains to the north. Justin went up to him and knelt beside him, wincing at the sharp stab of the rocks. "Where is the other man?" he asked.

"He is dead," Tagore said. The flesh of his face sagged. The eloquent long nose of the old man jutted with dignity toward the northern mountains.

"How?" Justin asked.

"That was for him to decide. There are many ways to will the body to die. He has gone into the shadows. We will not find him."

"Then how do you know he killed himself?"

"He had no other choice," Tagore said. "Like all of us, he was a monk who devoted his life to holiness. Yet this night he performed an act by which his karma was sullied."

"Karma?"

"The life force," Tagore explained. "Each of the Creator's beings on earth possesses a soul. In the beginning of life, this soul possesses all things, all possibilities. But as one's life grows, he forges by his actions the quality of that soul. The beauty or ugliness of his destiny is charted by the wisdom and care he places into his spirit. Do you understand?"

Justin nodded. "But why did the monk die?"

"He knew he could never again attain the spiritual purity necessary for our way of life," Tagore said. "His only course was to relinquish this life and wait for the next, in which he might justify himself."

Justin shifted his weight to sit, rather than kneel, on the sharp stones. "He must have done something terrible," he said.

"Not terrible. Necessary."

"What's that mean?" Justin asked.

Tagore fixed him with reproachful eyes. "You were not pleased with your food. Because there is so little edible vegetation in the area, he was obliged to kill the goat whose meat you ate. In doing so, he violated one of the laws of our religion."

"But it was *food*."

Tagore shook his head. "We had food. We would not have starved without the goat. And the beast was not attacking us. Its life was not taken in defense of our own. It was killed only for your pleasure."

The boy scrambled to his feet. "I don't believe you," he hissed.

Tagore only turned again to the mountain.

Justin was crying. "Did he know?" he asked in a small voice. "Did he know what would—happen to him?"

"Yes, my son," Tagore said.

"Then why didn't he tell me? I didn't have to eat the goat. Not if he was going to *die* for it."

Tagore took his hand. "One does not learn from words," he said. "And he obeyed because you are Patanjali."

That night, Justin took his blanket to the base of the mountain and left it there. He did not complain again.

Tagore and his men spoke little during their long sojourn. By day, they moved swiftly, stealing silently over the land, leaving only Justin's footprints in their wake. At night they watched, barely moving, listening for the faintest sounds, seeming to communicate with one another without words. Justin watched with them, trying to achieve the perfect stillness of his fellow travelers, but always he was aware of the sound of his own breathing, the obtrusive clumsiness of his own body. When he slept, he still shivered in the cold. When he walked, he alone, of all the men, frightened birds and small animals with the noise of his footfalls.

"I am not like you," he told Tagore.

"No being is like another. But you will learn what we know."

"Will you teach me?"

"Yes. That is why I have come," Tagore said.

"How?"

"In time, you will understand how."

"And when I learn?"

"Then you will understand how much you have yet to learn."

It was dawn. In the distance, the towering Himalayas rose out of a pink mist. Below them, just ahead of the group, was spread a large mountain lake, still as glass and surrounded by a purple ring of flowering wild rhododendron.

At the edge of the lake, one of the men wound his robe between his legs and walked slowly into the water. With a short bow toward the men on shore, he dived under and was gone.

They watched for some time, long after the ripples on the surface of the water had subsided and the lake returned to its perfect stillness. Justin began to panic. "What did I do this time?" he whispered.

Tagore smiled. "Nothing. He has gone to tell others of your arrival. Many will come to see you. As he has the farthest to travel, he must leave first."

"But he hasn't even come up for air."

"That is not necessary." With only a small nod from Tagore, the remaining three men folded their robes. Each in turn bowed to Tagore and the boy. Then they, too, entered the water and were gone without trace.

"How long can they stay underwater?" Justin asked.

"As long as they must. There are those among us who have lived in death for years."

"Lived in death?"

"That is what we call the suspension of breathing, the slowing of the bodily processes. In our practice, we learn to control our bodies through the union of our spirits with the forces of the universe. It is called yoga."

Justin made a face. "I've heard of yoga. It's where people sit around twisted into pretzels. They don't do what *you* do—walk without making noise, hold fire in your hands. They don't stay underwater for days, I know that," he said cynically.

"You know, you know, you know," Tagore said. "Tell me, is there anything you don't know?"

Justin was ashamed. "I'm sorry," he said. "It's just that

the things you do don't look like anything I've seen before."
He looked up. "I guess that doesn't mean it's not possible."

Tagore smiled. "A beginning," he said, "Now you will
swim the lake."

"Me?" Justin was horrified. "But I can't do that," he
said.

"And why not? Do you not have the same limbs, the same
organs as we?"

"You know what I mean," Justin said dispiritedly. "I
can't do magic."

"Ah," Tagore said, raising his eyebrows. "It is magic you
wish to perform."

"Your kind of magic."

The old man nodded. "Come," he said. He led Justin to a
small stream near the thicket of rhododendrons and picked a
hand-sized rock off the ground. "If this rock were made to
disappear—not hide, but disappear completely, never to exist
in the form of a rock again—would you consider such an act
to be magic?"

Justin looked at the rock. "Yes," he said.

"Very well." Carefully he placed the rock in the middle of
the stream.

"What did you do that for?"

"It is the magic you requested," Tagore said. "I have
placed the rock in water. You see it now, but in a century the
rock will be gone, disappeared forever. The flow of the water
will have worn it to nothing."

"I get it," Justin said, disappointed. "There's no magic."

"You are wrong, my son," Tagore said quietly. "It is *all*
magic." He sat down. Not a petal moved on the thousands of
blossoms around him. "When you accepted to eat with the
rest of us, you learned to endure hunger. When you gave up
your blanket in shame, you learned to endure cold. Those
small sufferings were like the first drops of water to come
into this stream. With many drops, there will be enough water
to flow eternally, with enough force to move through solid
rock. That is the magic you will learn, my son. It is great
magic, indeed."

Justin picked up the rock. "A century?" he asked.

"Only a century. Now cross the lake with me."

He wrapped his garments around his legs and led the boy
into the freezing water. "You will not die from the cold

because you have learned to endure cold," Tagore said. "Your little puddle is already growing into a stream."

He smiled, and then he was below the surface of the lake, pulling the boy behind him. Justin sputtered and coughed, trying to keep his head above water as he rushed away from shore. He was freezing. In a matter of minutes, his arms and legs felt numb, and his stomach knotted painfully.

"Tagore!" he screamed, gulping water. "Tagore!"

But the monk didn't surface. He continued through the water, dragging Justin's cramping, panicking little form with him.

He couldn't breathe. He was sure he was going to die. Feeling faint, he loosened his grip on Tagore's hand. To his surprise, the monk released him without any effort to hold on. But it was too late, anyway. Slowly Justin began to sink, falling into unconsciousness.

When he came to, he was still in the lake, but moving again, skimming once more over the surface of the water. He bucked in panic, filling his nostrils with water, cramping once again with the cold.

And again, the sure hands released him.

Justin understood.

He let himself go limp. Immediately the hands of his teacher enclosed his wrists. He felt himself being swept with Tagore's powerful movement underwater, and forced himself not to fight it. It was difficult. His body wanted to fight, screamed with urgency. But each time he felt himself involuntarily stiffen, the hands that held his wrists loosened tentatively.

Finally, to control himself as much as he could, he gulped in all the air he could and then submerged his head underwater. Without the fight for air, his body relaxed. When he could no longer hold his breath in his lungs, he brought himself up for another gasp. This time, he released his breath slowly, taking as long as he could. To his surprise, he didn't struggle when he came up for air again. It just filled his lungs as easily as . . .

As easily as breathing, he thought. That was all it was. Breathing.

His periods underwater grew imperceptibly longer with each breath. At last, when he could see the Rhododendrons at the far end of the lake, he stopped thinking about breathing, stopped thinking of his body. The only thought in his mind was a feeling of coming home, of seeing the tree again, the blue hat.

The tree?

Hail, O Wearer of the Blue Hat.

He stiffened. Tagore released him and emerged minutes later on the shore behind the circle of flowers.

Struggling, Justin swam the rest of the distance and walked over to join him. "I guess I don't learn very fast," he said, rubbing his hands over his wet clothes to warm himself.

"You are here," Tagore said, "so it was fast enough."

His robe was dry. He extended another to Justin.

"Where'd you get these?"

"They have been waiting for us for many years," Tagore said. He took him into a cave set at the base of the mountain and showed him the deep hole in the wall where the robes had been buried inside a silver casket, along with woolen cloaks and strips of cloth. "Ten years, exactly. That is how long it has taken us to find you."

"What if I'm not the one you're looking for?"

Tagore gathered sticks. "You are," he said.

Justin stripped down quickly and put on the robe.

"This, too," Tagore said, handing him a belt made of small bones.

"What are these things?" the boy asked, fingering the strange white rosary.

"The spine of a snake," Tagore said.

"It's not like yours."

"The snake is for you alone," Tagore built a small fire inside the cave, protected from the chilling winds outside. He took a dry bag of the tea mixture from the casket and cooked it in the bowl he always carried. "Tonight we will keep the fire," he said.

Justin smiled. "Why? I'm not weak."

"Because tomorrow we climb the sacred mountain of Amne Xachim. We will take no food until we reach the monastery of Rashimpur."

"Rashimpur." The boy rolled the name on his tongue.

Home.

He looked up suddenly from the fire. "Tagore, what is the blue hat?"

The monk straightened. "You know of the blue hat?"

"I heard something. In the lake. A voice, sort of. Not really a voice, more of a feeling . . . Oh, it's stupid."

For the first time since their journey began, Tagore raised his voice. "Do not call stupid that which you cannot explain!" He set the bowl aside and stood over Justin, his eyes blazing. "Your mind and body are young, but your soul is among the most ancient. When it calls to you through ages of death and wisdom, do not seek to ignore it, or to treat it with scorn. For it is the voice of Brahma, the Creator, which speaks, and without your faith, that voice will forever be silent."

For a moment, Justin thought the man was going to strike him. Then Tagore turned and walked back to the fire, his anger gone.

"It—the voice—said, 'Hail, O Wearer of the Blue Hat.' "

Tagore poured a portion of the gruel into another bowl and handed it to Justin. "Then it is time I spoke to you of yourself," he said.

"At Rashimpur," the old teacher began, "we practice a faith that is very old, nearly as old as the Sacred Mountain itself. It is said that when Brahma completed the task of creating the earth and its inhabitants, he was weary and sought a perfect place to rest.

"But the oceans, moving with the rhythm of the universe, made too much noise for the sensitive ears of the Creator. So, too, the plains with their shifting winds and the forests, filled with the chattering of the small creatures who dwelt there. Only the mountain remained as a place where Brahma could find complete peace. Yet even the mountains sometimes crumbled and fell from their heights, for this was the god's plan in fashioning the world. Change, death, and rebirth. Thus only can eternity be wrought, for without change there can be no life. Without life there can be no death. Without death, the spirit of Brahma's creations cannot be reborn to change and grow yet again.

"It was for this reason that Brahma created Amne Xachim, the Tower of Peace, the last mountain. As it existed for his use alone, Brahma formed the Sacred Mountain so that it would remain forever unchanged, its stillness and silence unique on all the earth.

"To shield it from the eyes of men, he hid it behind other, higher mountains which would draw their attention. But he wished to mark Amne Xachim in some way so that he himself might find it again when he returned to visit the earth. Toward this end he formed this lake at its base and ringed it with bright flowers, which bloom despite the cold mountain winds. Halfway up the mountain, near the cave where Brahma chose to rest, he placed another lake identical to this."

"At Rashimpur?"

Tagore smiled. "At Rashimpur. It is there still." He drank from his bowl and stirred the fire, enjoying the boy's anticipation.

At last he spoke again. "His work finished, Brahma entered the cave in the perfect stillness of the sacred mountain to sleep. But once inside, he could find no comfort. For he loved the earth he had created, constantly striving in its imperfection, constantly changing and growing and living. In comparison, the absolute stillness of Amne Xachim was like death without hope of rebirth, and it saddened him.

"So Brahma, in his supreme wisdom, brought life into the sacred mountain. For this life, he chose something of beauty and strength that would remain for the ages of the earth, something so silent it would not disturb the Creator in his centuries of sleep."

"The tree," Justin whispered.

Tagore studied him. "Yes," he said finally. "The Tree of the Thousand Wisdoms."

"I saw it." Justin tried to bring together the vision he had experienced as he passed through the lake. "A big tree, not like anything that grows around here, as wide as five men, with dark leaves and a bark like iron. A tree that grows without light." He looked to Tagore in bewilderment. "But I never really saw a tree like that. Not with my eyes."

"It is the tree, all the same," Tagore said. "It stands in the Great Hall of Rashimpur."

Justin spoke with difficulty. "How did I know that?"

"I cannot tell you," the teacher said.

Justin's eyes welled with tears that shone in the firelight.

"Do not be afraid," Tagore said softly.

Justin looked up at him, his blue eyes as weary as an old man's. "What's happening to me?" he asked. "Why am I seeing these things?"

"You are remembering," Tagore said. "This is as it should be. You see the Tree of the Thousand Wisdoms because the tree was beloved of Patanjali."

"That's what you called me. In Paris, when my father . . ." He drew a circle in the packed earth of the cave. It had been weeks since he'd thought about his father. The rigors of the trip had overshadowed the nightmare of that night when his father, bloated and bleeding, fell lifeless into the street.

"His eyes were open," Justin said quietly.

Tagore touched him lightly on the shoulder. "My son, your life is destined to be filled with hardship. You cannot escape it. Your father's death was but the first ordeal. There will be others. That is why we have searched so long to find you. In Rashimpur, you will be protected as you could never be in your other world. We will teach you how to bring your body into union with the forces of the universe, so that you will not fear physical danger. We will hone your mind and your senses so that you may seek understanding. But that is all we can do," he said.

Justin faltered. "But what do you mean . . .?"

"You will learn in time," Tagore said gently. "Do not try to learn too much too quickly. There is time."

"But the voice I hear . . ."

"It is meant for you." He held both the boy's hands and looked into his eyes, so deeply that Justin felt as if someone had entered his very soul. "Listen carefully to what I am about to tell you," he said. "And do not color my words with pride, for I give this as warning. There are men who possess extraordinary discipline, who can teach themselves to achieve far beyond their natural abilities. We at Rashimpur are such men. And there are others who are born with exceptional gifts, who can see past and present, who can move objects and create energy by the power of their minds alone. You of the West call these individuals psychics, or levitators, or other such names. But there is a third personality, very rare, whose very being cannot be explained. His is the hardest life, because he must live forever alone, his spirit removed from the rest of humanity. In order to dwell on the earth, he must learn to be like others, yet he will never be like others. You are such a one, Justin Gilead."

The boy's face was stony. "I don't want to be," he said.

"It is not your choice, as it was not the choice of Patanjali to be born the first incarnation of Brahma." He let go of the boy's hands and stirred the fire. It leaped to life. Tagore smiled at him from behind the flames, his features serene. "Shall I tell you of Patanjali?"

Justin shrugged.

"Very well. If you have no interest, I will not."

"No, go ahead," Justin said, betraying his eagerness.

"As I thought."

Tagore told the story of how Brahma, millennia after his first stay in Amne Xachim, returned to earth in the guise of a small snake. According to legend, the snake god lived in the Tree of the Thousand Wisdoms, but when he entered the world of men, he took the shape of a man and called himself Patanjali.

During his life, Patanjali developed the discipline of yoga, which he claimed united man with the stronger forces of the universe, and it is as the first teacher of yoga that he is remembered to this day.

Patanjali amazed the populace with seemingly supernatural feats of physical control, including holding his breath underwater or underground for astonishing lengths of time, lying on nails for long periods and rising unmarked, walking through flames, and changing his weight at will.

As he aged, Patanjali's physical strength weakened, but he had grown to be a sage of wide renown, leaving writings that are still read. His reputation grew to immense proportions, and from hundreds of miles away, followers claimed that the yogi was capable of such feats as animating dead bodies and becoming invisible.

Tagore related the famous story with the skill and expression born of many retellings. The boy sat, entranced, his eyes riveted on the face of his teacher.

"It was then that Patanjali discovered the great sadness of his long life," Tagore said.

"Why?" Justin jerked forward. "Didn't anybody believe him?"

"It is not known if the sage revealed himself to be the incarnation of Brahma, or if he even knew himself. All he explained about his own life was that he came to earth as a snake, and for this he suffered much persecution. Many did not believe him. Of those who did, the Shamans, or Black Hats, as they were called—practitioners of black magic who performed rituals of human sacrifice and held their followers in fear by claiming to control the weather—viewed the snake as an evil symbol, reckoned Patanjali as evil, and counted him among their own.

"The Black Hats summoned him to their temple, a vile

place filled with the skulls and backbones of the dead, to welcome him. But when he appeared, Patanjali mocked the Shamans by appearing in a blue hat, explaining that he was of the sky and the sea, which were filled with life, and that with his blue hat he denounced their unwholesome ways.

"The Black Hats were outraged. They challenged him to match his magic against their own before the wisest men of the region. Patanjali, who was a humble man, said that he knew no magic, but that he would be pleased to meet such wise men and learn from them. He invited them to Amne Xachim.

"There, before the sages and tribal leaders of the world as it was then known, the Shamans performed their conjuring tricks and incantations, speaking in inhuman voices and dazzling the onlookers with spells that produced flames out of air and terrifying visions in smoke.

"When they had finished, they demanded to see Patanjali's own performance. By this time, the yogi had grown to be an old man, frail and weakened since the days of his youth. He told them again that he possessed no magic, but that there was magic enough in every leaf of every tree to fill the world.

"Disappointed, the spectators jeered him and judged the Shamans in their Black Hats to be the greatest among them. As a gesture of their victory, the Shamans selected one of their number to punish the old man. He struck off Patanjali's right hand with a sword and threw it against the Tree of the Thousand Wisdoms. Then he plucked a leaf from the tree and tossed it down to the bleeding old man.

" 'Use this magic to heal yourself, then,' the Shaman said scornfully. And with that, the First Great Miracle of Brahma occurred. The cave was filled with a terrible noise. The severed hand of Patanjali had been transformed into a coiled snake whose hiss was so frightening it chilled the surprised onlookers to their depths. Moving with the speed of a lightning spear, the snake struck the Shaman in the forehead and killed him at once.

"The other Black Hats stood, rooted, fearful for their own lives. But when Patanjali rose, he carried only the leaf that the Shaman had plucked for him in derision, and placed it on the forehead of the dead sorcerer. It healed the wound without a mark. The snake disappeared, and the Patanjali's hand was restored.

"The Shaman, again whole, left Amne Xachim with the other Black Hats in shame. But the others bowed to Patanjali and praised him, saying 'Hail to thee, O Wearer of the Blue Hat.'"

Justin was transfixed. "Is that true?" he whispered.

"No one knows," Tagore said, smiling. "It is true that Patanjali lived, some two hundred years before the beginning of your calendar, and was believed, as we of Rashimpur believe now, to be the incarnate spirit of Brahma. It is true that he adopted the symbol of the coiled snake as his talisman, and the amulet that he wore has come down to us through the centuries. It is a powerful medallion, suffused with the spirit of the highest god, and may be worn with safety only by the true reincarnation of Brahma himself."

Justin blinked. "How do you know who that is?"

"Toward the end of his life, Patanjali invited a small core of his followers who were trained in the discipline of yoga to join him in Amne Xachim. They did, forsaking their worldly lives, and they transformed the cave into the monastery of Rashimpur. Before he died, he spoke of his spirit entering the body of a newborn infant. When that child was found, he was shown a number of objects, among them precious stones, toys, and ordinary rocks, covered in cloth. The amulet of the coiled snake was so covered. Yet the child grasped it immediately. Like you, he remembered small things of Patanjali's life. He grew to become the most holy of men and named his own successor on his death. The practice has continued to this day."

"But how does *he* know?"

The fire lay smoldering in its ashes. "My son, that is something only the Wearer of the Blue Hat can know."

They lay down in the cave. Outside, the wind from Amne Xachim howled. "Tagore?" Justin asked from the darkness.

"Yes."

"Did someone pick me?"

"Yes," Tagore said. "Ten years ago, on the date of your birth. His name was Sadika. With his last words, he dispatched us to find you. 'A small boy with eyes the color of blue ice,' he told us, for he knew we would not find you for many years. He instructed us to look for a boy from the West, one who learns of death from the game of *shah mat*."

"*Shah mat?*"

"Persian words. They mean 'the king is dead.' You call the game chess."

They slept that night and awoke the next day. Tagore wrapped himself and the boy in heavy cloaks and bound their heads and feet with the strips of cloth from the bottom of the silver casket.

"For the cold," he said. Then he replaced the casket in the wall and lifted the heavy stone back into place.

At the foot of Amne Xachim he knelt and said a simple prayer.

The climb to Rashimpur took four days. They traveled on a narrow footpath winding up the northern slope of Amne Xachim. They walked night and day, resting only when the boy could walk no farther.

Justin had grown thin and pale. The hunger in his belly gnawed at him like a living thing. When he slept, he dreamed only of death.

It was the same dream, recurring on each of the three nights of the journey. In it, he lay deep in a pit on foreign ground, straining to hear the songs of birds overhead for the last time as shovelfuls of earth crashed around his face. There was no pain in the dream, but a deep terror permeated every fiber of his body. For above him in the dream stood a man whose face he could see clearly, a man he had never met, yet whose features were oddly familiar. This man, he knew, would bring death, and in the dream that death was all around him, coming closer, curling around the corners of his spirit like gray smoke. Softly death came, as the earth slowly swallowed Justin up, and as it approached, the familiar stranger above him watched and stood guard, protecting death while it wrapped Justin in its soft gray arms.

He awoke screaming.

CHAPTER NINE

Justin tried to focus his eyes. A light drizzle was falling, and the rain felt cool against his fever-blistered skin. The sickness had crept up during the night, after his dream. He had not been able to sleep again.

An hour before, the starless sky had been pitch black. Now, streams of gray light were filtering through the ropey clouds to the east. With the light came the sounds of birds and insects. With some surprise, Justin saw the sky's reflection not more than a hundred yards from him, shimmering on the surface of a perfectly still lake surrounded by purple blossoms. Above him, the sacred mountain of Amne Xachim flattened abruptly into a shelflike plateau.

He squinted, hearing his breath hiss hotly out of him. The steep incline leading to the plateau continued farther up the peak, its brown earth and rock graduating to snow and, above the snow, clouds. But on the plateau itself the mountain seemed to form a solid wall of rock. And on the rock was etched what seemed to be the outline of a door.

"Tagore," he whispered.

The old teacher rose, staring at Justin's haggard face, stretched taut with fatigue and hunger and fever. He followed the boy's eyes upward to the cliffside.

"Rashimpur," he said.

The monastery was barely distinguishable from the mountain cliff. Built into the side of the mountain, Rashimpur sported no pillars, no statues or colored facades. Only the doorway, whose outline Justin had viewed from below,

74

interrupted the smooth wall of rock on the northern face of Amne Xachim.

"Why is it hidden?" Justin asked, blinking and taking deep breaths to steady himself as they made their way up the nearly vertical slope of the mountain.

Tagore followed behind closely. "It is hidden because there have always been men for whom faith has been inconvenient or dangerous. Patanjali knew this. Perhaps Brahma himself understood, and so formed the secret cave in which Rashimpur now stands."

"Do you mean the Black Hats?" Justin asked.

"It began with the Black Hats. Since the time of Patanjali's duel of magic with the Shamans, the Black Hats gave way to the Red Hats, who claim to have 'reformed' the rituals of the Black Hat. The Red Hats themselves have been taken over by the Yellow Hats, who were influenced by Christianity. In many areas, Buddhists have adopted our ways, but they do not revere Brahma. In some, as among the Kalmuks and the Buriats of Siberia and in the lamaseries of Mongolia, the czars and Chinese chieftains have sought to destroy the power of the yogis by placing their own men as heads of the monasteries there. And in other places, the old beliefs have been scorned by official decree. We of all the mystical faiths have been driven to live in secrecy by those who would destroy us."

"Who would do that?" Justin asked.

"Those who do not understand," Tagore said. "Those who fear any power other than that wielded by government decree. Those who believe that an army of soldiers with guns can erase the teachings of thousands of years."

"You shouldn't be afraid of stupid people like that."

Tagore stopped to look down at the boy. "At Rashimpur, many holy persons will come to see you. They will brave the greatest dangers to do so, traveling over harsh ground and bad weather. Still, it is nothing compared with the dangers they face each day, for many of them live in hostile lands where their very lives depend on secrecy. The Kirghiz of Sinkiang, now under the rule of the Chinese, were destroyed completely. So, too, were the lamaseries of Manchuria, because they failed to keep their existence secret. Most of those remaining may do so only in exchange for political favors—the use of roads built for religious purposes, now used as conduits for the military, the use of monks as spies to other lands. Many of our number have faced death rather than succumb to the corrupt demands of these others, preferring to see their monasteries obliterated and their ancient faith buried. It is only by the grace of Brahma that Rashimpur lies protected and hidden by Amne Xachim. No one but those in holy service know of the existence of Rashimpur. It must remain that way until we can live in safety and freedom.''

Justin stumbled near the top, but Tagore pushed him forward.

"You must enter Rashimpur on your own strength," he said.

Justin nodded, trying to steady the trembling in his hands. With a tremendous effort he pulled himself up to the plateau. There, he stood facing the rock face of Rashimpur.

The air was thin. Justin's head was spinning. His legs buckled, and he dropped to his knees. Tagore knelt beside him.

"Don't help me," Justin said sharply. "I will walk."

They entered the stone doorway.

Justin was dazzled by what lay inside. The walls of the Great Hall, illuminated by the flames from huge torches, were made of pure beaten gold. Its ceiling dome was of intricately wrought silver and encrusted with gemstones, so that the hall seemed to be ablaze with colored lights. The fragrance of almonds permeated the air.

There was no furniture in the vast hall. Yellow-robed men with shaved heads walked soundlessly on the mirror-smooth stone floor to where Justin and Tagore waited, bowing to both of them. At last a small man, identical to the others, came over and led them down the long hall to its far wall, which terminated in the massive trunk of a tree.

"The Tree of the Thousand Wisdoms," Tagore said.

As they drew nearer, Justin saw that in front of the tree stood a glass casket in which lay the body of an old man, the carefully preserved skin like parchment. The man's hands were folded across his chest, palms up. In his left hand was a diamond the size of a robin's egg. In his right, wound around the corpse's fingers, was the gold chain holding the amulet of the coiled snake.

"This is Sadika," Tagore said. "We have not buried him for these many years while we have searched for you. If you are the new incarnation of Patanjali and Brahma the Creator, then Sadika will be laid to rest.''

Justin was stunned. "If?" He had come with Tagore for thousands of miles. "*If* I'm the one? But you said I was.''

"I believe it is so," Tagore said. "But only Sadika himself can know for certain.''

"But he's dead," Justin argued, feeling faint.

"Our death is not as yours.''

He stared at the dead man, so restful, so at peace. He closed his eyes and again saw the gray smoke of his dream, now curling around the edges of the man's casket, enveloping the body. He opened his eyes and looked up, frightened. The casket was untouched. Tagore was looking only at him.

"What is it, my son?" he asked, his voice heavy with worry.

Justin felt heat. His eyes traveled up from the dead man to the tree, the strange dark tree he had seen in the water. Again he closed his eyes, and now he saw the tree burst into bright flame, the stench of burning flesh filling the Great Hall. And above it all loomed the specter of the man in his dream, the face strange yet familiar, watching the proceedings, unleashing the death he had brought with him. He reached out for the face in front of him, but his small hands clutched only at the air. And then he fell forward.

"Justin!" Tagore called to him, lifting the boy's unconscious body into his arms.

But Justin couldn't answer. Tagore's voice had come from far away, from another time, long past. For now, there was only fire and death filling the Great Hall, with the stranger, the Prince of Death, presiding over the devastation, guiding Justin toward his real destiny.

He awoke in a dark stone cell lit only by the flame of a small candle. Over him, Tagore bent, placing cold cloths on Justin's forehead. The old man's features relaxed when he saw Justin's eyes open. "My son," he said gently.

"How long?" Justin croaked.

"You have slept for three days.''

He had trouble swallowing. The burning fever had subsided, but the sickness had left him limp and weak. His robes were soaked with sweat and lay twisted around him. Suddenly he sat bolt upright, his eyes wide and glassy. "Rashimpur!" he cried. "The fire—the tree was on fire!"

"Hush," Tagore whispered, stroking the boy's face. "There has been no fire."

"There *was!* I saw it. It was all around. The Great Hall burned."

"The fire was in your body, burning from the fever." Tagore said. "Rashimpur is in no danger. There was no fire. You have been screaming about fire for these three days, but there is no fire."

"But the tree—"

"Silence," Tagore said, daubing the cool cloth over the boy's cheeks. "Those who have come to see you have begun to gather. You must save your strength. In two days' time you must go forth into the Great Hall, prepared to assume the duties left for you by Sadika."

Justin frowned, trying to pull the blurred image of Tagore into focus. "What duties?"

"They are to remain unknown to all but you. If you are fit to rule."

"But . . . how will you know if I'm fit?" Justin asked.

"I told you before that Sadika himself will tell us."

He cautioned the boy to silence and kept vigil over him for the rest of that night and the next day. Justin slept intermittently, accepting small bowls of rice and tea and fighting off the recurrent dreams of the familiar stranger who watched at the moment of his death.

On the third day, just as the first strings of dawn were seeping through the narrow slitted window of his cell, four monks bearing bowls of water and jeweled caskets entered and knelt before him. They were the same four who had left him with Tagore at the lake below Amne Xachim.

Wordlessly, they helped him off the stone pallet where he had lain since his first day in Rashimpur. They washed him with scented herbs in water and dressed him in another of the yellow robes, then led him into the corridor where Tagore stood waiting.

"Where are we going?" Justin asked.

"To the Tree of the Thousand Wisdoms," he said.

The torches in the splendid hall were all ablaze, giving the vast room a shimmering, underwater appearance. Visitors to the Hall lined both walls four deep, leaving only a path on the marble floor leading directly to the tree and the open casket beneath it.

The visitors were magnificently dressed in strange garb. As they waited at the rear of the hall, Tagore pointed out some of the visiting eminences. "The Dalai Lama of Tibet has come to pay Sadika his last tribute," Tagore said. "And beside him is Manjusri, the Saskya Lama." He nodded toward a small, round-headed man swathed in green silk robes, his feet shod in jeweled slippers. "Long before the establishment of the Dalai Lama, who rules Tibet today, Manjusri's predecessors were supreme in that holy land. Even the Mongol emperor Kublai Khan bowed before the ancestors of Manjusri, who are said to be the incarnations of the Bodhisat of Knowledge. He is reputed to be the wisest of men."

Tagore pointed out another, on the other side of the hall, a man in rags, his feet bare, who stood quietly in the shadows of the great torches. "That is the Ralpahi Dorje," Tagore whispered. "He is head of the Can-skya lamasery in Peking."

"Why is he so poor?" Justin asked.

"It is only in the eyes of the unseeing that the Dorje is poor," Tagore said. "He is also descended from an ancient line of holy men. He is considered in Buddhism to be a true saint. His miracles in healing have been seen by all. He chooses to live in poverty because true power comes from humility. He is the greatest of all healers."

"But I don't understand," Justin said. "Wouldn't people respect him more if he didn't look so dirty?"

"Only those whose faith is not strong enough to see beyond his rags," Tagore said.

There was a great clamor in the hall as four red-robed monks entered, bearing a sedan chair. It was jeweled from top to bottom, its bamboo poles lacquered a deep red. As the four monks set the chair down and drew open its curtains, a tall woman emerged. She wore a long garment made of many layers of crimson gauze, but as she moved, the fabric clung tightly to the curves of her body and showed the flesh beneath. Gems dotted the fabric. Her black hair glinted with jeweled pins, and on her fingernails, she wore long gem-encrusted sheaths. She fixed her eyes on young Justin, and, involuntarily, he sipped in his breath. Her eyes were of the darkest green, but they were dotted with flecks of a lighter color, almost gold, and they seemed to reflect all the lights in the great hall. Her face was beautiful, with high, sculpted cheek-bones and full, dark red lips, and Justin thought her the most beautiful woman he had ever seen. He could not pull his eyes away from hers.

"That is the Dorje Pagma," Tagore said.

Justin was stunned, then forced himself to look up to Tagore. "Is she a monk?"

"An abbess. She rules over the Samding monastery at the Lake of Yamdrok in Tibet. Both monks and nuns follow her, and believe her to be the incarnation of the Indian goddess Varja. She is the most powerful personage here. Her magic is very strong."

"As strong as the Shaman's?" Justin asked, remembering Tagore's story of the Black Hats.

"Stronger. Much stronger. It is said that she can control time itself. The goddess Varja is old, thousands of years. The Dorje's followers claim that she is not an incarnation, but the original goddess herself, living without time, without death."

"That's impossible," Justin said, noticing several of the visitors to the hall moving silently away from the jeweled chair of the Dorje Pagma.

"Nothing is impossible in our world," Tagore said. He smiled at the exodus of people to the other side of the hall. "They are leaving because they fear the power of Varja," he said.

"Why? Is she evil?"

"A goddess is a goddess," Tagore said. "She does as she wills. But many think the destruction of the monasteries at Labrang and Pemiongchi—formerly great centers—was brought about because of the wrath of Varja."

"How were they destroyed?"

"By—" Tagore's face changed. "The political governments of the countries where the monasteries had existed for thousands of years eliminated them," he said.

"They were burned," Justin said. "Just like in my dream. Burned." He had started to tremble.

"Be still, my son," Tagore said. "For if it is God's will, we will be destroyed. Not even Varja has power over the great Brahma. And if it is God's will, we will return. Do you understand?"

Justin said nothing. After a while, he looked up. "Tagore,

everyone here seems to do something better than everybody else. What do you do at Rashimpúr?''

Tagore smiled. "We of Rashimpur are the poorest of all," he said. "For we are not the wisest of men, nor the holiest, nor the most powerful. We have only our strength and will to take before Brahma in offering, as Patanjali did.''

"Strength?"

"I have told you of yoga. It is the discipline we practice here. With it, we' try to bring our bodies into union with the forces of the universe. We are known only for this.''

"You're the strongest ones.''

"It is as nothing,'' Tagore said. "But Brahma needs men of physicalness as well as those of spirituality.''

Justin smiled. "I think being strong is the best thing of all.''

They walked forward in silence. In the still hall, Justin felt Varja's eyes on him like molten lead. Clasping Tagore's hand, he made his way down the aisle to the base of the Tree of the Thousand Wisdoms. Torches above Sadika's casket illuminated the treasures in his hands; the diamond and the snake amulet sparkled in the light.

Tagore faced the crowd for several minutes. Justin wondered what the test would be. Then, without preamble, Tagore raised the boy's right hand with tremendous power and slashed it down the bark of the tree.

The pain was almost unbearable. Justin felt the skin and flesh of his right palm scrape off. Too surprised to cry out, all he could do was gape at his bleeding hand and try to hold back the tears that sprang to his eyes.

"Sadika!'' Tagore commanded. "Is this the child?''

Justin thought he was going to faint. A river of blood ran down his arm, staining the yellow robe he wore. The pain gave way to an electric throbbing that seemed to have no beginning and no end.

Tagore picked a leaf from the tree and placed it in Justin's wounded hand. Then, causing the most excruciating pain Justin had ever felt, the teacher closed his mangled hand into a fist around the leaf.

He began to shake. The pain was unendurable. He closed his eyes. And in the red darkness of his pain he saw the old man again, not dead and in his glass casket, but standing before him, holding out the two emblems of his office.

There was a gasp from everyone in the hall as Tagore opened the boy's hand. Justin's head swam. There was no blood. When his fist opened, all that fell from it was a withered brown leaf. The hand was unmarked.

Tagore raised the boy's hand high in the air. At that moment, the casket seemed to creak and move of its own accord.

The sight set Justin's teeth chattering. For, as Tagore held his arm in the air, the body of the old leader crumbled to ash before them. In the midst of the powdery remains rested the diamond and the gold amulet bearing the figure of the coiled snake.

"Hail, O Wearer of the Blue Hat," several voices called. Others took up the chant. "Hail, O Wearer of the Blue Hat."

Tagore repeated the words as he lifted the diamond from the casket and placed it in Justin's hands. Then, to the accompaniment of the chant that filled the hall, he placed the sacred medallion of the coiled snake around the boy's neck.

Justin felt the surge of power from the medallion like an electric shock that began near his heart and coursed wildly through every nerve and vein in his body. He fought for breath. Surely there was magic here, he thought, greater magic than he could ever control.

"Do not fear it," Tagore whispered.

Justin looked to Varja, the abbess of magic. Her green eyes were blazing, but she, too, bowed in respect to him.

"Hail, O Wearer of the Blue Hat," she said. A small smile played at the corners of her mouth.

Tagore began the procession out of the hall, keeping Justin in front of him. The medallion felt as if it were burning into his chest. The congregation filed outdoors to the rock shelf on which Rashimpur was built. Tagore knelt, and the others followed, even Varja in her misty jeweled crimson wraps. Alone, Justin walked to the edge of the precipice and stood facing the snow-capped Himalayas.

He could breathe more easily now. So this was where the amulet was at peace, he thought. Beneath the blue sky, which was the blue hat of the gods.

I will try to be worthy of you, he thought.

He held up both arms to the sky. The huge diamond gave off the fire of a thousand suns. The gold medallion on his chest warmed him. He felt strong.

Never will I betray you.

Never.

Alexander Zharkov sat alone in his Moscow apartment. Like his office, the apartment was spare and ugly, even though it was situated in one of the best buildings in the city and was spacious enough to house two families of six.

A pair of leaded-glass doors, now sealed shut, stood beside the armchair where he sat holding a file on Justin Gilead. But unlike the file in his office, this one was thick, bulging with papers. Its cover was red instead of the official green that signified a closed file.

The only light in the room came from an old brass floor lamp behind Zharkov's chair. At the other end of the room, near the doorway to the master bedroom, stood a small dining table with two straight chairs.

Beside it was another table, smaller, on which a magnificent teak and walnut chess board was set up, with a game in progress. Stacked neatly on the floor under the chess table were two piles of bound copies of *Shakmatni*, the official Soviet chess journal.

There was only one chair at the chess board, stationed behind the black pieces, because in this solitary game at home, Zharkov always took the black side. This gave white, who traditionally moved first, a slight advantage, and Zharkov had conceded that advantage to his invisible opponent.

The game had begun slowly, with white's pieces opening elegantly, following well-defined lines like a beautiful solo dance.

But after the first dozen moves, white had deviated from

the well-known opening "book" and moved other pieces into play in novel and interesting positions. The solo had turned into an ensemble ballet.

Zharkov's black pieces had joined the ballet and begun attacking almost at once. For a while, white's position seemed untenable and an early resignation inevitable. But slowly, white had consolidated his position, stood off Zharkov's onslaught, as piece after piece vanished from both sides in a series of equal trades.

The black and white dance continued, and the unbelievable had happened. White's king had moved, starting to march inexorably to the center of the board to join the contest. It was unthinkable. The king was at once both the most valuable piece in the game, whose capture ended the contest, and the weakest, most vulnerable, and hardest to defend.

Zharkov knew this opponent did not play a game of pawns, but to burst into the open with his king was impossible. Unless it signaled the beginning of an elaborate, deeply thought attacking scheme. Or did it mean merely that the invisible white opponent had lost his nerve and offered himself up for confrontation and quick slaughter?

For the first time since he had opened the red folder, seeing in his mind not its contents but the board across the room, Zharkov looked up. Rain was pelting against the glass doors. The room seemed suddenly dark. And there was a knocking at the big walnut door leading out of the apartment. It was delicate but insistent, as if whoever was behind it had been knocking for some time, although Zharkov hadn't heard anything in his concentration over the chess pieces.

He got up and opened the door. The face on the other side warmed him unexpectedly, as it always did.

Katarina Velanova was not a beauty in the classic sense, but her face held the subtle charm of the most complex chess. The quick, intelligent eyes of the woman never failed to fascinate him, shifting with a blink into dark, exotic pools and then brightening just as quickly into the simple joy of a schoolgirl.

She was drenched, her red cotton scarf dark with rain. Beads of water stood out on the clear pale skin—the only thing about her that was perfect—running down the long, sensitive nose and into the corners of her mobile mouth, which never seemed to smile the same way twice. She was tall, nearly as tall as Zharkov, and her eyes met his without the slightest hesitation. Wordlessly she placed both her hands behind Zharkov's head and kissed him. It was a perfunctory greeting, but the sudden touch of her full lips on his shot a quiver of excitement through him as she stepped briskly into the kitchen to set a kettle of water to boil.

She was that rarest of beings, a woman for whom passion was as natural as breathing. And yet Katarina was not a sensualist.

When he had first seen her at work at the KGB, Katarina's face had worn the stern, humorless expression expected of KGB researchers. Her co-workers, who spent their days looking through published information for the benefit of the thousands of Soviet agents who manned the largest espionage apparatus in the world, were mostly female, but they were not regarded as women.

They were automatons, office tools dressed in shapeless sweaters, their fingertips covered by rubber thimbles. They moved like whispers through the enormous KGB complex on Dzerzhinski Square and the modern eight-story building on the outskirts of Moscow that housed the First Chief Directorate for Foreign Affairs.

It had been five years before. Zharkov had just become head of Nichevo and had been in Ostrakov's office to review some manpower estimates on Allied and Western troop movements in Scandinavia.

The KGB man had issued a curt order over the intercom for some files to be brought into the office. Katarina Velanova carried them in. Her eyes boldly met Zharkov's. She smiled at him without embarrassment and nodded before leaving the room.

As soon as he began looking through them, Zharkov realized the files were unusual, because instead of merely reciting facts and statistics and numbers, they offered various conclusions about the Western motive for moving troops, and gave these conclusions a numerical weighting, ranging from most probable to least probable.

"Who prepared these files?" Zharkov asked.

"That bitch who brought them in. And this is the end of it for her," Ostrakov said. "She has no authority to draw conclusions."

"Maybe not the authority, but she has the mind for it," Zharkov said. "A mind of value."

Ostrakov had smiled lewdly and said, "Not a bad little ass, either." When Zharkov looked at him coldly, Ostrakov had said, "Don't play gentleman with me. She's spread that ass all over Dzerzhinski Square. I don't think there's a janitor in this building who hasn't been between her legs."

"I want her to work for me," Zharkov said.

"She's yours. I was going to fire her anyway. What Nichevo does is none of my affair."

Thank God, Zharkov thought. Kremlin policy did not allow for the existence of God, but as far as Zharkov was concerned, something special had to account for Ostrakov's not being able to stick his hands into Nichevo's business.

Katarina Velanova appeared in his office early the following week. It was dinnertime, and the Nichevo building was empty except for the handful of around-the-clock staffers who maintained security and watched the reports that were teletyped into headquarters.

"Comrade Velanova reporting for duty, Comrade Colonel," she had said briskly after being ushered into his office. But why was she smiling? he wondered. It was a knowing smile, as if she were privy to information he did not have.

"Do you like Colonel Ostrakov?" Zharkov said suddenly.

"I think the man is an imbecile," she answered without hesitation.

"And yet you have slept with him?"

"Who told you that?"

"I have been told that you have slept with everybody. Even with cleaning men."

"I have also slept with cleaning women," she said evenly. "Some of them have been of value. Ostrakov is not."

What kind of woman is this? he wondered. How could she speak to him this way? What guarantee did she have that he would not tell Ostrakov, so that by tomorrow she would have a one-way ticket to Siberia?

"You do not remember me, do you?" she asked. It was a simple question. Her eyes were frank, without a trace of coyness or seduction.

He tried to keep his voice flat and uninterested. "Have we met?"

"Long ago. You were meant to forget."

The woman exasperated him more by the minute. "Was it in Russia?"

"No," she answered, dismissing the subject. "I will be here first thing in the morning, Comrade Colonel, to begin my duties. But first I thought you might like to have this." Her eyes twinkling with subdued amusement, she handed him a thick folder.

It took him a moment to concentrate on the sheaf of papers. But by the third page, he could feel his breath coming in short, febrile gusts. Every word of the report—more than sixty pages—was about Justin Gilead. Nothing had been omitted. The names and addresses of Gilead's childhood guardians were included, as well as a listing of all the tournaments and matches he had played in and a complete record of all his games.

"How . . ." Zharkov began, but he lost the thought. He was absorbed in Katarina's sketches of Gilead's career with the CIA and her inspired guesses about what Gilead had managed to do for the United States while touring the world as an international grandmaster. There were neat hypotheses about his presence in Berlin in 1974, in Cuba during the peak of Castro's romance with the Soviet Union, in the Philippines in the late 1970s.

The information in the dossier had been gleaned from hundreds of sources, most of them obscure reports by field agents now long vanished. Compiling all the data had been a monumental task.

"Why?" he asked finally, laying down the folder. Outside, darkness was falling on the city, and the now powerful light from his desk lamp cast long planes of shadow over Katarina's face.

"Because you alone, of everyone in this nation of fools, know who Justin Gilead is," she said softly.

He snapped to instant attention. "Who are you?" he rasped.

The woman seemed to stand up taller. She said, "I will be here first thing in the morning, Comrade Colonel."

Without waiting to be dismissed, she turned and crossed the bare floor toward the open doorway.

"Stop," he said softly.

She turned. Their eyes met. Justin Gilead was important, and she knew it as well as he did. Of the nearly three-quarters of a million people who worked for the Soviet security machine, she was the only person besides himself who had seen that. Katarina's was indeed a mind of value.

He stared into her face beneath the fringe of her short, dark hair, taking in the enigmatic somberness of the brown eyes, the crooked long nose which, he was sure, reddened quickly in the cold. It was, in its way, rather a wonderful face. Looking into it, he lost track of time and thought. He wondered where he might have seen it before.

As if sharing the blank, electrifying buzz inside his mind, Katarina closed the door leading to the empty outer offices. She did not move from her place, and her eyes never left Zharkov's. Instead, she unbuttoned the white military-style blouse she wore and tossed it on the floor. Her exposed breasts were pale and rounded, and their nipples already stood erect.

Zharkov could not react. What she was doing was unthinkable, the grossest manifestation of decadence. Her behavior should have cost her her job, perhaps even earned her a stint in the city jail.

She stood staring at him. She made no move to entice him with movements of her body or sultry glances, but stood straight, her shoulders squared, as if for inspection. Her face changed in front of his eyes a dozen times or more. She looked by turns childlike and womanly, defiant, ashamed, easeful, tense. But she never broke the electricity with a single word, never gave him any encouragement after her brazen and inexplicable display. Zharkov could easily see her as a Committee informant. Forced by Ostrakov, perhaps, to present the Grandmaster's dossier to him.

No, he thought. Not Ostrakov. He could never have thought to assemble the folder. She had done it for someone else in the KGB, then. Or for herself. For the power women think they have over men by virtue of their sexuality.

She waited. Zharkov rose and walked over to her slowly. He could smell the warmth of her, her womanliness beneath the scrubbed cleanliness of harsh, strong soap.

When he came to her, it was not so much an act of lust as a huge leap of faith. He wanted to trust her, to take her as something that belonged by right to him; at the same time he hated her for filling him with fear and apprehension. Coming up in front of her in two long strides, he lifted her straight skirt upward with a jerk, and tore her silky underpants from her as if they were made of paper.

She closed her eyes. Zharkov cupped his hands around her

breasts, feeling the hot smoothness of her skin. Katarina's legs buckled at the knees. The place between them was wet and ready. He took her standing up, his hands clasped around the flesh of her buttocks, where the strong muscles pulsed and pumped and shivered with a wild, animal urgency.

She trembled once and then again, and he sensed himself reaching climax, but at the instant when he was ready to spend, he felt the muscles inside her body impossibly closing down on the shaft of his manhood, squeezing him, cutting off the flow.

For an instant, he experienced something akin to pain, and then she relaxed her muscles and he began thrusting into her again. But when again he was about to spend, she again tightened around him, making it impossible.

And he remembered. He leaned back from her so he could see her face.

She was smiling.

"Now you remember me," she said softly, then leaned forward and pressed the wet tip of her tongue into his ear.

"*She* sent you."

"Yes," she said. "I am to be here with you. To help you."

He felt her muscles go soft, and he knew that this time she would permit him to reach his climax, and he carried her upright, her legs locked around his back, over to the sofa in his office and lay down atop her and plunged into her over and over again with a furious passion that bordered on the sadistic.

Finally, he exploded in one giant thrust, and the two of them lay still, unmoving, the silence in the office broken only by their heavy breathing.

Afterward, there were no words of love, no soft caresses. She got dressed as if she were alone in the room, then walked out. Neither of them said good-bye.

She reported promptly the next morning. Zharkov set her to work to develop an intelligence system for Nichevo that could operate independently of the KGB.

They were always formally polite to each other in the office, and only occasionally did Katarina come to his apartment to spend the night with him. He never asked her what she did with her other nights; he did not need to.

The reports that crossed his desk provided that answer.

They told Zharkov what the KGB was planning, what its long-range policies were, who was winning the never-ending internal power struggles in the massive agency. He knew that Katarina bribed with sex the way some bribed with money, and a word here, a scrap of paper there, were all pieces in the protective fence she was erecting around Zharkov. She paid for the equipment with her body. They never spoke of it.

The teakettle whistled, bringing Zharkov's thoughts back to the sterile apartment where Katarina was standing, barefoot and laughing, in the middle of the floor. She was dressed in an old shirt of Zharkov's, the bottom half of her draped in a towel that fit her like a sarong. Her wet hair clung to her head in a cap of short, glossy black curls. There was no vanity in her, Zharkov thought, and yet she was beautiful.

"Playing chess?" she teased. She was used to Zharkov's periods of blankness, when he drew into his own thoughts and seemed oblivious to everything around him.

He smiled. "Remembering," he said, and touched her hair.

Her lips moved in a quick, uncertain expression before she turned away. It was the first time in nearly five years that he had shown her any affection.

"I have news," she said, handing him a cup. The tea was strong and sweet, heavily laced with vodka; the fumes stung his eyes. "Andrew Starcher's had a heart attack. He'll probably be retired as soon as he gets out of the hospital."

Zharkov sat bolt upright in his chair.

"In Lenin Medical Center. A nurse on the floor where he was brought lives in my apartment building. She says there was a big to-do over the foreign dignitary in intensive care. Apparently he'll be flown back to America as soon as he can be moved. Meanwhile the door is open for you."

He nodded, understanding immediately what she meant. The CIA's top man in Russia was ill; for a brief period, at least, his role would be filled by an inexperienced deputy named Michael Corfus. If Nichevo was to do any mischief, now would be an ideal time to do it.

The thought brought little joy to Zharkov. There were other things on his mind. Katarina read his expression and said, "What's the matter?"

He rose quickly and handed her the envelope of pictures that Ostrakov had given him. "Look at these."

Katarina sucked in a swift rush of air as she examined the photograph of the woman falling to the floor as her head exploded in a red spray. "I heard about it," she said, "but I didn't know it was this gruesome. The Samarkand? Are they insane?"

"Worse," Zharkov said with disgust. "They are stupid. Ostrakov hires terrorists and then wonders why they can't follow orders. The hotel was filled with tourists."

"Unbelievable. Is he in trouble?"

Zharkov shook his head. "He got out of it this time. The militia was called in. They've arrested two vagabonds, and they're calling Riesling an unidentified low-life. The two'll be executed before anyone can check anything."

"Riesling?" She looked up. "That's Riesling?" Zharkov nodded briefly, waving her on to continue looking through the photographs. "It's always strange," she said, "to see a face attached to the files I've read. Somehow, it's almost as if they aren't real people until—"

She stopped dead at the sight of the picture showing the gold medallion.

"Gilead," she said, in a soft, chilled whisper. "What does it mean?"

"I don't know," Zharkov said.

"Is he back?"

"I don't know that either. And I can't ask Riesling," he said bitterly.

"It may be just the medallion," she said. "Nothing for four years. If he were alive, we would have heard."

"He's alive," Zharkov said stubbornly. "I know it."

"Then kill him again." Her voice was cold.

"And again and again and again? When will he stay dead?"

"When you are man enough to kill him properly," she said stiffly.

But that wasn't the point, Zharkov thought. He was man—or beast—enough to kill anyone. But was Justin Gilead man enough to die?

Zharkov was silent as he and Katarina sat at the dining table over a Spartan meal of green vegetables and rice. He was intently reading the red-covered file on Justin Gilead.

Katarina watched him wordlessly as he pushed vegetables around his plate, only a few of them ever reaching his mouth.

Finally she said, "I know where Justin Gilead is."

He looked up quickly.

"Yes," she said. "He's a shoe salesman in Schenectady, New York. He has a fat wife and four children."

Zharkov appreciated her attempt to cheer him and smiled sadly. "No. He would be playing chess somewhere. I would have read about his games."

"Chess. Always chess. Was he that good?"

"Justin Gilead," Zharkov said, "was probably the most brilliant chess player who ever lived. He started playing again in 1970, when he was twenty-six. A year later, he was declared an international grandmaster."

"Then why wasn't he ever world champion?" she asked with a touch of asperity.

"You know the answer to that," Zharkov said. "You wrote this report."

"My report was filled with conjecture and speculation," she said. "Not with hard fact."

"All right. This is hard fact. For ten years, Justin Gilead was doing the CIA's work, harassing Nichevo. In every city he went to for a tournament, he managed to do some mischief before he left. Sometimes he did not show up for games and lost points on disqualification. Other times, he would adjourn a game that he had clearly won, and the next day would not come back to resume it. So he would lose another point for a forfeit. For ten years, he was an American agent and tried to play chess, too."

He began to recite as if from a memorized litany.

"In 1972, Nixon visited China. My father headed Nichevo then. He had an interesting welcome planned for Nixon. He had his top agents standing by in Hong Kong. Gilead played in a tournament in Hong Kong, and my father's agents were never heard from again. Gilead finished third in the tournament.

"In 1975, he played in a tournament in Toronto. Soon after the tournament, a dozen of our top people in Canada were expelled for spying. Gilead finished second in the tournament.

"In 1977, he played in a tournament in Djakarta. When it was over, the CIA arrested one of its own men who had been a double agent, working for Nichevo. Gilead missed the last three games and forfeited the tournament.

"In 1978, he played in South Africa. My father had carefully set up a supply route to get arms to the rebels there. Two weeks after the tournament ended, the South African police broke the supply line. Gilead tied for first in that tournament.

"And in 1979, when I took over Nichevo, I planned riots in Panama when the Americans gave the Panama Canal back. Gilead was playing in Panama City at the time. The riots never happened. My men were all arrested by the police. Gilead finished second in that tournament."

"And those were all Gilead's doings?" she asked. "Are you sure?"

Zharkov nodded. "My father knew and later I knew. The KGB never knew. It still doesn't. But then, the Committee never knows anything."

"Then why didn't you kill him all those years?" she asked. "You knew that one day you'd have to."

"He was too slippery. My father tried many times," Zharkov said. "It was only in Poland four years ago that we got the real chance. Katarina, I saw him in his grave. And now he lives." The Russian shook his massive head.

"Maybe he doesn't live," she said. "Maybe he was injured so badly that he's a vegetable now, lying in a nursing home, peeing in a pot."

"And maybe he is just waiting for his moment to strike," Zharkov said.

Katarina smiled and rose to clear away the dinner dishes. "I don't know about him, but I know *I'm* waiting for my moment to strike. Will you come to bed?"

He said distractedly, "In a moment."

"I know what that means," she said. "I hate Justin Gilead. If he lives, I want nothing more in life than to kill him for you." After she removed the dishes, she came back, kissed him softly on the cheek and walked quietly to the bedroom doorway. "All we know is that someone found his medallion," she said. "The Grandmaster may be a ghost."

Perhaps she was right. Perhaps the unkillable man had died after all. Not in Poland, where he had officially expired—Zharkov knew that Gilead had somehow, miraculously, tricked death then as he had tricked it once before at Zharkov's hands—but dead all the same. An automobile accident, an illness. Agents did die normal deaths more often than not.

But not the Grandmaster. Something inside Zharkov simply could not believe that the recovered medallion, handed to Starcher's aide, signified nothing. Justin Gilead was about to surface. Zharkov knew that as surely as he knew his own name.

He stood at the doorway to the bedroom. Inside, her face illuminated by the light from the other room, Katarina slept. The incessant rain beat on the windows like a beast trying to get in. Zharkov longed to lie with her, to permit himself to be enveloped by her warmth. But something pulled at him, uncomfortable, agitating, a force as inexorable as madness.

He looked at the chessboard. The white king stood defiantly out of his ranks, challenging his opponent to do combat.

Riesling . . . Kutsenko . . . Starcher . . . the Grandmaster.

The board told him that Justin Gilead was alive. He would live until the game was over, for it was the last recorded game that Justin Gilead had ever played. He had walked away from that position once and had never come back to finish the contest. The Grandmaster's life would not be ended until Zharkov had ended this game. And after four years, the game was still in doubt.

The Russian walked over to the chessboard and picked up a piece. It was the black queen, sleek, balanced, intricately carved, beautiful. The most deadly piece on the board. Powerful enough to topple the white king if the moves were right.

He set the queen down on a square where it gave check to the white king.

He knew it in his bones. The white king would lead an attack against him. And the white king would then be destroyed. Finally. Forever.

Zharkov put on a raincoat and an old cap with a visor and walked out into the rain. The black queen was waiting for him.

CHAPTER ELEVEN

He walked through the driving rain to the fashionable Sivcev Vražek district, where the core of Moscow's power elite kept their city residences. He could have driven—he had a Chaika limousine and a driver at his disposal—but drivers talked, and official Chaikas were easy to spot after midnight curfew. What he was about to do was dangerous, and although Nichevo was powerful, there were limits to its official power, and to Zharkov's.

Zharkov reached an area of shabby old buildings condemned but left standing despite the city's notorious housing shortage, as part of the Soviet myth of equality. Like the special stores where the cream of Soviet society purchased food and goods not available to the general public for a fraction of the price of the lesser-quality goods that ordinary people stood in line for hours to buy, and like the cars that "meritorious" members of the Party received, often as gifts, the elegant apartments in Sivcev Vražek did not officially exist. Their high windows were carefully shrouded with thick draperies. The buildings themselves were unkempt and moldering on the street side. Only from the rear courtyards could one see the gardens and the balconies, smell the fragrances of steaks and expensive perfumes, hear the luxurious whir of air conditioners.

He pressed the intercom inside one of the buildings. A woman's voice answered.

"Zharkov," he said. A buzzer sounded, and the drab metal door opened with a click, revealing a thickly carpeted lobby

95

decorated with gilt mirrors and French camelback sofas upholstered in silk. The two ornate elevators were unattended at
night, a sure sign of power. In even the lowliest buildings,
the entrances and exits of tenants and their guests were noted
by the *dezhurnaya*, usually old women who sat sullenly in the
lobbies and foyers, watching and listening. They were paid
little for their efforts, but if their observations led to an arrest,
they were rewarded with food or an apartment to share with
only three other families instead of the more common six.

But no *dezhurnaya* sat watch here. The eyes of the state did
not peer into the bastions of its privileged class.

On the seventh floor, on the wall beside Maria Lozovan's
door, was an Italian modernist painting of a woman stroking a
cat. Both figures were rounded and lush, obviously luxury
items. As was the painting, carelessly hung outside the apartment itself, Zharkov thought as the door swung open, offering him a waft of expensive perfume. As was the painting's
owner.

Maria Lozovan would have been a woman of notice in any
city in the world, but in Moscow she was nothing less than a
miracle. Cultured, charming, meticulously groomed, utterly
feminine, everything about her indicated that she had been
expressly created to adorn the arms of wealthy men. A blond
Georgian—that in itself a rarity—she possessed the high Slavic
cheekbones of her race and slanted eyes the color of copper.
No one knew her age. Zharkov guessed that she was anywhere between thirty-five and fifty, but probably on the upper
end of the scale, since he first learned about her activities
with the KGB when he was still a young man.

There were rumors that Maria had originally come to Moscow illegally, as a prostitute, and was set up by a rich patron
in an apartment, with residence papers permitting her to live
in the city. Zharkov didn't know or care about her life before
the KGB, and gave no credence to the stories about Maria
Lozovan that flew around the cocktail circuit of Soviet society.
She had been their favorite subject for years, ever since she
"retired" from service to marry.

Her marriage itself was a scandal of the first water. It was
well known that her husband, Dimitri, a minor executive for
Intourist, possessed neither the money nor the political pull
known as *blat* to afford the spacious eight-room apartment in
Sivcev Vražek. It was equally well known that Dimitri Lozovan

was the lover of a highly placed homosexual member of the Politburo.

The marriage between him and Maria had been arranged, basically, by the state as advantageous to all concerned. The Politburo member could continue his liaison with Lozovan openly, without fear of recrimination for his decadence, Lozovan was able to accept the gift of the large apartment and priceless furnishings, and Maria, in payment for her services as "beard" to the two men, was released from her assignments as a field agent to conspicuously lead the life of a Moscow socialite. Besides, there were other rumors that Maria had a lover of her own. A powerful man, of course; only the most interesting indiscretions were attributed to Maria Lozovan.

She obviously relished her role. All her clothes came from Paris and Rome, and twice in the last decade she had traveled to South America for several months at a stretch, returning each time with a face considerably younger than the one she owned when she left. "Plastic surgery," the gossips whispered. "The gall! How does she get away with it here?"

Only a handful of people not intimately involved with secret Politburo discussions guessed at some connection between Maria Lozovan's South American tours and the sudden eruptions of Communist uprisings on that continent, but they kept the matter to themselves. Nobody involved with Maria's activities was about to tell the truth about her, least of all Maria herself.

Like everything else about her, Maria's secrecy was a studied, cultivated quality. In fact, she appeared to have no secrets at all, chatting amiably at the parties she and Dimitri hosted about her work with the KGB. "Minimal, really," she would say with the lilting laugh that was always at the ready. "Codes and ciphers, that sort of thing. Mostly it was a lot of hard work with no reward except a kind of"—here she would insert a small sigh—"deep satisfaction that I might be doing some good in the world." A smile usually followed, one of a thousand practiced expressions of pleasure and mutual confidence with her listeners.

But Zharkov knew that Maria had spent six years at Gaczyna, and none but the most promising agents-in-training were sent to Gaczyna to study. Certainly not a code or cipher clerk. Certainly not an agent who would be retired upon marriage.

Gaczyna was probably the most unusual school in the world. It covered some 425 acres in an uninhabited part of the Russian interior stretching from the Tatar Soviet Republic to the Bashkir Soviet Republic. Agents who had been hand-picked by the KGB to serve abroad, either in deep cover or as illegals, were flown in special government aircraft to the security zone some thirty miles outside Gaczyna, where a military detachment searched the plane for weapons and explosives before permitting it to fly into the vast compound. The security zone circled Gaczyna completely, and no one was permitted to enter or leave without a special pass. The school did not appear on any map. Its teachers were assigned for life, and were not permitted to leave, ever. As far as even the inhabitants of the region knew, Gaczyna did not exist.

Zharkov himself had seen the school on only one occasion, and he had been stunned at his first sight of the place. For in Gaczyna, there were no school buildings, no desks, no blackboards. Instead, spread at distances of no more than a few hundred yards, were replicas of foreign towns exact to the last detail. There were streets, buildings, movie houses, banks, and bars. In the "English" towns, bright double-decker buses rolled down the streets. The American locales were dotted with blue mailboxes. Although most of the "classrooms" were English-speaking—no one in the area was permitted to speak Russian at any time—there were also facsimiles of some South American cities. Maria Lozovan had studied in these, as well as in the mock American areas. Her training had been exhaustive and detailed. Aside from her acquired ability to fit seamlessly into another culture, she was also well instructed in the use and identification of weapons, understood surveillance electronics to a degree, and excelled at what was called "silent sentry removal," which meant that she could kill with a wire better than any field agent in her class.

With these skills, Zharkov knew, Maria Lozovan still worked for the Committee. But sparingly. An agent as dangerous as she was was not to be wasted on inconsequential missions.

She served Zharkov a freezing cold Stolichnaya, thick as molasses, and sipped a glass of champagne. She was artifice itself, Zharkov thought as he watched her spin an interesting but trivial fabric of small talk around them. Not once did she question his motive for the visit; not once did she appear in any way perturbed at the late intrusion. She was dressed in some sort of silky pajamas, the kind of thing wealthy young matrons and expensive call girls wear around the house on off evenings, and her blond hair was perfectly styled, short and curly in front, with the back long and upswept. It was not a current hairstyle, but it was glamorous, and it gave her face an illusion of sexiness that it did not actually possess. Zharkov found himself studying the woman as if she were an exhibit in a museum. Her face was quite different from the early photographs of her in the files. The features were the same, but better. The slightly sloping nose had been replaced by a narrow, upturned button. Her jawline had been restructured into a square shape.

Zharkov, perhaps because of the potent vodka, felt an illogical urge to laugh. Only an agent of extraordinary vanity would go to the trouble of surgically reconstructing her face without changing her general appearance for cover purposes. And also because of the vodka, he thought he could discern the blunt features of a thug beneath the fine artificial lines. Something about her repelled him, on principle. She was the kind of enforcer his father had eliminated from Nichevo when it ceased to be Stalin's plaything and took on the dimensions of a serious organization focused on serious work. Nichevo had no place for crude killers anymore.

But Zharkov did.

"There is a man I want to question," he said bluntly, interrupting her chatter.

Her eyes slid toward him, amused. "So? The Committee will bring him to you. If you ask." A smile spread across her face.

"He's an American. A diplomat. He has immunity."

"I see. It would be quite against international law to bring him in for interrogation, wouldn't it?" She wagged a schoolmarmish finger at Zharkov. The gesture made him hate her.

Her complicity was obvious. She would work for him, for enough money. But she would want to maintain the thin charade of her innocence. He would have to endure the lewd dance between them for a time. Zharkov wanted to get her out of his sight, this whore of the KGB who killed for sport and then painted her lips to conceal the blood on them. He wanted to leave her silky presence, clear his lungs of her cloying perfume, wash his hands, burn his clothes. Instead, he accepted another drink and danced his role as she expected.

"It would," he said.

"But, forgive me, I'm just a housewife these days, you know," she said with a show of scatterbrained frustration that nauseated Zharkov. "Isn't the sort of thing you're thinking of somewhat out of the range of Nichevo?" She put her fingers to her lips. "Can we mention the name?"

Zharkov rose. "Madam, I've taken enough of your time."

"No, wait." She touched his arm, flashing the most ingratiating smile. "Do sit down, Colonel. I'm interested."

"In what?" Zharkov asked archly.

She sighed. "All right. Touché. You want someone to kidnap an American diplomat so you can interrogate him. The man I presume you want is Andrew Starcher, but since he's in the hospital, my guess is his assistant. The dark, ugly one. Am I close?"

Zharkov nodded.

"You needn't worry about speaking here, Colonel. My apartment isn't bugged." She gestured curtly toward a gilt-framed photograph of her husband's male lover. "For obvious reasons."

She poured herself another glassful of champagne. "The question is, why have you come to me? Everyone knows I've been retired for years."

"That is not the question," Zharkov said, pulling a stack of hundred ruble notes from his jacket. He spread them in front of her, arranging them in rows of ten. "This is the question."

She eyed the bills with something like love. "Of course, the Committee—"

"The KGB can have him when I'm through, if you want to prove your loyalty to the Committee. I just don't want that oaf Ostrakov to kill him before I've had my chance with him."

"Then this is a personal matter? Not Nichevo business?"

"That's not your concern."

"They'll blame you. There'll be an incident," she said.

"Will there?" Zharkov asked coldly.

Maria Lozovan thought. "Of course, there are alternatives, believable alternatives." She still had not touched the money.

"I thought as much." He laid out five new rows of bills.

Maria smiled up at him. "You were right, Comrade Colonel. This was the question."

She scooped up the notes in both hands.

"And that is your answer."

It was nearly three o'clock in the morning when Zharkov returned to his apartment. The first thing he saw upon entering was the chessboard set up with the black queen in play. How dangerous was Maria Lozovan to him? What prevented her from taking the money and spilling what she knew to the KGB?

Only her greed, he thought. She might have guessed that there was something to come after the relatively minor task of capturing Michael Corfus—a more impressive, more expensive assignment.

As for himself, he decided that he risked little on the surface. Even if Maria Lozovan turned him in, what would the Committee do to him? At most, it might chastise him for interfering with the diplomatic-immunity laws with a low-ranking American agent. But the KGB itself had done much worse to people of far greater importance. Corfus's kidnapping would be presented to the Americans as the act of anti-Western radicals. Then, to make it stick, a few troublesome dissidents would be taken from the political prison at Lubyanka and hanged. *Nichevo?* the Committee would say. Who cares?

Still, there might be questions. Why had Zharkov done it? Why use an agent of Lozovan's caliber to get to someone as politically innocuous as Starcher's aide?

They *could not* find out about the Grandmaster. Zharkov would not permit it. Justin Gilead was his, and his alone. He had hunted Gilead for the whole of his life, and he would not allow Ostrakov or his clones to find the great beast before he did.

He stripped off his clothes and crawled silently into bed with Katarina.

He embraced her, feeling the warmth of her body rush through him like molten metal. He remembered the first time he had met her—God, was it fifteen years ago?—when she had led his initiation into the rites of love and into the service of a woman who was more God than woman, who had tied him to her with the power of her body and her sex, and had promised him the world. In return, he had to promise her his loyalty.

Katarina had been trained by her and saved by her, just for Zharkov. He pressed his body against her back and with his left hand stroked the nipple of her left breast. It responded instantly, hardening, furrowed, and in her sleep, Katarina, created for one purpose only, moaned slightly with pleasure. He slipped his other hand through the small valley between her hip and his mattress and then put his hand between her legs. She was, as he knew she would be, wet there. He dipped his fingers into her moistness, then brought his hand up, to anoint her breasts with her own juice.

He felt her shudder. She turned to him, then rolled him onto his back and climbed on him, easing him into her. In the misty moonlight that filtered into the master bedroom from the window overlooking the garden behind the building, he could see her eyes flashing as she straddled him and then began lifting her body up and down, enveloping him, sinking down powerfully on him, swallowing up his manhood with her womanhood. Then she leaned forward; her hardened nipples grazed his chest. Her tongue touched the inside of his ear, and he heard her say softly, "I am going to fuck you as you have never been fucked before, Alyosha."

And he knew he would surrender himself to her completely, that he would think of nothing but his body and his pleasure, but as he closed his eyes so he could concentrate on nothing but his own throbbing sex, he saw again, in his mind, the chessboard in the other room and the white king moving out to meet his pieces. So naked, so vulnerable, so pitifully exposed. The game would be his.

The game was moving, moving beautifully, and it would be a game not of pawns, but of kings.

And he would win.

And the Grandmaster would be his.

Half a world away, a man quietly sat in a darkened room, his legs folded under him. Outside, waves lapped against the hull of a boat, but the man did not hear them. The unlighted room smelled of waste and rotted food, but the man did not notice the scent. A bowl of food sat untouched on the hard floor next to him. The man sat staring straight ahead at a point in the darkness ahead of him, his eyes unfocused, unseeing.

His frame was gaunt and wasted, and his mind held no thoughts, no visions, no great plans, no master strategies. It was, like his body, useless and rotted.

But sometimes, alone, in the silent frightening dark, the man remembered music and the scent of almonds.

Book Three

NICHEVO

The day after the ceremony investing Justin as the Wearer of the Blue Hat, Tagore tied narrow tubes of cloth weighted with small stones to the young boy's wrists and ankles. He led him to the small lake to the east of Rashimpur.

"Swim," he commanded.

The boy struggled for a few yards. "I can't," he said. "Help me."

"Swim."

He made it a quarter of the way across before losing consciousness.

The next week Tagore led him to a narrow footpath at the base of Amne Xachim. "Run," he said.

"Where to?"

"To the place where you can run no more."

Justin ran until he dropped, exhausted, the dust of the footpath biting into the raw flesh beneath the stone bracelets he wore.

Tagore was waiting for him. "Farther," he said.

A month later, he took the boy farther up the mountain to where the scrub grass sprouted in scattered clumps beneath the snow. A thirty-foot-high boulder rose out of the ground, its slick surface covered by a thin layer of ice.

"Climb," Tagore said.

The boy looked at him reproachfully. The weights binding him had completely removed the skin around his wrists and ankles. At night, when he slept, the weights were removed, and his flesh healed into paper-thin scabs. But each morning they were rubbed raw again, the pain permeating him during every waking moment. His back and arms and legs ached constantly with a dull throb. His fingers were cracked and blistered. The exercises Tagore saw him through every morning left him paralyzed with fatigue and dizzy from the arcane methods of breathing the monks taught. He was made to stand for hours, his arms outstretched until there was no more feeling in them, to breathe with such depth that he felt his ribs would crack, to lie outside in the cold until his shivering gave way to numbness. He hated Tagore.

"Climb," the teacher repeated.

Justin climbed.

Halfway up the boulder, he slipped and fell. Tagore caught him effortlessly.

"I can't," the boy cried. "I won't. Not with these weights. It hurts too much."

Tagore grasped him by the cloth on his back and propelled him off the ground, onto the freezing boulder. "Climb," he said.

Enraged, Justin climbed to the top of the rock. His arms and legs and face were already beginning to bruise from his fight with the massive boulder, but he didn't care. Defiantly, he looked down at Tagore. "I did it," he said triumphantly.

His training had begun.

From the monks, Justin learned the Hindi dialect of the region. From special tutors summoned by Tagore, he learned Russian, Chinese, Italian, French, German, Polish, Spanish. From ancient books he learned mathematics and astronomy. From Tagore he learned strength.

The small weights disappeared from beside Justin's pallet. In their place were new weights with stones twice their size.

He was taken back to the small lake. "Swim," Tagore said.

By the time he was twelve years old, the stones he wore around his neck, his waist, his wrists and ankles weighed more than a hundred pounds.

When he was thirteen, he swam the length of the lake without a breath.

When he was fifteen, the weights were removed. He could outrun a rabbit.

When he was sixteen, his sleeping pallet was replaced by a

floor of sharp rocks laced with thorns. That same year, he learned of sex.

At seventeen, he could walk over fire.

By the time Justin was nineteen, he could change his heartbeat at will, registering different pulses in various parts of his body. For six weeks, Tagore shut him inside a sealed cave with no food or water. When the cave was opened, Justin rose and left in silence.

At twenty, he was left inside the cave for five months. This time, Justin did not wait for Tagore to come to him. He left the cave when he was ready. In front of the cave, the rock slab that had sealed the opening lay split into fragments.

Justin had grown into a nearly perfect specimen of young manhood. The scars where he had carried the heavy weights had disappeared, and his skin was bronzed and hardened from his years spent in the rugged mountain climate. The boy's stick-thin limbs had filled out with muscle.

When he moved, it was with the grace of a tiger. He had learned how to walk without disturbing even the dry leaves underfoot. He could endure a degree of pain that even the disciplined monks of Rashimpur found astonishing. He exercised for weeks on end without sleep or food. He had grown tall, more than a foot taller than most of the monks at Rashimpur. During devotions, he towered above them, his electric blue eyes surveying all he saw with detached grandeur.

"Your body has grown well," Tagore said.

"I have done my best." A small spark flashed in his blue eyes. His teacher had never complimented him before.

Tagore became an old man. The crinkles around his eyes and mouth had deepened into furrows, and the skin over his beak nose was stretched and spotted. Justin had always thought of Tagore as a big man, the greatest and strongest of all the remarkable men at Rashimpur. Now he looked at him as a man would regard an equal, and he noticed for the first time that his teacher was just barely taller than the other monks, his small bones as fragile as a bird's.

Tagore smiled with his eyes. "You have done your best," he said softly.

"Yes . . ." He was puzzled. "And you, too, Tagore," he added. "Your training has given me everything."

"Ah," Tagore said. "And with my training and your body you are prepared to rule over Rashimpur?"

Justin's face broke into a sudden smile. "Yes," he said, exultant. "I did not want to announce myself ready for the task, but yes, I am ready."

"And for what reasons do you feel you are adequately prepared for this task?"

Justin stammered. "I—I don't understand. I'm the strongest of all the monks of Rashimpur. I have trained all my life to be the Wearer of the Blue Hat. And I wear the amulet of Patanjali. It is my destiny to rule. I am grown now. It is time. You have said so yourself.

"I said only that your body has grown well. You have learned next to nothing about your soul."

"That's not fair," Justin said. "I practice my devotions longer than any. I have carried through the Nine Steps of Renunciation. I have learned all of the eighty-four positions of the Asana, and even the longest mantras. I have been the best *chela* in every exercise of the spirit. The monks themselves have acknowledged my ability."

Tagore sat silently for several moments. "My son, a *chela* is a pupil only. The Wearer of the Blue Hat does not look to others for proof of his merit. He must know in his own heart of his place."

"But I am the best," Justin protested. "I do know it."

"Is that why you chose to smash the rock sealing the cave rather than to wait inside for us?"

Justin's frown disappeared. "I knew it was time. I wanted to prove that I could leave of my own will."

Tagore spoke quietly, his voice full of sadness. "Was it so difficult for you to wait, unnoticed, in silence?" he asked.

Justin didn't answer.

"Come."

They walked through the Great Hall to the Tree of the Thousand Wisdoms. Tagore stood before it, his shoulders stooped with age. "Do you remember when the holy ones came to see you by this tree?" he asked.

"Of course," Justin said.

"Was it painful when I scraped your hand along the bark?"

Justin smiled. "Yes," he said. "At that time, I thought it was the worst pain in the world. In my dreams, this tree possessed a bark of iron."

"But you are much stronger now," Tagore said.

"I hope so," Justin said lightly.

Tagore raised his hawklike head. "Very well, my son. Pass your hand along the bark once more."

Justin looked from his teacher to the massive tree. "I don't want to damage it," he said.

"The Tree of the Thousand Wisdoms cannot be destroyed. Never. Even by one so prideful as you." There was the faintest trace of anger in his voice.

Justin nodded curtly. He raised his hand as high as he could reach and grasped the bark of the tree. Then, with all his strength, he swept his hand downward.

The pain was as hideous as he remembered. Like metal spikes, the bark of the tree speared and cut the palm of his hand to bleeding strings. Blood poured out of him.

Justin gasped once with the white-hot shock that seared through him, but he quickly brought himself under control. This was, he reasoned, Tagore's final test for him. If he could endure this pain, he could endure anything. He would be ready. He closed his eyes. Slowly his blood vessels contracted. The bleeding stopped. He willed his throbbing nerves to silence, and the pain subsided to a dull thumping. At last, he was prepared to face Tagore.

"There is no more pain," he said proudly. Tagore said nothing. Justin plucked a leaf from the tree. "May I heal it now?" he asked.

"If you are the one who heals your wounds, yes," Tagore said.

Justin grasped the leaf with his wounded hand.

He screamed.

The touch of the leaf was like fire. He dropped the leaf and it fell, blood-soaked, to the floor. The throbbing pain had returned, greater than before. Justin tried to will it into submission, but the pain raged unabated.

Tears sprang to his eyes. "It's terrible," he groaned, pleading with his eyes. "I can't stand it."

"You can," Tagore said coldly. "And you will. And one day perhaps you will understand where a man's strength lies."

He turned his back and walked away.

The next day Justin sought out the old teacher. His hand was wrapped in cloth, and there was no pride in the blue eyes. "Please help me to understand," he said.

Tagore gave him a roll of coarse rice paper. "Kneel before the tree and crumple this paper into a ball," he said.

Justin looked up. "And then?"

"And then smooth the paper flat. When you have finished, begin again, crumpling the paper and smoothing it on the floor of the Great Hall. You are not to speak during the task. You are not to move from your place. You are not to come to me again. Go."

Trembling with anger and shame, Justin took the rice paper to the Great Hall and knelt before the Tree of the Thousand Wisdoms. From his position on the floor, the tree looked once again as it had when he was a boy, forbidding, darkly grand. The tree where the spirit of Brahma lived.

As Tagore had instructed, he crumpled the paper into a ball and then smoothed it flat on the stone floor. It was no effort. It did not even pain his damaged hand. The exercise required no skill, no strength, no endurance. As the monks passed, unseeing, in front of him to gather for devotions, he flushed with humiliation. Those others were to bow to *him*, he thought angrily. They always had. It was not his place to stay on his knees in full view of his followers, performing a task unfit for the lowliest *chela*. He was Patanjali. He was the Wearer of the Blue Hat.

Tagore walked by him without a glance. The old man has lost his senses, he thought, hating the stooped figure who shuffled down the long hall. Justin began to rise. There would be a confrontation, and it would be now.

The moment his knees left the ground, the old man whirled around and fixed him with a stare so cold and unforgiving that it felt like a dagger entering Justin's heart. Involuntarily, he sank to the floor again.

The old man was a magician. A mind reader. An evil, fanatical old lunatic.

Who had given him the body of a god.

Stifling his rage, he crumpled the paper again.

The sun set and rose again. And set. Food was brought to him once a day. He ate alone, in silence, kneeling in the Great Hall. At night, one of the monks took him to his cell, now cleared of the spiky rocks, and Justin lay down on the bare stone floor, trying to hold back his tears of shame. Autumn gave way to winter, and when the small doorway to the hall opened, gusts of windblown snow showered the torches like sparks. In spring, he heard the songs of birds outside as he knelt in his small spot, crumpling and smoothing the rolls of paper that were brought to him every few days.

Another year passed. He would never be strong again, he was sure. Tagore had given him the useless task to perform in order to take away his strength—the strength he had spent a lifetime of discipline acquiring.

To counteract his failing muscles, he began to use the time in his cell at night to exercise. Alone, fighting off sleep, he breathed and stretched, working one muscle against the other. He worked a crack in the wall until a small rock broke loose. With this he chipped away at the wall, night after night. After a few months he had loosened a section of rock and broken it into small pieces, which he knotted into his robes. Using the weights as he had as a child, he performed his exercises, teaching himself how to move again. Now, when sleep came, Justin welcomed it.

He grew accustomed to silence. Each morning he focused all his attention on the short walk from his cell. His legs fairly danced with the pleasure of walking. Kneeling before the ever-present paper, he began to observe details of the tree that he had never before noticed. Minute pockets of sap formed on the bark during the autumn season; in spring, the blackish trunk took on subtle shades of green. He grew to tell the time of day by the shades of light and dark cast by shadows in the hall. Each grain of rice he ate became a new experience for him, and for the first time he tasted a variety of flavors in the food he had once regarded as bland. He felt the response of his organs to every breath he took, every miniscule shiver of excitement.

Gradually his world, which he had thought was shrunken into one odious task, had exploded into a thousand universes, each bursting with experience. Suddenly, he found that there was barely enough time in each day to sift through all the wonders that entered his mind. The world was not Rashimpur. It was immense. And it was tiny. He meant nothing to it. And everything.

As he was smoothing out his paper, one of the monks bade Justin to follow him outside. The beauty of the sunset that melted around Amne Xachim was achingly beautiful. His nostrils filled with the cold air, and he shivered with its sweetness. His mind reeled with the thousands of sounds and songs of the mountains, all filled with breathtaking wonder. He stood on the edge of the cliff where he had stood on the day of his coronation. Once again, he felt power surge through him as it had never done since. He touched the amulet on his chest, and again he heard the ancient music he had heard on the day he met Tagore. It had been mysterious then, unknowable. But now he heard it, and knew distinctly what the music was. It was the sound of the wind, of the birds, of the still water in the lake, of the movement of the earth and its births and deaths. It was the sound of present and past and eternity. It was being. It was life.

This time he did not stop the tears that came to his eyes. Never had he thought he would see anything so lovely, hear anything so beautiful, and yet the sights and sounds that intoxicated him were things he had seen all his life. Tagore had been right. It was all magic, every molecule of air.

Another figure walked silently to the cliffside and stood beside Justin.

"Come inside," the old man said.

In the Great Hall, Justin slipped wordlessly to his place on the floor, but Tagore took his hand and raised him up.

"Pull your hand down the bark of the tree," he said.

Justin obeyed without hesitation. The pain would come, but it would leave. The tree would wound him, but that wound would heal. And even during the worst of the pain, he knew, the wind outside would still sing. The sun would still set. Amne Xachim would continue to live, and so would his immortal soul. He feared nothing.

With all his strength he pressed against the black bark of the tree, seeing its tiny sap tears with his new eyes, savoring its thousand hidden colors, feeling its ancient strength beneath his hand. In his mind, he joined with the tree, became the tree itself. In one swift motion, he swept his bare palm down the bark.

The bark fell in a strip at his feet.

Aghast, he stared at the peeled-away bark and at the white stripe that ran the length of the tree. He looked at his hand. There was not a mark on it.

He turned to Tagore. The old man was kneeling on the hard stone floor, bowing to him. Justin reached down and helped the old man to his feet.

"Do you remember?" Tagore asked gently. "When I first

brought you here? You wanted magic. To show it to you, I placed a rock in a stream.''

"I remember," Justin said. They were the first words he had spoken in three years.

''Which is stronger?" Tagore asked, lifting the crumpled sheet of paper from the floor. ''The rock or the water?''

Justin knelt and bowed to him.

By the time Justin Gilead was twenty-six years old, he had learned every lesson but one.

In that year, he learned how to kill.

CHAPTER THIRTEEN

The dreams had grown worse.

Through each step of Justin's development, the strange yet familiar face of the man he had come to know as the Prince of Death had entered Justin's world as he slept, bringing with him the destruction of Justin's life. He told Tagore about the dreams, of the fire and destruction he saw, of his own death and burial. But Tagore told him only that the will of Brahma would prevail and that dreams were only dreams.

"But I've seen other things. The tree. I knew about the Wearer of the Blue Hat. You believed me then."

"Yes," Tagore had said, and dismissed him.

But the old man had taken the diamond left to Justin and buried it deep within the walls of the Great Hall of Rashimpur. "This is yours," he said. "If you leave this place, you must take the diamond with you. Break it into small pieces and sell them. The diamond will keep you until you are able to return here."

Justin watched sadly as the old monk sealed the stone into the wall. "My dreams are true, aren't they," he said.

"I do not know. Only the Wearer of the Blue Hat can know."

The dreams weighed more heavily on Justin than did the rocks he carried as a boy. At first, the Prince of Death had visited him rarely. Each time, it had taken Justin days to recover. But now the dreams recurred every night. Every night the man whose features he knew by heart appeared, bringing with him the soft, gray curling smoke of endless pain. Before, he had come alone; but recently the man in Justin's dreams was led by a woman. She was beautiful and ageless, robed in crimson, with jewels in her black hair. She, too, was someone Justin had seen before. The Dorje Pagma, abbess of the Yamdrok Lake monastery in Tibet, the one called Varja, the goddess. In the dreams Varja pointed the way to Rashimpur, for the Prince of Death to walk forth.

He stopped sleeping. The nights came and went, each spent looking out the narrow slotted window of his cell. After a week, he wrapped himself in a woolen cloak and spent the cold nights outdoors, keeping vigil on the rock face of Amne Xachim.

Tagore went to him.

"He is coming," Justin said. "You do not believe me, but I know this. The abbess, the one you call Varja, has shown him the way."

Tagore did not answer for a long moment. "I believe you," he said at last. "I have always believed you."

Justin turned his blue-circled eyes from the darkness of the mountains to the old man.

"Sadika, your predecessor, prophesied it himself," Tagore said quietly. "You are to be the last Wearer of the Blue Hat. The ages of Rashimpur are to end with you. I could not tell you earlier, because it would have frightened you. Forgive me, Patanjali."

Justin stared, stupefied. "That can't be true," he said.

"Long before your birth, Sadika told of the trials we would all face after his death." He wrapped his cloak around him tighter. "He, too, saw the flames of destruction that were to engulf Rashimpur," Tagore sighed. "And he, too, saw the figure of Varja leading the way."

"Then why did you invite her here?" Justin asked, the despair in him welling. "Why didn't you kill her before she started?"

"My son, Varja already knew of Rashimpur. And we do not kill out of fear. That is for the weak. Such an act would have destroyed us far more completely than it would have hurt her. No, Justin. Varja has her destiny, just as you have yours."

"And the man? The Prince of Death?"

"He, too, must live out his life according to Brahma's great plan."

Justin spoke bitterly. "The great plan to kill us all."

There was silence. "Not all," Tagore said softly. Then he asked the drawn young man next to him, "What is karma?"

Justin thought. Karma, he knew, was everything. Good and evil, incarnation after incarnation. It was a man's spirit, created by his actions. The obstacles and joys he experiences in a present lifetime, carved inexorably from the previous one. Karma was destiny, at once fixed and changeable, understandable, yet beyond reach. The beginning and the end. Past and future, together in the present.

Justin struggled with the answer. At last he said, "Karma is the circle."

Tagore nodded slowly. "You must allow the circle to complete itself."

"I don't understand," Justin said.

"The man, the one you call the Prince of Death, is as much a part of your life as I am. As necessary to you as the air you breathe. You can no more deny yourself the pain he brings than you can the peace brought by Amne Xachim. I told you once that your life would be the most difficult of mortal lives. I have tried to train you here to prepare you for that life, for it has not yet begun. It is your karma to meet this man. As it is your karma to vanquish him or be vanquished by him."

"I will kill him the moment I see him."

"You are forbidden by ancient law to kill except in defense of a life in immediate danger. If you kill this man now, you will break the circle of your karma. And the snake within your circle, whose power rests in the amulet you carry, will remain forever coiled. It is not time yet."

"Should I let him destroy us first?" Justin said with a cruel edge to his voice.

"You will not decide the matter," Tagore said.

Justin looked deeply into the old teacher's eyes. "Tagore," he said, "you have been more than a father to me. I respect you above all men, and I love you. But this time you are wrong. I rule over Rashimpur, and I will decide. The man will die."

"When it is time."

"And when will it be time?" Justin asked angrily.

"You will know. Until then you are forbidden."

Justin turned away from him and sat once again facing the black night mountains.

"It is not I who forbid you," Tagore said, rising. "It is the karma of Patanjali, and the will of Brahma."

Justin did not answer.

"Farewell, my son," Tagore said, and left.

The next morning, just after dawn, a procession of soldiers appeared on the narrow footpath at the base of Amne Xachim. Justin watched them in silence for a moment. Then, checking to make sure that he wasn't seen by the other monks at Rashimpur, he stole away, alone, scaling down the cliffside to wait for them among the rocks.

Too far away for the untrained eyes of the marching men to see him, Justin stole toward the group, watching as they made their slow progress up the mountain. They climbed along the narrow mountain route as Justin had as a boy—wearily, with painstaking effort. The first time Justin walked to Rashimpur, the journey had taken four days. Now he could run it easily in less than six hours.

The men were more than a day's journey from Rashimpur when Justin reached them, careful to conceal his movements and stay out of their sight. There were twelve of them, dressed in some sort of military uniform, their long overcoats crusted with dirt from what had obviously been a long overland journey through the mountain passes on foot. Justin studied them carefully, searching for the face he had seen so often in his dreams. But none resembled the familiar stranger who had come to him night after tortured night since childhood.

The soldiers stopped for food and rest at high noon, laying down the heavy backpacks and weapons they carried. They spoke in Russian, but what they said puzzled Justin.

One of them complained about the endless journey, and others joined in, calling their group the losers in a wager. Even when the leader of the group demanded silence, he did so in a halfhearted way, his disgust at his position clear.

Justin watched the men for some time. A couple of the soldiers dozed. Without a sound, Justin made his move, bursting into the small encampment and removing their weapons in one swift, continuous motion. A young soldier scrambled for his rifle. Effortlessly, Justin kicked it out of his hands as he reached for the leader of the troop and pinned him to the ground.

"Where is he?" Justin shouted, sickened at his own actions. His karma, he knew, was already lost. By attacking first, he had violated the most basic laws of his people. But Rashimpur would not be destroyed. He vowed it, and if that vow meant the loss of his soul, then so be it. "Where is the one who leads you?"

No one answered. Two of the soldiers looked at each other, apparently surprised that the young monk with his shaved head and flowing yellow robes could speak Russian. The officer in Justin's arms struggled to free himself. He yanked the man's arm harder, and the officer yelped.

"Where?" he demanded. "I swear before you that I will kill every one of you if you keep your silence."

The soldiers stood in awed bewilderment. Most of them were young, Justin noticed, still young enough to be called boys. They shivered as they watched him, their eyes round and frightened. One of them, the youngest-looking member of the group, glanced upward, behind Justin toward the plateau where Rashimpur stood. He swallowed hard and blinked.

Justin didn't move. Something was wrong, he knew it. Very wrong.

"You will not decide," Tagore had said of the destruction of their home. And then the machine-gun fire came from overhead, punctuating the still air from the cliff face of Rashimpur. The guns, mixed with the screams and wails of the dying, the terrible noise, sending down fumes of acrid smoke. The boy whose eyes Justin had followed were downcast in shame.

Justin whirled, the soldier still locked in his grip, and he saw it. Thick gray curls of smoke were pouring out of the doorway leading to the Great Hall. The vision had come to pass, after all. Rashimpur was burning.

"No!" he shouted, tossing the soldier away like a rag and darting at full speed up the stony mountainside. Shots were fired behind him, but he paid no attention to the soldiers below now. The only thought in his mind was to reach the monastery before it was too late. To reach Rashimpur and to find the Prince of Death.

The hours of running up the colossal steepness of Amne

Xachim seemed like days. His heart pounding, he forced his legs harder, willing himself upward.

The Prince of Death would not escape him. He would be there, waiting, and Justin would see that he died for daring to invade the monastery. He hoped that the other monks had not already killed him. For he would be there, Justin knew. He felt the presence of the man as surely as if he were standing in front of him.

He approached by the small lake to the east of the cliff face and dived into the water. He scaled the final cliff of the ascent in bounds, thrusting his hands into the rock and pulling himself up, choking on the heat and smoke that poured out of the rock face above, his ears ringing with the cries that faded into a silence that was even more pernicious than the sounds of death.

At last he stood on the plateau. His teeth clenched, tasting the bitterness in his throat, he made his way silently through the rank smoke to the doorway. His face collapsed as he took in the most horrifying spectacle of his life.

The walls were lined with soldiers, their weapons in firing position. On the floor of the Great Hall were strewn the bodies of the dead monks, their yellow robes stained dark, with blood. The air was filled with the acrid stench of spent gunfire. The hall was utterly silent.

He took in the sight, unbelieving, his eyes wandering from one end of the desecrated hall to the other. And then he saw the Tree of the Thousand Wisdoms. Burning. Smoke billowed out of the ancient tree, its leaves blackened and fallen in clumps of ash. The shock took Justin like a wave. He groaned and felt something in his chest turn to water.

Tied to the tree was the charred and mutilated body of Tagore.

He walked toward it hesitantly, as if in a dream. It *was* the dream, come hideously to life. Flames licked around the massive tree's trunk, lapping onto the frail legs of the old man. He had been stripped naked, and his chest had been punctured. His skin was blistered and blackened. Dried blood was splashed around his shattered knees.

"Tagore," he said softly, approaching the body. The old man was tied to the tree with steel wire, which had sawn his wrists to the bone. With a snap, Justin broke the wires and held the limp form of his teacher in his arms.

The features of the old face were composed. There was no torture in it. It had taken all his strength, Justin understood, just to die at peace.

Slowly Justin's sadness solidified into something hard and alien within him.

Hate.

He stood in front of the smoldering tree with Tagore in his arms, turning to face each of the dozens of soldiers flanking him, their bayonets fixed on him. "Where is he who leads you?" he screamed, anguished. "Show your face to me!"

One man moved. He stepped from the shadows at the far end of the hall, near the doorway. His steps were measured, careful. He walked with perfect authority. As he drew near, Justin saw his face. With sickening gratification, he recognized the man.

The Prince of Death had come at last.

The two men stared at each other for a long moment. The man's impassive face betrayed nothing. He wore his blond hair short, like a brush, and although he was young, it had already begun to gray. He was not a big man, but the set of his shoulders beneath his uniform showed a power of will rare even among the disciplined monks of Rashimpur. His weathered face held the beginnings of furrows from his nose to his chin, lines that would deepen with age.

But it was his eyes that most held Justin's attention. They were a colorless green-gray, shallow-set and heavy-lidded, burning with deep intelligence. They were reptile's eyes, spilling out of the expressionless face to take in everything around him at a glance, eyes that judged instantly and without emotion. Cold eyes, unburdened by arrogance, unfettered by passion, as if they saw all things before them as equal, and equally disposable. The eyes suited the Prince of Death. They were exactly as Justin remembered them from his dream.

The Russian spoke first, in a quiet, cultivated voice. "I am Lieutenant Alexander Zharkov of the Army of the Union of Soviet Socialist Republics," he said. "I require the use of this building." There was no challenge in his words, no unspoken threat. It occurred to Justin that the mass murder of every living being at Rashimpur meant nothing to this man. The monks had been destroyed because they had been in the way.

"This is not your land," Justin answered, trembling. "Your

government does not rule this area, and no one rules Rashimpur.''

Zharkov hesitated for the briefest moment. "The building is mine," he said softly.

Slowly Justin lowered the body of his dead teacher to the floor, his eyes never leaving those of the quiet, intense man who stood before him. "It is not yours." The menace between them was palpable.

Zharkov made a swift, jutting motion with his chin, and the soldiers moved instantly out of their formation. But before they could reach him, Justin was in the air, the power of his legs striking out with every muscle in his body focused. With awkward slowness, Zharkov whirled away, a flash in the lizard's eyes betraying sudden fear. Justin's foot struck the man's shoulder, snapping it with a loud crack. Zharkov fell to the ground with a rush of breath.

Justin prepared for a new attack, but it was already too late. He felt the bayonet tip enter his back, below his last rib. As he acknowledged the pain, he saw the blood-smeared shaft emerge from the front of his body and recede again.

He gasped, watching the blood pump out of his belly in rhythmic spurts as the steel spear tore through him again.

And again.

With a shudder, he fell. His legs splayed apart, twitching uncontrollably. He struggled for air. At last he lay back, his hand covering the wound in his side, the gush of blood subsiding between his fingers.

He looked up. The last sight he had was of the Prince of Death who stood over him, his face twisted in a pained grimace, while soft gray edges of smoke curled around him like a shroud.

CHAPTER FOURTEEN

Water.

It was all around him, cold and soothing, its blue clarity marbled with threads of dark blood seeping from his wounds. Justin's eyes opened slowly. He realized that he had automatically suspended his breathing.

In the stillness of the water, he heard his own heart beating in a rhythm so slow that it seemed to have no rhythm at all. This remarkable ability, drilled into Justin every day since childhood until his body could perform it without thought, had saved his life. Silently he thanked Tagore for the arduous training. He would need it all now.

The calm of the water was shattered by something of great weight falling into it near Justin. Bubbles frothed above a sudden gush of mud. When the water cleared, he saw the floating yellow robes of one of the monks, sinking, then rising slowly to the surface. There was another splash, and the face he saw stared into the depths of the water with sightless eyes. He must be in the small lake near Rashimpur, he thought numbly. The soldiers were dumping the bodies of the dead into the water.

Justin's injuries were too severe for him to move, so he remained motionless, rocking with the impact of each yellow-robed body that was thrown into the lake, focusing his will on the broken blood vessels in his side. There was no time for sorrow. He had to direct every fiber of his body and spirit toward his own healing. The sorrow would remain, he knew. The horror would last forever.

124

Concentrating, he willed his heart to beat even more slowly. The water felt warmer, so he knew his temperature was falling. The blood from his side thinned to a trickle. His thoughts narrowed to a white dot of light that he willed in front of him. He had no consciousness of anything outside the white light. He grasped it with his mind and brought it closer. Then, when the dot of light was large enough for him to enter, he willed a dot of black light inside the white, and withdrew himself even farther. When the black dot revealed yet a third light, he was in the trance state of deep consciousness where he knew he had to be in order for his body to heal. He rested inside the small white light until his eyes opened again. The water was dark now. Outside, it would be night.

Like a snake—semiconscious, his limbs blue from the cold, his mind clouded—he slithered onto the shore of the lake and lay beneath the rhododendron bushes. The blossoms were trampled and muddy from the boots of the soldiers. Overhead hung a thin moon, dim and shrouded by mist. The monastery of Rashimpur was invisible and silent, but the lingering stench from the fire remained. Slowly Justin deepened his breathing. The new oxygen made him dizzy at first, then filled him with energy. He sat up, then stood. His heart sped up to his normal waking rate. Tearing a strip of cloth from his robe, he tied a crude bandage over his wounds.

He tested it with a slap. The pain was bad, but the bandage would hold. He clenched a fist; his fingers worked. Good, he thought. He would need his hands.

He was ready.

Two sentries guarded either side of the plateau where Rashimpur stood. Justin edged silently up the cliffside behind the left guard and waited for him to mark his paces. When the sentry approached the far end of the plateau, out of sight of the other guard, Justin wound his forearm around the man's neck. A low gurgling sound issued from the man's throat as his arms windmilled in panic.

You are forbidden to kill. Tagore's voice rang out in the hate-filled recesses of Justin's mind. He had never killed before. The man's flesh was clammy, and he stank of fear. Lice crawled in his filthy hair. This is a man who bore me no ill, Justin thought. He has endured hardship and loneliness and has gone unclean in service to another. He lives only to do another's bidding. He is a soldier, not a leader. The rationality of his years of tutoring came back to him: The taking of life is wrong, rarely justified.

Your karma will be destroyed, Tagore's voice echoed. But Justin's karma was a foreign thing now, burned in the fire of Rashimpur, as dead as his soul.

Forgive me, all the wise and holy who have gone before me. The hate inside me is too great.

He broke the man's neck.

The second time, the killing was easier. The sentry died quickly under Justin's hands, soiled now with the sweat of his first kill. Then he made his way inside, where the soldiers lay sleeping on the floor of the Great Hall. Tagore's body was gone. He lay, Justin knew, at the bottom of the lake with the others.

His movements were soundless. He had learned to walk with such stillness that even the air around him was not disturbed. He was careful to strike each blow with such speed that the soldiers would make no noise to awaken the others as they died. There was no more hesitation in his attack. Reason had no place in his thoughts. He felt no pity. It was only his hate that Justin was feeding now, and the hunger in him grew with each death. It would not be satisfied until the last man had died by his hand. He would make sure that the last man was Zharkov himself.

Zharkov would not die silently. Justin wanted to see him suffer, watch him in the extremities of his agony, hear his pleas for mercy. He wanted to look into the composed lizard's eyes at the moment when the life in them was extinguished. Only then would he begin to sorrow for the lost love of Tagore, for he would allow himself no rest until then. *He would see his eyes.* For that, the loss of his immortal soul, doomed to wander the earth for endless ages of suffering, was not too high a price to pay.

One last perfect moment with the Prince of Death.

In minutes, the Great Hall had become a massive crypt for the second time. The soldiers lay in their bedrolls, undisturbed except for their bloodless, fatal wounds. Zharkov was not among them.

Justin paused after his work to breathe in the air, thick with death. Death was his karma now, his essence. He understood it in the depth of his heart. Death was all he wanted, first Zharkov's and then his own. He himself needed Zharkov's death; the spirit of Tagore, now desecrated by Justin's actions, would require Justin's death.

He pitched his hearing low. All life, he was taught, carried sound. Even the growth of plant could be heard by ears sensitive enough to perceive it. He listened now, in the death-filled stillness, for the sound. Because Zharkov was alive.

It came from the monastery's kitchen. He followed it through the dark corridors, the torches on the walls now extinguished forever. His heightened hearing picked up the low wail of the wind behind the rock facade of Rashimpur, and the scurrying of a thousand invisible night creatures. But behind them was another sound, one that Justin would never forget.

The sound of fire.

Zharkov sat at the stone cook's table, facing the doorway. He was bent over scrolls containing maps of the area. Occasionally he marked the maps, writing notes along the edges. Behind him, in a stone grotto, burned a small cooking fire, which cast huge shadows tinged with gold.

Zharkov's jacket was open. Strapped to his chest was a pistol in its shoulder holster.

"I remember you," Justin said.

Zharkov grabbed for the gun, but Justin was prepared this time. He swung his arm downward and knocked the weapon out of Zharkov's hand. It clattered to the floor. With his eyes on Zharkov, he picked it up and threw it through the narrow slot opening of the kitchen window. Justin could hear it strike the ground outside and tumble down the cliff face.

"Your men are dead."

The reptilian eyes wandered slowly in the direction of the Great Hall. He was listening. At last he said, "You couldn't have reached me if they weren't."

Justin marveled at the coldness of the man. There was not a flicker of panic on Zharkov's face. No surprise that a man he had watched die was standing in front of him. Not the slightest pity for the soldiers who he surely knew were lying, lifeless, outside the room.

Zharkov spoke again. "I remember you as well. The chess match in Paris." He spoke quietly, without a trace of emotion. "You beat me then."

"I will beat you again," Justin said.

Zharkov shrugged slightly. "I presume the old man lied to me. I asked who the leader of your sect was. He said it was he who ruled the monastery."

"You killed the wrong man," Justin said.

"I guessed as much. He spoke through an interpreter. He did not know my language. I understood that the Wearer of the Blue Hat was educated to speak many tongues."

Justin tried to conceal his shock as the man continued. "Also, you wear the amulet of the coiled snake. You are the leader."

Then Justin understood. The vision in his dreams had been real. "Varja," he said. "The woman led you here."

Zharkov's eyes remained locked into Justin's. "Then you understand why all had to die. I knew of their skill in combat. I could not risk my men so early."

"It is too late now," Justin said coldly.

There was silence. "I have been instructed to occupy this building. If I do not take it, then others who come after me will."

"Let them come. You will be long dead."

Zharkov did not flinch as Justin inched closer to him, his footsteps as silent as dead air. Justin's heartbeat quickened; the moment he had given his soul for had come. He would see those lizard eyes roll into a nightmare death.

At that moment, Zharkov drew back and kicked him in his wounded side with the heel of his boot. Justin reeled backward, the unexpected pain ripping through him. As he staggered away, Zharkov's hand snaked out to tear the amulet from Justin's neck and throw it into the fire. While Justin was recovering from the blow, Zharkov pulled a short knife from his belt and lunged at him.

Nauseated with pain, Justin lurched forward and grasped the knife by the blade. The exercise of crumpling and smoothing the rice paper for three years had made his palms as hard and unyielding as slate. He twisted the knife away. Then, swiftly, he yanked Zharkov by the hair and dragged him over to the fireplace. With one hand he reached into the flames to find the amulet.

Zharkov struck out blindly. Justin was surprised at the man's strength, but his struggle fired Justin's hate. He slammed Zharkov's head into the stones of the grotto. The distance was only a few inches, not enough to kill, but the force of the blow, undirected, unfocused, filled Justin with shame. He did not want to bludgeon his enemy to death like a terrified barbarian.

Zharkov moaned. His legs skittered in place for a moment, then stopped. The hooded eyes fluttered open briefly and then closed as Zharkov fell limp, his short hair bristling through Justin's fingers.

This was not how it was supposed to be, Justin thought, anguished, as he watched the inert form beside him. Zharkov was unconscious, the pulse in his neck still throbbing rhythmically. For the Prince of Death simply to die, unaware and painlessly, was not enough.

Tagore had been right. It was not yet time. One did not answer meaningless deaths with more meaningless deaths.

Justin retrieved the amulet from the fire. It had already begun to melt. The coiled snake had lost its intricately carved scales, and a drop of molten gold rested on the base of the disc.

Zharkov came to groggily, the lizard eyes unfocused. Justin held him fast.

"I cannot kill you yet," Justin said. "It is not time. But we will meet again." He pressed the fire-hot amulet into Zharkov's neck. The Russian screamed and bucked, trying to get away, but Justin's arm around his throat was like iron.

The skin on the soldier's neck smoldered and blackened, and once again the terrible stench of burning flesh filled the air. When Justin drew back, the imprint of the coiled snake, raw and blistered, remained.

"Remember me," Justin said.

He returned late the next night. Zharkov was gone. The bodies of his soldiers still lay on the floor where Justin had killed them.

He removed the heavy stone from the wall and took out the diamond that had been kept for him there. The Great Hall was in ruins. Its gold-covered walls were blackened with smoke, and the tree—the sacred Tree of the Thousand Wisdoms, which had healed him and taught him to see through new eyes—now stood leafless and broken, a charred hulk.

"Tagore said nothing could destroy you," he said bitterly.

He gathered a handful of ash from the base of the tree and

walked outside to the edge of the plateau where Rashimpur stood. The wind whistled in tuneless mourning through the silent mountains.

Justin wanted to pray for the souls of the dead, but he knew he was no longer fit to pray. He had destroyed his karma and had gone against the will of Brahma. Worst of all, he had not been able to save a single life except his own and that of the man he hated more than anything on earth. They would both have to live now.

"Weep, sacred mountain," he said. "Weep the tears I have no right to shed." He opened his hands. The ashes were swept upward in the wind, flying into the silent night.

In Havana, the sun is hot . . .

An image of improbably colored palm trees swirled through Andrew Starcher's mind. In Havana, the sun was hot. It hung in the sky, bright and dangerous, a drop of molten gold at its base, and the coiled snake inside it darted out and wound itself around Starcher's heart, squeezing, killing him . . .

He sat up with a start. The pain was excruciating. The intravenous tubing in his arms stabbed him, and the ball of muscle inside his chest seemed about to burst. Monitors above his head squealed in protest. Their smooth waves peaked into jagged irregularity. Within seconds, a team of nurses was hovering nearby, forcing him back down in the bed, covering his face with a plastic oxygen mask.

"Don't sit up like that," one of them barked in Russian. "Can you hear me? Blink if you can hear me."

With an effort, Starcher squeezed his eyes shut. The sweat on his forehead ran in thin streams down his temples.

It had done this to him. The medallion. The touch of it had been enough to stop his heart. No one would ever believe him, but it was true. The coiled snake possessed the same power its owner had, the same electric quality Starcher had noticed when he'd first met the young man named Justin Gilead.

Starcher remembered the day well because he had just gotten word that he was going to be reassigned back to Europe. For a year, since taking the bullet in Berlin, he had been working unwillingly as a trainer for new CIA recruits at the complex in Langley, Virginia. Nursemaiding a bunch of twenty-one-year-old Yalies was a long step down from the feverish excitement of cold war Europe, and he wanted to get back. It was 1970.

There was a man at Langley then, not a recruit, but a prisoner. Langley always had its share of weirdos storming the doors and demanding to become spies for the U.S. government. Everyone from shopping bag ladies to seedy degenerates in their sixties, it seemed, had bought the James Bond myth of glamour and adventure in the espionage trade and wanted to be a part of it. These were almost invariably turned away at the first guard station, but the young man being held in isolation was not one of these.

Gilead had come in three days before, without the knowledge of any of the security guards. This in itself was adequately alarming to have him questioned. Starcher, because of his long background in Europe, was told to talk to him. "Something's going on here," the operations chief told him, "so find out what's going on. I think the Russians sent this guy."

"Not your usual way of infiltrating the enemy," Starcher said dryly and went to a guarded room where the intruder was being held.

His first reaction to the young man was wonder at the man's ice blue eyes, and then surprise at his youth. He could not be older than his mid-twenties. His shirt was open; a golden snake amulet hung at his throat.

"I've come to talk to you," Starcher said.

"I'm used to it by now." The voice was soft but pitched deep. He spoke evenly, although he must have been tired of repeating his story to everyone who came to the room.

"My name is Justin Gilead. I want to work for you people. I ask no salary. Someday I will want a favor."

"What kind of favor?"

"I can't tell you specifically. It won't be illegal; it'll just be a piece of information I need."

"Can't tell me specifically or won't tell me?" Starcher asked.

"Either way," young Gilead said. His accent was American, although he could produce neither passport nor identification.

Starcher sat on a chair at the small desk in the room while Gilead stood with his back to him, looking out a barred window. The CIA man opened the folder he had brought with him and glanced at its contents.

Justin Gilead was twenty-six. He had been born in New York City and spoke a dozen languages. He did not know how to drive a car. He had no living relatives. He said that his occupation was chess player. He had spent his childhood being raised by monks in India. As a reference, he gave the name of a professor at Columbia University in New York, Anna Tauber.

Starcher talked to him for two hours, and Gilead neither changed his story nor betrayed by any slip of word or fact that he was anything other than what he pretended to be.

He said that he was going to begin playing international chess. With that as a cover and an entrée into various countries, he would be able to do a great deal of work for the CIA. He insisted that all he wanted in return was someday a favor—"a piece of information," he repeated.

Starcher got up to leave the room, more confused than he was when he entered.

"How long will I be staying here?" Gilead asked him.

"I don't know."

"You seem like a reasonable man, Mr. Starcher. Do you think I have any chance of getting my request granted to serve with you people?"

"Honestly, I think you have two chances: slim and none."

"I've come around to that way of thinking myself. I guess I'll be leaving here, then."

"They might want you to stay."

"What they might want and what I do are two different things," Gilead said. He smiled at Starcher, but it was a cold smile, without humor or mirth. A mouse might see a cat smile that way.

"What do you think?" Harry Kael asked Starcher after he came out of the isolation room. Kael was chief of security at the time.

Starcher shook his head. "I don't know what to think. I don't think he's a Russian agent, if that's what you mean. If the Russians wanted to plant somebody in here, they would have prepared him. They wouldn't have just had him march in."

"I never trusted chess players," Kael said. "Every one of them I ever see in the papers has got a sneaky, devious, pinched little face.'' Kael's face was as open as a Boston saloon at high noon.

"Is he a chess player, then?" Starcher asked.

"That part checks out. There actually was a Justin Gilead, a kid who was born in New York when this guy says he was. He was a chess player. A child whatchamacallit.''

"Prodigy?" Starcher suggested.

"Right. His old man was some kind of hot-shot writer or something. Got murdered in Paris in '54. Went by the name of Leviathan. The boy was with him when he bought it. Police assumed the kid got hit, too, although they never found the body. Made all the papers.''

"I remember now. The boy was a chess genius.''

"A master at the age of ten. You play chess?''

"No," Starcher said.

"It's a tough game. Maybe that's what pinches their faces. You play for years, maybe you get a little better. Then once in a while a kid like that one comes along. Takes all the marbles before he's out of diapers. Master at ten, that's nothing to sneeze at. I just wish I knew what he was up to.''

"Maybe he's telling the truth," Starcher said.

"Come on, Andy. There's nobody like who this guy says he is.''

"Have you checked out the college professor?''

"Who? Oh, her. Wrote her a letter. She doesn't have a phone. Didn't get an answer yet. Let's face it. This kid's a spy or a nut. We can't use him either way.''

"I didn't think nuttiness was a drawback in our kind of work," Starcher said, and both men laughed.

Starcher thought that, back in the old days of the OSS, a man of Gilead's apparent intelligence and abilities wouldn't have been pigeonholed as a lunatic without first checking his background with some thoroughness. But then, you took chances in the old days. You looked for the exceptional man, not the one whose graph matched the standard agent's profile. Starcher thought that maybe age was making him sentimental. Even in the old days, Gilead's story would have been hard to swallow. Which was exactly why he wanted it to be true.

The next day Gilead was gone from the isolation room.

"I can't understand it," Kael told the men who had assembled in the empty chamber. Two guards on duty all night, no tools inside, the window's not broken . . .'' He pointed to the small glass block high up on the wall. "He must have gotten out through the heating duct, but he couldn't have breathed in there. Ten to one he's dead in the system somewhere," Kael said with a disgusted sigh. "I'll call in a cleanup crew."

The crew found nothing but dust clumps. Justin Gilead had vanished.

CHAPTER SIXTEEN

Starcher had two weeks to kill before he was due to report to his new post in Paris, and decided to spend the time in New York City. But the theater and the opera seemed flat and boring to him; his thoughts wandered too often to the strange young man, Justin Gilead.

The decade of the seventies, Starcher felt, would see deep changes in the way America and Russia faced each other in the world. In the generation since the end of World War II, the two superpowers had squared off like street gangs in a tire-iron fight, scrapping for every advantage, every inch of turf. But now the national borders were set; spheres of influence had been long since established. The spy business would become less confrontational and more subtle; the battles of the next generation would not be overtly for space and power, but more often to win the minds of men and women. It would require a different kind of spy operation, and perhaps a different kind of spy.

One afternoon, he took a taxicab to Columbia University and found the office of Professor Anna Tauber, who taught Eastern religions at the university's Department of Asian Studies.

"Ah, yes. My friendly neighborhood CIA," Dr. Tauber said amiably from behind a desk crowded with papers, books, bits of discarded sandwiches, moldering tea bags, and unopened mail. "I read your letter. Unfortunately, I haven't had a chance to answer it yet."

"I didn't write the letter, so I don't know what's in it," Starcher admitted.

"The usual bullying government pap. Wanted to know about Justin. Turn over any records on him, blah, blah." She pursed her lips and emitted a sound that clearly expressed her views of the Central Intelligence Agency. "What'd you say your name was?"

"Starcher. Andrew Starcher."

"You're southern. Any relation to the Virginia horse-trading Starchers?"

"That's my clan," he said with a smile.

"Met some of them when I worked on Johnson's Human Rights Commission. Big family. Nice. You must be the black sheep."

She spoke without a trace of humor. Starcher couldn't help liking her, with her steel-wool hair and rubbery lips and old-fashioned two-toned glasses that left red welts on the bridge of her nose. "I'm afraid so," he said. "My family was very disappointed when I didn't grow up to be a plantation boss."

"Well, you're here on business, and I've got a class in forty minutes, so start talking. Hold it." She slammed two fungus-encrusted coffee cups on the desk in front of him. "Go rinse these out at the water fountain down the hall." With surprising agility, she swiveled her chair around and plugged in a plastic teapot sitting on the windowsill. Starcher noticed that there was a small tear in her dress just below the armpit. "The water'll be hot by the time you get back."

He obeyed. When he returned, Dr. Tauber had tossed over a fresh tea bag and a copy of Alan Watts's *The Way of Zen* for him to use as a coaster. "All right. What do you want to know?" Suddenly her face broke into a wide smile. "That's a hell of a thing to ask the CIA, isn't it?"

"Before we go any further," Starcher said, "I ought to tell you that I'm not here for the CIA. The CIA's forgotten about Justin Gilead."

"And you haven't?" she asked.

"No."

"Why not?"

Starcher faltered a moment. "He's kind of hard to forget."

"He is that, isn't he?" Dr. Tauber said with a grin. "Will you be able to use him in your work?"

"I don't know. Maybe. The world's changing."

"That's CIA double-talk. Tell me the truth. You folks think he's some kind of foreign spy or something."

"I don't," Starcher said, but she ignored his answer.

"I told him you would." She banged her fist down on the desk, causing a pile of mimeographed papers to cascade off the side. "He wouldn't believe me. These kids all have stars up their ass. Oh, they have their little protests, but underneath it all, they think old Uncle Sam's on their side."

"I believe the same thing, Dr. Tauber."

"Bullshit. Right now, at this moment, you're probably thinking I'm a Red, too."

Starcher blinked. She had read his mind.

"Well, I'm not. I've voted in every election since I was twenty-one years old. I've served under three presidents in one capacity or another." She lowered her eyes. "And I lost both my sons in the damn war."

"I'm sorry," Starcher said.

"It's past," Dr. Tauber said quietly. "While Mama was marching and picketing and talking at antiwar dinners, her two kids were getting poured into plastic bags. They believed." There was a long silence. "And Justin believes, too." Her features softened. "So how do you stop the young from believing there's a difference between the good guys and the bad guys?"

"You don't," Starcher said, sipping his tea. He knew Tauber was no Soviet sympathizer. She was just an old lady who'd had to bury her children. "Mr. Gilead claims that you're the only person he knows in this country."

"Could be," she said without surprise. "He sure didn't know anyone when I met him."

"Where was that, Dr. Tauber?"

"At the boat. I've got this ratty old houseboat at the Seventy-ninth Street Boat Basin. Call it *Rook's Tour.*"

"You play chess?"

"Got a nineteen hundred rating," she said proudly. "That ranks me near expert. Which doesn't mean doodly-squat, since master's the only rank that counts in serious chess, and that begins at twenty-two hundred. Anyway, Justin. I was out on deck one Saturday this past summer, playing against myself. I remember I was setting up a Sicilian defense . . . a dragon variation. Well, never mind that; you're not interested. And I see this skinny kid dressed in rags about four sizes too small for him. Italian."

"Gilead?" Starcher asked.

"No, Starcher, not him. The clothes. He said he bought them from one of the crew on an Italian steamer he bought passage on. Illegal, of course. Didn't have a passport. Hell, he didn't even have a wallet." She laughed.

"What kind of currency did he have on him?" Starcher asked.

She sat back silently, studying him. "All right. He wouldn't have gone to you people if he'd had anything to hide. He had a pocketful of diamonds."

"*Diamonds?*"

"You heard me. But I'm getting ahead of myself. As I was saying, I was playing against myself, and kind of absorbed in the play, when I noticed Justin standing on the pier. I asked him what the hell he wanted. And you know what he said?" She laughed uproariously. "He said, 'I want you to move the bishop to king four.' "

"Yes?" Starcher asked impatiently.

"Well, it opened up a whole new defense. I could follow it for five or six moves, but then I lost the line, so I told him to play it out with me. He beat me in twelve moves. Never saw a strategy like that in my life. I knew then I'd found a genius."

"About the diamonds, Dr. Tauber . . ."

"I don't know where he got them. I didn't ask. All I knew was that he was hungry and dirty, and the best damn chess player I ever met. We played four more games, and then I gave him a sandwich. He took all the lunch meat out of it; I remember that. Ate the bread. Then I let him take a shower and bunk on the boat overnight. I half expected to find my radio gone with him the next day, but he was still there. He tried to give me a diamond, but I wouldn't take it. Hell, I said, I ought to pay you for showing me that defense."

Starcher glanced at his watch. He wanted the woman to take her time with her story, to remember everything she could, but her forty minutes was running out. "He said nothing about the diamonds?"

"I told you, I didn't ask," she said vehemently. "Oh, hell. I did ask."

Starcher waited.

"He didn't steal them, I'd bet my life on that. You see . . . How much has he told you about himself?"

"He told a rather bizarre story about living in the Himalayas," Starcher said flatly.

"Then you know," she said with some relief. "That's true."

Starcher stared at her.

"The region around Amne Xachim near the Tibetan border has been of interest to scholars for centuries because of the Patanjali legend." She looked up. "Do you know what I'm talking about?"

Starcher said he didn't. She glanced around, annoyed. "Then how do you expect to know anything about him? What time is it?"

"Three forty-five."

"I've got to get to my class." She raised herself out of the chair with some effort and lumbered over to the three bookcases that lined three walls of her office, picking out an armload of books. "You'd better read fast," she said, thrusting the books toward Starcher. "I want those back by tonight." She gave him the address of her apartment on West Eighty-sixth Street. "Now, out. You can read in the library."

Starcher read until his eyes were bleary, comprehending next to nothing about the strange customs and religions in the ancient lands that came to be known as India, Nepal, Burma, and Tibet. He had nearly decided that Anna Tauber was a well-meaning but shaggy-minded academic when he turned a page and saw a drawing of the revered medallion bearing the image of the coiled snake, owned by the monks of Rashimpur and prized as the most sacred amulet of the sect.

"The drawing is based on verbal testimony," the text explained. "No contemporary Westerner has ever seen the medallion or, for that matter, Rashimpur itself. All that is known about the monastery is that it stands somewhere in the vicinity of Amne Xachim, a mountain that is held to be sacred by both Brahmans and Buddhists."

Was the golden medallion the same one he had seen around the neck of the young man in the isolation room at Langley? Of course not, Starcher told himself. A cheap imitation purchased at a flea market in Katmandu. Or New York City, for that matter.

The text went on: According to legend, the high priest of

the Rashimpur sect is the direct reincarnation of Patanjali (and thence Brahma) himself, and is selected at the moment of his birth by his predecessor. At the time of the priest's death, the monks of Rashimpur set out to find the successor according to the directions of their dying leader.

"There is evidence that the leaders chosen often hail from far distant lands, and themselves have no knowledge of their place in the ancient rites until their arrival at the monastery. In 1653, a twenty-one-year-old Swiss clerk named Karl Behrmann disappeared from his native village of Dorhoffbatten, leaving his young wife and two sons. Sixty years later, when Behrmann lay on his deathbed, he composed a letter to his sons outlining his strange adventure on the other side of the world. Although Behrmann did not disclose the location of the monastery, he described its "golden wonders and immortal delights," including a tree that grew in the center of the edifice with neither light nor water. In the letter, which was preserved by the Behrmann family until 1879, when it was destroyed by fire, Behrmann admonished his now elderly sons 'not to mourn my absence nor hold my memory in bitterness, for I was called to fulfill a destiny so removed from the ken of mortal men that none but the past keepers of the medallion and the Eye of Rashimpur can know my heart.'

"The reference to the Eye of Rashimpur is obscure, but some scholars believe it to signify the legendary diamond revered by the monks of the sect and held by its priest, along with the coiled snake medallion, as symbols of his office."

Starcher closed the books and went to Dr. Tauber's apartment. When she opened the door, he handed her the books.

"Do you expect me to believe this?" he asked the professor.

She took the books from him. "I don't expect you people to believe anything. It was my obligation to show you the truth, even if it doesn't mean anything to you. The curse of the educator."

Starcher stood silently in the foyer of the apartment crammed with Far Eastern artifacts. "I'd still like to ask you some more questions."

Tauber laughed. "So you're not as closed-minded as you're supposed to be, after all." She walked away from him, into the apartment. "Come in. Sit down. Coffee?"

He shook his head. She poured him some anyway.

"Dr. Tauber, I'd better explain to you now that if you're involved with this man in any sort of activity subversive to the United States or its intelligence services, the consequences are going to be unpleasant."

"Here they come. The threats. Cream and sugar?"

"You don't seem to understand. I was thinking of using this man with the Central Intelligence Agency. I'm not about to accept a bunch of hocus-pocus as adequate background."

"You're the one who doesn't understand, Mr. Starcher. Justin Gilead is probably the most unusual man in the world. He speaks twelve languages. He can run twenty miles without breaking a sweat, for God's sake. He can swim more than a mile underwater." She was shouting. "You want the truth about him? I wish I could give it to you. I know that when *Rook's Tour* sprung a leak, he dived down under it and stayed there twenty minutes and patched it. And he wasn't wearing air tanks. You want the truth? I don't know. Everything he's told me about Rashimpur checks out with what little I know, and his knowledge of the area, in which I do have some expertise, is far too accurate to be extracted from books. Aside from that, he's twenty-six years old. He might be lying, but in my opinion, no one could know as much as he does without firsthand experience."

"He said he'd work for us for nothing, but that he'd want a favor someday," Starcher said.

Dr. Tauber shrugged.

"What's the favor?" Starcher asked.

"Damned if I know," she said.

"Do you know where Gilead is now?"

She was silent.

"I should have guessed," Starcher said.

Rook's Tour was a dilapidated houseboat whose blue and white paint was peeling off in strips.

"Justin Gilead," Starcher called from the pier.

After a few moments the young man he had talked with at Langley appeared. He was wearing jeans and a T-shirt. Over the shirt hung the gold coiled snake medallion.

"I'm Andrew Starcher. I met you at Langley." He extended his hand. Gilead refused it.

"Yes. You were the last of the pests," he said coldly. "Did you think of more questions?"

"The same one I asked before. What favor will you want?"

"Same answer as before," Gilead said. "I can't tell you specifically."

"Tell me generally."

"Why should I?" Gilead asked.

"Because I'm going back to Europe in a few days. Because if what you've told us is true, I could probably use you."

"Where in Europe?" Gilead asked. His eyes had not left Starcher's throughout the entire conversation. He hadn't seemed to blink.

"I'm going back to Paris. After that, I should be assigned to Moscow," Starcher said.

"Russia," Gilead said. "All right. There's a Russian named Alexander Zharkov. Do you know who he is?"

"Yes," Starcher said, trying to disguise his surprise. "Do you?"

"Yes. He is the son of Vassily Zharkov who is the head of Nichevo. He'll take over when his father dies."

"What do you know about Nichevo?" Starcher asked.

"Not as much as you do," Gilead said. "But I know what it is and what it does."

"And what's this favor you're going to want?" Starcher asked.

"Someday I'm going to have to kill Alexander Zharkov," Gilead said. "When that day comes, I'll want you to tell me where to find him."

"That's it?" Starcher said. "That's the favor?"

"Yes."

"You won't want any help?"

"No," Gilead said. "I won't need any help."

"What do you have against Alexander Zharkov?" Starcher asked.

"He stole something that belonged to me," Gilead said.

"What?"

"My life." He fingered the medallion around his neck.

"Is that the real coiled snake of Rashimpur?" Starcher asked.

"Yes," Gilead said.

"I don't know whether I believe you or not," Starcher said.

"You will," Justin Gilead said.

*   *   *

Before going to France, Starcher returned to Langley to find something out, and the next day he went again to see Gilead on *Rook's Tour*.

"Bad news," he said. "I'm afraid our deal's off."

"Why is that?" Gilead asked. He was busy on the deck of the boat splicing rope, his back to Starcher.

"Alexander Zharkov," Starcher said and got a moment's satisfaction when he saw Gilead's back stiffen and the young man turn toward him, fixing him with his cold blue eyes. "He's probably dead," Starcher quickly added.

"Oh?" Gilead said blandly. "Who told you that?" Starcher could have sworn that he had seen the young man sigh in relief.

"I just came back from Langley. Zharkov was out on some kind of secret army patrol in India about eight months ago. Some border problem. The whole patrol vanished. Everyone's presumed dead."

"Zharkov's alive," Gilead said.

"You don't seem to understand," Starcher said. "The whole patrol, Zharkov included, vanished. Not a word from them for eight months."

"*You* don't seem to understand," Gilead said. "The patrol *is* dead. But Zharkov's alive."

"How do you know that?" Starcher snapped. Gilead's patronizing attitude was beginning to annoy him. "How do you know the patrol's dead? How do you know Zharkov's alive, when he's been lost in the damned mountains for eight months?"

"I know the patrol's dead because I killed them," Gilead said simply.

For a moment, Starcher was stunned speechless. Then he said, "And Zharkov?"

"I didn't kill him," Gilead said. "I let him live."

"Why?"

Gilead turned back to the large coils of rope on the deck of the houseboat, and bent down to resume his work. He spoke quietly, almost as if to himself, but Starcher heard every chilling word clearly.

"Because it isn't time yet," he said.

CHAPTER SEVENTEEN

Starcher had almost forgotten about Justin Gilead. He had been five months at his post in Paris, the first in what he knew would be a long career-concluding series of desk jobs, and he hated it. Of course the work was important. Coordinating European activities of the CIA and "friendlies"—pro-Western nations—was critical to maintain the West's position in the world, particularly with Nichevo roaming about, but still Starcher longed to be in the field again.

He kept filing routine requests for reassignment, which were routinely rejected. Then one gray wintry afternoon, his deputy came into his office in the American embassy and put a single piece of pink paper on his desk.

"One of our analysts just put this together," he said. "I figured you'd be interested."

The brief report had been culled from Soviet publications, internal information, and hints picked up by men in the field.

Alexander Zharkov was alive. According to the memo, Zharkov had shown up in Moscow and reported that he and his entire patrol had been ambushed by hostile tribesmen while on secret duty in India a year earlier. Zharkov had been injured and had suffered amnesia. For a year, not knowing who he was, he was cared for by the monks at a small monastery in the Himalayas. Then his memory returned. Before leaving the monastery—because he did not know what he might have told the monks while an amnesiac—he "eliminated" the monks. There was a possibility, the report

145

said, that Zharkov would be presented with a medal for his "bravery and heroism."

"Thanks," Starcher said and dismissed his deputy with a nod. When the young man left, Starcher read the report again. He didn't believe Zharkov's story for a moment, but there seemed no doubt that the young Russian was alive. And Justin Gilead had known.

How?

Had his story been true?

Had Gilead himself slain the entire patrol and let Zharkov go free? If that was true, where had Zharkov been for the past year?

Justin Gilead showed up at the office that day, and Starcher had a chance to ask him those questions. But to Starcher's announcement that Alexander Zharkov was alive, Gilead only said, "I told you that. Don't give me facts I already know. That's not our deal."

The CIA chief's attempts to get any more information out of Gilead were exasperatingly fruitless. Finally, Starcher said, "Where have you been?" He noted that despite the chill weather, Gilead was wearing only a suit jacket. His shirt was open at the throat; the snake amulet hung around his neck.

"I've been playing chess," Gilead said. "I had to get my grandmaster ranking, so I could play anywhere. I'm ready to work now."

"Just like that?" Starcher said. "You think it's all that easy? You haven't been trained."

"In what?"

"Self-defense. Weapons. Codes. Tradecraft. How to know you're being followed. What to do about it. So many things."

"Those are all fine for your employees, Mr. Starcher," Gilead said calmly. "But I'm not one of your employees. I'm a chess player." He reached into his jacket pocket, extracted a slip of paper, and handed it to Starcher.

"That's a list of the tournaments I'll be playing in for the next six months," Gilead said. "I'll keep in touch. If there's anything you want done near any of those cities, you just let me know. If it helps to disrupt anything Nichevo's doing, so much the better." He smiled; it was a rich smile that involved his entire face, and it warmed Starcher as much as Gilead's ice blue eyes usually chilled him. "Don't worry so much. I'll be all right," Gilead said.

"You'll be a piece of meat that I throw to the dogs," Starcher grumbled.

Gilead answered, "Some meat's poison, and some dogs die." He rose from his chair, and Starcher said, "Wait. We haven't talked about anything yet. Expenses. Salary. Anything."

"I don't need any money, Mr. Starcher," Gilead said as he walked toward the door. "I just want to work, and I want you to live up to your end of the bargain."

Starcher nodded and rose from behind his desk. He picked up the one-page memorandum on Zharkov and walked across the room to hand it to Justin. "I thought you might want to see this," he said.

Gilead read it quickly, his face impassive, then handed it back. "The part about killing a monastery of monks is true," he said. "The rest is all lies."

"They're giving him a medal," Starcher said.

Gilead again fingered the amulet around his neck. He said, "I've already given him a medal to wear. He has it on his throat."

When Gilead left, Starcher went back to his desk, opened its bottom left drawer and took out a file folder. Inside it, he put Justin Gilead's tournament schedule, but before he returned it to the drawer, he penned across the top: "The Grandmaster."

That was 1971. Justin Gilead, at twenty-seven, was to be Starcher's best field agent.

At first, Starcher used Gilead very sparingly, and on only the smallest and safest of projects. Pick up a document in one country and deliver it to another; interview someone who claimed to know about some internal frictions in one of the Soviet Union's satellite states.

Starcher ran these operations privately, keeping Gilead's involvement secret even from his superiors at Langley. Time, Starcher knew, was on his side. The world of intelligence and espionage was passing from its monopoly by paid, salaried agents, into a freebooting world of informers, dissidents, interested citizens, and ideological volunteers. The day was not long off when a Justin Gilead would not be dismissed out of hand by the CIA, but welcomed to work with them.

Meanwhile, Gilead was handling all his assignments from Starcher with efficiency and quiet competence. The big break came in 1972 when President Nixon was planning to visit Communist China. The CIA was quaking, knowing beyond a doubt that Russia would be planning something to prevent the two other superpowers from forging any kind of alliance, so Langley put out a nervous call to its administrative personnel all over the world to report any contacts they might have with anyone who lived in China, worked there, visited there, who might have heard rumors about what was being planned. Starcher sent in the name of Justin Gilead.

At the last minute, on the eve of Nixon's flight, the CIA got word from an informer network that Chinese assassins on Nichevo's payroll were standing by in Hong Kong, ready to kill the American president. Langley flooded the area with personnel, looking for the killers. Andrew Starcher made a quiet call to Justin Gilead, who was playing in Hong Kong in a Far East chess open tournament. The would-be assassins vanished, as if they had slipped off the edge of the earth. When the smoke of confusion had cleared away, it was obvious even to Langley that Justin Gilead had somehow been responsible.

Starcher was called back to CIA headquarters to discuss the matter. He acknowledged that he had been using Gilead on small missions for over a year. "I was testing him," he explained.

"Where did he come from?" the director of operations said.

"He came here one day to sign up, but it didn't work. Later on, he looked me up in France, and I thought it was worth a try. He globe-trots around, and being a chess player is a great cover."

The meeting ended with Starcher being commended wryly for his wonderful way with recruitment and being told not to keep Justin Gilead to himself. "If he's that good, let's all use him," the chief of operations said.

"It's okay by me," Starcher said.

But it wasn't okay by Gilead. The Grandmaster himself told that to the first CIA official who came to talk to him. "I work only for Starcher," Gilead said.

"Why's that? We're all on the same side," the CIA official said.

And Gilead, who did not want to tell anyone at Langley

that he and Starcher had made a deal for Alexander Zharkov, said simply, "I trust him. I don't trust any of you."

So Gilead's assignments continued to come from Starcher, but now, more often than not, they were given to Starcher by the operations desk in Langley.

There was the Russian spy ring in Canada, the Nichevo agent in Indonesia, the Panama Canal, the South African arms supply line. Gilead was on the scene when Frank Riesling was almost caught in East Germany, and somehow the Grandmaster got him out, leaving Riesling babbling about somebody who ripped his way through the steel walls of a building.

Throughout the CIA, the legend of the Grandmaster grew. Starcher was, at first, proud of it. But then he grew fearful. If Justin Gilead's work for the Company was made known, he would become a prime target for the KGB. Or for Nichevo, whose plans he seemed most often to thwart.

Gilead was playing in a tournament in Belgrade when there was an explosion and fire in the hotel he was staying in. Gilead's room had seemed to be the center of the blast and was literally blown apart. No sign of his body could be found.

Starcher put in a nervous twenty-four hours before Gilead showed up at his office in Paris.

"I thought you were dead," Starcher said.

"Obviously not."

"But they tried to kill you?" Starcher asked.

Gilead nodded.

"Justin, this is getting too dangerous. I think it's time you retired. You're not getting paid to do this."

Gilead shook his head. "It wasn't the first time they tried to kill me," he said.

Starcher sat back heavily in his chair. "It's happened before?"

"A half-dozen times," Gilead said. "Don't worry about it. I don't."

"How the hell can you sit there and tell me you're not concerned about the Russians trying to kill you six, seven times?"

"Because they can't do it," Gilead said. He rose from his chair. "Stop looking so worried," he said, then told Starcher that he was taking the next few weeks off and would be in

Paris. "My chess game needs work. If you need me, I'll be at the Strand Hotel."

The next day, Starcher got word that Vassily Zharkov had died and his son Alexander had been named to head Nichevo. He went to the Strand to meet Gilead and told him the news in the cocktail lounge.

Gilead nodded. "Good," he said.

His time was coming. He went back to his room and his chessboard.

It took Starcher a moment to realize where he was.

He saw the American guard standing near the door of the Moscow hospital room. The fever had broken. He felt cold and wondered if he was dying. For nearly twenty years he had harbored a secret fear that there might be a God and that if there was, he would not approve of Starcher's way of life. He had even, in his less coherent moments beginning with that day at Langley in 1970, speculated that on his day of judgment he would be forced to confront not Jehovah but Justin Gilead.

It must be close now, he thought. Death's embrace must be terribly close to bring the Grandmaster into his thoughts with such insistence.

He should have objected to Gilead's being used so frequently. If he had not permitted the CIA to run him so often, the boy might have had a chance to live a little longer.

Wait a minute, he thought, trying to organize his confused thoughts. Gilead was alive. Riesling had said so.

But that couldn't be true. He had seen the burial pictures himself, courtesy of Nichevo.

Starcher lay there in the dark, remembering. Outside, he could hear the rough voices of nurses speaking Russian in the hospital corridor.

Justin Gilead. But his death hadn't been the CIA's fault. It had been Starcher's. His fault . . . his responsibility that Gilead had died so young.

It was May of 1980. Alexander Zharkov had been head of

Nichevo for one year. Starcher had met Gilead in a shabby apartment on the Bahnhofstrasse in West Berlin. There had been little communication between them in the past three months, a fact for which Starcher was grateful. Gilead had been run too often, too hard by the CIA. By now, his life was constantly in danger. Starcher knew all that, but he also knew he owed Gilead this assignment.

"You're going into Poland," Starcher said without preliminaries. There was no point in offering Gilead a drink or engaging in casual conversation with the man. Gilead was as asocial as an automaton and seemed to find vaguely distasteful any activity or avenue of thought not related to his work or to chess. It was, Starcher thought at the time, as if Gilead were driven by a personal demon that helped him to endure the Agency's cavalier treatment of his life.

"You'll travel to Görlitz in southern West Germany tonight. It's only a few miles from there to the Polish border."

"What's the border like?" Justin asked.

"Mountains," Starcher said with some embarrassment. "Three hundred miles of them."

"The entire southern border," Justin said.

"That's right," Starcher said. "Let me tell you what's happening. Since the 1968 uprising in Czechoslovakia, there's been a big underground movement there. They hide, they wait, they disrupt, and then they hide again. A couple of months ago, a third of the Czech government was ousted on orders of the Soviet Central Committee."

"What's that got to do with Poland?" Gilead asked. "You said I was going to Poland."

"I'm coming to that. There's a movement growing now in Poland, mostly among the laboring groups. With the food shortages, a rebellion's a real possibility. They're talking about it openly up in Gdańsk in the North. Now what's happening is that some Czechs are making it across the Carpathian Mountains into Poland, and they're trying to spread the word in the cultural centers like Kraków and Warsaw that if the two countries unite, they can kick the Russians out."

"And the Russians?" Gilead asked. "Do they take this seriously?"

"They've sent troops and tanks. We don't know how many, and the men we send in there just don't come back.

That's your job. Travel through the Carpathians, estimate the troops, what kind of hardware they've got and so on.''

Justin looked at him steadily. They both knew that Gilead had never received that kind of training and probably could not bring back much information about Soviet weapons in the area.

"I'm not qualified," Justin said.

"I know that, Justin. You've got every right to turn down this assignment. But you asked if the Russians are taking this seriously. I know that Alexander Zharkov himself is in the area now. Nichevo's there. That's how seriously the Russians are taking it.''

"I'll go," Gilead said immediately. "I can live in the mountains, and I speak Polish.''

"Good luck," Starcher said. "And good hunting.''

Starcher lay in the dark of the hospital room, his open eyes fixed on the gray ceiling. Justin Gilead went to Poland for one specific purpose; to find Zharkov. And in the cruelest of ironies, he found him. Zharkov's face, in fact, was probably the last sight the Grandmaster saw before he died.

A frown furrowed deep into his brow. Riesling said Justin Gilead was still alive. How could that be? He had seen the pictures. The Grandmaster was dead.

If he was alive, where would he be? What would he be doing? Why hadn't he come forward, at least to spit in Starcher's eye for conning him into doing a job he was utterly unprepared to perform?

Oh, what did it matter anymore? Starcher thought. *Nichevo?* as the Russians were so fond of saying. Who cares? What can anyone do? Why bother? Nothing would ever remove the stain of guilt from Starcher's past. All Starcher remembered now was that he had never spoken with Gilead the way he'd wanted to, had never laughed with him or tried to comfort him in his deep and inexplicable sorrow. In the end, he'd helped to kill him.

He sighed, closed his eyes, and tried to sleep.

Nichevo?

Book Four
_____

THE GRANDMASTER

CHAPTER NINETEEN

POLAND, 1980

Justin Gilead crouched in a narrow mountain path. Fruit trees were in blossom, showering their fragrant petals in blizzards of color. In the distant valley, a small village with its central wooden church looked as if it had been preserved, intact, since medieval times. Ahead of him, the bodies of five men hung by their necks from a line of tall spruce trees.

They were all young, their clothes ragged. One was covered with blood: He had been shot before he was hanged. Nearby, a group of Russian soldiers sat talking beside a modern army tank. They were passing around a bottle of vodka, apparently oblivious to the swinging bodies.

Gilead had seen much the same sight many times over the past 150 miles. He had followed the foothills of the Carpathian Mountains on foot, watching the young Czechs as they made their way over the treacherous, waterlogged passes into Poland. Sometimes he helped them to safety in the tiny, welcoming villages of the *goral* highlands on their way toward Kraków and Warsaw, but more often he just watched them go the way these five had gone. The Russian patrol of the mountain border was scant, but effective enough to handle the few Czechs brave or crazy enough to cross over. Tanks were stationed every five miles or so, with jeeps running constantly between the postings. Along the length of the newly reinforced border were hanged bodies, some of them women, some so young they had not reached their full height. They

waited in warning for those who would try to follow them,
their bulging eyes open to the high spring wind. Gilead
thought bitterly that the Russians were always predictable.
Faced with a crisis, they always reverted to barbarism as a
response.

A jeep buzzed in the distance, growing louder. It was
coming from the village, loaded with embroidered blankets
and food. It was a common enough sight these days. The
soldiers stayed near the forest at the base of the mountains
while their C.O. ventured into the villages to take supplies
and liquor for his men and interrogate the residents about any
foreigners who might have passed through on their way north.

The *goral* were mountain people. They cared little for
politics. They didn't participate in counterrevolutions. They
disliked strangers. But they were still Poles, and Poles were
not Russians. When someone broke a law, the *goral* did not
denounce the offender to state authorities. More likely, they
sent him to the village pastor for a public beating, to which
the villagers would bring food and musical instruments. After
the whipping, if the lawbreaker was one of their own, he
would be forgiven and invited to join the festivities. If he was
a stranger, he would be expelled in a shower of stones before
the feast began. But no *goral* would volunteer any information about criminals to the Russians, no matter how serious
the crime.

Occasionally, the border guards found Czech troublemak-
ers hiding in *goral* homes. When this occurred, the entire
village was razed to the ground. Word traveled fast in the
mountain villages; no strangers had been found for several
weeks. Even when Justin, with his fluent Polish, ventured
into the villages, he was treated with suspicious silence.

He kept to the forest. Although the soil in the region was
poor for farming, there was plenty of food among the dense
trees. He lived on tender new spruce shoots, on sorrel, thistle,
and nettle. It felt good to be outdoors again, after the years of
sitting in tight little rooms staring at chess pieces. He was still
marking time, waiting for a message he hoped would soon
come, but here, at least, he could breathe clean air. Sometimes he could aid the Czech travelers, finding food for them
and directing them past the Russian troops. They often asked
him to work for them against the Russians by poisoning the

water supplies in the tanks, but he refused. He had killed enough.

At night, he would search for the dead left behind by the Russians and bury them. Then, pressing the gold coiled snake medallion to his chest, he would pray, as he had prayed every night since he left Rashimpur, for the sign from Tagore.

It is not time, the old man had said. Everything in Justin's life had been destroyed, and still it was not time. He had let Zharkov, the Prince of Death, escape, and until he found him again, Justin knew, all the deaths at Rashimpur would have been for nothing. He waited only for the sign, but there was no sign. Tagore was as dead as the Tree of the Thousand Wisdoms, the tree that Tagore had sworn nothing could kill.

He had been dreaming again. The dreams had stopped after the destruction of the monastery, but now, in the forest, the recurring dream of being buried alive had returned. It was always the same: Justin lay in a grave, hearing the birds sing overhead, unable to cry out as clods of earth fell upon him, suffocating him. And nearby, so near that Justin could feel the man's energy, stood Zharkov, watching.

The jeep drove up to the soldiers, who quickly hid the bottle of vodka. If the officer in the jeep had been their regular commander, they might have offered him a drink. But not this officer, not this colonel. Rumor had it that he was some high muckamuck from Moscow and the man solely in charge of preventing Czech incursions into Poland. The soldiers didn't know him, and they did not trust him.

The colonel, his hat perched squarely on his head, got out and motioned to the others to unload the supplies. Standing apart from the men, he looked for a long moment at the hanging bodies.

"Cut them down," he ordered finally. "They've served their purpose." He turned away and took off his hat, and in that instant, Justin froze.

Zharkov.

The Prince of Death had returned.

Justin rose shakily. "Zharkov," he called. Then, louder, "Zharkov!"

All five soldiers looked up. "It came from up there," one of them said. But Zharkov did not move, did not speak. He scanned the forest like a machine, his gaze shifting slowly from one side to the other. Finally, his Tokarev drawn, he moved cautiously up the hill. "Follow me," he ordered his men.

Zharkov moved through the woods as if drawn by a magnet. Justin stayed ahead of him, tantalizing him with sound, moving swiftly and without disturbing the forest floor when the soldiers came too close.

It was almost delicious. One more murder and Justin could at last prepare himself for death. Zharkov had for so long been the only thing Justin had to live for. With Zharkov's last breath, the circle of karma would be almost complete. Afterward, it would require only Justin's own suicide. That would be all the penance Justin could give Tagore.

"Do you remember Rashimpur?" Justin hissed. "I told you we would meet again."

A volley of machine-gun fire splattered off some rocks above Justin. A shower of earth trickled down the side of the mountain.

Justin climbed higher, out of the woods, to where the vegetation was sparse and the earth slippery with loose shale. His feet skidded, sending up a cloud of dust.

"There he is!" someone called. There was another burst of gunfire, striking very near. Justin darted upward, throwing himself behind a cluster of large rocks. The bullets pinged off them. Above him, a ledge of shale trembled.

"Hold your fire," Zharkov shouted. The gunfire stopped. "Who are you?"

"The Wearer of the Blue Hat. The one you failed to kill during the massacre of Rashimpur." Justin stood up in full view of the soldiers. "Will you fight me now? Alone? Or will you use your dogs on me again?"

"You have no weapon," Zharkov called. "Come down peaceably, and you won't be hurt."

Justin laughed coldly, "Is that what you told those five men in the forest?"

Zharkov moved closer. "I will fight you alone," he said.

"Without your gun."

Zharkov's hooded reptilian eyes met those of his soldiers. He tossed the Tokarev to the ground. "Lead. I will follow."

After a moment, Justin nodded. Then he turned and ran up the mountainside.

"Now," Zharkov shouted, dropping to the ground. The soldiers opened fire.

Justin groaned as a bullet caught him in the right calf. As he fell, the ledge of slate above him toppled, raining rock.

"It's going to go, Colonel," one of the soldiers shouted.

"Clear out!" Zharkov yelled, shielding his head from the falling shale as he snatched up his pistol and crawled toward Justin.

"Colonel!"

"I said clear out." He skidded and slipped up the melting hillside to where Justin lay, his trouser leg soaked with blood. "You swine," Zharkov whispered, and yanked Justin up by his collar. The young man's eyes opened groggily. "You ask if I remember Rashimpur." He raised Justin as high as he could, then sent him crashing to the ground with a shriek of pain. "I remember. You gave me something that would never let me forget you."

He clasped the medallion around Justin's neck, ready to yank it off. The touch of it was terrifying, electric. He released it, cursing. *"Bljad!"*

Zharkov got to his feet and stood over Justin as the young American groaned. He pointed the Tokarev at Gilead's head. "Your time has come," he said coldly, "Grandmaster." The name dripped with contempt.

But even as he began to squeeze the trigger, the mountain rumbled like thunder. Huge chunks of earth crashed around the two men. A rock fell and struck Zharkov's right arm, knocking loose the pistol and shattering his elbow.

The Russian looked skyward and saw the rocks coming down toward them. He swore again, stepped forward, and kicked Justin's injured leg. More rocks hit near them. Zharkov turned and fled.

He ran, fell, then rolled down the moving earth. One of the soldiers came out of safety to help him. When Zharkov reached the base of the mountain, he turned and saw Justin's arms shoot upward, as if to ward off the avalanche. One wrist snapped backward under the weight of a flying rock. Then, with a terrible din, the whole side of the mountain seemed to slide off, enveloping the soldiers in choking dust.

Zharkov stood watching, the lapels of his coat pulled over his face so that he could breathe, until the mountain settled. The others stood with him, exchanging glances among one another. The eyes of their commander were fixed on the earth-covered spot where the strange young man had lain.

One of the soldiers spoke. "Shall I take the jeep for reconnaissance, sir?"

"Stay where you are." Zharkov climbed to the place where Justin Gilead had been, and shifted the earth around with his feet. "Dig him out."

"But . . ." The soldiers looked at him incredulously. "We have no tools."

"Get some from the village. Use your hands, damn you!"

It took hours to dig the body out of the deep rubble. "Get a doctor," Zharkov said.

While the envoy was gone, Zharkov took a camera from the tank and snapped pictures of Gilead from all directions.

"Is he important, sir?" one of the soldiers asked.

"Only to me," Zharkov said.

The doctor, a frightened old man, looked at the body and then at Zharkov. "But he's dead," he said quietly.

"Check, fool. Be sure."

The doctor knelt down, placing an ancient stethoscope in his ears. He frowned, listened, checked the body's reflexes, pulled open the eyelids, listened again to Justin's chest.

"He's dead," he said. "When did the"—he stumbled over the word—"accident occur?"

"More than three hours ago. He was buried under the rock."

"Ah." The doctor put his few instruments away. "Quite dead, I'm afraid. No one could live without air for that length of time." He looked around sheepishly. "I'm sorry . . ."

Zharkov waved him away. The old man stumbled through the forest, walking nearly a half-mile out of his way to avoid passing the five hanged bodies.

Zharkov prodded the body with his toe. "It was easy to kill you, after all," he said softly. "She had told me it would be difficult, but you were easy."

"Sir?"

Zharkov looked at the soldier sharply. "Dig a grave. Bury him here."

"But—"

"That's an order!" Zharkov snapped.

"Sir, he's wearing some kind of necklace. It looks like real gold."

"Leave it," Zharkov said. "I want it to die with him. Take

photographs of the corpse after it's in the ground. Then we'll move on.''

The grave was dug. Two soldiers grabbed Gilead's body as if it were an old carpet, ready to toss him into the hole.

"With care," Zharkov barked.

"He won't mind, sir. Dead men rarely do," one of the soldiers said with a querulous attempt at a smile. It slithered off his face at a glance from Zharkov.

"You swine," he croaked. "You cannot even recognize a god in your filthy presence."

In the late afternoon sun, the birds overhead sang violently. It was a song heard long ago, in a child's dream.

The water. Dark water. Swirling yellow robes of drowned men. Can't breathe, can't breathe . . .

Justin came to consciousness in panic. Water again, suffocation . . . Was he back at Rashimpur? Had the nightmare never ended? For a moment, he saw the future: He would emerge from the dark water of the lake, bind his wounds, go to the monastery. He would find the Tree of the Thousand Wisdoms burned, the monks dead. He would kill for the first time and for the second, would wallow in an orgy of death, and meet its prince.

But what surrounded him was not water. From a slight motion of his fingers, he could feel something damp and gritty. Earth. He had been buried alive. The dream had been complete.

The Prince of Death had triumphed.

There was nothing to do now. His body had automatically slowed itself to keep him alive, just as it had before. But before, he had had a reason to bring himself back to life. There was no Rashimpur anymore, no precious home. Even Tagore, whom he had thought would live forever, was dead. Justin stilled the panic of death inside him, and prepared to die.

"It is not time," a voice called. It was a sound out of space and time. Tagore's voice.

It *is* time! Justin wanted to scream. It's time for me to die. I've failed in every way. Leave me alone!

But the voice would not be silent. Instead, it was joined by a thousand others, the wails of the dead calling to him.

"Hail to thee, O Wearer of the Blue Hat," they chanted.

"Hail to thee, Patanjali!''

And through the deep earth, the scent of almonds came to him.

His fingers moved. Almost against his will, his muscles strained. Above him, the ground heaved. He was traveling up, out of the void of death into the place of penance. He would not, he knew, be allowed to rest. The pain he felt was agonizing, the shock of movement horrible. Some of his bones were broken. When he lay beneath the ground near death, the pain had disappeared, but now each movement intensified it.

This was his punishment, he thought. His karma had been broken; as penance, he would not be allowed to die until he had made it whole again.

The suffocating heat was replaced by cool air. He crawled out of the hole in the ground that had accepted him so willingly, only to spit him out again. The dead did not want him among them. He was soiled. He was unfit to join them.

Above him shone pinpricks of light. Stars, he thought. I'm free.

Free to die again.

How many times must he die before he could rest?

He lay near the grave, exhausted, and slept.

CHAPTER TWENTY

He awoke in hot sun, sweating. His hands and clothes were filthy. His left wrist was swollen to twice its normal size. He wore only one shoe, and his right leg was bleeding. Beside him was a deep hole cut into a hillside. Below him was a forest. In the distance, through the trees, he could see a small village. He had no idea where he was, who he was, where he had been, or what he was doing alone on the side of a mountain. His thoughts came scattered, in pieces. They formed themselves in a dozen different languages, then fled before he could capture them.

He staggered to his feet, fainted, pulled himself up again. The medallion around his neck glinted in the sun. What was it, he wondered. A snake? Was he a rich man to wear gold as an ornament?

Outside the village, a farmer and his family were picking stones out of a hard, barren field, preparing for the spring sowing. The wife—a thin, wizened woman with a face carved in sharp planes—stood up as Justin limped toward them, her hands on her back.

She watched him for a moment, then flew at him angrily. "Get out of here! We don't want trouble. The Russians are near. Find another way to where you're going. Shoo!"

Justin looked at her uncomprehendingly. His head was swimming. The woman was no more than a blurred form, her voice a distant sound, growing fainter. He weaved where he stood, trying to focus his vision.

"What's wrong with him?" the farmer asked.

"Been shot, from the looks of that leg. My guess is the Russians already had him. Look at his feet. He's only got one shoe." She walked briskly toward Justin. "Go," she said, pointing emphatically westward. "Do you understand?" She shook her head. "Stupid Czech. He doesn't know a word I'm saying."

Justin held out a hand to the woman. She backed away. Unable to stand any longer, he shuddered, tried to walk, and fell.

The man bent to see the wound on Justin's leg. "He's been hurt pretty badly. His eyes are in fever."

"We can't keep him here," the woman said. "The Russians will burn everything we have."

The man threw his cap to the ground. "The Russians, the Russians," he said hoarsely. "We are not Russians. This man is dying, and we will help him, by Christ."

He picked Justin up in his powerful arms.

"All right, then," the woman shouted after him angrily. "But take him to the village. Don't keep him here."

The villagers were already celebrating the departure of the Russians. The bell of the small, carved church rang jubilantly, and the dirt streets were filled, the inhabitants relieved to be able to leave their homes without fear of being stopped by soldiers.

"Franek!" someone shouted to the farmer, waving a bottle. "Look! Now we know it's a special day. Even old Franek has come into town. What have you brought us?"

The farmer prodded his horse along in silence to the doctor's house.

"What's the matter, Franek? Is someone sick? Where's your wife?" A few people gathered around the cart as Franek tied his horse. Sighing, he uncovered the man lying in the back.

"A Czech," someone gasped.

"Are you crazy? Get him out of here."

"He will see the doctor before he leaves," Franek said obstinately, lifting Justin out of the cart.

"We will all burn," a woman whispered. "It is a bad omen."

Franek pounded on the door, drowning the woman out. The doctor came out, pulling his wire eyeglasses over his ears. In his hand he still clutched a dinner napkin. "What is it? What's the commotion?"

"He's got a Czech," someone called.

"Oh, Franek," the doctor said dispiritedly, looking at the man in his arms. His hands went to the man's dirty face, then pulled back abruptly.

"What's wrong?" the farmer asked.

"This man . . . I saw him yesterday. He was . . ."

"He was what?"

"Dead," the doctor whispered. "I was sure of it."

A murmur rose in the crowd. The villagers crossed themselves. Others came to see what was going on.

"He was with the Russian division. The soldiers were concerned."

"A Russian?" Franek asked incredulously.

"Bring him in," the doctor said. "Quickly."

The big farmer laid the unconscious man on the road. "No." He stepped back and folded his arms. "As a Christian, I couldn't let the man die on my land. But by God, I'll go no farther than this for a Russian."

The crowd became noisy. The little doctor tried to lift Justin under the arms, but he was pushed away.

"Stone him!" someone shouted.

"Kill the Russian!"

The sound of horse's hooves galloping down the narrow street sent the crowd into shrieks of fear. But it was only a small boy, Franek's son. "Father! Father!" he called.

"Dimitri?"

The farmer pushed through the growing mob as the boy dismounted.

"Mother made me come," he said breathlessly. "I went to the mountain to see where the stranger came from. There was a hole there. A grave, it looked like. I found this inside." He produced a shoe.

Women wailed. Instinctively, the doctor crossed himself. Franek took the shoe from the boy's hands and threw it into the street. The people stepped aside, as if the shoe were some evil talisman.

"Risen from the dead," someone whispered.

"He is the Undead One."

The crowd backed off, leaving a circle of space around Justin.

"Look. He wakes."

Justin blinked. He propped himself up on one elbow, holding his hand to his forehead. Then he looked, surprised, at the mass of people gathered around him. His face was strained, uncomprehending.

Franek's son, standing in the inner ring of the circle, picked up a small stone and hurled it at Justin. It struck him in the forehead, leaving a bright gash. The little doctor ran to stop the boy, but others had already picked up rocks and thrown them. Justin rolled onto his side, trying to shield himself from the attack.

"Stop it!" the doctor yelled. "You're killing him, can't you see?"

"Get out of the way!" Someone knocked the doctor to the ground, while the rocks continued to thump against the stranger's huddled body.

Suddenly a young woman dressed in gray rags rushed into the clearing, picking up stones and hurling them into the crowd.

"That's for you, scum-eating bastards!" she shrieked, oblivious to the shower of stones directed now at her as well as the fallen man beside her.

"Stop, stop," a voice called from the outer ring of the crowd. The mob parted as a fat, balding man wearing a cleric's collar bustled forward.

The woman in the clearing flung back her arm to take aim at the pastor, then stopped. Instead, she dropped the rock in her hand and spat on the ground.

"The witch," someone said. "Come to take her own."

The pastor held up his hand. "What's this?" he asked sternly.

"Ask them," the woman said contemptuously. She stooped to wrap Justin's arm around her shoulders. She was small, not much over five feet, but the sinews in her neck and forearms attested to a life of hard work. She got him into a standing position. "Let me pass," she said.

"Who are you, child?" the pastor asked.

"Don't go near her," someone said.

"Better listen to him," the woman said nastily. "I might turn you into a frog."

The pastor stepped back, shocked, as the woman shoved past him. The doctor came up to explain.

"She means no harm, Father."

"Is she from around here? I've never seen her before."

"Her name is Yva Pradziad. She lives in the hills east of here. Keeps to herself, mostly. The villagers here say she's a witch, but there's nothing to that. She makes some herbal medicines, and occasionally delivers babies for the hill people. I don't think she can help him, though."

"Leave him, my son," the priest said. "Whether he's a Russian or a Czech, it is better that he is with her than here in the village. We cannot put the lives of all our people in danger because of one stranger."

The doctor nodded. "It's funny, though. I was sure he was the one the Russians called me to see yesterday."

"And?"

"And he was dead."

The priest pulled himself up to full height. "Don't speak heresy, my son."

"But they found his shoe in an open grave," a woman whispered, moving in between the two men. "And he wore a snake, the symbol of the Devil, on his breast."

"Whoever he is, he did not rise from the grave," the priest said loudly. "And anyone who says so will be punished both in heaven and here on earth. By me. Those who wish may come with me to the church, to light a candle for the soul of this man."

The villagers followed meekly, whispering among themselves. Only Franek and his son left. The doctor stayed behind, feeling ashamed. He should never have spoken. The villagers were good people, but the strain of superstition in them was strong. They would never, he knew, believe that the poor, wounded stranger was anything but a living spirit of evil, just as they would never forgive Yva Pradziad the sin of living without a husband and family. Such a woman would, in their eyes, always be a witch, and the doctor was too much of a gentleman to explain to them how he knew she wasn't.

The first and only time Yva had come to see him was nearly three years before, when she was only sixteen. She was a scrawny thing, as bedraggled as a stray cat, carrying in her arms a baby already blue and stiff.

She had been expelled by her family when they discovered she was pregnant. Alone, she built a shack for herself in the rocky hills where the soil was too poor to farm anything but roots. The work must have been too hard; she'd had no milk, and the baby took sick within two days after its birth. It was already dead by the time she reached the doctor.

Her reaction to the infant's death was stoic, but when he suggested that she see the pastor about burial, she turned on him violently.

"They'll never let me bury my child here," she spat. "They'll say he was conceived in sin. My parents told me."

The doctor could not think of anything to say. He offered her a tonic for herself, but she refused. She snatched up the tiny body of her dead son and left. She never came to him again. Occasionally, he saw her in the village, trading turnips for lye to make soap, but she never spoke to him or anyone else. Yva had her own world, spare, hard, and independent. She earned some food by nursing the isolated mountain people who distrusted doctors, with her medicines and poultices, but for the most part she lived on the animals she killed in the traps around her house and the food she could find in the forest. She had managed to live a solitary life in a hostile climate, among neighbors who despised her, and for that, he admired her.

Perhaps the stranger would live. It would give her some company, at least for a while. He hoped, for her sake, that her medicines were adequate.

"Hey, Doc," someone whispered nearby, startling the doctor.

The surprise quickly turned to disappointment. The man beside him was Józek Szulc. Józek was one of those men whom the doctor had come to realize were a necessary evil in any country occupied by a foreign power. Owning no land, Józek nevertheless always had a supply of ready cash from the sale of black market goods, Russian products, army supplies, and food. In a land perennially short of even the meanest food supplies, Józek would regularly come into town with whole calves for sale at exorbitant prices. He was gone frequently and never disclosed the destination of his travels, but he usually came back with treasures considered priceless by the austere *goral* people: nails, salt, tea, insecticide, cotton cloth, dyes, paraffin for canning, boots, tires, and, most valued of all, meat.

If others believed, as the doctor did, that Józek was a thief and a conniver, they took pains not to let Józek see their disdain. The doctor himself had relied on Józek more than once for urgently needed supplies of penicillin and antiseptic.

"Yes, Józek?" the doctor said blandly.

"You saw him up close, didn't you? The Undead One?"

The doctor sighed. "He's just an ordinary man."

"That's not what I heard. Did you get a look at the medallion around his neck?"

"It was a necklace of some kind."

"Of pure gold, I hear. Forged in the furnaces of hell."

"Oh, come now, Józek . . ."

The wiry little man laughed. "I don't believe those fairy tales, either," he said. "These fools say anything. That's why I'm checking with you. Was it gold?"

The doctor blinked exasperatedly. "I really don't know. It could have been."

Józek sucked on his tooth, his eyes squinting into the sun. "Think he's going to live?"

"I can't tell you that, either," the doctor said sharply.

Józek shrugged. "Just asking. The medallion won't be any use to him if he dies."

The doctor excused himself and went inside, slamming the door behind him.

CHAPTER TWENTY-ONE

Yva Pradziad's house was surrounded by animal traps. Before she began to set them, the local children amused themselves by breaking the oilskin windows and throwing piles of horse dung inside. After a rash of scraped ankles and broken toes, they left her alone. She hadn't been bothered in more than a year.

The house was no more than a crude shack, with a small garden carved out of the rocky, uneven ground behind the traps. Inside, the only furnishings were a large wooden table, a broken chair, splinted and tied, set in front of the stone fireplace, in which hung a kettle and an old iron frying pan, and the straw bed where Justin lay.

He had walked, mute and uncomplaining, from the village with her, but as soon as he entered the house he had fallen unconscious. Working only with some boiled rags and a sharp green stick, Yva probed the wound in his leg. The bullet had passed through, but she reopened the wound and cauterized it with a hot poker. She bound the leg, put a splint on his broken wrist, cleaned the caked mud off the stranger, pressed his face with cold cloths, and, for good measure, wrapped a poultice around his chest. That was the extent of her knowledge.

The stranger slept all night without waking. By morning, his fever still hadn't broken. There were medicines, Yva knew, that could help him. She had nursed fevers before, and wounds, but nothing as serious as this.

By night, the fever was worse. The stranger lay soaked in

his own sweat, the straw beneath him hot. She smoothed his forehead; strands of his black hair stuck to her fingers.

She sat back on the broken chair and looked at him. Even in fever, with perspiration pouring from him, he was beautiful. His face was smooth and chiseled as if by an angelic sculptor, and his bare body was lean and hard. It had never occurred to her before that men could be beautiful; she had thought beauty was the special possession of women, like the women she saw sometimes on a Sunday morning on their way to church, their faces glistening, their hair shining. But this man was beautiful, too, and his beauty was all the more powerful to her for reason of having been so unexpected.

She took a cupful of broth from the large black kettle hanging at the fireplace and, when it had cooled somewhat, pressed it to Gilead's mouth. She opened his lips with her fingers and allowed some of the broth to dribble in, but it only rolled out the side of his mouth. He would die, she knew, without food and without medicine. And he was just too beautiful to let die.

Yva reached into an old jug in the corner of the room. Inside was a scrap of cloth tied around some money. There were only a few zlotys; not enough for a doctor, and a doctor was what the man desperately needed. Even if the doctor in the village did not fear Yva as a witch, he was still one of *them*. And she would not ask one of them for a favor. She would have to pay.

"Yva! Yva Pradziad!" a voice called from the bottom of the hill below her house.

Recognizing it, she picked up a rock as she stepped out the door and hurled it at Józek. "Can't you leave me alone, scum?" she screamed.

"Hold it, Yva! I only want to talk. But I don't want to get caught in your traps."

"Then talk from down there, Russian ass-kisser."

Józek spread his arms wide. "Now, is that any way to talk?"

"I'm only saying the truth. Everyone knows you make money from the Russians, only they're all too gutless to say so. They're afraid you won't sell them your precious Russian luxuries. Well, there's nothing I need from you." She spat elaborately.

"I'm not here to sell. I'm here to buy," Józek said pleasantly.

Yva cocked her head. "Buy? Buy what?"

"Your friend inside." He thrust his chin toward the house. "Is he dead yet?"

Her face pinched into a grimace. She picked up another rock and threw it expertly, striking Józek on the shoulder. "Get out of here!"

"Wait, Yva. Wait." He held his shoulder with his hand. "I want to buy the medallion around his neck. Even if he's not dead, he won't miss it." He ventured a step forward. "I'm offering you a lot of money for it, Yva. Three hundred złotys. More than you'd get anywhere else, even in Kraków."

"It's not mine to sell," Yva said.

"Think about it. Aren't you taking care of him? Maybe he's a Czech, a renegade. Then you're risking your own life to save his skin, aren't you? Ask him. He'd be the first to tell you he owes you something."

"He can't talk," Yva said. "He's still in fever."

"Well," Józek said with satisfaction, "then some money for food will do him more good than a silly necklace, won't it?"

Yva stood in the doorway for a long time, looking from Józek's mocking figure at the foot of the hill to the sick man lying on the straw. Finally she walked over to Justin and unclasped the medallion's chain. It felt hot to her touch. She wrapped it in a scrap of cloth and then picked her way between the familiar animal traps to Józek.

"Where's the money?" she asked sullenly. Józek produced a crisp roll of bills.

"Now, was that so hard?" he asked, smiling.

"Get out of here."

Justin awoke two days later. The damp straw beneath him hurt his skin. He was in a strange place, a country shack. Vaguely, he remembered walking here, but he did not recognize the young woman who bent near the fireplace on the other side of the room. Was he supposed to know her?

He strained to see, craning his neck with exhausting effort to see her face. She turned, still squatting, saw him, covered her mouth with her hand in disbelief. She came over to him, speaking words his mind could not yet follow, and held a cup of cool water to his lips. For the first time he noticed a plaster cast on his left wrist.

By nightfall, he could sit up. The evening breeze felt cool. The woman he did not know fed him some soup. It was delicious. He ventured toward the open door, but the woman stopped him, cautioning him with gestures and the peculiar language he did not understand.

Little by little, the words began to make sense, although Justin still did not speak. Several days after he first came to consciousness in the straw bed, he was well enough to walk outdoors. He found the woman in her garden, pulling weeds. He stooped beside her.

"So, my handsome simpleton has come to help me, has he?" she said, rumpling his coal-colored hair. She demonstrated how to pull the weeds from the earth.

The earth. Touching it, he felt again the nightmare sensation of earth weighing down on him, suffocating him. Of clods of earth falling on him as birds sang and a man watched overhead, the Prince of Death with a face Justin could not remember . . .

"What's the matter, bored already?" the woman said teasingly.

Across the valley, past the distant forest, in the mountains. Over there the Prince of Death waited, faceless and patient, *over there,* and Justin had to reach him or his karma would not be complete, but it was not time . . . was not time; the Tree of the Thousand Wisdoms burned, and so the time was past, come and gone, and his soul was in damnation, and still the Prince of Death waited for him . . .

He ran.

"Stop!" Yva called, rushing after him. "The traps! You'll be hurt!"

Justin howled as the trap closed over his ankle. Yva knelt beside him, straining to open it. "Stupid!" she shouted. "Don't you know anything?"

He moved her hand away, grasped the trap by both of its rusty sides, and pulled it apart, sending the spring mechanism flying.

Yva checked the wound on Justin's bare foot, then examined the broken trap. "Dumb as a beetle, but with the strength of an ox," she said. "Even with a broken wrist. Well, that's something, anyway!" Scolding, she led him back to the house and handed him a broom. "Sweep up," she said, showing him how. "As long as you're healthy enough to run, you might as well make yourself useful."

The straw bed was split into two parts, but Justin abandoned it. At night, he slept outdoors, where the sight of the stars brought back distant memories: of high mountain passes above a lake surrounded by flowers; of a gold-domed hall where a tree stood, a tree with a bark of iron that fell at his feet; of an old man who handed him a diamond and a gold snake enclosed in a circle.

The snake obsessed him. At times, it was no more than a feeling, but sometimes he could picture it as clearly as if it were a real thing, gleaming, powerful, with a drop of molten gold at the base.

Two weeks later, the woman who had become a constant in his life was gone all morning. When she returned, she was smiling. Under her arm was a board of some kind, warped with water and time. It was marked with a checkerboard. She set it in front of him.

"You leave this alone, now, understand?" She took his hand, pulled it near the board, then slapped it away. "Don't touch," she said, shaking a finger at him. He nodded in understanding. A few minutes later, she returned with an apronful of wood chips. Some were dark and some were light. She placed them carefully on the three end rows on each side on the black squares. "This is a game even you can play," she said, moving her light piece diagonally onto another black square. "It's called checkers. Go ahead. Do the same thing I've done on your side." She pointed encouragingly toward his hand, then tapped the square he was to move to.

Justin looked at the board, feeling something awaken inside him. He moved the center left piece in the front row two spaces forward.

"No, no, you can't move that way. I showed you where to put it."

Justin looked at her uncomprehendingly.

Her face softened. "Oh, that's all right. I got the board for free, anyway. You can play whatever crazy way you want." She left him with the board and the blocks of wood.

Justin stared at the board for hours. Invisible lines of force seemed to connect the pieces on the checkered background, but there were not enough pieces. He went to the woodpile and returned with thirty-two more scraps of light and dark wood.

"Don't you bring a big mess in here," Yva shouted, but she didn't try to stop him.

He placed the pieces side by side on both sections of the board. Now the lines of force worked. They were aligned now, at rest. He moved white's center right piece forward two squares. Then he opened black's game by moving the queen bishop pawn forward by two. Already the lines of force stretched into possibility.

You are the game.

As he shifted the shapeless pieces of wood over the board, the mush of unrelated information in his mind receded. What was past and unknowable for him no longer mattered. Here was a world of logic and order, and he had found his way to it again. He was home.

He didn't sleep that night. Instead, he took Yva's skinning knife and whittled the pieces into recognizable shapes: a horse's head; a castle tower; the bland, faceless soldiers of the front rank . . . *Chess.* The game was called chess, and in it were hidden the secrets of thought and power.

Things came to him like a barrage of bullets. A game long ago with a small boy, ashamed of a radio transmitter under his sleeve, the yellow robes swirling around him in a dark alley, the scent of almonds, the music, *the coiled snake.*

Instinctively, his hand slapped against his chest. There was nothing there. Was it imagined, the coiled snake in the circle, the center of his life? What did all those memories mean?

He ran to the fireplace and pulled out a piece of blackened wood. No, it could not be imaginary, because he could see it clearly. Sweeping the chess pieces off the table, he set the charcoal on it and began to draw. First, the eyeless head, with its tongue darting, then the coiled body, only occasionally dotted with scales, then the circle around it, the circle of destiny, of karma, closed, with a molten drop of gold . . .

"What have you done?" Yva screamed behind him. He looked over his shoulder, startled back into reality. Yva was angry, her features pinched. She was pointing to the drawing. "You've ruined my table!" she shouted. "Look, I can't even get it out. You've dug into the wood." She slapped a wet rag on top of the design. "It'll never come out, you worthless dummy!'' She picked up his whittlings and threw them across the room. "You're good for nothing, like your toys.''

Justin backed away, feeling whatever thoughts had briefly possessed him recede into blankness again.

He ran to the forest, and spent the rest of the day and night sitting, waiting for the precious thoughts that had left him to come back. They were his past, the elements that made him something besides a stranger locked in the present. He had to find them again.

The days passed without notice. One day he removed the cast from his wrist. His leg no longer hurt. Justin walked and ate from the woods, and found contentment. By sunrise of a day when the breeze blew warm and he could smell the scent of wheat from the nearby farms, he found a small stream. In its center was a rock so large that the water eddied around it. He picked it up. "In a hundred years, the rock will have disappeared," he said out loud. His words were in English, and behind them, he could hear the soft, remembered voice of Tagore. He said the words again in Hindustani, German, Russian. He repeated them in Polish.

Polish is what I've been hearing here, he decided. I'm in Poland. *Poland*. Think. Why Poland? Where did I come from?

Suddenly he thought of the woman who had been looking after him. Since he'd first awakened in the tumbledown shack, he'd taken her for granted as a presence, chattering, scolding, feeding. She was the mother he had needed, and like a child, he had accepted her without question. But she was not his mother. She was young and almost pretty and, except for him, it seemed, entirely alone.

He retraced his steps back to her. He did not remember how long he had been away, and did not know if she would permit him to return. But she was his only link to his own past, and he had to find her.

Yva was seated at the big table still marked by Justin's drawing. Always working, she had a scrap of sewing on her lap as she ate from a bowl. She sat bent over her food like an old woman. Justin knocked on the door frame.

"It's you," she said breathlessly, rising. Her face brightened visibly in front of his eyes. She *was* pretty, like a cut stone, her sharp edges giving her distinction. Hers was the face of one who had suffered and survived.

"I have your toys," she said quickly, bringing over a box filled with Justin's whittled chess pieces. "You see, I wasn't really mad at you. I knew you didn't know better, but see?" She pressed them into Justin's hands. "Oh, how I wish you could understand me, even just a little."

Justin held his hand out to her and touched her cheek. "Thank you," he said slowly, "for all you've done."

"You can talk!" she gasped.

"I couldn't until now. I didn't remember. Something happened, and . . ."

"But you're speaking Polish," she marveled. "Then you're not a Czech after all."

"I don't know. I speak other languages, too. I don't know which is my own. There are so many things I don't remember." He looked into the box, with its small figurines. "This game is called chess," he said, trying to think. "And there's a wise man named Tagore, and the Prince of Death is somewhere beyond the woods . . . It all sounds so crazy."

"No, no, it's wonderful. Come. Eat." She led him to the table. He saw the mark on it and rushed to it.

"And *this*," he said, tracing the drawing with his fingers. "I see this all the time. It's something terribly important to me, I know, but I can't remember what it is. Have you seen this before?"

She looked down. "It's just a picture," she said.

"No. It's something else. Something powerful, part of me. But what could a coiled snake mean?"

Wordlessly, Yva brought him a bowl of soup.

That night, as Justin lay outside beneath the stars, Yva came to him. Her head was covered with a cloth, as if she were in church. "There is something I must tell you," she said.

He sat up. In the moonlight, her rough features softened.

"The coiled snake was on a gold medallion you wore around your neck," she said. "I sold it to buy food and medicine."

He stared at her.

"I sold it. Do you understand? While you were sick."

"Where did you sell it?"

"A man came. Józek, from the village. But you can't go there. The villagers think you're the Devil."

And so I may be, Justin thought. All he had known since

he first came to consciousness here were voices and images outside human experience. "Why?" he asked.

She shrugged. "I don't know. They say you rose from the grave. Some think you're a Russian. But of course, you couldn't speak then—"

"A Russian?"

"The doctor saw you with the Russian soldiers in the mountains. Don't you even remember that?"

"I remember . . . strange things," he said. "But the snake . . . It was a necklace?"

"Yes. I'll get it back for you, I swear it. Please forgive me, if you can." She rose quickly.

He touched her long skirt. "Don't go," he said.

"What's wrong?"

He swallowed. "I don't know. I'm so confused. The snake . . . everything seems jumbled together. I'm not sure what anything is. I don't even know my own name."

She sat beside him, her strong hands holding his. "It will come back," she said. "When I get the snake back for you, it will come back." She stroked his hair. "My name is Yva."

"Yva," he repeated softly.

"It was the name given to the first woman, in the Bible. She and her husband, Adam, lived in Paradise until she found the snake." She laughed. "You see, just like yours."

"And after?"

"Well," she went on as if she were telling a bedtime story to a child, "then they ate an apple because the snake told them to. The apple was knowledge that they were forbidden to have."

"The secrets of thought and power," Justin said, remembering the lines of force on the chessboard.

"That's very good. You get smarter every day. Anyway, after they listened to the snake, who was the Devil, and ate from the Tree of Knowledge, God was displeased with them. As their punishment, they had to leave the beautiful garden where they lived, to wander and toil on the earth for the rest of their lives."

"Did you take me from the village, Yva?"

She smiled. "Yes. Yes, I did. They were cruel to you there."

"Why did you save me?"

She looked down at the ground. "Because you were so beautiful," she said.

Justin stared at her questioningly, and finally she raised her face and then kissed him. He was afraid at first. Something inside him feared the lips of women.

But this was no fearsome experience. Yva was a simple girl, and he felt nothing but softness and warmth.

"Perhaps you are the first woman I ever kissed," he said sincerely.

She laughed. "I doubt that." She put her arms around him and pulled him down to the ground with her, and he buried his face in her hair.

She had said something that stirred uneasily in the far reaches of his memory. Had there been other women? Or just one? And why did the trace memory fill him with both joy and loathing?

It had all been so long ago . . . so long ago . . .

CHAPTER TWENTY-TWO

In Justin's sixteenth year, Tagore sent him to the palace of the abbess Varja to learn the ways of women and pleasure.

"But we do not need women here, my teacher," he said, "and my pleasure comes from learning the ways of Rashimpur."

The old man smiled. "The pleasure you will find with Varja's acolytes is of a different character. It is a pleasure of the senses, of the body."

Justin made a face. "But they're nuns," he said guiltily.

"Not as you know them, my son. The abbess finds her acolytes as young children, and then trains them in the ways of sensual expression. This does not displease the spirits," he added. "Brahma, Siva, and Vishnu—the creative, transcendental, and preserving powers of the universe—recognize the female force as both necessary and magical. The enjoyment of the senses is as meaningful to them as the denial of those same pleasures, for without enjoyment, there can be no sacrifice."

"Then why aren't there women at Rashimpur?"

"It is the main denial of our sect, Patanjali. The monks here seek all their lives to attain spiritual purity. This is not to say that women are impure, but only that their company is so intoxicating that to give in to a life lived with women would deter us from our chosen path. Do you understand?"

"I guess so." In fact, Justin didn't understand at all. The life he led at Rashimpur was orderly and full. There were classes, devotions, and work. There was Tagore, the greatest of all men, to guide him. And most important, there was the discipline of yoga, in which Justin learned every day to accomplish things he had always believed to be impossible. What would women be like in such a place?

He remembered girls he had known at the various schools he'd attended. They were tolerable but useless; not one of them could even climb the rope in gym class to the top. His Uncle Sid's wife Arlene had walked around in nightgowns most of the time, smoking cigarettes and painting her fingernails. She had hair the color of Mercurochrome, and it never moved, even in the highest breeze. That would be no sort of person to have at Rashimpur.

"I don't see why I have to do this," Justin grumbled.

"You will do it because it is necessary for you and because Varja herself has offered to initiate you in your first rites." With a flick of his eyelids, he dismissed the subject. "I have explained the route to Varja's palace to you. Can you find it alone?"

"Yes," Justin said, resigned to his fate.

As was his custom, the old man bowed to him, and Justin returned the gesture.

"Remember that you are the son of Brahma. Do not displease him with unseemly conduct. Be a welcome guest in the great house of Varja, for she is powerful beyond your knowledge. But keep the preserving spirit of Patanjali within you."

Varja's palace was small in comparison with the monastery at Rashimpur, but it was exquisite. Constructed of ancient rock in the Indian style, its low, domed roof of black iron gleamed in the sun.

Justin stood in an open field near the front entrance, shivering with apprehension. What was he supposed to do in there? He would be the only male among a hundred women. Would they try to harm him? Would they make fun of him and laugh behind their painted fingernails?

A young woman came out of the building. She was small and heavily veiled. On her feet were satin slippers that curled fancifully at the toes. She fell to her knees in front of him and bowed, touching her forehead to the ground.

"Welcome to the dwelling of the great goddess," she said.

"It is the honor of my brothers and their ancestors that I be permitted into the presence of the abbess and her acolytes," he answered formally in the arcane Hindi dialect he had learned just for this occasion.

She rose. Behind the thick white veil she wore, the girl's features showed fleetingly. Justin couldn't see all her face at one time, but he saw enough to know that she didn't look anything like the woman he'd expected. She was not a female version of the monks at Rashimpur. For one thing, she was nearly as tall as Justin, and he towered over the other men in the monastery. Her skin was very light, and, though her hair and eyes were dark, her hands, covered with jewelry not only on the fingers but up to the wrists, were pale and blue-veined, like his own.

Her coloring shocked Justin. He didn't think anyone in this strange part of the world looked like him. He longed to ask her where she came from, but restrained himself. He did not wish to appear rude and overly inquisitive before he even entered the palace.

She moved aside and gestured for him to walk ahead of her into the palace. The path led through a magnificent ornamental garden, replete with curved stone bridges over streams that must have been created artificially. Low, spreading trees shaded small stone benches, and huge goldfish swam in a shallow pond. Everywhere, flowers blossomed in a profusion of color and sweet perfume. Beside it, the bare, windswept peaks around Rashimpur seemed bleak and desolate. It was hard for Justin not to linger in the garden, breathing in its lush fragrance and succumbing to its visual perfection, but he made himself keep the pace he had set. It would not do for the girl to think him weak.

She led him into an unoccupied room lit by spade-shaped brass oil lamps. The walls were covered with silk that billowed with the breeze from the garden, causing the pale colors of the fabric to shine in the light. More than a dozen huge cushions, covered with gold and silver brocade, were arranged on the floor around a pastel rug intricately woven into fluid designs. The ceiling was of hammered silver. It was the most opulent room Justin had ever seen. Even the Great Hall of Rashimpur with its magnificent Tree of the Thousand Wisdoms paled beside it.

The girl bowed again, and disappeared. Within a few minutes, a line of young women filed in through the mosaic doorway with its onion-shaped arch. Some of the women carried strange-looking musical instruments. Others brought with them books, clothing, pallettes, clay, and armloads of bright flowers. They came in silently, smiling but keeping their eyes averted, and arranged themselves on the cushions. After the last one had entered, the veiled girl came in and led Justin to the corner, where he would be flanked by the women, and gestured for him to sit down on the largest and most comfortable cushion.

"The goddess Varja accepts your most honored presence," the girl said softly, assuming an attitude of prayer as she knelt at his feet.

"Is she coming here?" Justin asked hesitantly.

The girls giggled. "No," the veiled one said. "This place is for your welcome. We hope to make you comfortable and easeful here so that you may be initiated into the rites of love in the proper state of mind."

The proper state of mind? Justin wondered. How hard was this going to be, anyway?

One of the girls began to play. In her lap she held a seven-stringed instrument; gourds served as sounding boards at each end of the fretted fingerboard, which extended downward in a curve to the floor. The music it made was droning and soft. To Justin's ears, which had never heard anything but Western music, the sounds struck him as discordant, but he smiled anyway, lest he offend the musician.

"This is Rakhta who plays the *vina*," the veiled girl said. "It is a sacred instrument, formed in the shape of a woman. Its music is the sound of darkness and the sea, where the female spirit originated." She pointed out another young woman of striking beauty who was arranging heaps of orchids in translucent pastel bowls. "Dakini arranges the flowers from our garden. Flower arranging, like music, is one of the womanly arts. So are poetry, sculpture, disguise, and many others."

"Do you have to learn them all?"

"Yes. We must master sixty-four arts, including dancing, writing, painting, reading, perfumery, gardening, languages, carpentry, chemistry, logic . . . Many."

"Which languages do you speak?" Justin asked, hoping to learn more about the strange-looking Caucasian girl.

"Here we learn all the dialects of the region, plus the ancient languages of religious rites . . ."

"Do you speak English?"

The girl bowed her head. "Yes," she said. "It is understood that English is your language. For this reason, I have been selected as your companion, if I do not offend you too severely."

Justin grinned. "It will be a pleasure to speak my native tongue again."

One of the women added a final dab of ink to a drawing, blew on it for a moment, then presented it to Justin, bowing low as she offered it.

Justin took it from her, then uttered an involuntary gasp as he noticed the subject of her art. The drawing depicted a man and a woman, dressed in ornate finery from the waist up, but utterly naked below. Their feet were joined at the soles, and their hands rested on their bent knees. At the center of the picture, the man's penis fully penetrated the woman.

Justin felt himself flushing deeply. He swallowed and forced himself to look at the young woman who had given him the drawing. She was very pretty, and no more than twelve years old, with the soft, rounded cheeks of childhood still accentuating her oval face.

"This is Saraha," Justin's guide said. "She is our best artist."

The young girl smiled shyly.

"Yes, it's . . . wonderful," Justin said, hearing his voice crack and feeling horribly ashamed by it. If the girls heard him, they made no show of noticing. The veiled girl took the picture and set it aside.

"And what is your name?" Justin asked.

"My name is Duma, but it will be difficult for you to remember us all," she said. "But we have another name. Saraswati is the name given to the feminine counterpart of Brahma. Here, we are all Saraswati. Whatever you wish, Saraswati will provide it."

"Is that what you call Varja, too?"

"The goddess Varja is only Varja," she corrected quickly. "The spirit of Saraswati is within her, but Varja cannot be interchanged with any ordinary woman."

"But no one can be interchanged . . ." Justin began, but Duma's stiffening posture made him drop the subject. He didn't understand why the tall girl's approval was so important to him, but it was Duma he sought to please more than the mysterious abbess who owned the palace. "I'd like to call you Duma," he said lamely.

"As you wish."

"Why are you the only one wearing a veil?"

She hesitated for a long moment, dropping her head. "Because I am too ugly to be presented to your sight," she said softly. Then she rose. The movement was so quick that she seemed to float off the ground. She ran to the garden.

"Don't go," Justin called, going after her. She stopped at his command. "I'm sorry if I offended you," Justin blurted. "My teacher has told me that, to the eyes of seeing men, even the grossest disfigurements are invisible. Brahma knows only what is inside a person's soul."

Duma lowered her head. Maybe women were different, he thought. Sid's wife Arlene seemed to be a lot more concerned with how she looked on the outside than how much she understood about life. Maybe to a woman, an ugly face was the end of the world.

"Please come back," he said. He felt his face reddening. "I'm—I'm not comfortable in there alone."

"But you are not alone," she said, astonished. "The women will be with you to pleasure you and prepare you for Varja. I am not permitted to participate in those rituals."

"Then why are you here?"

Duma hesitated, seeming not to know what to say for a moment. Finally she said, "I was told that you possessed the curious mind of the Westerner. Since I, too, am a foreigner, I was selected to act as your guide. It is a great honor, considering the unpleasantness of my appearance."

"But why are you in this place at all?" Justin persisted. The folds of her white veil trembled in the breeze. "The goddess Varja rules over time," she explained. "Next to the creative force of Brahma himself, there is nothing more powerful than time. The goddess knows our destinies, because she understands time."

"You mean she can foretell the future?"

"Yes. There is one in time to come who will possess me. One whose destiny will be entwined with mine. He will desire me, despite my ugliness. It is for him that I was brought here."

"Where'd you come from?" Justin asked.

She shook her head. "I have already spoken too much."

She put her hand gently on his shoulder. "Come. You must begin what you were sent to accomplish."

She led him back to the harem. At the doorway, she knelt. "I will remain here, if you wish."

Justin nodded and walked desultorily inside.

The girl named Saraha, who had given him the drawing, came forward and knelt before him. In the background, the droning instrument played on, while a third girl, also very young, rose and glided in a sensuous, swaying motion to the middle of the floor. She was dressed in a brassiere of chained silver, which left her nipples exposed, and a loose silk skirt that hung low on her hips. Flowers were in her hair, and she wore a wide silver collar. She began to sway, finding rhythms in the tuneless music that was so alien to Justin.

Justin glanced at the doorway. Duma sat, as she had promised, the veil and the light from the garden behind her completely obscuring her features. She was a shadow of reality in this bizarre place where Justin felt more frightened than he had been even on the night his father was killed.

The dancer whirled, her perfumed skirts rising higher until Justin could see her thighs and, beyond, the mound of flesh downed with short pubic hair. He gulped, ashamed of looking, but unable to take his eyes away from the undulating female body in front of him. He was so transfixed that he didn't notice when two more women came to sit on either side of him, until they began to unfasten his garment. Involuntarily, he reached up to swat at the intruding hands. The women drew back with curious glances at each other. To Justin's astonishment, he saw that they were completely naked.

One was small, with breasts still budding and tender; the other was fully developed. The place between her legs was dark with long silky hair dappled with moisture. Gently, she took Justin's hand, questioning him first with her eyes for permission. Frantic, Justin looked for Duma. When she caught sight of him glancing nervously at her above the heads of the other girls, she nodded slowly.

The mature girl slid his finger along the cleft of her sex. When she maneuvered herself to let it penetrate her, Justin felt an aching in his groin that he thought would make his heart stop. He had experienced erections before—once when he had seen a pair of rutting mountain goats, he had nearly exploded with his own excitement—but he had never permitted himself to spend his seed. Tagore had told him that to fondle one's genitals was contrary to the discipline of yoga. Sexual pleasure was something that a man could enjoy only with a woman, and he was taught to curb his instincts.

Until now. Apparently it was all right for him to have an erection in this place. The deeper he probed into the dark, wet crevice, the more out of control he felt. His penis seemed to take on a life of its own, growing huge beneath his wraps, embarrassing him wildly. What if the women should see it? What if it just exploded, right here on the cushions?

The other girl leaned forward, almost across him, and rubbed her nipples across his lips. They were swollen with her first flush of womanhood and felt to Justin like wisps of air. His lips parted. Experimentally, he touched one of the nipples with the tip of his tongue. A thrill like a faint electric shock coursed through him. He opened his mouth wider and took the soft, soft disc into it until he could suck it. From deep in her chest, the girl moaned.

His breath came fast and hot. He could feel perspiration beading on his forehead and upper lip. A woman's body was a powerful thing.

He permitted the women to remove his robe. They were all over him, fluttering, caressing his chest, his neck, his buttocks, teasing him softly with their fingernails and teeth, using their tongues to stimulate him in areas where he had never thought to seek pleasure. The musician slowed her rhythm to a persistent, steady beat; the dancer followed suit. Undulating so that her belly heaved with each thrust of her hips, she spun slowly, unclasping her skirt as she turned. When she faced him again, moving as sinuously as a snake, she wore only the silver halter and a girdle of silver chains high on her hips. She bent backward, nearly touching her head to the floor, while her hips continued to push. The exposed vulva was glistening with wetness, and gave off a faint odor that affected Justin like a drug.

Saraha, at his feet, turned to face him. With her small hands, she spread his thighs apart.

What's she going to *do?* Justin thought, panicking. Not with her mouth!

She took him easily, her practiced tongue flicking, then holding lightly as he slid into her up to the hilt. She squeezed him with muscles at the back of her throat. The pleasure was so exquisite that it was a hair's breadth away from pain. His eyes were heavy; he wanted to sink into the cushions of silk and flesh around him and cry out with his ecstasy.

But instead, his gaze wandered toward the shadowy figure in the doorway. Duma sat, unmoving, veiled, and tense as a statue. He could not see her eyes, but he knew she was watching him. And for a reason he did not comprehend, he felt a great sadness coming from her. Duma was the only one of all the women around him who was not a complete stranger; and yet his pleasure excluded her. It was not that the women did not please him; there was something else, something about the lonely figure in the doorway that drained his pleasure as soon as he saw her. Because, for all the skills the women possessed, something was missing, an essential he could not name, and the sight of her reminded him of it. He felt lonely.

"I'm sorry," he said, getting clumsily to his feet. The women whispered, shocked, among themselves. He strode toward the garden.

Duma leaped up and hurried toward him. "What is wrong?" she asked anxiously.

"It's nothing," Justin said, brushing past her. It was difficult for him to walk. His belly ached. His senses, still filled with the tastes and scents and sensations of the harem, reeled. He sat down on a stone bench, wrapping his robe around him. He buried his face in his hands.

"They—they did not please you?" It was Duma, standing a few feet away. Her hands were clasped in front of her.

Justin looked up, but unable to speak, he covered his face again.

"It was my presence," she whispered. "My spirit destroyed the love force."

"No," Justin said with an effort. "It wasn't you. It was me. Something was missing."

"Perhaps if they were to try again . . ."

"No!" He hadn't meant to shout. But the girl bowed to him and left. He was relieved. He didn't understand his own feelings, let alone hers.

Inside the harem, the women were chattering in a fury. He had doubtless offended them all, Justin thought. He would be considered not only a coward but a boor as well. Tagore would not be pleased. At the moment before completion, he had failed. But why? Perhaps he was not Patanjali after all. Perhaps he was not even worthy to become a man. The monks had made a terrible mistake, selecting as their leader a boy who was afraid of women.

He stayed in the garden, alone, until long after dark. The sound of soft, feminine voices stilled. When he was sure the harem was empty, he went inside.

Duma was waiting for him.

"I have prepared a sleeping pallet for you," she said.

"You shouldn't have stayed awake on my account."

"It is my duty," she said softly. She bowed again to him, then rose.

"Wait," he called. She turned around. For a moment, he longed to tear the shapeless veil from her face, see whatever scars or deformities it hid, shame her with her own ugliness. He wanted to blame her for his failure. It would take some of the sting away. But he knew that she had done nothing, that the fault was his alone.

"I'll leave tomorrow," he said at last.

"But the goddess Varja will not receive you for many days to come," she explained, her voice strained.

He could not offend the goddess with so grave an insult. There was nothing to do but bear the derision of the women for however long it took the abbess to meet him. Tagore would still be displeased with his performance, but at least he could not accuse Justin of endangering Rashimpur by his rude behavior.

He nodded to her. "All right."

She took a tentative step nearer. "Would you like me to send someone to share your pallet for the night?" she asked hopefully.

Justin laughed bitterly. "No. No, thank you. I prefer to sleep alone."

He stayed awake, his thoughts a jumble of fear and self-reproach, until the first gray streaks of light appeared in the sky.

He didn't want to sleep. He didn't want to be in this place, this playpen full of girls. He had no desire to meet the terrible Varja, whom the legends said could eat a man whole and spit out his skeleton. He wanted to talk with Tagore, not with the deformed young girl who talked from behind a veil.

But mostly, he wanted to see Duma's face.

He got up slowly and walked to the inner entrance to the harem. He made no sound, although his heart was pumping furiously. What if Varja caught him? He had seen no men, but Tagore had said that the goddess ruled over both sexes. Were the men invisible? Anything was possible in this place. Had she eaten them whole? Would Justin's own skeleton be spat out in some desolate place with the others?

To his right was a room. It was little more than a tiny enclave, with no door. Inside, a plump young woman slept.

Beyond it was another room. He recognized the occupant as Saraha.

The sleeping rooms. *She's in one of these.* He moved swiftly, checking each room. When he reached the end of the hallway without finding Duma, he reproached himself angrily for his childish curiosity.

What difference does it make what she looks like? he asked himself. There's nothing special about her anyway, except that she goes around all covered up while the others live as naked as jaybirds.

Nevertheless, he turned around, walked back the entire length of the hall, and searched the other side.

What if she's so horrible that I turn to stone just looking at her? he thought, seized with sudden fear. That would really shame Tagore. Taking a deep breath, he stepped back a pace.

He turned to go back into the harem. But before he could take the first step back to reason, he glanced over his shoulder at the corridor of silent rooms. Duma was inside one of them. And suddenly, he didn't care if she was ugly or not. She was his friend, his first and only friend, and he had to see her.

His mind shut off like a machine. His reason was gone. There was no fear of Varja now, no self-recrimination, no struggle with his better judgment. He wanted to look at her, just look at her, just once.

He would never mention it to her or to anyone else, he decided as he raced down the hall, checking every room. Rakhta's *vina* was propped in the corner of one; books and scrolls were stacked neatly in the corner of another. And then he saw it. Hanging on the wall like part of a bride's trousseau was the long white veil.

His breath caught. Trembling, he moved silently inside the room. She was sleeping on a mat on the floor, her long brown hair streaming out behind her. She was turned away from him. She was wearing a white cotton shift, and in her hands—they really were pretty hands, he thought, regardless of what the rest of her might look like—she clutched a thin sheet of pink silk.

He tiptoed toward the other side of the mat, the thrill of adventure rising in him. He had never been disobedient to the monks at Rashimpur; he hadn't dared. But here, so far from home, alone, with no restraints . . . He was supposed to be learning how to be a man, after all. Wasn't a man supposed to be independent, especially around women?

Just as he bolstered his confidence sufficiently to reach the foot of Duma's mat, the unthinkable happened. His toe caught on the corner of her pallet, throwing him off balance. My toe! he cried inwardly in the half-second before he fell. To look on the forbidden face was bad enough, but to betray himself by his own clumsiness was a shame too great to bear. It was the end. He would have to run back to Rashimpur and beg the monks to accept him into the lowest beginning classes. He landed on his hands with a thud.

Duma woke immediately, sitting bolt upright. "What . . . what? It's you," she said, aghast.

Justin's hoarse intake of breath was louder than the sound he made hitting the ground.

She was beautiful!

She blinked, rubbing her eyes with the backs of her hands. Her skin was white as alabaster, making her large, dark eyes even more striking than they would have been on an olive-skinned girl like the others of the harem. Her nose was long and delicate, its tip chiseled. Her mouth was larger than the other girls', the lower lip thick and full.

"I've never seen a face like yours before," he whispered.

As soon as he spoke, Duma's eyes darted toward the veil hanging on the wall. She pulled the sheet over her head.

He knelt beside her and lowered her hands forcibly with his own. "No . . . don't cover your face. Your beauty pleases me," he said in formal Hindi.

She stared at him in bewilderment.

"Will you come to the garden with me, just for a little while?" he asked. She didn't respond. Her features remained fixed in an expression of stunned suspicion.

"Oh, God, I'm so dumb," Justin said in English. "I forgot

the lateness of the hour. Please forgive me for intruding on you.'' He bowed and backed away.

''I'll come with you,'' she said.

''You will?'' He felt he was grinning like a baboon, but he couldn't stop himself.

She smiled back. It was a brief, tentative thing, as if she were unused to happiness. Then she rose, put on a wrapper of bright blue silk, and reached for the veil.

''Leave this,'' he said, taking it from her.

She watched him replace her covering on its hook, then bowed her head and nodded slowly. Justin thought he saw the trace of a smile on her lips again.

''Why do they consider you ugly?'' Justin asked. The sky was glowing pink with the dawn. Fat droplets of dew gathered on the clusters of small, hardy orchids that grew only in the garden of Varja's palace. The ground was veiled in thick mist.

''It is obvious,'' Duma said. ''My nose is as long as an elephant's trunk. My mouth is large and coarse. My skin is white.''

''So is mine.''

''It is different with me,'' Duma said cryptically.

Justin didn't understand how it would be different, but then, he thought, women were strange people with odd values. ''I think you're the prettiest one here,'' he said.

''You are kind,'' she answered, clearly not believing him. ''Perhaps the one I am fated for will be as kind.''

''How can you be so sure this—this person will turn up? Nobody can read the future.''

''Varja can.'' Duma's eyes grew wide. ''She can foretell incredible events. She predicted the downfall of the monasteries that were destroyed by the soldiers. She says there is more destruction to come.''

''Has she warned them?''

Duma looked surprised. ''Of course not. Varja is not concerned with mortals. She is a goddess.''

''Doesn't she care?''

Duma shrugged. ''The lives of ordinary people are too short to warrant Varja's time.''

''But if she's immortal, she has all the time in the world.''

She screwed her face into a grimace. ''I don't understand

these things,'' she said. ''Anyway, the people who die don't mind. The monks of every monastery that's been ruined have sent the goddess their most precious relics as parting gifts.''

''Why would they do that?''

Duma looked at him as if he were a small child. ''She is a *goddess*. They worship her, as everyone does.''

Justin frowned. The monks at Rashimpur did not worship Varja. They didn't even call her a goddess. And Tagore had said that Varja's immortality was a legend. Nobody had even mentioned that she could see the future.

''What does she do with them?''

''She keeps the relics in the Sacred Chamber, her special room. You will see it during your rite of passage.''

A sudden fear crept over Justin. ''What's she going to do to me?'' he asked.

Duma smiled. ''Do not fear. It is a great honor to pleasure the goddess. She herself will initiate you into the Well of Love. This is very rare. It is because you are to head the monastery at Rashimpur that she accords this honor to you.''

''You mean I'm going to have to . . .'' He remembered the bizarre drawing of the two figures sitting on each other's backsides. ''How will she do it?''

''Oh, the usual way,'' Duma said offhandedly.

Justin looked down.

''It's very simple. The woman lies on the bottom, and the man gets on top of her.''

''But how does it *feel?*''

Duma stared at him for a moment, then turned her eyes away, embarrassed. ''I don't know,'' she said quietly. ''I've never done it either.''

He brightened. ''You haven't?''

''But I've watched. It looks easy, and the partners always seem to enjoy themselves.''

''Well, I don't know . . . How old is Varja?''

''She is as old·as the forests and the sea, as old as the world, the heavens, and Brahma himself.''

Justin raised his eyebrows. He wasn't sure he wanted to assume the ridiculous posture in the drawing with a woman who was even older than Tagore.

''It's getting to be light,'' Duma said. ''I must return.''

Justin stayed in the garden, endlessly watching the tangerine-colored fish swim circles in the little pool. Spending more time in the palace of Varja no longer seemed like a terrible ordeal. In fact, he began to wonder what the time without Duma would be like.

She was the first friend he'd ever had. As a child, being shifted around from one relative to another during his father's long absences, he'd had no opportunity to be close to anyone his age. Even the other boys he met at the occasional chess tournaments he played in were opponents, not friends. There was usually little socializing during the tournaments, anyway. At Rashimpur, there were others of his age, but there had been too many difficulties. In the first place, Justin had spent the past five years just learning to speak the languages the monks used. No one in the monastery, with the exception of Tagore, spoke English, and Tagore had curtailed their English conversations as soon as Justin had learned an elementary vocabulary in Hindi. But the major obstacle with the other *chela* at the monastery was that Justin was set apart by his position. He was Patanjali, the Wearer of the Blue Hat, and the other young boys were not willing to risk the wrath of Justin's dormant spirit by accidentally offending him. They treated him with courtesy and deference, but never with intimacy. The short time he spent in the garden with Duma was his first real conversation with someone his own age.

After I leave this place, I'll never see Duma again, he thought, and the thought made him sad. She was so like him, and yet so different. And she was beautiful, no matter what she thought of herself.

When daylight broke fully, the women brought him baskets of succulent fruits, a bowl of rice, some smoked fish, some odd pickled vegetables, and a dish of spicy chutney. He ate, but he was preoccupied. He was looking for Duma, waiting for her to awaken. When she finally came into the room, again draped in her heavy veil, he nearly ran to her.

"Will you join me for breakfast?" he asked.

The room fell into an immediate silence. "It would not be proper," Duma whispered.

"Why not?"

"Because I am unpresentable. Please pick one of the others."

"I don't want to eat with any of the others. I want you. And can't you take that thing off?"

There was a low murmur in the room, and he heard a few

giggles. Saraha, who had placed herself next to Justin, moved to make space for Duma.

"All right," Duma said. "If you insist. But I must not remove the veil."

He accepted her condition. For the moment. He had a plan. "Duma, you've got to get more confidence in yourself," he said as he took the first bite out of a pear.

"How is that possible?"

"I'm going to teach you. Is the garden always deserted? I haven't seen anyone in it besides us since I got here."

"It is more seemly for women to remain indoors," Duma said formally. "But since you are our honored guest, we will accompany you to the garden if it is your wish."

"It is my wish," Justin said. "But not everyone. Just you."

Duma bowed slightly in acquiescence, then followed him out.

Near the farthest corner of the garden, where the others could not see them, Justin took Duma by both shoulders and sat her down on a bench beside a huge white azalea bush in full bloom. "Now," he said, "I've been thinking about this for a long time, and I think it'll work. But first, you've got to get rid of this." He lifted her veil.

"No, you mustn't . . ."

"No one will see," Justin assured her. "Besides, if I don't think you're ugly, then what's the harm?"

"It is only your strange eyes that find beauty where there is none."

"That's not true. My eyes are as good as anyone's. It's your eyes that don't see what's really there. Now, look into my eyes."

"Why?" she asked, smiling shyly.

"Just do it. Okay, what do you see?"

"I see myself," Duma said.

"Keep looking. And say, 'She's beautiful.' "

"Who is?"

"The girl in my eyes."

"But I can't. That would be a dreadful lie."

"Do you dare to call your honored guest ugly?"

"Oh, no," she said, confused. "That's not what I meant."

"Your reflection's in my eyes, isn't it? It's part of me. So say it."

Duma peered guiltily into the turquoise eyes. "She is beautiful," she said softly. She looked miserable.

"Say it again. I command it."

Duma hesitated. "She is beautiful," she said finally.

"Once more."

"She is . . ." She stepped back. "I don't look so different from you, after all."

"Except for one thing. You're more beautiful." Duma could see from his face that he meant it. He plucked a sprig of blossoms from the bush and eased them into her hair behind her ear. "Now come with me," he said gently.

He led her by the hand to the goldfish pond and made her bend over it. "Now what do you see?"

The swimming fish caused the surface of the water to ripple, but he waited with her. Softly he placed his hand around her waist. Duma was a giantess compared with the other women, but in his arms she felt small and fragile. She made a point of not looking at him, but he could feel her trembling.

"There," he said. "The water's still."

For a moment, Duma's face shimmered in the water. With the white flowers next to her skin, she looked like some sort of forest sprite. Then a fat, shiny fish leaped in an arc out of the water, and Duma's reflection disappeared.

She straightened up slowly. When she did, Justin was facing her. "She's beautiful," he whispered, raising her chin and kissing her on the mouth.

There was a rush of activity from the harem. When Duma turned to look, five or six women had gathered at the doorway.

"Oh, no!" she gasped. "I forgot to replace the veil." Amid the women's exclamations, she pulled the veil over her face and ran toward the palace. But before she reached the doorway, she turned to face Justin once more. Then slowly, deliberately, she raised the veil once more from her face.

And Justin knew what it was that he had missed so much.

The days passed quickly, and they were filled with Duma: She was constantly with him, and he was never bored. She taught him the basics of painting and sculpture, and persuaded Rakhta to show him some chords on her *vina*, although Justin never did accustom himself to the sound. In time, the other girls became used to the young man who had spurned their advances, and accepted him as part of the household. Justin gardened, filling the harem with huge bouquets of flowers. He delighted the women, and himself, with displays of strength learned during his six years at Rashimpur. He read the books of poetry that the women studied, and kept them spellbound at night with the stories and legends Tagore had told him.

And always there was Duma. She refused to wear her veil any longer, and, to her surprise, none of the others objected. Wherever Justin was, she was at his side, and together they filled the palace with laughter.

She was changed. She took his hand easily, smiled often; the weight of a hundred years seemed to lift off her shoulders along with the ungainly veil. But the one unspoken question remained hanging like a cloud over them all: What will happen when he leaves?

"Patanjali, are there no women at Rashimpur?" Saraha asked, her fat cheeks dimpling.

"No, little one, there are none at all," Justin said.

"Then will you take us with you?" She looked despondent as some of the older girls giggled. "He is the only one who has not required us to give our bodies," she exclaimed to them angrily.

Duma stopped her. "It is an honor to give pleasure to those whom Varja deems worthy of us."

Saraha made a face. "I still don't like it. They never even talk to us. Patanjali is different. Oh, will you take me with you?" she asked eagerly.

Justin touched her hair. "This is not in my power," he said softly.

Saraha's eyes moistened. Thrusting out her lower lip to control her tears, she left the room. An uncomfortable silence settled in the air.

But no more than two hours later, the plump little girl was back, her chubby face radiant. "I have asked her," she announced breathlessly.

"Asked whom, Saraha?" Duma asked.

"Varja. I have gone to Varja herself!" The girl practically squealed with excitement.

Duma blanched. "Saraha, you should not have done that. It is forbidden to disturb the goddess before one is called."

"It was all right," she reassured the group. "I asked her if we could all go to Rashimpur one day for a visit. Then we can see Patanjali again!''

"And she said yes?" Duma asked.

"Almost. She told me to visit her in the Sacred Chamber tomorrow to receive her answer."

The girls clapped their hands over their mouths.

"It is a miracle," one of them said.

Duma explained to Justin. "We have never left this place, not even for a day. We have been here since we were children. These palace walls are all most of us remember."

Justin looked around at the women, as if for the first time. "How did you all get here?"

Duma lowered her eyes. "For many of us, like Saraha, the selection to serve in the palace of Varja was an honor for the entire village of the girl's birth. Saraha was picked because she has no marks. She is perfect," Duma said proudly.

Saraha hugged her. "Oh, Duma, you're perfect, too. You're the smartest of all of us, and the nicest. What does it matter that you were . . ." Her eyes slid guiltily toward Justin.

"It's all right," Duma said gently. She held up her head and looked Justin square in the eye. "I was sold by my family to Varja when I was five years old," she said. "This was not my doing, and so I feel no shame."

"Where are you from?" Justin asked.

"A cold country; I remember little about it. But it is the same place where the man I will be given to now lives."

Justin felt a stab of jealousy. "You should be allowed to choose your own mates," he said.

"Oh, we don't mate," Saraha said. "Only Duma. She's special. The rest of us—"

"Silence!" Duma snapped.

Her anger surprised Justin. Then he looked at the women. "You're all young," he said with wonder. "If you don't mate, then what happens to you when you get old?"

Saraha blinked, thinking. "I don't know. Do you know, Duma?"

A sound rose in Duma's throat. With a choked sob, she ran into the garden.

"Duma," Justin called, going after her.

"Leave me alone!" she cried.

The other women left. Justin said good night to Saraha. He spent the rest of the night alone. It was not until late the next morning, after they heard the scream, that Justin began to understand Varja.

The doors of the Sacred Chamber, usually locked, were flung wide. Rakhta was the first to pass it, the first to see the white-draped bier in the center of the room. On top of the bier, high above the heads of the observers who rushed in after Rakhta's warning, lay Saraha. She was dressed in a sari of white brocade. Her hair had been combed into a formal style, with silver ornaments. She was not breathing.

Justin stood staring in horrified silence until Duma gently took his arm. "We shall go now," she said.

"Did Varja kill her?" Justin asked when they left the Sacred Chamber.

"It is not death," Duma said fiercely. "It is life-in-death."

Justin was puzzled. Life-in-death? That was what the monks practiced. It was the state in which he had first seen Sadika, before the old leader permitted his spirit to leave and his body to crumble to ash. But only the most experienced practitioners of yoga could accomplish the feat of stilling the life processes for more than a week. Saraha was twelve.

"But life-in-death is a voluntary process," he said. "It could not have happened to her against her will."

Duma turned to him quickly. Her eyes were red-rimmed and feverish. "It is not we who practice life-in-death," she choked. "This is Varja's punishment on Saraha for wanting to leave the palace."

"But how . . ."

"You wanted to know what happens to us when we grow old?" she raged. "You have seen it! And there is more. There is much, much . . ." She sobbed.

Justin put his arms around her. For a moment she sank against him with relief, but she pulled herself back. "No. Do not touch me. Varja is a jealous goddess. There is danger for both of us. For all of us, now."

"Duma . . ." He looked at the somber faces of the women. They seemed to edge away from him in a group. "Please tell me. What do you call life-in-death?"

After a silence, one of the older women spoke. "It is the way Varja keeps us eternally beautiful," she said evenly. "We are made to sleep. And when Varja determines that we sleep no longer, we wake."

"And we are always beautiful," another girl said.

"I don't think that's true," Justin said simply.

"It is! There have been those among us who have been restored after life-in-death. When they awaken, they are no longer wicked. They are obedient to Varja. They carry her magic with them."

"Who among you?"

"They are not permitted to remain after they are brought back," Duma said.

Justin had no more to say. The women had seen the victim of an irrational vengeance, yet they accepted and defended Varja.

"Soon the night of your rite of passage will arrive," Duma said.

On the thirtieth day of his visit, Justin was escorted at sunset into the Sacred Chamber of Varja.

He had been permitted no food or drink that day, and the hunger and thirst accentuated his fear of the goddess.

His preparations had begun at dawn, when Duma came to wake him. She was again wearing the heavy veil, and her movements were stiff and formal.

"Our sister Saraha has been removed from the Sacred Chamber," she said.

Saraha's body had remained on view for three days, since the morning when the lifeless young girl was found. Justin had watched the body many times, looking for the inevitable decomposition of death. But there was none. The girl had remained as fresh and lifelike as she had been when she was living among them.

"What has Varja done with her?" he asked.

Duma shrugged. "We do not see the punished ones. But it is said that sometimes the goddess prepares the minds of those who live in death to assume a new life outside this place."

"How does she prepare their minds?"

"We are mortals, Patanjali. Perhaps you, as the son of Creation, can understand how the goddess transfers her thoughts to another, but I cannot. All we know here is that the unfortunate ones who have displeased Varja appear to die, but do not die. They remain forever young; that is all we know."

"But what happens when the women here grow older?" Justin asked.

Duma turned her head. "No one grows old here," she said quietly. "Saraha's turn came early, but her fate would have been the same ten years from now."

Justin could hardly believe his ears. "You—you *all* . . ." He couldn't bring himself to finish the thought.

She took his hand. "It is not painful. No one has ever cried out. There are no marks. And perhaps there is another life, after the time of life-in-death, as the stories say."

"I won't let her do that to you," Justin said.

Duma smiled. "It will not happen to me. I am not worthy of life-in-death. Because of my ugliness, I will be the first among us in the palace to leave."

"To whore for some man you don't even know," Justin said with disgust.

Duma's eyes were level. "If that is Varja's wish," she said softly. She got to her feet. "Come. The ritual of your manhood will begin tonight. This is your last day with us."

Justin was stunned. "My last . . . How do you know?"

"The goddess Varja sent for me. She is pleased that you have refused to take other women into your bed. So she will be the first," Duma said dully.

"But I want you to be the first! I've been waiting for you!"

"It was not to be," Duma said. She spoke breathlessly, whispering over the catch in her throat. "You were sent not for me, but for Varja. When this night is over, you will return to your life, and I to mine. Nothing will have changed. Our destinies are not to meet."

"No, Duma," he said, clasping her tightly by her shoulders. "It was always you. I stayed only because of you. I wanted so much for you to like me . . ."

"Stop," she gasped. She pried his hands loose. "You will not look on me again. It is best." She left the room quickly.

Duma alone was absent from the Sacred Chamber as Justin arrived. The other women stood with their backs against all four walls. Each was dressed in her finest clothes and wore a small transparent veil over the lower half of her face. In the center of the room, where Saraha's funeral bier had been, now stood a huge cube of white silk that billowed with the softest breeze.

When the room was utterly still, two of the women drew

apart the thick flowing fabric of the enormous cube in the middle of the room, facing Justin. Behind it was a bed of embroidered silk pillows, heavily scented. A woman lay in the center of it. Justin had no doubt about who it was. He was seeing the goddess at last, and the sight filled him with disgust.

Varja was painted like a ceremonial doll. Her face and body were covered with intricate patterns in red and black. Small gemstones swirled in lines from her chin to her temples. In the center of her forehead was painted a realistic third eye, unblinking and terrifying. Not an inch of bare skin surface showed.

The terrifying abbess he had seen for the first time at his own investiture had been breathtaking; now Justin realized that her beauty had come from her externals—the shimmering jeweled robe of crimson, the palanquin in which she rode, which was worthy of a goddess. But up close, was she a beauty? He could not tell because the artful painting hid her face and body from his eyes.

The cushions she lay on were supported by a large, flat, black-lacquered platform. On it, around the edges of the bed, was a collection of artifacts—polished bronze bottles, jade and silver bowls, golden statuettes.

As the curtains parted, the women lining the walls dropped to their knees, their heads bowed almost to the ground. Justin stared at her sullenly, refusing to kneel to Saraha's killer. The moment was tense. Varja, in her submissive position, edged upward slightly, her painted eyes narrowed. The women along the walls tensed, shifting their heads to look at the boy who defied the goddess.

Justin swallowed, feeling his face flush, but he did not move. Varja was no deity as far as he was concerned. She was an obscene, painted grotesquerie who lay exposed in front of him like the cheapest harlot, and he would not bow to her.

Then he felt a soft brush of fabric behind him, and a scent he recognized, sweet and gentle as spring. He didn't have to turn around to know it was Duma. Her long fingers rested on his shoulders with gentle authority, and when they pressed him downward, he did not resist. The goddess Varja was a slut, not worthy of even his attention; but for Duma, he would do anything. He knelt, but his eyes never lowered, and never lost the look of contempt they held.

Her pride satisfied, Varja lay back down on the mounds of silken pillows and gave a signal with a flick of her two-inch-long fingernails to the woman closest to her. The woman was the oldest of the group. She acquiesced with a bow, then reached into the folds of the cloth surrounding the bed to extract a bowl of gleaming gold. Handling it carefully, she passed the bowl to the next in line, and so it progressed until it reached Justin. He stared at the bowl for a moment; then his gaze shifted disdainfully back to Varja.

Duma accepted the bowl. "You must drink this," she whispered.

"What is it?" Justin growled, his eyes never leaving Varja.

"It is the cup. It is part of the ritual."

"What's in it?"

Duma sighed. "I do not know. But it is very important. If you do not drink, it will offend the goddess."

"She offends me," he said.

"Please, Patanjali." Her face was covered, but the pressure of her hand around his expressed her urgency. "If you displease the goddess, she will punish us all."

He turned to face Duma. "Tell her I'll drink if you can remove your veil."

A small gasp escaped Duma's lips. "Patanjali, I cannot . . ."

Before she could finish, Justin took hold of the veil himself and raised it. "So that the beauty of all incarnations of Saraswati may please Brahma," he said formally.

Varja's eyes flashed with an evil glance at Duma's face, but she said nothing. Then Justin nodded curtly and drank a small sip from the golden bowl.

The taste of the milky liquid was bitter and pungent. He swallowed it with difficulty. As he gave the bowl back to Duma, Varja smiled. It was a tight, evil expression, her jaws strained and her eyes hard. She nodded once, slowly, and the women began to leave, bowing as they rose.

"Not you," Justin said, taking Duma's hand.

"Patanjali, I cannot . . ."

He didn't hear the rest of what she said. He was reeling, stumbling to remain on his feet. His vision blurred. The drink. Whatever was in it was having a powerful effect. He clasped Duma's hand more tightly. "She stays," he said, forcing himself to speak Hindi. The volume of his words surprised him. He could not control his voice.

Varja took her eyes off him and shifted them toward the girl. There was malice in them, but she said nothing. Instead, staring intently at Duma, her tight-lipped smile like a cat's, the goddess pulled aside the silk covering over her lap and spread her thighs wide.

, Duma lowered her head. She was shaking. On the inside of Varja's thighs were painted a hundred figures depicting couples engaged in sexual acts. Justin felt a shudder of revulsion.

"Very well," Varja said at last. "She may stay." They were the first words Justin had heard her speak, and they were filled with a perverse triumph. "Come," she commanded.

Justin looked at Duma, trying hard to focus on the girl. The room was swimming around him. "Please do as she says," Duma whispered. With some difficulty, Justin mounted the bed.

The cup. Swimming around the soup of disjointed images in his head was the cup Tagore had given him to present to Varja. It sat on the low ledge that surrounded the bed, along with many other artifacts, some very old—a staff, jeweled and gilded, and a rock that glittered . . . the stone of Dinrath. It had belonged to the monastery at Labrang. Tagore had told Justin that the monastery had burned to the ground. Soldiers, he said. Fire.

Mixed with the swirling, vague sights in the room was a sudden remembrance of a dream. A dream of fire, burning the Tree of the Thousand Wisdoms, burning it all to the ground . . .

But fire melted gold. The stone of Dinrath should have vanished in the flames.

They give their relics to Varja. They worship her.

Something was wrong, very wrong. The monks at Labrang did not worship Varja any more than those at Rashimpur did. Tagore had told Justin that the stone had been stolen.

Stolen?

"Show me your manhood," Varja commanded.

Justin looked down, confused, at his limp member. The stone of Dinrath. Fire. Something in the drink. Fire to come. He gasped involuntarily as he spotted another relic on the ledge. It was a golden vessel from the monastery at Pemiongchi. Also burned.

"You stole them," Justin said groggily. "You led the soldiers to the monasteries to destroy them. You took the relics from their rightful place."

Varja ignored him, looking with contempt at his groin. With a flick of her hand, she commanded Duma to prepare him.

He felt the girl's slender, trembling fingers untie the cord at his waist, then touch his bare skin.

"Duma," he said softly. "Duma." He felt himself harden at her touch. It was all so confusing. There was a woman in front of him, tattooed and leering, her legs opened in invitation. There were the relics of the lost holy places surrounding the ugly, wanton thing, focused, it seemed, around the unblinking third eye in the center of her forehead. There was the misty unreality of the chamber, and a feeling of nausea in Justin's stomach.

Tagore should never have sent me to this place, he thought. The monks didn't know. Varja is evil, a ragged, smelly, contemptible thing.

And then there were the soft white hands on him, hands that smelled of kindness and desire. Duma was touching him, and Duma became all there was in the strange, convoluted world of the milky white liquid he had been made to drink. *Duma, I have always wanted you. I will always be yours. The man you were promised for will never own you, I promise. I will kill to prevent it, if I have to; I will even leave Rashimpur. But I will never let you go because I love you as I have never loved anything. I love you, Duma.*

"Come to me." The woman's voice was deep and passionate and wet with experience.

The tumescence between his legs was unbearable. He leaned forward, searching. "Duma," he sighed. "Duma, it was always you." He opened his eyes. And there, in front of him, lay a three-eyed monster with foul breath and paint melting from the sweat on her face.

Then Duma screamed, and Justin saw the knife at his throat. One of Varja's hands was clasping the amulet around his neck while the other brought down a razor-sharp blade.

In an instant Justin was in the air, not fully realizing what was happening, his mind still murky from the drug, but following the instinctive commands of his body. He had been trained to respond quickly, without thought, at a sign of

danger. In that blinding moment when he saw the three-eyed
woman lunge for his throat with the jeweled blade glittering
in her hand, he ceased to remember that she was a goddess,
or that he was in her presence at the request of his mentor, or
that the knife might be a painless part of the ritual. All he
knew was that someone was trying to kill him. He responded
by first knocking the blade out of Varja's hand, sending it
clattering to the floor while the goddess watched its trajectory
with amazement, and then slapping Varja hard across her face
with the back of his hand. She reeled as she let go of the
medallion around Justin's neck.

Duma propelled herself backward, aghast. She struck the
wall behind her. Her face was ashen, and the fingers she
raised to her mouth were shaking with fright.

Biting the inside of his cheeks to stay alert, he grasped her
by the arm and forced her toward the doorway.

"Leave. Now," he said.

"I cannot," Duma answered breathlessly. "You struck the
goddess . . ."

"Your goddess tried to kill me for my amulet, and she
won't think anything about killing you."

"Patanjali . . ."

He threw her bodily into the hall. In the same motion, he
whirled around to return to the bed where Varja still lay,
stunned, the paint on her face smeared. He picked up the
bowl of milky liquid that he had been made to drink. There
was still some of the concoction left in the bottom. With a
sound of utter disdain, he flung the liquid in Varja's face.

"You're no goddess," he said with disgust. "You're nothing more than a pillager of monasteries and a killer of men
and women." His anger had cleared his head. Every other
emotion had been replaced by a searing rage. He pulled back
his arm to strike her again, then let it go. No violence would
bring back Saraha. No matter how strong his hatred was, it
would never restore the monasteries that Varja had looted and
destroyed. All he could do now was to save Duma, because
she would surely be Varja's next victim.

Duma was sprawled on the floor in the corridor outside the
Sacred Chamber. "I'm sorry," Justin said, picking her up as
deftly as he could manage. "Let's get out of here."

"But the others. My home—"

"I will tell the monks at Rashimpur. They will help the

others. But your home is with me." He pulled her through the garden and out into the open fields.

The night sky was swirling with stars. Despite his fear and concern for Duma, he could hardly keep his eyes open. He tripped over a stone, landing painfully on his face. "So clumsy," he said, struggling to right himself.

"Even Patanjali is not completely immune to life-in-death. But he is very strong." She stroked his face with her long fingers. "I suspected that Varja meant to kill you with the drink she offered, but I could not believe she would do such a thing. Now I believe. Oh, Patanjali, will you ever forgive me? I should have known."

Justin smiled. "How could you have known? I didn't know myself."

"The drink. It was the same as one I remembered."

Justin was startled to alertness. "She gave it to you?"

"Not me. Another." Duma put her arm beneath Justin's to help him walk. "When I was quite young, perhaps six or seven, I tried to escape from this place. There is something evil in Varja's palace. I could almost smell it. I cried myself to sleep every night after I was brought here. Then one day a friend—an older girl who was kind to me despite my ugliness—ran away, through the garden, just as we came. I begged her to let me come with her, and she allowed me."

"Where did you go?"

"Far away. To the west, it seemed. We traveled for many days. But Varja found us."

"How?"

"She has men. They live beneath the palace. They are"—she choked—"they are vile men who live like beasts. Varja lets them use us whenever they want. We were not permitted to speak of them to outsiders, but they are always in the palace. They'll come looking for us soon." She pointed into the distance. "There is a small cave nearby. My friend and I passed it when we escaped, but we did not stop there."

"What happened when Varja's men found you?" Justin asked, trying to keep himself awake by talking. "Were you punished?"

"I was made to wear the veil from that day. Varja said that my ugliness would someday be known to all the world. But I was very young, and the goddess had plans for me."

"You don't have to worry about those plans anymore, Duma."

Duma slowed. "Varja's plans are always fulfilled," she said softly. "My friend was not so fortunate. She was given the bowl to drink, as you were. I was made to watch her. Her punishment was life-in-death."

"Like Saraha."

Duma nodded. "And like Saraha, she never returned. The others speak of those who return after life-in-death, but I don't believe the legends are true. My friend is dead. And Saraha is dead."

They walked in silence to a cave in the foothills of the great Himalayan peaks that surrounded them.

"They will not find us here," Duma said. "It is dark, and they will walk beyond this place, to where my friend and I escaped before. You can sleep here, Patanjali."

"No, I mustn't—"

"It's all right. You will not succumb to life-in-death now. You are only tired."

Justin felt himself sinking into the cold earth of the cave floor. "But I should watch . . . for you . . ."

Duma smiled. "I will watch, Patanjali. There is no danger now."

"Duma," Justin whispered, taking her hand. The stillness of the cave enveloped them like a womb. "Will you stay with me forever?"

Duma lowered her head. "I cannot stay with you at Rashimpur."

"Then we will leave Rashimpur."

"But you are the leader of the monastery. You are Patanjali."

"And you are the woman I love. I did not choose to be Patanjali. I don't even know if I am what the monks say I am. But I know what you are." He caressed her face. "And I choose to be with you. If you'll have me."

Duma looked at him with sad eyes. "We cannot chart our own destinies," she said at last. "If we are meant to be as one, then we shall be. But if we are not . . . if anything should happen . . . I will always remember, Patanjali. I will always love you. I will save my heart for you."

"Do you promise?"

"I promise."

"Then I do, too. Duma, I will have no woman but you."

Then he touched her, and she held him, and he loved her in the quiet cave, feeling the pain of her first experience, entering her darkness, exploding with joy, and he was glad he had waited for her, and he knew that if he'd had to wait forever, he would have waited, because no other love was possible for him. And wrapped in the warm smoothness of her flesh, feeling her beating heart next to his own, Justin slept.

Rough hands awoke him, yanking his head backward, dragging him out from the cave into a night bright with fire.

Duma was gone. In the distance, in front of a huge bonfire, wavered the shapeless forms of women whose screams pierced the stillness of the mountain night.

"Duma!" Justin shouted, but there was too much noise and confusion for him to hear even his own voice in the sudden din. Big men with black-painted faces held him down as his wrists and ankles were tied.

"Patanjali!" someone called from the distance. It was not Duma's voice, but one he recognized from among the women at the palace. As his eyes adjusted to the sudden brightness of the fire, he saw that the women were bound together in a circle surrounding the fire. He searched for Duma, but could not see her.

"What do you want with me?" he shouted.

The men didn't answer. Then, from the directions of Varja's palace came the jeweled palanquin of the goddess, borne by four men. When it approached Justin, the silk curtains of the carrier parted, and Varja, again resplendent in floor-length robes, stepped out.

"What have you done with her?" Justin rasped.

"Your accomplice will serve you no longer," she said. Her face held a look of malicious victory.

"You've killed her, you filthy whore!"

Varja raised her hand. "Ah, but you underestimate me, Patanjali. Killing is far too easy. Killing her, or killing you. No, my young fool. You shall live. For now."

She took a black cloth bag from a cord tied around her waist and poured the contents into her hand. It looked like black soot. She sprinkled the powder over Justin's face and body.

"And this shall be your destiny," she intoned in the formal dialect of her sect. "To live with such suffering that you yourself will seek death. To die with each breath of life. To be betrayed by all the gods. To be trusted by no one. To find no shelter from pain and sorrow throughout all your days. To see that which you love wither and die and be turned to dust. To be betrayed by your own heart. This to you, Patanjali, is the blessing of Varja and all the power at her command. And then, on the day that I will it, you will die and be no more."

Then she raised her hands high, and the men who served her left Justin to form an outer circle around the women. Justin watched, horrified, as they drew long sabers and held them aloft.

"What are they doing?" Justin asked, stunned. Surely . . . Not the *women* . . .

She lowered her arms. It was a definite, unmistakable command. And as Justin screamed with horror at the realization of what was about to happen, the guards hacked the heads off the women, one by one, and kicked the bodies into the flames.

"This is the beginning," Varja said softly as she mounted her palanquin. Her eyes gleamed. She was smiling.

At daybreak, after the men were gone, when the fire had settled to smoldering ashes and the stench of burning flesh had disappeared, Justin was able to release himself from the thick bonds that tied him. He walked to the site of the fire, feeling as if he had died along with the women.

There was nothing of Duma. A few bones and undistinguishable shapes—burned meat—rested among the coals. Nothing else remained. Nearby, he could hear the shuffling of hyenas coming to feast on the dead, to lick the charred bones of his love.

Using his hands, Justin covered the pit with earth, then walked back to the monastery at Rashimpur.

Varja's curse had already come to pass, he thought. He would seek his own death, and welcome it when it came.

The sooner the better.

CHAPTER TWENTY-THREE

There was a noise from the base of the hill in front of Yva's small house. Justin sat bolt upright.

"Yva!" a voice rang out. "I have to talk to you now, Yva. It's important."

"It's Józek," Yva said, scrambling to her feet. She pressed her fingers to her lips and gestured for Justin to stay down. Hurriedly, she put on her dress and called, "What is it?" as she picked her way down the hillside among the traps.

Józek was visibly nervous, his thin fingers twitching. "The medallion," he said without preamble. His eyes darted in all directions. "I—I sold it to a Russian soldier."

"Pig!" she began.

"There isn't much time. Listen to me," Józek said, shaking her, his voice hushed and irritated. "That was a week ago. I went to Kraków and sold it to a soldier there. Today they came—to my house—to take me back to Kraków. There was this big-shot officer from Moscow. He had the medallion, and wanted to know where I got it. They kept me for six hours. I had no water; I was terrified."

"And so you told him," Yva said simply.

"I gave him the long route, through Lubsana. They won't be here for a while. Yva, you have to get that man out of your house, out of the area. He's wanted, a criminal maybe. If the soldiers find him here, they'll destroy everyone in the village. As it is, they'll know I led them on a goose chase around Czeskow."

213

Yva stuck out her chin. "Why should I believe you? You don't care anything about the village. And neither do I."

Józek hung his head. "They brought the doctor along, too," he said. "They wanted to know if it was the same man he'd looked after before. This man rose from the *dead*, Yva. There's something terrible about him." He shook his head. Spittle formed in the corner of his mouth. "The Russians want him bad. He must be a big underground leader or something. The doctor told me to warn you. He's in the village now, telling everybody to bury their valuables in case of fire." He scanned the dark house on top of the hill. "We have to move fast. I'll help you carry him out. Can he move at all?"

"Don't come," she said, pushing him back. "He can move. He's—he's already gone."

"Well, all right," Józek said uncertainly. "I'm not going to stick around to find out if you're telling me the truth or not. I only came because the doctor's a good man. But don't let the Russians find your pretty boy here."

Yva ran up the hill without another word.

"You have to leave," she whispered to Justin. "Now. There's no time to explain, but get out. Get as far away as possible for the next few days." She spoke while she gathered some dried fruit and a jug of water.

"Are you in danger? I'll wait nearby, where I can watch."

"No! The soldiers are looking for you. If they find you here, they'll kill you, and me, and everyone else for miles around. Just listen to me, and don't argue." She thrust the parcels at him and pushed him toward the door. "They'll be coming from Lubsana, to the west. So head east, and keep moving. Things ought to be clear in a day or so."

Justin felt helpless. Why was he running again? "I don't know any soldiers," he said. "What do they want me for?"

"They say you rose from the dead. What difference does it make? Don't waste time thinking. Just go." She shoved him into the darkness.

The jeep came within twenty minutes. To Yva's surprise, there was only one man inside, a Russian colonel.

Yva rushed outside. "What's your business?" She shouted.

"I am Colonel Alexander Zharkov. I am looking for a man named Justin Gilead. An American."

An American! In her wildest dreams, Yva had not imagined

that the beautiful boy with no memory was an American. She wondered if Justin even knew it himself. "There is no one here except me," she said.

Zharkov got out of the jeep. "I'll see for myself, if you don't mind."

"Wait," she said, picking her way among the hidden traps. "I'll bring you up." The traps were her only weapon. It would be wise, she knew, not to show her hand too quickly.

Zharkov scanned the inside of the house cursorily, kicking the straw of the bed, flinging Yva's few articles of clothing to the floor. At last, he came to the large wooden table covered with sewing materials. He swept them away with one arm. Beneath, etched into the grain of the wood, was Justin's drawing of the coiled snake.

Zharkov looked at her levelly. Slowly he took out his pistol. "Where is he?"

Yva swallowed. "I never knew his name. He left several days ago. I took his medallion as payment for looking after him. I was going to turn him over to the authorities when he was well . . ."

"How many days?"

"Three," she said without hesitation. "He was sick until then."

"What did he tell you about himself?"

"Nothing. He couldn't talk."

Something in the fireplace caught Zharkov's eye. He walked over to it, keeping the Tokarev trained on the woman. Reaching into the flames with a poker, he pushed out the charred corner of a checkerboard.

"You're lying," he said evenly. He threw the board at her feet. "I'll be back."

After he left, Yva sat down, shaking. The danger was momentarily past, but he would come back with his men. That was a certainty. They would comb the woods for a man traveling on foot. They would guess his direction once they realized that Józek had given them the wrong route. They would alert the other villages to look for Justin. And Czeskow . . .

There was a cry and a thump from in front of the house. For the first time since she'd buried her dead child, Yva crossed herself. The Russian officer had found the traps.

Peering out the door cautiously, she watched for movement. Zharkov lay on the slope, his arms flung wide, his head bleeding against a rock.

Yva scrambled down the hill to him. First, she picked up the Russian's gun, which was lying a few feet from his right hand, and threw it as far as she could into the shadows. Then she searched the unconscious man for the medallion.

She found it in the inside pocket of his uniform jacket, still wrapped in the piece of dirty cloth she had put it in. She opened the cloth to be sure. The medallion was the same, and again it felt warm in her hand.

"It is not yours," she mumbled softly to the unconscious Russian officer. "Not yours."

She slipped away quietly and moved, with unerring instinct, down the hill to the base of a large tree. Using a rock for a tool, she dug a hole by the tree and buried the medallion. Then she placed the rock over the hole as a marker.

Done. Now, whatever they did to her or to her house, the medallion would be safe for Justin. She said his name aloud. "Justin Gilead. An American." The thought of the strange young man's powerful body, his tender yet strong arms, made her heart beat faster.

She scooped dirt into her apron until it was full, then, laboriously, handful by handful, pushed it all into the gas tank of the jeep.

It was more than six miles to the village. Yva ran the whole distance, planning, praying, regretting that she hadn't shot the Russian officer with his own gun while she'd had the chance.

But maybe things would be all right anyway. The Russian would find his way back to his troops in time, she knew, but that time might be enough for Justin to get away.

She found the doctor, rushing from one house to another, warning the inhabitants about the approaching destruction.

"I need to speak to you," she said.

The doctor, exhausted and hoarse, took her arm. "Have they come?"

She nodded. "One. But the rest will come. He knows the stranger was there. There were things I couldn't hide."

The doctor sighed. "Then at least we have warning. Many have fled already. Thank you for your concern."

"My concern isn't for you, or these people," Yva said

flatly. "I want you to give the stranger a message if you see him again. I . . . may not."

"Nonsense, dear. You'll come with my family."

"No!" Yva shouted. "That would be suicide. The Russian officer will be looking for me. I'll be safer in the woods. But I want you to tell the stranger, if he comes back, that the medallion is at the bottom of the hill, by the tree. He'll understand."

"All right," the doctor said, "But you—"

"That message is only for him, understand? No one else. No one. In exchange for this message, I'm warning you to get whoever you care to out of Czeskow."

She walked back to the cabin. It was nearing dawn. She longed for sleep, but there was still much to do. Zharkov would be back with his men in a few hours. It was enough time to pack some provisions and a blanket before she set out to find Justin in the forest, but not enough time to hesitate, even for a moment.

She stopped at the bottom of the hill, near the tree where the coiled snake medallion was buried. The rock marker had not been disturbed. The jeep, useless now, remained where the officer had left it. Zharkov himself was gone, the trap sprung, as she had expected.

But a faint, shadowy glow shone behind the brown oilskin windows. A lamp. Had Justin returned already? Had he been tricked by the calm into believing that nothing would happen?

She rushed up the hill. "Justin?"

"Yva."

"What are you doing here? What—"

The Tokarev was pointed directly at her face.

Zharkov grabbed the shoulder of her dress and pulled her into the room. "Where's the medallion?" It was a command.

"It's—" She looked around. There was no place for her to go now. "It's in Czechoslovakia by now."

Zharkov's jaw clenched. "Where did you meet him?"

"Why should I tell you? Filthy Russian pig. It wasn't yours."

"Tell me where he's gone!" Zharkov's voice was strangled. He grabbed the girl by the neck and slammed her against the wall, jamming the Tokarev into her temple. "Where?"

Yva's heart pounded. Her eyes unwillingly welled with tears.

"Where?" Zharkov repeated, pounding her skull against the wood. She was *his*, he thought, the Grandmaster's woman, and it gave him satisfaction to hurt her. "Is this how he takes care of you? Is this how he looks after you?"

She managed to turn her head slightly. The round, frightened face gathered into a mask of hatred. In one last, defiant gesture, she spat in his face.

Zharkov fired the Tokarev.

The man who did not know his name was Justin Gilead returned to the house the following night. There were soldiers in the woods, heading east; they would long ago have passed Yva Pradziad's house.

There seemed to be light everywhere, light and sound and excitement. The lights usually visible from the village were oddly extinguished, but there were other lights from the roadways, and the sounds of horses and cattle carried from isolated places on the wind.

He walked around the house silently, watching, listening. No sound. No light. Had she left? No soldiers. He entered quietly, surprised to find that he could move without disturbing even the pebbles under his feet. He had to have learned that somewhere. Perhaps in the place where he'd gotten the medallion.

"Yva," he whispered. Eve, the first woman. His mother, his teacher, his friend.

He found her, bloody and decapitated. What remained of her face was splattered over the fireplace. A box had been tossed into the new ashes. Across her body were strewn its contents: the chess pieces Justin had whittled from scrap wood.

Justin moaned. A vision of a mutilated old man tied to a burning tree came to him, followed by a nightmare sequence of still photographs: bodies in a lake, a golden hall filled with dead soldiers, a ring of headless women around a bonfire. And now there was yet another picture. Once again, someone who loved him had died in his place. Once again, the Prince of Death had triumphed.

The sound stopped in his throat. In the distance, through the numb, senseless blackness, he saw the village of Czeskow burning.

There was nothing left.

CHAPTER TWENTY-FOUR

_er_ squinted at the figure coming toward him through the ▓ to his hospital room. It was a fat man, young, from his ▓. His face was obscured, but the overhead fluorescent ▓ts shone through the mass of fuzzy hair on his head. The ▓an spoke softly to the American guard in the room, and the guard left.

"Corfus," Starcher said. He had not spoken in so long that his throat was unused to producing sound.

"Shhh. I had to get special dispensation to come here. Any plumbers come around?" He smiled broadly at his own joke. The KGB was famous for stashing surveillance devices in the most unlikely places, on the off chance that the subject in question would do or say something for the hugely overstaffed secret police to dissect and analyze.

"I don't remember. You'd better take a look around."

Corfus searched the small curtained area around Starcher's bed, pausing when a sullen nurse entered for a spot check. After a long, cold look at Corfus, she left, and Corfus pulled a small disc of plastic the size of a button off the electronic buzzer attached to Starcher's bed.

"Thar she blows," the young man said, grinding the button under his heel. "There's probably more. Hold on." He took a portable tape player from his pocket and turned on loud rock music.

"They never stop, do they?" Starcher said.

Corfus leaned over the bed and spoke softly in Starcher's ear. "You're being flown back to HQ."

"When?"

"As soon as you're stable. They're afraid the goon squad'll put a bomb in your bedpan to make you talk."

Starcher exhaled. He seemed to disappear into the folds of the sheets. "I guess this is it, then."

"Hey," Corfus said, pushing the old man's hair out of his eyes. "You'll be back."

"Like hell," Starcher said mildly. "Not at my age."

There was a long and awkward silence. Corfus put his hands in his pockets and shuffled his feet, then stepped forward again. "Andy," he said quietly, "I don't know if you're still interested in the Riesling business, but I think I've got something."

Starcher eased himself up. "What is it?"

"The stuff in his pockets. Remember those fake passports? He was trying to get someone—two people, a man and a woman—out of the country."

"And?"

"And what he said to me. The stuff about Havana. I think it might tie in."

"A code?" Starcher asked.

"Maybe. The thing that kept sticking in my head was Havana. Why Havana? And then I read today in *Pravda* that there's going to be a chess challenge match in Havana in a couple of months. U.S. versus U.S.S.R. I don't know. It might just be a red herring."

Starcher thought. "Riesling never operated in Cuba."

"Okay," Corfus said with a nod. "But just for argument's sake, let's say he couldn't get Mr. and Mrs. X out of Moscow, or wherever they are. Maybe he turned his stuff over to me so that someone else could get them out."

Starcher blinked.

"And then I started to think about who would want to defect. It wouldn't be anyone military, because Riesling dealt with civilians, am I right? Scientists, that kind of thing. So when I read the piece in Pravda—"

"A chess player."

"Bingo. So I started going over some past issues to see if I could rout out anything about the big-deal chess players over here. Any problems. What I came up with was this." He leaned back to hand Starcher a Russian newspaper clipping. The date, October 5, was scribbled over the top:

Tass

HELSINKI—The International Consortium of Pediatricians convened early today at the Privm Hotel in Helsinki, Finland. The main event of the day will be a symposium on the relation between prenatal care and birth defects. The symposium will be conducted by Dr. Lena Kutsenko, chief pediatrician at Moscow University Medical Center.

"Ring a bell?" Corfus asked.

"Not Ivan Kutsenko," Starcher whispered incredulously.

"The same. Her husband's the world chess champion. Pride and joy of Mother Russia."

"Riesling's cover was as a journalist for Associated Press in Helsinki. And he started his last run the day after this clipping."

"It fits, Andy. She could have approached him. I don't know chess from dominoes, but I've heard rumors that Kutsenko's awful nervous about the Havana match. There's some talk out that if the team doesn't win, he may follow Boris Spassky to the land of nonpersons. Russian chess champs aren't allowed to lose."

"Well," Starcher said, "it's a good theory . . . but *Kutsenko*."

"There's something else. I tried to get hold of Lena Kutsenko at Moscow University Medical Center. Guess who's out of a job."

"They fired her?"

Corfus shrugged. "She's not there. They said she left because of ill health, but they wouldn't say when. It makes me wonder if it isn't tied in somehow with the incident at the Samarkand."

Starcher snorted. "I wouldn't be surprised. Damn, I wish I weren't out of this. Grabbing Kutsenko would at least give some credibility to this travesty we're running over here. The KGB boys practically laugh in my face as it is. They've got God knows how many thousands of agents operating in the States, while all we've got is an embassy and a handful of . . . hell, they might as well be commandos for all the cover they've got."

He was breathing heavily under the strain of his anger. "The balls of them, shooting Riesling in a public place.

Arrogant bastards. And it's not just us. The West in general is about as threatening to them as a Chiclet. Remember Ben Barnes?''

Corfus said he'd read about the case. The Agency had come out of that one looking like the fool of the Western Hemisphere. After an espionage ring in New York was uncovered, seven highly placed Soviet agents including a Russian mole named Morody Gotst, who went under the name Ben Barnes, were arrested. The Soviets agreed to a trade, but there were so few Western spies in Russia that the Soviets could only produce one prisoner in exchange for the seven convicted Soviet spies, and the prisoner they did have was no more than a low-level intermediary—utterly out of Barnes's league. It was a bad trade, but the best the Western powers could manage. After the incident, there was a flurry of arbitrary arrests of Western tourists in Moscow. These innocent people were offered, in what Starcher considered an act of brazen arrogance, as trades for convicted Soviet espionage agents incarcerated in the United States and Western Europe.

"They've got all the latitude," Corfus said. "They can sit in on sessions of Congress, go through the CIA files . . ."

"We're a joke to them. But with Kutsenko . . ." He curled his hand into a fist and laughed out loud, then lowered his voice again while the rock music tape blared on. "Mike, see that whoever replaces me follows through on this, will you? I'd give my arm to see the faces in the Politburo if Kutsenko ducked out."

"I'll see to it, boss," Corfus said, smiling.

Starcher nodded. "I guess this is good-bye, then."

"I guess so. You'll be going home soon. I've turned in all the paperwork."

"Good," Starcher said. "You've done well, Mike. Maybe I'll see you again."

Corfus took his hand. "I hope so." He clicked off the tape playing rock music and the room was marvelously silent.

But as Corfus lumbered away, Starcher knew he would never see him again. American spies didn't have reunions the way the Brits did, with their toasts and honors to their secret heroes of yesteryear. There was something ludicrous in the practice anyway, Starcher thought, as if a charade of camaraderie could dispel the truth that intelligence agents were as disposable as Kleenex. They functioned while they could, and then they disappeared. No good-byes, no gold watches. A short silence, perhaps, before the quiet walk down the road to where death waited.

The snow was swirling into whirlpools as Corfus walked toward the metro on Ulyanovskaya Street. The old ladies with their brooms were out in force, but they seemed more to chase the turbulent snow than to sweep it as the wind hurled itself against their stocky, heavily-clothed bodies.

Corfus never could get used to the sight of women laborers. Moscow, even in winter, offered a panorama of sexual equality, from the women who poured pitch into the potholes, to the old *babushkas* who cleaned the streets. The Soviet ideology had triumphed: wherever there was work to be done, there were women to perform the lowest, dirtiest tasks. Corfus remembered an old joke about two Russians swilling vodka and playing cards. A third entered, asking where their wives were. "The masses," came the reply, "are in the fields."

Up ahead, a woman swathed in sable stepped from a silver Mercedes 450. The top of her fur hat bobbed up and down comically as she walked around the car as if surveying a lot for a subdivision.

"Excuse me," she shouted above the wind to passersby. "Could you . . ." Her accent was atrocious, very Western. Probably American, Corfus thought, dressed in her new Russian sable while the Russians could hardly keep themselves warm. No wonder they hate us, he said to himself.

The people on the street gawked disdainfully at her expensive trappings and moved on. "Oh, Christ," she finally shouted in despair. "Doesn't anyone in this godforsaken country speak English?"

"That's my cue," Corfus said, striding up alongside the car. "Michael Corfus, American embassy, at your service." He gave an elaborate bow.

"Thank heaven," the woman said with a desperate relief in her broad New England finishing school tones. "You can't imagine how awful it is being stranded out here in this horrible weather among these rude people. No one even stopped to ask what the problem was."

Corfus laughed. "As far as the average Muscovite's concerned, anybody with a fur coat and a Mercedes doesn't have any problems."

"And as far as you're concerned?" she said.

"Your only problem is that you're stuck in a snowbank. You back out and I'll push."

A moment later, the woman's car was back out in the snow-slicked street.

"Marvelous," she said. "Thank you so much. You said your name was . . . ."

"Corfus. Mike Corfus."

"Beatrice Kane. Can I give you a lift?"

"No, that's all right."

"I insist. Actually, I'd prefer it if someone else drove for a while. I've had just about all I can stand of Moscow winter traffic. Or Moscow, for that matter."

She slid over into the passenger seat, and Corfus got behind the wheel. He had never driven a Mercedes. "Are you a tourist?" he asked.

"In a way. My husband's a furrier here on business. This is his idea of a vacation for the two of us."

"The garden spot of the totalitarian bloc," Corfus said, craning his neck to see above the snarled traffic. "Where are you from?"

"Boston originally. Now I live in Los Angeles."

"I thought Californians all had tans."

"I detest the sun," she said wearily. "How long are we going to be tied up here?"

The steam of cars inched forward.

"Your guess is as good as mine." He checked his watch: 4:45. There was no point in returning to the embassy now.

"Mike, I wonder if I might ask you a favor, as one American to another?" She looked up at him appealingly.

She was a beauty, Corfus thought. A hothouse Stateside

flower, *princessus americanus*, pampered and coddled into a state of perennial youth. "Do you want me to drive you home?"

"I can't tell you how much I'd appreciate it. John and I are staying with some friends of my husband's outside the city. They're very rich, I think, although no one around here will admit to that. Zak works for the Kremlin."

"Zak?"

"My husband's friend. I couldn't begin to pronounce the last name. But I'm sure he's important. The house has twelve bedrooms and an indoor swimming pool. Too bad they're such dreary people. They've all gone off to spend the day at a mink farm somewhere in the hinterlands. I opted to go shopping. What a waste."

"I suppose the government stores are a far cry from Rodeo Drive," Corfus said.

"Never again. If I need clothes while I'm here, I'm going to have them imported. Anyway, if you'd be kind enough to get me out of this swamp, I'll see that you get home comfortably. They took Zak's driver with them, but they ought to be back by now. You can stay for dinner and meet everyone. Oh, please."

Corfus almost laughed out loud. The idea of a CIA agent having dinner at the illegal mansion of a high-level Kremlin employee was too good to resist. "Madam, I see my mission, and will not fail," he said.

"Good," she said softly. She placed her hand on his knee. It was a fine, manicured hand with a huge diamond on its third finger. It rested on his thigh, weightless, for a moment, then began almost imperceptibly to move upward. Astonished, he looked over to her face. The fur of her hat was dappled with melted snow. Beneath it, she smiled at him with waiting copper-colored eyes. "Good."

He edged out of the traffic and onto the Moscow Ring Road, trying to ignore the advances of Mrs. Kane. The boys at Langley would never believe this, he thought giddily. Corfus had always been the lump, the joker, the one girls sought as a "friend," the extra man at dinner. His work at school had been excellent, and he'd distinguished himself sufficiently at Langley to be sent, at the age of twenty-five, to Moscow. But the bald fact of being unattractive to women had bothered him like a sore tooth since high school. The biggest compliment he'd ever received from a girl was that he bore a resemblance to the conductor of the Metropolitan Opera. And now he was sitting next to a gorgeous woman of obvious means who was trying everything short of rape to get at him.

"My husband is a very successful man," she purred. "Unfortunately, he has little time for anything except business." Her free hand caressed his face and trailed down his chest. Corfus sucked in his stomach. "And his mistresses," she added.

"I'm sorry to hear that," he said. His voice came out an octave lower than he'd intended.

"You're so proper," she said, unfastening his belt. "Don't you find me attractive?"

"I find you distracting," he said, laughing excessively.

"The roads are clear now. You won't need all your concentration. Turn right at the crossroads ahead."

He followed her directions onto a narrow uphill road that the snowplows hadn't yet reached. "I don't think—"

"Pull over." She smiled. "I want to give you a present. Come over here."

He slid over on the seat. "I don't believe this," he said under his breath as she undid his fly expertly. He was so hard he was beginning to ache. She stroked him with her slim fingers until the pressure inside him was almost excruciating, then touched him with her lips, teasing, enveloping him, sucking him into her mouth until he was about to burst.

"Oh, God," he said. "I'm sorry . . ." He came in a violent spasm, closing his eyes and seeing color, feeling a pleasure so exquisite that it was nearly pain, and then it *was* pain, something jabbing hotly into his groin, and he cried out, but it sounded so weak, so far away. He was aware that he was losing consciousness fast. All he could focus on were his own clenched hands grasping tufts of fur from the woman's hat. They looked like an animal's paws.

Maria Lozovan opened the passenger door and tossed the plastic hypodermic syringe outside. Some of the Thorazine had seeped into the lining of her sleeve. She examined the spot with annoyance as she got in behind the wheel. Corfus's bulk was sprawled over the front seat. Using both legs, she kicked him onto the floor.

"Disgusting ox," she said.

_____CHAPTER TWENTY-SIX

The woods around the cabin sixty miles outside Moscow were quiet. The house had been a real dacha back in the days when Zharkov's father had it built, with tidy lawns and flower gardens where his mother planted pansies and marigolds. Now the grass lay long and flat beneath the snow, and the cabin itself was crumbled to disrepair.

There was a single light burning in the basement. Zharkov could see its dull yellow glow behind the snowbanks. He entered quickly, pushing back the cobwebs and making his way down the rotting wooden slat stairs. The place stank of urine. At the bottom he stopped, unable to believe what he saw.

Corfus was tied, naked, to a metal chair. His shoulders were covered with small dark circles which, on close inspection, turned out to be burns dusted with gray ash. A pile of lipstick-marked cigarette butts lay strewn on the floor beside him. His head lolled forward. Zharkov raised it carefully. The man's eyes were strapped with adhesive tape. He moaned.

"My God," Zharkov whispered. He released the head with distaste. His hands were wet with sweat and oil, and there was blood on them from Corfus's right ear, which was streaming.

Behind him, he heard the clatter of shoes on the stairs. Maria Lozovan smiled when she saw him. She was carrying a tray with a large bottle of water and a gasoline funnel.

"What have you done?" Zharkov rasped. "When did you bring him?"

"Yesterday," she said crisply. "There was no point in your coming before now. These cases usually take a little time before they're ready to answer questions." She winked, as if she were giving advice on baking. The man's torture seemed to have no effect on her whatever.

"Are you mad?" he asked. His voice was nearly inaudible.

She flushed, setting the tray down with a clatter. "Colonel Zharkov, perhaps you failed to realize the gravity of your crime when you had this person brought here. When we discussed alternatives to handing him over to the authorities, it seemed clear—"

"Not this!" He pointed his arms toward Corfus, his fingers outstretched. "Look at him! This isn't war. Look at what you've done to him! *Pizda*," he swore at her. *"Xer tebe v rot."*

"I did what was necessary," she said coldly, ignoring the insults. "Surely you didn't believe that you'd get him to talk just by asking him. That sort of naiveté has no place in our line of work."

"Our line of work?" Zharkov snapped. "Your line of work is being a Committee whore. Your line of work and mine are not the same." Zharkov's arms were trembling. He picked up the funnel. "What's this? Another one of your 'persuasive' tactics?"

She didn't answer. He grabbed her wrist roughly. "I asked you what this was for." He thrust the funnel near her face.

"It's for water," she said, avoiding his eyes. "Sometimes it's helpful if the prisoner . . ." She glanced at Zharkov. His gray, hooded eyes were wide with rage. He held her wrist so tightly that it shook. She spoke softly and quickly. "It helps if the prisoner is interrogated with a full bladder."

With a sound like a wounded bull, he threw the funnel against the wall.

Maria Lozovan backed away. "Comrade colonel, I assure you there was no other way—"

In a fury, he flung his arm out toward her, cracking the back of his hand against her face. She reeled backward, gasping. "Get out," he said.

She crouched on the floor where she had fallen, her hand held to her face. "You're the one who's mad, not me," she hissed. "If you speak against me, the charges against you will be doubled. You've broken international law and acted without the knowledge of your superiors, and I can prove it. I've got proof that you came to my apartment, Zharkov, and proof of what you wanted, so you can't do a thing to me.''

He picked her up bodily and threw her face down against the stairs. "I told you to get out," he said.

One of her front teeth was chipped. She pulled herself slowly up the stairs, sobbing. When she reached the top, she spat at him.

Zharkov raised the pitcher of water to Corfus's lips. He began to untie the ropes around the prisoner's legs. The skin on them was rubbed raw. "Bitch," he said as he freed one leg. Corfus's toes were blue. Zharkov massaged the foot gently. "Can you feel this?"

Corfus made a sound.

"What?"

"My eyes," he said in Russian.

Zharkov dropped the foot. The man spoke Russian, as he suspected he would. He had understood the exchange between Zharkov and Maria Lozovan. Zharkov forced himself to look at the creature trussed in front of him, naked, disfigured, grotesque. In a pathetic gesture, Corfus dragged his free leg near the other to cover his privates.

It was not supposed to happen this way, Zharkov thought with disgust. If Maria Lozovan had done what she had been told and nothing more, Zharkov would have questioned Corfus, learned what he needed to know, and a few days later Corfus would have wound up in a small Russian hospital, suffering from a severe case of alcoholic delirium. After being sobered up for a few days, he would be expelled by the Russians as *persona non grata*.

Neat, simple, painless.

But not this way. Not this brutal torture of the American spy. And he knew he shared some of the blame. He had expected that Lozovan would do only what she had been told to do. He should have considered that she would jump at the chance to practice the brutal, stupid, mindless sadism she had learned at all her KGB spy schools.

Too late now. Corfus spoke Russian, and he had heard Zharkov's name, and now he could not go back to the Americans under any circumstances.

He was a pawn, and sometimes pawns had to be sacrificed to win the game.

Zharkov saw his hands near the man's leg, poised as if they were still holding the foot. They looked suddenly to him like killer's hands.

"How—" He swallowed. The question had come to him so easily, despite the condition of his subject. He should untie the man first. At least his legs. At least put a blanket around him. At least let him piss into something besides his lap. "How do you know Justin Gilead?" he asked.

"I'm cold."

"His code name is the Grandmaster."

"Please." He pressed his lips together and opened them. Strands of saliva showed. "I don't understand."

"A CIA agent known to you gave you a medallion belonging to the Grandmaster. What do you know about this man?"

"The medallion." His lips almost forced a smile. "Kiss of death." His face contorted. He sobbed.

"What did he . . . Listen to me." He tried to shout down Corfus's uncontrollable weeping, but the American wasn't paying attention. Lozovan had gone too far.

"What are you doing with me?" Corfus screamed. "You're breaking the law of every country in the world! For what? I'm the fucking liaison officer, for Christ's sake. I can't mean anything to you. What do you maniacs want, Zharkov?"

Zharkov slapped him across the face. Corfus's head reeled back. "Tell me about the Grandmaster."

"I don't know him. I never met him. He was dead—"

Zharkov slapped him again. "What do you know about the Grandmaster?"

Corfus sighed, his breath ragged, his shoulders shaking. "Fucking maniacs," he sobbed.

"What did the agent Frank Riesling tell you?"

"Reisling?" Corfus grew still. "The medallion."

"Justin Gilead's medallion," Zharkov said.

"Is that what you killed him for?"

Zharkov slapped him again. A thin stream of blood trickled out the side of Corfus's mouth. "What did Riesling say?"

Corfus was silent. Zharkov took his Tokarev from his shoulder holster and held it to Corfus's temple. "What did he say?" His voice was a whisper.

"He said the Grandmaster was alive."

Zharkov swallowed. "Where?"

"I don't know."

Zharkov pressed the revolver hard against the man's head. Corfus leaned back, his lips blubbering.

"I told you, I don't know! You're going to kill me anyway." Mucus streamed from his nose. He tried to wipe his face on his shoulder. "Cuba. Maybe Cuba."

"Cuba?" Zharkov pulled the gun away. "In the chess tournament?"

Corfus nodded wearily.

Chess! Of course it would be chess. The plan was working. Ivan Kutsenko, the Russian chess master, would be the pawn to draw the white king out. "What is the recognition code?"

"It'll change."

"What is the code?"

"Go fuck yourself."

Zharkov kicked the chair across the room. Corfus landed on his face, his legs splayed out beneath the chair.

"I asked you what the code is!" Zharkov shouted.

"In Havana . . ." A small pool of blood was forming on the floor under Corfus's nose. Zharkov strained to hear him. "In Havana . . . I can't remember."

Zharkov kicked him in the stomach. Corfus retched, skittering along the cement floor with the chair on his back like a crab's shell. Its metal legs clanged when they struck the cinder-block corner.

"The code, Mr. Corfus," Zharkov said quietly.

"The sun. In Havana, the sun is hot." Corfus tried to raise himself up. His elbows, poised in push-up position, trembled violently, then collapsed.

Zharkov stared at the inert form for several minutes, then held the Tokarev out at arm's length and prepared to fire.

"My eyes," Corfus breathed. "My eyes hurt so much."

Zharkov dropped the gun at his side. "It'll be easier if I don't remove the bandage," he said softly.

"I want to see you."

What accounts for the bravery of weak men at the moment of death? Zharkov wondered. Would he, when his time came, be as strong as this young man whose sole reason for dying was that his life was inconvenient for one man?

Zharkov righted the chair and pulled the thick adhesive

tape off Corfus's eyes. The eyelids were raw and blistered. On the floor were two small pads of cotton. Zharkov picked them up and sniffed them. They had been soaked in some sort of solution.

"Warts," Corfus said.

"What?"

"She told me the stuff on the bandage was used to take off warts." He laughed, but tears were running down his face. His eyes, swollen slabs of flesh around two narrow slits, squinted to get a better look at Zharkov. "You know, I never knew you existed until last week."

Zharkov nodded curtly, his jaw clenched.

"Why are you doing this?" Corfus whispered.

Zharkov stared at the man. How could he explain? Who among the mass of mortal men would understand the workings of a world far beyond their ken?

"Because the golden snake must be killed," he said quietly. Something—Corfus's pitiful condition, perhaps, or a vestigial connection with humankind, long discarded—impelled Zharkov to touch the man's savaged face.

Corfus wept silently.

He thinks I'm mad, Zharkov thought. He doesn't understand. He can't.

Zharkov stepped behind the fat man and backed off a few paces. He raised the Tokarev slowly, with the formality of an execution. Corfus swallowed hard. He turned as much as he could manage in this, the hour of his death, to face his killer.

For a moment, their eyes met and locked. Each saw nothing but sadness in the other's. Then, shaking violently, Corfus turned his head away, and Zharkov fired.

CHAPTER TWENTY-SEVEN

He took the body to a ravine in the woods. As a boy, Zharkov had been cautioned against going near it. "In the snow, you could lie there until you died, and no one would find you," his father had said. It was a deep, narrow chasm, damp with rotting leaves in summer, deceptively shallow-looking when filled with winter's snow. He dropped Corfus into it, and the body sank. Only an arm and the sole of Corfus's foot showed.

The snow was coming down heavily; within an hour the body would be completely buried. Zharkov searched for some sticks and threw them on top to conceal the exposed limbs. It looked like a grave. It looked like Poland, he thought, except for the snow. Like Poland, with another grave . . .

Stop it, he told himself, forcing his gaze away from the ditch with its grisly buried treasure. He would have to leave, return to Moscow, allow the snow to do its work, see Katarina. He ached for her.

He walked slowly to his car, through the snowy, dense woods. He never wanted to see the place again. He would sell it.

But the body . . .

And there was Lozovan. She had fled, frightened of Zharkov's unaccustomed anger, but when she returned home and stared in her many mirrors and saw the tooth Zharkov had broken and remembered how he had called her a whore and worse, that fright would turn to anger and to a passion for revenge. He would have to deal with Lozovan.

Another to die.

He veered the car off to the side of the road and skidded to a stop. He pressed the palms of his hands against his face.

Why was this so different? He had killed before. He was a soldier, and in the line of duty he had ordered the massacre of hundreds. With Nichevo, he had set plans in motion that would kill people by the thousands, and he had never felt any remorse. The monks at Rashimpur had fallen beneath the bullets of his patrol like so many dominoes. He had felt nothing then, when the yellow robes of the identical little brown men had burst with red smears. Even when the burned hall of the monastery had quietly filled with his own dead, he had feared only that he might not escape, might not live to fulfill his destiny.

As he had fled down the steep slope of Amne Xachim, he had felt the throbbing humiliation of the coiled snake burned into his flesh, but he had also felt the exhilaration of being alive.

Death was for enemies, not for him.

So why now? Why did he feel so sorrowful for having killed Corfus?

Because, he realized, it had not been Justin Gilead against whose head he had placed the muzzle of his pistol. Corfus was only a pawn. Zharkov needed the white king.

Oh, Katarina. He needed her. He would go to Katarina and use her body to squeeze the filth out of his.

In Moscow, he parked his car five blocks from Katarina's home and walked. She was still awake, dressed in a bathrobe. An ashtray spilling over with cigarette butts sat on the table beside the telephone.

"Where have you been?" she asked frantically. "What's going on?"

"What's happened?" he asked.

"Ostrakov. About a half-hour ago. He came here. What have you done?" Her face was pained. She picked a cigarette from a pack, and as she lit it, she saw her hand tremble.

He nodded. So Lozovan had already contacted Ostrakov, and the KGB general had instantly come looking for Zharkov. He must feel that he was playing a very strong hand, if he had had the nerve to come to Katarina's house looking for the Nichevo chief.

"He knows, Alyosha. He knows everything about us. There was a tape . . ." Her face crumpled. She wiped her eyes with the back of her hand, her fingers still holding the trembling cigarette.

"What tape?" Zharkov said. His voice was flat, expressionless.

"In the bedroom. He showed me." She waved vaguely toward the wall. There was a hole beside Katarina's bed where the forced-air register had been. "The landlord sent a man to replaster the ceiling about a month ago. I had to go to work, so I let him stay here after I left. I never thought . . ."

Zharkov kicked fiercely at the hole. "That swine," he snarled.

"Why are they doing this?" Katarina asked softly. Her eyes were red, and her short hair stuck out in comical peaks. She looked too young to smoke. "Are you in trouble?"

"No. It's Ostrakov who's in trouble. I am finished tolerating his stupidity and his arrogance."

"Are you sure?" she asked.

"Very sure."

"I was frightened," she said softly, "but somehow I knew that. I knew you would be all right."

As he turned to her, she was snuffing out her cigarette. He reached for her and pulled her onto the bed, still conscious of their violated privacy. He gently removed her clothes. The touch of her, her smell, faint and sweet, filled him up and enveloped him. She smelled as she had when he had first met her, those many years ago. So many years . . .

Rashimpur had been destroyed. The monks were dead. Only Justin Gilead had escaped, and Zharkov—alone, weary, the burn throbbing on the skin of his throat—had begun the long journey home. He was not sure of the direction he would take among the endless snow-covered peaks and and bottomless chasms of the highest mountain range on earth, and he hadn't brought many provisions with him.

On the fourth day, he realized that he was hopelessly lost.

On the sixth day, he ran out of food. He tried to forage for something to eat, but there was little he could be certain was edible among the sparse vegetation. He filled his belly with water. And, afterward, with snow. Winter came early in the mountains.

At night, when the cold rush of wind froze him to his bones, he would huddle in his inadequate clothing, shivering until he slept. When he awoke, his toes would be blue and numb. His fingers would barely move.

He forced himself to walk, even though he had no idea where he was. More than once he had cursed and then wept at the sight of a familiar boulder or patch of scrub grass, because he knew he had spent the last of his energy traveling in a circle.

On the twelfth day, he began to hallucinate. Crouching behind a dry bush for a moment's rest, his arms wrapped around himself for warmth, he thought he saw faces. Black-painted faces belonging to men in strange garb. They skulked in the darkness, these phantoms, their eyes glowing occasionally from a ray of moonlight.

But unlike phantoms, he could hear them, too. They were not like the silent monks of Rashimpur who walked like wisps of air. These were men who ran awkwardly like other men, who stood and watched the dying soldier and then hastened away from him in his need.

So real did they appear that Zharkov called out to them for help. He scrambled to his feet and tried to chase after one of the elusive shadows, but they seemed to dodge him deliberately.

"Help me," he screamed. "Can't you see I'll die here?"

He thought he heard a faint laugh.

Exhausted, he leaned against a boulder and slid to the ground, his feet splayed beneath him.

Around him was silence. So he had been alone, after all, he thought. There had never been a horde of painted men. It was cold. He tugged at his cuffs to cover his bare hands. The fabric sprung from his fingers; he was too weak to close them. He rested there, against the rock, until he no longer felt the wind or the cold.

At least it would be an easy death, he told himself.

He closed his eyes and allowed himself to sleep, knowing he would not awaken. But before he slept, he thought once again that he heard the coarse laughter of men behind him.

Zharkov was wrong. He did awaken. He awakened screaming.

He was bound and tied on a table in a filthy pit. Surrounding him were the grease-smeared men of his nightmare delusion. But these men were real. Swarming around him like curious dogs, they poked and prodded Zharkov with dirty hands while they shouted to one another in a strange guttural language he did not understand.

He surmised from the seeping water and mildew on the walls lit by primitive stone oil lamps that he was underground. There were no windows, and the stench of crowded male bodies was oppressive. On the wall opposite was a huge fireplace in which the parts of some large animal were roasting. As the fat dripped, sizzling, from the shanks of meat into the flames, Zharkov realized that he had been aching with hunger for days.

Had these strange men rescued him? Would they feed him? Or was he there for another purpose?

The meat, he thought with a rising panic. Could they be cannibals? Why else would they keep him tied and strapped?

One of the men walked toward him with a knife. Zharkov screamed again. The man looked startled for a moment, then looked at his knife and at Zharkov again, and laughed. The others joined him, showing gaping mouths filled with rotten teeth as the man teased Zharkov with the blade. But when the laughter died down, the man merely cut the ropes binding Zharkov's hands and feet.

Zharkov stared at his wrists for a moment. He was being set free! But for what? He was too weak from hunger to survive outside any longer. He tried to pull himself into a sitting position, but even that was too much effort.

The man who had cut his bonds grunted and gestured with his chin for Zharkov to move. Zharkov shook his head in fatigue and desperation

The man raised his leg and kicked Zharkov off the table.

He landed on a bare earth floor crawling with cockroaches. Slapping them away in disgust, he finally wobbled to his feet. Then one of the men tossed something his way. It was greasy and burning hot and, Zharkov realized after the initial shock of catching it, aromatic. It was a shank of meat.

Zharkov dug into it savagely, tearing off slabs with his teeth, feeling the warm, oily juice pouring down his chin. It was delicious. He thought he could never get enough, until the heavy lump in his stomach churned sickeningly. He turned aside and vomited. The cockroaches covered the spill in a swarm.

After that, he forced himself to eat sparingly. He remained in the stinking underground hole for what seemed like several days, although he never saw sunlight. The men left him alone. They gave him food—always meat—from time to time, but otherwise attempted no communication with him. His questioning gestures were ignored.

In time, his questions stopped. He lived like an animal scratching at the lice on his head, sleeping on the infested floor with the rest of the men. At least, he thought, he was gaining a little weight, and the paralyzing numbness in his limbs had gone.

Then one day a crack of light appeared high overhead. The men stopped their activity at once and looked up, squinting, in silence. The light broadened.

A door. Zharkov's heart pumped wildly. The place he was in was not a pit, after all, but a cellar of some building. But there was no stairway leading to the high door. It seemed to be cut out of the stone wall as an observation point.

Into the bright light of the doorway appeared the silhouette of a small, bent figure. Like an insubstantial shadow, it wavered in the light, turning its small head slowly right and left, as if searching for someone. Then it seemed to find what it wanted, and a thin arm rose and pointed at the mass of men below.

Several hands shoved Zharkov forward. The dark figure in the doorway nodded slowly in assent, then lowered a narrow rope ladder into the pit.

When Zharkov reached the base of the rope, the figure on high nodded again, and he climbed up, leaving the stink and squalor of the black-painted men behind.

The individual at the top of the ladder was an Asian of indeterminate sex. The head was shaved and the face expressionless, but the eyes shone with what Zharkov could only describe as malice. Although he could not understand why, the whole bearing of the little creature unnerved him.

Zharkov was led first to a large, steaming bath chamber where he washed gratefully and dressed in robes that had been laid out for him. Then the androgynous guide took him as far as the entrance to a large, dark room.

Even from outside, Zharkov could smell the strong incense. The guide gestured for him to enter, but for some reason he hesitated. Something frightening was inside that room. Zharkov didn't know how he knew that, but he was certain. Something frightening and deadly and almost unbearably compelling.

He felt beads of sweat form on his brow. "What's in there?" he asked, although he didn't expect an answer.

The guide answered in flawless Russian. "The goddess Varja awaits. She has sent for you."

"Why?" Zharkov asked.

The guide's eyes again smiled malevolently. "She owns you." Even the voice of the small, bent Asian was without gender.

Zharkov contained his annoyance. "What about the men? In the cellar."

"She owns them, too," the soft voice said.

Zharkov suppressed a shudder, then went inside. Those steps into the woman's chamber changed his life forever.

He slept after their lovemaking. When he awoke, Varja was gone. The androgynous gnome stood near him.

"Where is she?" Zharkov snapped.

"The goddess Varja commands you elsewhere."

"Commands?" He stared imperiously at the little guide.

"Commands," the Asian repeated with assurance, then gestured toward the door.

Zharkov followed. He was taken to another room. It was smaller and painted stark white. There were no furnishings in it except for a large white dais in the shape of a cube. On top of the cube, covered by many layers of white silk, rested a long object.

He waited alone in the room for some time before Varja entered. She was wearing a long gown of black brocade studded with rubies, like a thousand red eyes that saw into his soul. Zharkov trembled in her presence. As before, the very sight of her mesmerized him and infused in him a sense of utter, unquestioning obedience.

She held out her hand. Every finger on it was covered with precious rings, and an enormous ruby bound her wrist. Zharkov fell to one knee in front of her and kissed it.

"You have pleased me, my prince," she said. "As reward, I have called you here to show you a gift that I will give you in years to come."

"Whatever you have chosen to give me, goddess, whenever you choose for me to receive it, I will treasure."

She smiled. "You will most certainly treasure this," she said. "It will be of great help to you later, and pleasure beyond counting. It will be yours to use as you please, and destroy when you choose."

He rose. "But I could never destroy a gift from you."

"Not now, perhaps, but someday. When you are truly my disciple, when the suffering of men and the weakness of your spirit and the need of your flesh no longer concern you, you will destroy my gift. Then will you return to me, pure, strong, complete. Then will you be my mate for all the ages of evil to come."

She made a quick gesture, and the sexless gnome appeared carrying an embroidered footstool. The Asian placed the stool beside the dais, bowed once, and departed.

He climbed to the top of the cube and removed the thick silk wrapper. Beneath it was a girl, no more than fourteen or fifteen years old, tall and dark-haired and beautiful.

And dead.

"Her name is Duma. I have saved her for you," Varja whispered. "Enter her."

Zharkov felt a knot in his stomach. The girl's skin was cold as ice.

"Do not disobey me!" the goddess shrieked, her eyes flashing.

He turned back to the body. Swallowing the lump of nausea in his throat, he spread the girl's stiff legs and opened the robe he wore.

His organ was shriveled. Surely the goddess asked too much. Surely he could never . . .

At first he thought the low hiss in the room was his imagination. But when he turned toward Varja, he understood that in this place of magic, anything was possible.

Black smoke was issuing from the goddess's fingers like serpents' tails. Her eyes were rolled back in her skull, exposing only the whites, and from her mouth poured strange sounds as ancient as the magic mountains themselves.

And as Zharkov breathed in the acrid smoke and his ears filled with the droning, savage sounds of Varja's words, his mind raced backward, back beyond memory, before his own birth, through empty centuries to the time of his ancestors. What he saw in his half-conscious state were only impressions, brief pictures: a tree with a bark of iron . . . a saber, flashing with inner power . . . Black Hats, the mark of a magic long buried . . . an old man, a severed hand, a golden snake . . .

"No!" Zharkov screamed.

A golden snake bearing death, death for ages, death forever.

"The Wearer of the Blue Hat has returned," Varja warned.

Zharkov clutched his forehead. It felt as if a dagger had just pierced it. A dagger . . . or a bite from a golden snake.

"He became the snake and destroyed our kind, but I have kept our power alive," the goddess said. "This time, he must die. He must die . . . he must die . . . he must die . . . This time you failed to kill him. The next time, you will not fail . . ."

Her voice receded in his mind, replaced by the thunder of his own obsession. The golden snake! Like Jehovah destroying the kingdom of Edom, the golden snake had obliterated the sacred cult of the Black Hats and the unbounded power they possessed. Only if he killed the snake would his own kind be permitted to thrive again. Thrive and rule, with Zharkov himself, the Wearer of the Black Hat, to lead them . . .

His flesh quickened. He kissed the belly of the dead girl beneath him, and her cold, lifeless body filled him with aching desire. His hardness throbbed for her. With one deep thrust he entered her, groaning in twisted pleasure. The room was warming, Zharkov realized. And not just from the heat of his own loins, but from the flesh beneath him as well. What was once a cold slab of meat was emanating heat and lust and the sweet fragrance of a woman.

The body was coming to life.

"Take her, Prince of Death," Varja said, her thousand red eyes glowing. "Take her with your body now. Later you will love her. And later still, you will kill her. For me."

"For you, my goddess," Zharkov said, closing his eyes to the exquisite pleasure of the girl's awakening limbs. She rolled her hips to his rhythm, raising her knees to let him penetrate her more deeply. Her hands, once still, clawed at his back like a cat's. She lifted her breasts to give him suck. Then he galloped her, and she cried low in her throat, pressing him to her. At the moment when he burst, frenzied and hard as iron inside her tight wetness, the girl's eyes fluttered open.

They were blank eyes, neither worldly nor naive. There was nothing behind them, no feeling, no fear, no joy, no remembrance. They looked past Zharkov into space.

The smoke cleared away in an instant. Varja spoke. "You

have awakened from life-in-death to aid him who now controls you."

"Yes, my goddess," Duma said. She still did not look at Zharkov.

"You will be taught everything you need to function in the world of men. When you are prepared, you will be sent to him."

"I understand."

"Do you remember any of your life before the moment of your awakening?"

"No, goddess."

"Whom do you serve?"

"I serve the great goddess Varja and those she selects to carry out my destiny."

Varja smiled. "Then it begins," she said with satisfaction. "Our time has come again at last."

On the dais, Duma looked into Zharkov's eyes for the first time. He thought he saw something like disappointment register in them fleetingly, but the reaction vanished as quickly as it came, if it had come at all. The girl's face was as blank as a mannequin's.

CHAPTER TWENTY-EIGHT

At seven-thirty in the morning, Zharkov went to Sergei Ostrakov's office in full dress uniform. He waited in an anteroom until Ostrakov arrived minutes later, smiling.

"My dear comrade, come in," he said, taking Zharkov's arm. Zharkov brushed his hand away.

"Why did you place Katarina Velanova's apartment under surveillance?" he asked bluntly.

"Alyosha." The general spread his arms and grinned broadly. "It will all be explained to you soon. But I can tell you that my orders originated from the highest sources. The highest, you understand."

"And did these high sources order you to break into Velanova's home in the middle of the night, too?"

Ostrakov made a disapproving noise with his mouth. "You are so dramatic, Alyosha. There was no breaking in. Comrade Velanova invited us inside most graciously. She is a charming woman, your friend. You ought to marry her."

"My private life is no concern of yours."

Ostrakov shrugged. "How much you have changed, Alyosha. I'm only suggesting that one could do worse than to marry a beautiful woman who is also a loyal Party member. A very loyal member."

"What you're suggesting is that she's working for you against me. It won't work, Ostrakov. I've used the same ploy myself."

"Alyosha! I meant nothing of the kind." He smiled mirthlessly. "Perhaps your position has made you suspicious."

"Bugging Katarina's apartment may have had something to do with that. But, of course, what should one expect from thugs?"

Ostrakov's face reddened with anger. "Nichevo is an insulated pocket in the security system. It makes its own rules, runs its own projects. Through the years, its director—first your father, now you—has become nearly inviolate. Above the law, as it were. Nichevo could become a dangerous organization."

"I'm not here to discuss Nichevo. What did you want with me last night?"

"Comrade, I came to bring you good news. Great news. The hour was late, but I was sure my message would have more than made up for the small inconvenience. Unfortunately, you were nowhere to be found. Playing tricks on sweet Katarina already, eh?" With his hands, he formed the exaggerated shape of a woman in the air. Zharkov had to control an impulse to hit the man.

"You know perfectly well where I was," he said, "since the whore who works for you reported all to you. What did you want?"

His voice was growing colder, and his lizard-lidded gray eyes locked on Ostrakov's, forcing the KGB official to look away.

"The premier wishes to see you," Ostrakov said.

"Kadar?"

"The *vozhd*," Ostrakov whispered. "He wants to see you. Now."

The *vozhd*, or great leader, had had no time for Zharkov since his inauguration three months before. The only time Zharkov had even met the man was at a formal reception during the inaugural ceremonies. Kadar had been polite—part of his new image, which was already being cultivated by a staff of underlings for the selling of the premier to the world—but the leader's ill feeling toward Zharkov had been evident even then.

Konstantin Kadar had been head of the KGB since 1955, under Premiers Malenkov, Bulganin, Khrushchev, Kosygin, Brezhnev, and Andropov. Under his direction, the Soviet secret service had become the largest and most powerful police organization in the world. Kadar could, almost at will, execute nearly any person in the world without reprisal, and frequently took that option. The political prisoners at Lubyanka—some of whom could not even recall their "crimes" against the state, all of whom had been tried secretly—referred to Kadar as Little Josef because of his Stalinesque methods. Others had labeled him more succinctly "the Butcher."

Everyone in Russia was answerable to Kadar, except the premier and Nichevo, which had been formed as an independent organization before Kadar's rise to power. Through the years, Kadar had used every device available to obliterate Nichevo, or at least bring it under the control of the KGB. He had gone to each of the six premiers he served and warned him against Nichevo and its potential to overthrow the government, the possibility that it was a hub of foreign espionage activity, the foolishness of allowing an intellectual like Vassily Zharkov to run such an autonomous operation as Nichevo, and the consummate unwisdom of replacing Zharkov with his own son after his death. But none of the leaders had taken his advice. Not one.

What at last became clear to Kadar, what only a handful of people in the Soviet Union and absolutely no one outside it knew, was that Nichevo—so secret, so special to those in ultimate power—was the personal tool of the premier himself.

"The czar's army," Kadar had called Nichevo during a violent quarrel with Zharkov's father. It was not far from the truth. Nichevo originated under Stalin, and Stalin was nothing if not a czar.

After the execution of Premier Aleksei Rykov in 1938, it was evident that in a country with Russia's centuries-old tradition of violence, even the head of state was not safe from government factions vying for power. V. M. Molotov nominally held the office of premier after Rykov, but the real power was already in the hands of Stalin. Stalin was not about to permit the execution of another head of state, particularly if the head was his. He formed Nichevo, drawing it like a cloak around him, then fabricated the myth that the organization was of no importance to him.

The general populace of the intelligence community scoffed at Nichevo from the beginning—at its thugs, its childish projects, even its joking name. The brighter ones wondered aloud why a brilliant and acclaimed political scientist like Vassily Zharkov would toy with such a ridiculous organization, and so another myth was fabricated: Zharkov became Stalin's "nephew." When they heard this new piece of manufactured information, even the bright ones laughed. To make it legitimate, Zharkov was married off to one of Stalin's nieces.

And then came the purges.

First, Stalin wiped out the landowners and dissidents. Next came his enemies. They fell by the thousands, and among them were some of the highest members of government. The NKVD—the old name for the KGB before it accrued its almost total power—was the instrument used to carry out the murders. Then, because the leaders of the NKVD knew too much about his crimes, Stalin ordered them removed, too.

The order went to Vassily Zharkov, head of Nichevo, who carried it out ruthlessly, implacably, quietly.

Nichevo had come of age, and it was untouchable. The KGB had no control over it. Nichevo belonged to the *vozhd* alone and answered only to him.

Now it belonged to Konstantin Kadar who hated it.

And very shortly, Zharkov would give him even more reason to hate it.

"The *vozhd* wants to see you. Immediately," Ostrakov was saying. He had a broad smile on his face.

Zharkov nodded. "When I am through with him," he said, "I will have more to say to you."

"We shall see," Ostrakov said.

"Yes, we shall," said Zharkov.

Zharkov waited in the Kremlin for three hours before he was taken to the premier's opulent private library. It was a small room, once used as the personal retreat of Czar Nicholas I.

Konstantin Kadar, seated behind an intricately carved rosewood desk, dominated the room. He was a tall man, slim but well muscled for his sixty-four years. His head, elegant and oval-shaped, looked more German than Russian, with its fringe of silver-white hair, its long nose and tight lips. It was not the face of a policeman, Zharkov thought, except for the eyes. Behind their old-fashioned metal-framed glasses, Kadar's eyes were as flat and dead as a shark's.

"Sit down, Colonel Zharkov." When he spoke, nothing moved but his lips. He waited until Zharkov obeyed, not moving a muscle. Zharkov had the feeling of being in the presence of a huge stone idol.

When Zharkov was seated, Kadar arranged some papers into a neat pile and laid them carefully on the desk in front of him. "They call you a prince. Do you know that?"

"No, sir," Zharkov said.

"A prince," Kadar repeated softly, leafing through the papers in front of him. "A scholar, a soldier, a scientist. A chess prodigy at the age of eight. The son of the illustrious Vassily Zharkov." Kadar looked up as he spoke the name, his thin lips wrapping around his teeth. "A chess master at ten. Accepted into the university at fifteen. Honors in senior levels in engineering and physics. Recruited into the intelligence service at seventeen. I remember you, Colonel. You didn't finish the program."

"I was removed to be enrolled at the Institute of International Relations."

"It was unnecessary. We would have used you in the KGB. You were a bright boy. You would have made an adequate analyst."

Exactly, Zharkov thought. Kadar would have liked nothing better than to bury Vassily Zharkov's son in an intelligence analyst's job for the rest of his life. Vassily had permitted the boy to train for two of the three years required of the KGB intelligence program—enough time to learn the basics of tradecraft, without being slotted into a specialty.

"But why should I go at all?" young Zharkov had protested to his father. "Kadar hates you. He'll make my life miserable."

"Because you must learn everything. For Nichevo, you must know everything. Two years of personal unhappiness is not too high a price to pay," the elder Zharkov said. "And he will not dare to make your life too miserable."

Nichevo would be his destiny; both Zharkov and his father had known that from the beginning. There was only one place for a man like Alexander Zharkov in the Soviet Union, and that was at the head of Nichevo. Not the KGB, with its hundreds of thousands of agents enmired in a morass of bureaucracy so deep that most of them spent their time either duplicating the efforts of others or wastefully watching one another. Not the Kremlin, where the gamesmanship of power politics counted above ability. Certainly not in science or law or economics, where only part of Zharkov's mind would be put to use, and that part for projects not of his choosing. Only two endeavors could tax a mind like his to its limits: Nichevo and chess.

And Nichevo *was* chess. Small, independent, and deadly, there was no room for mistakes in Nichevo, just as there was no room for mistakes in the game. The wrong man at the head of Nichevo could destroy it, and there was only one right man, with his genius and careful education and his father's formidable power behind him. For Zharkov, it was always Nichevo, only Nichevo.

"Graduated from the institute at twenty-one," Kadar continued, sounding bored. "Enlisted in the army. Attained rank of full colonel"—he set down the papers—"when you seized Nichevo at age thirty-five."

"I was appointed to the position by Premier Brezhnev," Zharkov said flatly.

"Because your father left no records."

You ought to know, Zharkov said to himself. Kadar had personally raided Vassily Zharkov's office within an hour after Zharkov was taken to the hospital. He found nothing.

"My father was very careful," Zharkov said. "Nichevo is, after all, a secret organization."

Kadar clasped his hands together, extending his index fingers, and rested his chin on them. For the first time, the shark's eyes registered a response, and Zharkov thought with some amusement that the word "records" must be the most frightening in the world for tyrants. It must haunt their dreams, the thought that someone, somewhere, was in possession of facts and history that could be used to tell the world what kind of men they were.

"It is now *my* secret organization," Kadar said. "It exists for me. You are aware of that, aren't you?"

Zharkov nodded. "Under certain circumstances."

"Under *any* circumstances. I own Nichevo. I own you."

He waited, and Zharkov said, "Do you also own the microphone that was planted illegally in my friend's apartment?"

For an instant, Kadar seemed shocked with Zharkov's rudeness. The shark's eyes flashed briefly in anger, then appeared to cloud over again as Kadar said, "Few things are illegal when one is trying to uncover a traitor."

"Traitor?" Zharkov asked.

"For instance, the evidence does not indicate that you have a weakness for young men. So why did you wish to see this Mr. Corfus alone?"

"For information," Zharkov said.

"And that was not an isolated instance of your seeking out Americans," Kadar continued as if Zharkov had not spoken.

"What are you talking about, Premier?"

From the bottom of his pile of papers, Kadar took a photograph. It was from the Samarkand Hotel, showing the gold coiled snake medallion dangling from Frank Riesling's shattered hand. "Look familiar?" Kadar asked.

"It once belonged to an agent," Zharkov said.

"An American agent, Colonel. One you have met several times."

"We have met twice as adults. By coincidence."

"And is the mark on your neck a coincidence as well?"

Ostrakov, Zharkov thought. Lozovan had told all she knew about Corfus to Ostrakov, and Ostrakov had taken it, and his filthy tape recordings from Katarina's apartment, and all he knew about Zharkov and had laid them all on the premier's desk. Kadar must now feel that he had a noose to put around Zharkov's throat if he wished. The Nichevo head restrained a smile. He wondered how far Kadar would go.

"I think the Tribunal would be most interested to see the emblem you carry. It is perhaps the same as this Justin Gilead's?"

Zharkov was silent. Kadar dangled a green folder between his fingers, toying with it like a boy about to tear the legs off a fly. "It seems you have a lot in common with Mr. Gilead. You even played chess together as children. A very early association. Perhaps your father arranged it, Colonel. Since he conveniently destroyed Nichevo's records before his death, one has no way of knowing just how extensive are your family's relationships with the CIA. Perhaps that is why you told General Ostrakov to let the chess player Kutsenko go when it is known he plans to defect?"

Zharkov was still silent, and finally Kadar snapped, "Have you nothing to say?"

"I have a great deal to say, Premier. I thought you would prefer my waiting until you ended this charade."

"Charade?" Kadar repeated incredulously.

"Yes. Charade," Zharkov said. "You know I'm no traitor." He rose from his seat and stood behind the chair, his hands gripping the top of the elaborately carved oak back.

Kadar fixed his dead, indifferent eyes on Zharkov's face. "Explain yourself, Comrade Colonel. I hope for your sake that it is a good explanation."

"Certainly," Zharkov said. "First of all, I have always known how you hated Nichevo. My father warned me about you."

"No agency must be above the state. That is what I hated," Kadar said. He stopped as Zharkov raised a hand.

"What you mean is that no agency must be above you, now that you are premier," Zharkov said. "Well, Nichevo is. And will continue to be."

Kadar's lips tightened. "I suppose I should be impressed by this display of authority."

"It is not a display," Zharkov said simply. "Only fact."

Kadar half rose out of his chair. "I could press a button now on my desk and you would be shot where you stand. Without hesitation or question."

Zharkov picked a piece of lint off his jacket. "No man is invulnerable to a stray bullet, Premier Kadar. Not even you."

Kadar flushed. "Are you saying that my personal guard has been infiltrated by Nichevo?"

"I am saying that Nichevo will go on. As it always has."

Zharkov saw Kadar hesitate. The thought that his palace guard might not be totally loyal to him had evidently never crossed his mind before. He had not been premier for long.

"Say what you have to say," Kadar said finally.

"Thank you. First of all, my father was a very great man. You hated him too much to realize that. It was your loss."

"He was an intellectual. He dabbled in the affairs that some of us *work* at, day after day, year after year, for our country," Kadar said.

"Did you ever wonder how this 'dabbler' managed to survive through six different premiers?" Zharkov asked. He answered his own question. "Because it suited him that you and others should regard him as a dabbler. He told me once that few things are more powerful than being regularly under-estimated by your enemies. You proved the wisdom of that."

"I? How?"

"Many years ago, my father told me to watch out for you.

He said that one day you would be premier and you would try to destroy Nichevo and me. He told me what to do about it."

"And what was that?" Kadar said, with a small bemused smile.

"You thought my father left no records." He took a moment to savor the quick twinge of alarm that registered in the premier's eyes. "Actually, all the Nichevo records remain intact. But they were not meant for you to find."

"Such as? What kind of records?"

Zharkov shrugged. "Which officials have money secretly hidden in foreign bank accounts. Which ones have mistresses and where they keep them. Who likes to sleep with young boys. Whose drunken automobile accidents killed innocent pedestrians but were covered up by the police. Did you ever wonder why my father always seemed to prevail over you when you sought to bring him up short in meetings of the Committee? Because he never walked into that room without having enough votes in his pocket to ensure victory. That was another of his lessons: 'Never fight unless you are sure to win.' "

"These records," Kadar said nervously. "Where are they?"

"They are not in Katarina Velanova's apartment," Zharkov said sarcastically.

"I could arrange to get their location from you."

"Perhaps. And by that time, the records would be gone. They would be in someone else's hands. Perhaps someone not nearly so discreet as I am. As my father was before me."

Kadar wheeled in his chair, pressing the tips of his fingers together, and looked out the inch-thick window that protected him from the capital city of the nation he ruled. "And the file on me?" he asked, his back to Zharkov.

"It is the largest of all."

The premier slapped his hands on the arms of his chair. "What is it you want?"

"I told Ostrakov to leave Kutsenko alone and to make sure his wife is reinstated in her post at the hospital. I want that done. Kutsenko is just a pawn in a bigger game."

"What game?"

"I saw to it that Dr. Lena Kutsenko went to Helsinki and made contact with that CIA agent, Frank Riesling. The one that Ostrakov's gorillas shot up like some Chicago massacre. I ordered the extra patrols at the Finnish border to make sure that Kutsenko could not get out along Riesling's regular escape route. The chess player plans to defect during the world challenge chess match in Havana three months from now.''

''And you will help him to defect, I suppose,'' the premier said dryly.

Zharkov smiled. ''To a point. Havana will be swarming with CIA agents.''

''And?''

''And the CIA will be blamed for the assassination of Fidel Castro.''

Kadar spun around in his chair. The shark eyes had come to life.

''Don't sputter, Comrade Premier,'' Zharkov said. ''I know it has been a plan of the KGB for the last three years to eliminate Castro when it becomes possible to do so. Cuba costs us too much, and it causes entirely too much trouble in the world. It is unsettling, and Castro is unstable. Nichevo is going to do for you what your own men were incapable of doing.''

Kadar rested his chin on his fist. His glance darted around the ceiling in thought. ''Why did you kidnap Corfus?''

''I needed to know the password by which the CIA contact in Havana will identify himself to Kutsenko. He is the man on whom we will blame the killing of Castro.''

''You could not get that information and let Corfus live?''

''He was already dying when I saw him. Lozovan saw to that. The American did not deserve the kind of death she arranged. So I gave him an easier way to die.''

Kadar looked down at the papers on his desk. ''And this Justin Gilead. Who is he?''

''He was an agent of the CIA, I thought I killed him in Poland four years ago, but I have learned he is still alive. I don't know where.''

''Is he important? The Committee knows next to nothing about him.''

''The Committee has never known anything that requires thought,'' Zharkov said. He saw Kadar bristle. ''Important? Justin Gilead is perhaps the most dangerous man on earth.''

''Come, now,'' Kadar said with a forced urbanity. ''No man is so powerful as that.''

Zharkov fixed him with a look that sent a shiver up the

premier's neck. "There are things even the premier of the Soviet Union cannot know about men. Or power," he said finally.

Neither man spoke for several minutes as Kadar made a show of riffling through the papers on his desk. Zharkov was the first to break the silence. "He will be in Havana."

"Gilead? Is he a chess player, too?"

Zharkov nodded. "A grandmaster. *The* Grandmaster."

He rose, unasked.

"You have a great deal of confidence, Comrade Colonel," Kadar said. "No one else would have spoken to me the way you did."

"And remained alive," Zharkov finished.

Kadar attempted a smile. "Times change."

"Nichevo does not change."

The premier rose. "We have never had this meeting," he said. "I know nothing of what Nichevo is doing, in Cuba or elsewhere."

"That is correct," Zharkov said, and prepared to leave. He stopped near the doorway. "One more thing. Did you authorize Ostrakov to put a microphone in Comrade Velanova's apartment?"

Kadar made a dismissive gesture. "Of course not. Ostrakov's games do not concern me. Who is this woman to you?"

"A woman," Zharkov said. "If Ostrakov was acting on his own, I will have to repay him for that particular 'game.' "

"You are a chess player," Kadar said, the dead eyes lighting with a hint of amusement. "What will be the nature of your countermove?"

Zharkov deliberated for a moment, then said, "I will trade queens," before walking out.

Zharkov's instructions to Katarina were brief: "Leave the office now. Buy some men's clothes that fit you and wait for me at my apartment."

"What is going on?"

"I'll explain it all later," he said as he hung up the telephone in the street-corner booth.

He drove to one of the old districts of Moscow, a neighborhood with a heavy concentration of Arabs, where young Russian women with painted faces huddled from the cold in doorways, occasionally calling out to passersby. Prostitution was officially illegal and severely punished, but as long as the activity remained confined to certain areas, the law managed to look the other way.

From another street-corner telephone, he called his office. Katarina had already left, and he spoke to one of his assistants. "Velanova has been terminated," he said. "She will be transferred for work on the Trans-Siberian railway. Prepare the necessary documents at once and put them in her file."

He heard the man stammer. "To Siberia, Colonel?"

"Do what I tell you."

The young women were lined up in the identical doorways of identical tumbledown buildings. With their bare knees showing below their heavy winter coats, the girls looked like worn, uncared-for dolls on a toymaker's shelf.

"Looking for some fun, mister?" one of them called. She was squat and fat with yellow strawlike hair. Zharkov shook his head and continued to move down the line of doorways.

"You," he said, pointing to a tall, thin woman with a cold-reddened nose. "Take off your hat."

"That'll be fifty kopeks," a fat blonde called from another doorway, and two other women laughed. The tall girl stepped forward warily and removed the brown knit turban she wore. Her hair was dark and cut short like Katarina's.

"You'll do." He motioned her to follow him down the street.

"He picked Galina," one of the girls whispered, giggling. "Maybe he's short of cash."

In the fading light, Zharkov examined the woman's face more carefully. "How old are you?"

"Twenty." She looked ten years older. "Do you want to go to my apartment?"

"I have a car." He led her to the Chaika. She fingered the leather seats as if they were made of gold. "You must be very rich," she said admiringly, as she got into the passenger seat.

He pressed the button that locked all four windows and doors. "I am an official of the Committee for State Security," he said, unbuttoning his overcoat to show his uniform. "Hand over your papers."

She threw herself against the door, banging futilely on the closed windows.

"Be still," he snapped. "No one's going to hurt you. Where are your papers?"

From her pocket she produced a grubby plastic wallet, but even as she handed it to him, she was pleading, "Please. Don't send me to prison. I won't do it anymore."

"All I want is for you to take a train ride," Zharkov said.

The girl's face froze. "Where to?"

"The north. For a real job."

The girl's face twisted in bewilderment for a moment, then sank into blankness. "Siberia," she said. "You're sending me to Siberia."

In the warmth of the car, Zharkov could smell the odor of her fear.

"You'll have handsome wages. If you save your money, when you come back you'll have enough to make yourself beautiful, perhaps buy a nice apartment and a car."

"You're crazy," she said. "Let me out of here."

He took her wrist and held it firmly. "If I accuse you of

prostitution, you'll go to prison. If I accuse you of picking my pocket, the term will be even longer. Suppose I say you tried to steal my car. You will never get out of prison. You will do as I say.''

The girl looked up at him miserably. ''Why are you doing this to me?'' she squeaked, trying to hold back the tears. ''There were so many others.''

Because you don't matter, Zharkov thought. Because no one will miss you, no one will look for you, no one will care when you disappear off the face of the earth. He started the car. As he drove, he took a packet from his coat and handed it to her. ''These are your new papers,'' he said.

She looked at them suspiciously. ''Katarina Velanova. Who's she?''

''She is you, from now on,'' Zharkov said.

''I don't like this. I want to get out.''

They were stopped for a traffic light and Zharkov turned and stared at her icily. ''Don't make me kill you,'' he said.

She lowered her eyes. ''You people can do anything.''

Zharkov pulled into the parking lot near the massive railway station. The train carrying the Siberian work volunteers was on a distant track. There were three cars, two for men and one for women. There were rows of wooden benches inside, but most of the passengers were crammed onto the floor. They were rough-looking people, each with a personal reason for volunteering to work in the hostile Siberian climate under primitive conditions. Some were going for the high wages, but an equal number were traveling to escape the law. They went because virtually no questions were asked of the volunteers.

In the women's car, the passengers sat sullenly, jockeying for space on the seats and floor. The eyes of the women turned silently toward the young woman as she and Zharkov approached.

''I'm not going in there,'' the young whore told Zharkov.

He jerked her arm forward.

''This is some kind of fucking concentration camp!'' She swung at him. ''I'm not going, I tell you. You're pulling some kind of trick.''

A uniformed soldier came over. His blue shoulder boards indicated that he was a sergeant. ''Anything wrong, Colonel?'' he asked politely.

"This person has been reassigned to work on the railway," Zharkov said.

"I'll look after her personally, Comrade Colonel," the sergeant said, saluting. He shoved Galina roughly into the train car. The other women cursed and complained loudly as the girl tumbled over them.

"You're a pig!" Galina screamed through the open car door at Zharkov.

"Shut up," the sergeant said lazily. He was a young man, but he had obviously heard last-minute pleas as desperate as Galina's before. The women cackled.

When he turned away from the train, Zharkov noticed four people standing far across the platform, watching him. It was common for the worst criminals, who were fleeing to Siberia, to wait until the final few minutes before jumping onto the train, just in case there was a last-minute police search of the railroad cars for someone wanted for a crime.

His attention was caught by one woman. She was probably forty, but she looked sixty. Her face was ravaged by a long badly healed knife scar, and her complexion was blotched, red, and alcoholic.

But what he noticed was the back of her right hand as she reached up to push back a tendril of dirty-looking hair that had spilled from under her black cap onto her face.

A word was tattooed across her knuckles. Zharkov recognized the mark as the kind usually done in prison to prisoners by other prisoners. Usually the tattoo spelled out the crime the person had committed. It was the hardened criminal's stupid, self-destructive way of thumbing his nose at society.

As Zharkov walked toward the group, the train's engines rumbled to life and the four people started running toward the railroad cars. Zharkov intercepted the woman and grabbed her by the right arm. Even through her coat, her arm felt muscularly stringy. He looked at her hand. The word tattooed across the back of her hand was "Murderer."

"Going to Siberia?" Zharkov said.

"Yes."

"I suppose you will find the climate there much more comfortable than here," he said.

"I just want to leave Moscow," she said.

"Before the police catch you?"

"I—" she started, but Zharkov interrupted her.

"Don't worry. Come over here. There is a favor I want you to do."

A few moments later, he released the woman, who ran toward the train. She just got into the women's car before the army sergeant closed the doors.

As he walked back to the parking lot, Zharkov thought it was a game of pawns after all. Every chess game was a game of pawns, and no game was ever decided until many pawns had fallen.

Katarina was waiting in his apartment. She was wearing the men's clothes Zharkov had told her to buy, and she looked like a slender, hairless youth.

"You make a handsome boy," Zharkov said with a smile.

"Alyosha, I've been sick with worry all day. What's going on?"

"In the car," he said. "We're in a hurry."

Driving away, he told her about his meeting with Kadar. She asked, "What does that mean, to trade queens?"

"It means that your life is vulnerable right now to Ostrakov's hoodlums," Zharkov said. "That's why I'm getting you out of here."

"Where will I go?"

"Officially, you've gone to Siberia. Didn't you always want to be a railway worker?" He tried smiling at her, but her face was glum and unhappy. "Anyway, here are your new papers," he said. He handed her the cheap plastic packet he had taken from Galina, the prostitute. Katarina did not even look at them, but stuck them in her pocket.

After a moment she asked, "You're not really sending me to Siberia, are you?"

Zharkov smiled. "No. You're going to Cuba."

"But why?"

"Because you'll be safe there." He was unable to keep the exasperation from his voice.

"And you?"

"I will be safe," Zharkov said. "Kadar cannot move against me without first finding my records, and he will never find them."

"How can you be so sure? He can tear this country apart. He can find them."

"He can't find them," Zharkov insisted.

"Why not?" She was nearly shouting. "Alyosha—"

"He can't find them because they don't exist," Zharkov said.

Katarina's eyes registered surprise, then amusement, then admiration.

"It was my father's advice: 'What you never wish found, commit only to your own memory.' " He pulled into a small side street and stopped the car. He scanned the street and said, "Good, here's my man."

A tall, thin man with an uncombed scraggly beard was approaching the car. "That is Felix," Zharkov told Katarina. "He will take you to Primorsk, and the two of you will get on a trawler. At sea, you'll transfer to another ship, which will take you to Cuba." At her worried look, he said, "Don't fret. You'll be perfectly safe. Felix is Nichevo, and he's been in Cuba many times."

Katarina's pertness had dissolved. She looked down at her hands. "Why does it have to be this way?" she said, choked.

He touched her face. "There is no answer that will make this easier. But things will not always be this way. When I have kept my promise to Varja, you will be at my side."

"When will I see you again?" she asked as she opened the passenger door of the car.

"Soon. When I come to Cuba. Go now. There isn't much time."

She threw her arms around him and kissed him until he pushed her away. Then she stepped from the car, closed the door quietly, and walked off with Felix toward a waiting car down the street.

Maria Lozovan had not wasted any time. Her broken front tooth had already been repaired when she let Zharkov into her apartment. She was dressed in fashionable Western-style pants and a thin silk blouse through which he could see her bare breasts.

She looked at him triumphantly and said, "I trust you've come to apologize."

"I've come to do what the *vozhd* ordered me to do," Zharkov said.

"Good," she said with satisfaction. "It is good for a man like you to crawl a little. It reminds you that you are human, after all."

"Not here, though," Zharkov said.

She arched a penciled eyebrow. "Where, then?"

"Ostrakov's. I want a witness to my abject apology and my admission of wrongdoing," Zharkov said.

He waited until she got a fur coat, then led her to his car. A few minutes later, they were speeding toward the outskirts of Moscow.

"This isn't the way to Ostrakov's," she said, an edge of panic creeping into her voice.

"No, it isn't," Zharkov said, and when she turned to look at him questioningly, he punched her jaw viciously and she slumped unconscious against the passenger door.

Slow down.

The big Chaika almost skidded on the snow-slicked road. Ahead, barely visible through the storm, stood the cabin and, beyond it, the deep woods where Corfus's body lay in the ravine.

Maria Lozovan had regained consciousness. She cringed in terror as Zharkov dragged her roughly from the car and pulled her through the snow toward the ravine. He tossed her into the snow, then took a long branch to brush snow away from Corfus's already frozen body. "That's your work, bitch," he snarled.

"What are we doing here? Where is Ostrakov?"

"I thought this would be cozier with just the two of us," Zharkov said. "As to what we're doing, we're just taking a quiet stroll in the country. No acid on the eyelids, no cigarette burns to mar your well-oiled skin."

"I have always been loyal," she protested huskily. Tears formed in her eyes as she rose to her knees.

"To yourself, Maria." He shrugged. "Unfortunately, that is not enough. You betrayed me to Ostrakov. Later, if it is in your interest, you will betray us both to the Americans."

"I wouldn't . . ."

"Who can foretell the future?" Zharkov said smoothly. "Particularly when you have none."

She pressed her hands together in front of her, as if she were in church, a supplicant to God.

"Why are you doing this, Zharkov? Why?"

He liked looking at her, kneeling there before him that way. "You wouldn't understand," he said.

"I will. I will."

And because it amused him, he said, "All right. Forty-one years ago, two boys were born. They shared the same birthdate, but they were to face very different destinies."

She stared at him. Her face was expressionless, but she nodded to urge him to continue.

"Because they were not simply boys. Each was the latest in a line of ancestors that goes back centuries. One was to become the Wearer of the Blue Hat; the other was to be the Wearer of the Black Hat. Each was to serve a different god. And they would battle, as all those who came before them have battled through the centuries. The winner will possess the world."

He stopped and waited. Finally, Maria Lozovan said, "Who? Who are these two?"

"You know only one. I am the Wearer of the Black Hat, and the world will belong to me. When the Grandmaster is dead."

She was weeping again, and suddenly her life no longer amused him.

"Look down there," he said, pointing toward the ravine. "Look at your handiwork."

She turned and stared blankly down at Corfus's corpse. Beside her, Zharkov drew the Tokarev from his coat and waited. He waited to see her eyes. And when she looked up at him finally and saw the barrel of the weapon inches from her face, and a flash of terror and panic glazed the copper-colored irises, Zharkov had what he wanted.

Feeling the satisfaction of justice, he fired. Her forehead blew away, spattering two nearby trees with red.

He kicked her body into the ravine atop the American's and brushed snow over both corpses. He turned and left without a backward glance.

Sergei Ostrakov's voice was bluff and hearty as it sounded over the telephone answering machine in Zharkov's apartment.

"Alyosha, this is Sergei. I don't know, but I think there might be some misunderstanding between us. We've got to get together to clear it up. Call me as soon as you get in."

And then, with a little trace of desperation, he added, "No matter how late it is."

He was tired, and he thought of ignoring the call until the next day, but finally he called Ostrakov's home and told the KGB officer's aide that Ostrakov should come right over.

When Ostrakov arrived, Zharkov was sitting at the chessboard in the dining room.

"Alyosha, how are you?" he began heartily.

Zharkov turned in his chair. "You have spoken to the *vozhd?*" he asked.

Ostrakov nodded. "He wanted to be sure that you and I—"

Zharkov interrupted him brusquely. "Have you brought the tapes you made in Velanova's apartment?"

"Yes," Ostrakov said. There was a faint quaver in his voice.

"Put them on the dining table."

Ostrakov took a small paper bag from the leather briefcase he was carrying and placed it on the table. "They're in there. All of them. And no copies were made. None. None at all."

"Ostrakov, if you ever try that with me again, you will be a dead man," Zharkov said.

The KGB officer stood silently near the table.

"Is that clear?"

Ostrakov was silent for a moment, then nodded.

"Maria Lozovan is dead," Zharkov said.

"I guessed she would be."

"She knew too much about Corfus's disappearance," Zharkov said.

Ostrakov nodded. "She couldn't be trusted with that kind of secret," he agreed.

"Anyone else who might talk about it will also be killed," Zharkov said.

"No one else knows," Ostrakov said.

"Except you," Zharkov said. "Think about that for a while." He turned away from the KGB officer and looked again at the chessboard. "You'll forgive me for not offering you a drink, but I'm busy," he said in dismissal.

A few moments later, he heard the door to his apartment open. Then he heard a hiss from Ostrakov. "It's simple, isn't it? Simple for all you smart people. I don't know how you got away with it this time, Zharkov. But you won't always."

"We'll see," Zharkov said without looking up.

"Just one last thing, Colonel," Ostrakov said. "You might think you were very smart in trying to get Velanova out of town."

Zharkov paused. He could feel himself holding his breath.

"But she's dead, too."

Zharkov turned to stare at Ostrakov.

There was a flicker of frightened triumph in the KGB man's eyes. "You didn't know that, did you? Well, she's dead. They found her body tonight alongside the railroad tracks. Someone stabbed her."

"Who did it?" Zharkov asked.

"Who knows? With a train full of criminals, anyone could have," Ostrakov said. "You shouldn't have sent her to Siberia."

Zharkov concentrated on looking sorrowful. "I thought she'd be safe," he said.

"You thought wrong." Ostrakov turned triumphantly and walked out the door.

Zharkov turned back to the chessboard where he stared at the pieces, arranged in the play of Justin Gilead's last game.

It had all worked out for the best, he thought. His position was stronger than ever. Katarina was on her way to safety. The day would come, perhaps sooner than he could even expect, when he would lead this giant nation. And more, perhaps. Varja's power was unlimited. He could set his sights beyond Russia, beyond the East, if he wished.

Oh, yes. Beyond the East.

But first there was the Grandmaster to finish off. That was next.

Before he went to bed that night, Zharkov made three telephone calls. The next day there was a brief item in *Izvestia*:

Boris Godofsky has been forced by illness to withdraw from the Russian chess team, which will meet an American team in a challenge match in Havana, Cuba, in sixty days.

His place will be taken by Army Colonel Alexander Zharkov. Zharkov is considered one of the Soviet Union's finest players, and this match will mark his return to top-level competition after an absence of many years.

The Russian team will be headed by Ivan Kutsenko, world chess champion.

Zharkov read the news item in his office and smiled. The game had begun.

Book Five

THE GAME

_____CHAPTER THIRTY

Andrew Starcher felt like a very old man, lying in the same bed he had slept in as a child. Except for the funereal array of flowers sent by family friends—most of whom had never met him and had no idea what he'd done with his sixty-six years on earth—the room was exactly as it had been the day Starcher left for boarding school. The cheerful blue and white wallpaper, the crisp white curtains, the tiny Hepplewhite writing desk sitting beneath the Remington painting depicting a scene from a buffalo hunt.

Below, at the bottom of the curving walnut staircase, the bell was ringing again. More visitors. In a house with sixteen permanent family residents, many of whom were involved with the government in one quiet way or another, Starcher and his convalescence were only a minor facet in the day-to-day activities, a fact for which he was immensely grateful. For a man who had lived almost the whole of his life in secrecy, it was abhorrent to lie in this child's room in pajamas, on display for anyone to see. He despised the cheerful intrusions of the well-wishers who cared even less than he did about the physical condition of an old man come home to die.

As soon as he was able, he'd bribed the gardener to fit a bolt onto the bedroom door so that he could lock out the visitors, but his sister had gone on the warpath. Finally, she agreed to keep people off the second floor until he was well enough to move back into his own house.

It was the insignificant victory of an old man turned crotchety with infirmity.

He lay on the bed day after endless day, working crossword puzzles and reading magazines and wishing, now, that even the unwanted visitors would reappear for a moment or two.

To amuse himself, he had copies of *Izvestia* delivered daily, and he read carefully the growing crescendo of Russian warnings to the American imperialists that Cuba was not to be tampered with. What was it all about? Starcher wondered. He read *The Washington Post* and *The New York Times* every day, too, but there were no reports of any unusual American activity concerning Cuba.

The more he thought about it, the more convinced he was that the Russians were planning something, some kind of a swindle. He thought for a moment about calling Corfus in Moscow, but he realized immediately that such an act was ridiculous. Corfus might not even be assigned to Moscow anymore, and if he was, he certainly wouldn't tell Starcher anything over an open transatlantic telephone line.

In the fourth week of his convalescence, he read another bitter Russian attack complaining about "growing evidence of American provocation" against Cuba, and he realized that, without his work, he was a useless thing.

He got out of bed, dressed, stared at himself in the mirror for several minutes, decided something was missing, and stole a family car from the driveway and smoked a cigar clandestinely as he drove away from the house. It was a deep and smoky Dutch Masters. It made him feel better than the gallons of medication the doctors had poured into him.

And he decided not to go back to that child's room again.

One of the guards at the entrance to the Langley complex was an old-timer.

"Well, well, Mr. Starcher. Long time no see."

Starcher puffed his cigar between his teeth. "Just back for a visit, I'm afraid."

The guard smiled sympathetically. "I'm due to retire next year myself. The time sure goes fast." Starcher waved and started to drive through the gate, but the guard stopped him. "I've got to ask you who you're coming to see, sir."

"Oh . . . of course." He was an outsider now. No special privileges. Langley was no longer home, any more than his family's house was. "Harry Kael," he said, "director of security."

"Director of operations now. Is he expecting you?"

"No . . . will you buzz him?" An appointment to see Kael, of all people. The time sure did go fast.

Kael was a little fatter, a little balder, but in general the same fast-talking overgrown college boy he'd always been.

"Starcher, you old fart," he said cheerfully. "Didn't expect to find you lurking around here for another six months. What'd you do, fire all your doctors? And put out that cigar. It's not good for you."

"At my age, all the things that are good for you are disgusting," Starcher said. He gestured around the big office. "So when did this all happen?"

"Couple of months. Just about when you got sick. Going pretty well."

"Need any help?"

Kael smiled and shook his head. There was pity in his eyes.

"I didn't think so. How's Moscow?" Starcher asked.

"Still not applying for statehood, if that's what you mean. New guy we sent over to replace you's got his hands full. Rand. You know Rand? Hungary, 1956."

Starcher nodded. "He'll be all right. And Corfus is a good number two."

Kael mumbled something and lit a cigarette.

"What's the matter? Anything wrong with Corfus?"

"Well . . ." He inhaled deeply. "Forget it, Andy. You don't need to know this kind of shit anymore."

"If it's about the man I left in charge of my job, I want to know about it. What's happened to Corfus?"

Kael hesitated for a long moment. "All right," he said at last. "Corfus is missing. Has been since before you left Moscow. The Russian police are looking for him. That's the official line."

"What's the unofficial line?"

"Classified."

"Well, maybe you'd better declassify it to me."

"You know I can't do that, Andy. Even for you."

Starcher rose angrily. "Don't give me that crap. If Corfus has been missing since I was in that Russian hospital, then he never got the information about Cuba to this Rand fellow."

Kael choked on his cigarette smoke. "What about Cuba?"

"Maybe that's classified," Starcher said, and immediately

felt childish. "All right. Remember Frank Riesling, the agent who was getting some Soviet bigwigs out through Finland?"

"The one who got blown away in the hotel? How can I forget? The Reds called it a mugging. If that was—"

Starcher waved him down. "Never mind about that. The point is, Corfus figured out who Riesling was trying to get out of Moscow that day. We weren't sure, but it's very possible that the man was Ivan Kutsenko."

Kael looked blank.

"Kutsenko," Starcher repeated, searching for a reaction. "The world chess champion."

"Oh," Kael said finally, and stubbed out his cigarette.

" 'Oh?' That's all?"

"What's the big deal about a chess player?"

"Jesus Christ," Starcher sighed. "Don't you guys follow anything but Monday night football? In the Soviet bloc countries, chess is the most prestigious peacetime confrontation there is. It's a very big deal. And the best chess player in the world might want to come over."

Kael said nothing.

"If Kutsenko were a ballet dancer, you'd be jumping at the chance," Starcher said grumpily.

"It's not that . . . How do you know he wants to come over?"

"Long story. But before he died, Riesling said something that we think was a recognition code. 'In Havana, the sun is hot, but it's good for the sugar crop.' The World Open Chess Tournament's going to be held in Havana. I think Kutsenko'll be waiting for us. An easy pickup, and a big slap in the face for the Russians." He puffed mightily on his cigar. It was good to be in the thick of things again. "So what do you think?"

"Screw Kutsenko. I'm not even going to take it up with the director."

"Why not?"

"Unreliable source."

"Who? Me? Riesling? Corfus?"

"Corfus," Kael said quietly. "See, the official line about him being missing may not be accurate. Hell, Andy, let's just leave it at that, okay?"

"No," Starcher said. "Don't do this to me, Harry. I was your senior officer when you came here, and I was Corfus's immediate superior. If something about Corfus is suspect, I have the right to know about it. Hell, I might have started it.''

"All right, all right," Kael said. "If it's serious, you'll end up being involved, anyway. The fact of the matter is, the Russians have been acting funny about Cuba."

"I know. I've been reading *Izvestia*," Starcher said.

"Naturally, I should have known. Anyway, the Russians have ships all around Cuba. Not doing anything. Just sitting there in the water, waiting."

"For what?" Starcher asked. "We haven't done a thing in Cuba since 1962 besides take in refugees they didn't want."

Kael said, "You really don't know what's going on, do you?"

"Of course not," Starcher said. "I've been sick. Remember?"

Kael hesitated as if weighing some alternatives. Finally, he said, "Okay. Your replacement, Rand, he got a phone call from somebody saying that the Russians know we've got something big planned in Cuba. And that they got the information from Corfus."

"Corfus? This has got to be some kind of a trick," Starcher said.

"Well, maybe. Ever hear of somebody named Lars Saarinen?" He lit another cigarette, coughed, and put it out in an overfilled ashtray that was still smoldering.

"The name sounds familiar, but—"

"In connection with Frank Riesling," Kael said.

"Oh, of course. The ship captain. He used to run Riesling in and out of Russia. Why?"

Kael took off his glasses, wiped them on a rumpled Kleenex lying amid the clutter on his desk, and replaced them. "Well, it seems that your man Corfus pulled some strings with the Finns to get Saarinen an exit visa to the States."

"Saarinen isn't a Soviet. He's a Finnish national. A Finn doesn't need special consideration to get to America," Starcher said.

"He does if he's in jail," Kael said. "Saarinen was picked up for smuggling. Corfus apparently got him off scot-free."

"Well, so what?" Starcher said. "Saarinen helped us. Why shouldn't we help him?"

"How simple you make it all sound," Kael said. "Saarinen's in Miami now. We've got him under surveillance."

"What the hell for?"

"Because he sailed his freaking boat across the Atlantic," Kael snapped. "Suppose Corfus was a double and working for the Reds. Then maybe this goddamned Finnish fucking pirate is a Russian spook, too. He's in Miami, dammit. He could be in Cuba in a couple of hours if he wanted to be."

"That's a lot of ifs," Starcher said. "If Corfus is a spy, if Saarinen's part of his network . . . if, if, if . . . and you still don't know what the hell the Russians are doing in Cuba."

"Suppose there was something funny about Riesling, too," Kael said.

"Such as? The man was murdered by the KGB in front of a hundred witnesses," Starcher said.

"Exactly. What was Riesling doing in Moscow?"

Starcher began to speak, but Kael stopped him.

"Riesling did small stuff, right? Scientists, writers, you say maybe a chess player. Nothing big. No hardware, no documents."

"No, nothing big. Only people," Starcher said, his lips tight.

"You can can the humanistic slobber," Kael said irritably. "The fact is he wasn't doing anything really big, but the Russkies blew him away as if he'd just pissed on Lenin's tomb."

"So what do you think happened?"

"Maybe the KGB was afraid that Riesling had found something out, like the fact that Corfus was a double. Maybe he was going to tell somebody, and maybe they shot him up so he couldn't."

"That still doesn't say what happened to Corfus," Starcher said.

"He's probably living in some villa right now on the Crimean, spilling his guts about CIA operations."

Starcher shook his head. "Everybody's a Red, I guess. Corfus, Saarinen, Riesling. Me, too?"

"Andy, you know I don't think that, but I think maybe you turned your operation into the freaking British Secret Service with everybody on their honor and not a check on any one of them. You remember? You even started using that chess player who wasn't with us. What was his name, Gilead?"

"He was a Communist agent, too?" Starcher asked.

Kael shrugged. "Maybe. I don't think you'll like this, but we're running a tighter ship in Moscow now, Andy."

Starcher stared at him for long seconds. "Are you going to tell the director about the possibility of Kutsenko wanting to defect?" he asked.

"No. We've discussed Cuba. We're staying the hell away from there. Let the Russians bluster and then wind up with egg on their faces when nothing happens. We had a meeting yesterday. We were almost going to stop the American chess team from playing there, but what the hell trouble can chess players cause?"

Oh, you fool, Starcher thought. He sat for a moment, quietly angry. Corfus was missing. Kutsenko wanted to defect. The head of Nichevo had joined the Russian chess team.

The Soviets were definitely planning something in Cuba. And these idiots, Kael chief among them, were just sitting still, doing nothing. The fools. Didn't they know? Didn't they care?

But who was Andrew Starcher, anyway, he thought bitterly. He could see the answer in Kael's patronizing glances toward him. Just an old retired CIA man, sick, probably senile, his head filled with old cold war plots. Kael would have a big laugh with his buddies in the coffee shop when he told them about Crazy Andy and all his worries.

He stood up stiffly and said, "Thanks for the time, Harry. Sorry to bother you."

"No bother," Kael said. "I'll give you a call sometime when I get some free time. Maybe we can grab lunch when you're feeling better."

"I'm feeling fine now, Harry," Starcher said.

The younger man nodded and seemed ready to offer Starcher his hand, but the white-haired Virginian turned away and walked from the office.

He drove back to the house, smuggled his box of cigars into his room, and sat there smoking until well past dark.

Something big, something important was going to happen in Cuba, and the CIA didn't know about it and didn't care to know about it. What to do? he asked himself. What to do? The question hung in the darkness as he looked out over the rolling Virginia hillside.

The genes of two centuries of Starchers who were American patriots, who had fought in every one of the nation's wars, who had given their lives and their honor to their country, answered him.

He would have to do something about it himself. And maybe, just maybe, he would not have to do it alone.

He opened the top drawer of the small dresser and looked inside it. In the back, he found, wrapped in a dirty piece of paper, the medallion of the coiled snake.

He put it in his jacket pocket and left the room, the box of cigars clutched tightly under his arm.

CHAPTER THIRTY-ONE

New York's Seventy-ninth Street Boat Basin was just as Starcher remembered it, a mishmash of boats, dilapidated and grand, jammed together beneath the hot sun of an unusually warm November day. There was activity on the docks, pretty girls in shorts, children, a lot of haggard-looking executive types snarling at the attendants as if they were office boys. Starcher walked past them to the dilapidated blue and white houseboat where a stumpy old woman, her hair now completely white, sat reading a newspaper.

"Dr. Tauber?" he called from the pier.

She looked up, adjusted her glasses, rose.

"I'm Andrew Starcher. We met several years ago—"

"I know who you are," she growled. "And I'd appreciate it if you'd get the hell out of my body bag. What gives you jokers the right—"

"I don't work for the government anymore," he said tersely.

She sat back down in her tattered plastic lawn chair with an elaborate rustle of paper. "I'm not surprised," she grumbled. "You're as old as the frigging hills."

Starcher smiled. "So are you. So you must know how tired I get standing out here. I've come a long way. I'd appreciate a cup of coffee and a chair."

Dr. Tauber pretended for a moment not to hear, then set her newspaper under a rock with a great sigh of disgust. "You Rhett Butler types never know when enough is enough, do you? Well, get aboard. I won't have it on my conscience that some old fool keeled over from a bum heart in front of my boat. But no coffee.'' She poured him a martini from a pitcher on the deck alongside her feet. "You coming from Virginia?'' Tauber asked. Starcher nodded, the glass to his lips.

"What for?'' She raised a finger directly in front of his eyes. "And don't tell me you're a tourist. You don't have the eyes of a tourist.''

"I'm here to find Justin Gilead,'' he said.

She snatched the glass from him. "That's what I thought. Now you can kindly scuttle your butt out of here.''

"Do you know where he is?''

"Maybe I do and maybe I don't. But you characters aren't going to get your grubby hands on him again. Not this time. Not after what you did.''

Starcher felt his heart racing. "Then he is alive,'' he said.

"I didn't say that.''

"Listen to me.'' He clasped both her hands in his own. "I have to talk to him. I've got to see him.''

"No.'' She yanked her hands away. Her face was stony and bitter. "Now you listen to me, mister, and listen good. You're not talking to him; you're not taking him anywhere, understand? He *can't* talk to you. He can't go anywhere, thanks to you.''

"I—I don't understand.''

"Oh, no? I would have thought you understood better than anybody. You did it to him.''

"Did what? Dr. Tauber, you've got to believe me. Justin Gilead was lost in Poland in 1980. He's officially dead. There are pictures to prove it.''

"You people think you can turn the whole world upside down and inside out, don't you?''

"*We* people didn't do it. We had documented facts from the Soviet government.''

"And you took their word for it,'' she said. "Nobody bothered to look for himself. Nobody bothered to find out if he was dead or not.''

"That's what I'm doing now,'' Starcher pleaded. "I'm retired, but I'm here looking for him. If he's alive . . .''

She burst out laughing, harsh and loud. "Alive? *Alive?*'' She slapped her hand on his back and pushed him. "I'll show you how alive he is.''

She opened a door with a key and shoved Starcher inside.

The room was nearly pitch dark, and it took Starcher a moment to see at all. The portholes were covered with nailed boards. There was a small cot inside, no other furnishings. In the far corner crouched a figure, emaciated, withered, mute, his pale eyes luminous in their sockets.

It was Justin Gilead.

"Maybe you'd like to give him your regards from the CIA," Dr. Tauber said bitterly, closing the door behind Starcher.

Starcher stood in the darkness for what seemed like an eternity, staring at the remains of what had once been a man of great promise. He was a dull, frightened creature now, his thin arms encircling his knees, his hair long and untidy. Gilead's fingernails, Starcher noticed, were as long as a woman's. His face, once almost too beautiful, was drawn and etched with deep lines around the slack mouth.

For a brief, crazy moment, Starcher wished that Riesling had never spoken his last words. It would have spared him this sight of the dead man who hadn't quite died, who had lived on the fringes of death for four years.

"I'm sorry," he said hoarsely. He realized from Gilead's expression that the words hadn't registered. "Oh, my God, I'm sorry. I'm sorry you didn't die." Starcher blew out a gust of air and sat down on the small cot. He felt warm tears streaming down his face. He tried to think of something to say, but his brain would produce no words.

He stared at the ceiling, felt the blackness around him. Oddly, the darkness seemed to impart a perverse kind of comfort. Perhaps Justin Gilead had found that, too. Starcher hoped so. Whatever had happened in Poland, it had been enough to drive Gilead into this dark hole. He hoped that the young man had found some comfort here.

He sat in silence for a long time, staring at the figure in the corner, as still as a wood carving.

No words came. He had traveled all this distance to find Justin Gilead, hoping that Riesling was right, that he was still alive, and now the only thought in his mind was that death would have been more merciful. Anything would have been better than seeing this silent, mad stranger who occupied the shell of the body that had once been the Grandmaster.

How could he apologize? What could he say? What words

would give enough comfort to make up to Justin Gilead for the loss of his sanity? He had been a young man when Starcher last saw him, and now there was only . . . only this *thing* left.

"I'm sorry, Justin," he finally said. "For both of us." He got up and walked around the room. Occasionally, a child's shriek from outdoors broke the silence; otherwise there was only the dull clunking of Starcher's footfalls on the wooden floor and the droning of his voice, talking to a man who wasn't listening.

"I didn't really come to bother you," he apologized. "I thought I'd come here and recruit you all over again. You and me, off on a spy mission to Cuba, to save the world from Zharkov and his men." He laughed bitterly. "I should have known it was just an old man's dream. I'm sorry I wasted your time."

He turned toward the door, then stopped and pulled the dirty brown paper from his jacket. "I nearly forgot. Here's something that belongs to you." He held it out at arm's length. Justin made no move to take it. Starcher unwrapped the package gingerly and spilled the contents into Justin's lap. For the first time, Justin's head moved.

He stared at the glittering thing nestled in the space between his chest and his indrawn legs. Finally, his thin arms moving as awkwardly as the wings of a newly hatched bird, he picked it up and put the chain around his neck.

"Well, that's something, anyhow," Starcher said. "Good luck to you, Justin." He closed the door behind him gently and walked off the boat, nodding silently to Dr. Tauber as he passed.

Justin Gilead coughed. For a moment, the dim half-light that had surrounded him for as long as he could remember exploded in a frenzy of color and motion. His breath came in violent, ragged gasps. Sweat poured off him, trembling at the tips of his shaking fingers. His eyes opened wide in horror. The pain was horrible, a searing, powerful force that hollowed his body and set his senses on fire.

Hail to thee, O Wearer of the Blue Hat

He was floating. He was somewhere long ago, in a faraway mountain lake, guided by a strong hand to a sacred mountain, and in his soul surged the power of a thousand generations, calling to him amid the sweet scent of almonds.

Hail to Thee

O Patanjali, the pain of this body is too great

Wearer of the Blue Hat

I am not worthy

Hail to thee

Not worthy

Not worthy

And past was present and present was future and what had been was what now was and would always be. The circle was forming again, and Justin screamed with the agony of it.

"Help me," he whispered.

Hail to thee . . .

"Help me, Tagore!"

I warned you that you, above all others, would suffer, came a voice from deep within him. *That, among all men, only you would find no solace in this world.*

"I am not the one you sought!" Justin cried out. "I have failed again and again. I have destroyed myself and everyone who was dear to me. I have even killed you, my father." He sobbed. "I am finished. I cannot live in this place. Let me die. Let me go to the fires of hell, but let me die now."

You are not finished. You have not yet begun, the voice said. *Follow him who awakens you, for it is he who shows you the path toward your destiny.*

"I have no destiny," Justin screamed. "I have lost my youth. I have lost my health, my strength, my will. I cannot do anything now."

You have waited, O Patanjali. You have waited for the moment when you could face again the Prince of Death, for the moment when you alone could save the world from his evil.

"I can save no one," Justin said weakly. "It is too late for me."

It is not too late. And then the voice came again, Tagore's voice coming to him through the thick film of death and despair:

It is not too late. It is time.

It is time.

It is time.

*   *   *

Justin became aware that his face was pressed to the wood floor. His fingernails, broken and bloody, left long streaks where they had scrabbled in Justin's pain.

Had he spoken? Or was this just another madness in a life filled with insanity?

He sat up. The darkness beckoned to him. Like a woman, it caressed him in its soft, forgetful embrace.

Come back, Justin. You're safe here. Pick up your terrors, your old friends, and come back . . .

But he could never go back. The scent of almonds was too strong, and the medallion, burning like a sun against his chest, filled him with light.

Starcher turned when he heard the old woman scream.

"Justin! Come back! Stop him, somebody. He doesn't know what he's doing!"

Starcher's face contorted in pity at the sight of Justin, withered to skin and bone, walking stiff-legged and bent up the pier. Some men abandoned their work on their boats to stop him.

"Starcher," he shouted, his voice thin and weak.

Starcher ran toward him. "Leave him alone," he said, disentangling Justin from strange hands that held him. Dr. Tauber came running forward, but Starcher silenced her with a glance.

"What is it?" Starcher asked.

Gilead struggled to speak. "Take me with you." Painfully he pulled himself up to his full height. "You owe me a favor, remember?" His voice was soft, almost inaudible. "I told you long ago I would ask for it."

Starcher looked the man over. From what he could see, Gilead wouldn't last out the week. But a promise was a promise. "Zharkov's going to Cuba to play chess," Starcher said.

A look of profound relief passed over Justin's face. "So am I."

Dr. Tauber could restrain herself no longer. She blurted out, "But why, Justin? It's been so long."

"Yes. Why?" echoed Starcher.

Justin Gilead raised his head slowly. His face was far older than its years, the skin ravaged and gray, the thick black hair now matted and long and streaked with white at the temples. But the clear, cold ice eyes held Starcher's with the same inexplicable authority they had possessed a decade and a half ago.

"Because it is time," he said.

CHAPTER THIRTY-TWO

Starcher drove southward until the megalithic skyline of New York City was well behind him before he spoke.

"We'll get you to a doctor."

The dirty, half-conscious passenger next to him lifted his head weakly. "No doctor," Justin said.

"Don't be ridiculous. You need—"

"No doctor. You can get me ready."

Starcher took out a cigar. He smiled as he crackled the cellophane wrapper between his fingers. "For what?"

"For Cuba."

"Now? In the condition you're in?" Starcher lit the cigar. "You've got to be joking."

Justin leaned back in the seat. His eyes closed slowly, then opened again. "Stop."

"What's the matter?" Starcher asked, pulling off the road in a skid.

"I need water."

"Oh, Jesus," Starcher sighed. "Look, just hold still, all right? I'll pull over at a gas station somewhere."

Justin wrapped his bony hand around Starcher's. "Here," he said quietly. He got out of the car and walked stiffly over a debris-covered embankment toward a river.

Starcher puffed angrily on his cigar, thinking that Justin would come back even filthier than he already was. He checked his watch. It was 3:15. He found a station on the radio that played big band music from the forties. Those were the days. Before the infirmities of age and guilt. Before the Grandmaster came into his life.

Justin Gilead had come back to Starcher, the son he had fed to the dogs. He had come back to show Starcher what he had done to him. He came back dead, in order to rot in Starcher's arms. It all ends badly, he thought. There's no good way to get old, any more than there's a good way to die. But at least Kael and the other idiots at Langley didn't know of Justin, couldn't arrest him as a Communist agent. "Ruby" was playing on the radio, and Starcher closed his eyes and remembered Jennifer Jones.

A horn blew, and a wave of thunder seemed to roll over Starcher. He awoke, terrified, to see one sixteen-wheeler passing another and blaring its horn in salute. "Ruby" was no longer playing. He checked his watch. It was nearly 3:30. Justin was nowhere near.

He got out of the car and walked hastily toward the river. The embankment was a disgusting sight, with broken bottles and scraps of paper and fly-covered food everywhere. The river itself was a slick, filthy mess, its Plasticene surface broken only by a few soda cans bobbing in the foamy scum near the water's edge. Justin was nowhere in sight.

"Gilead!" he called. "Justin!" He walked downstream, picking his way through the trash and the trees with their blackened, soot-heavy leaves. "Justin."

There was no answer. It was 3:36.

Some children trying to set fire to some rags in a bottle whispered excitedly to one another when he approached.

"Did you see another man come by here?" Starcher asked. "Or in the water? Did you see anyone swimming?"

The boys quickly pulled down their pants, waved their exposed cheeks, and darted off, giggling. One waited long enough to say. "A man went in. But he didn't come out. I watched."

It was 3:41.

Starcher felt his heart thumping. "Justin!" he shouted. But he knew it was no use shouting anymore. The man had come back to life only to drown before the day's end. Starcher climbed, wheezing, back to the car, put on his hazard lights, and waited for the police.

From the top of the embankment, he saw something emerge

from the river. "Jesus Christ," he muttered and clambered out of the car.

It was 3:47.

"Where in hell were you?" he shouted, stumbling toward Gilead.

"I was underwater."

"For half a fucking hour?"

"Was it so long?" Justin smiled. "I missed it."

Starcher gaped. "You didn't stay under all that time." He turned away, then turned back to face Justin. "Did you?"

Justin took a deep breath. His eyes were sparkling.

"What are you so happy about? I almost had heart failure looking for you, you crazy middle-aged fool."

"I thought it was all gone," Justin said quietly.

"What was? What are you talking about?"

Justin looked at him for a moment as if appraising the old man. Finally he picked up two rocks the size of baseballs and held one in each hand, weighing them, flexing his fingers around them.

"Come on, let's get back to the car," Starcher said. "We've still got a long . . . ."

But Justin's eyes were turned inward. His breathing was deep and fast. The rocks trembled in his hands.

"Justin . . ."

He brought his hands together. The motion was so swift that a sound like a thunderclap issued from them. The cars on the roadway slowed down. One swerved, grazed a guardrail, and lumbered on.

As Justin released his hands, a fine spray of dust shot upward into the air like a fountain.

Starcher's mouth hung open in astonishment.

"That's what I have inside me," Justin said.

Starcher tossed away his long-extinguished cigar. He felt as if he were seeing Justin Gilead for the first time. "You did stay underwater all that time."

"I did."

Starcher sighed and got into the car. "You're not anything like the rest of us, are you?"

Justin looked over, his eyes weary and sad. "No," he said.

CHAPTER THIRTY-THREE

There were seven weeks till the chess match in Havana.

Justin's transformation began immediately. He exercised from five in the morning until noon, ate ravenously, then ran. Within two weeks, he increased his distance from a quarter-mile to fifteen miles. In the evenings, he lifted weights in Starcher's basement, devoured the books in Starcher's library, and played chess until the small hours of the morning. He slept little, and was up at five the next morning.

Starcher often watched him from the kitchen window. The house was small, in contrast to his family's other holdings, sparsely furnished and with the vaguely shabby air of a bachelor's quarters. He had never thought of it as anything but a place to sleep at night when he worked at Langley, but now, with Justin's presence, things changed. The strange young man who shared Starcher's days was inexplicably coming to life again, like a dead plant suddenly blossoming through its withered brown husk. Justin was still bone thin, still uncommunicative and alien, but the bones were being strapped over with hard flesh, and something inside him seemed to be expanding, releasing, energizing.

What is he? Starcher wondered for the thousandth time. The Company had missed the opportunity of a lifetime in not training Gilead while he was still young. Even now, at forty-one, after four full years of privation and suffering, he was astonishing. The hollowed sockets around his joints had begun to fill out, and the wasted appearance of his face had changed, focused, intensified.

Maybe this is enough, Starcher thought. A man who had been ready to give in to whatever strange demons possessed him was healthy again. This had been Starcher's gift to the young man who had once come, earnest and gifted, to him, and whom he had sent to be slaughtered in Poland.

But there was more. Justin Gilead was more of a man than most, but somehow also less. He had no concept of casual conversation. He evinced no desire to leave the small house near Langley to seek more stimulating company. Yet he could crush rocks in his bare hands. Starcher had seen him swim underwater for thirty minutes without coming up for air. He always slept out of doors, on a path of gravel. He could catch butterflies in his hands. When he walked, he made no sound.

He was, Starcher imagined, like a sleeping giant now awake, his body aged inexorably into middle age, but with some extraordinary spirit within him just beginning to kindle to youthful life.

And when that spark was in full blaze, Starcher knew, its light would be dazzling.

Starcher got the impression that Gilead was merely tolerating him, putting up with him as a means to an end. That end was Zharkov. Justin seemed to give his total attention to the retired CIA officer only when they talked about the trip to Cuba.

Gilead's air was cool, as if Starcher and not he were the houseguest, and during their conversations Starcher usually wound up displaying his annoyance.

"Have you figured out how I'm getting to Cuba?" Justin asked matter-of-factly, as he did every morning.

"Have you figured out how you're getting on the American chess team?" Starcher countered.

"Don't worry about that. I'll get on the team."

"Why aren't you doing anything about it now?" Starcher asked.

"You know why. If I do anything too soon, your friends at Langley will get wind of it and find out that I'm still alive. Since they've decided that everybody who ever lived is a Russian spy, they'd be coming after me with an armed posse. I've got to do it at the last minute. How will I get into Cuba?"

"I'll get you in. I'm more concerned with how you're going to get out."

"After I do what I've gone there to do, I don't really care if I get out or not," Justin said.

"Well, I do," Starcher snapped. Justin shrugged and left the room to return to his exercise.

The next morning, he would reappear and ask, "Have you figured out how I'm getting into Cuba?"

One day, Starcher handed Justin a list of four names. "These are the American players who are making the trip," he said.

Gilead looked at them and nodded. "Needham," he said aloud. "That's good. He owes me a favor. I'll be going in his place. Did you figure out how I'm getting into Cuba?"

"You know," Starcher said, "I've been reading a book. I don't know anything about chess, but I've been reading about the Fischer-Spassky match."

"A wonderful match," Gilead said.

"I couldn't tell if it was a wonderful match or a blowout," Starcher said. "But Fischer had a second. Are you allowed to have a second?"

"Of course," Gilead said.

"Good. Then we're both going to Cuba."

Gilead smiled, surprised. "When did you become interested in chess matches?"

"Forget chess. I'm interested in what Zharkov is doing in Cuba. What he's got planned. And there's Kutsenko. If he wants to defect, I want to get him out. Somehow, I don't think you're going to concern yourself with either of those things very much. That's why I'm going to go."

"It'll be dangerous," Gilead said. "Zharkov's going to try to kill me. You're sixty . . ."

"Sixty-six," Starcher snapped. "And still alive. If you're worried about taking me along, those are all the credentials I have to offer." His dark eyes were frosty and unyielding.

The Grandmaster nodded slowly. "They're enough."

"Good," Starcher said, still blustering. He lit a cigar, blowing out an enormous, joyful cloud of smoke.

"Maybe you ought to figure out how we're going to get into Cuba," Gilead said.

Starcher sat down and stretched his legs out in front of him languidly. A big grin spread across his face, making him look twenty years younger. "I have."

CHAPTER THIRTY-FOUR

Starcher permitted the bellhop to carry only one of his bags up the sumptuous stairway of the Miami's Fontainbleau Hotel. It was nearing Christmas, and the hotel was filled, mostly with New Yorkers.

"Pretty fancy," Justin said as Starcher tipped the bellhop and closed the doors on the suite. "Was that a ten you gave him?"

"A hundred. To come in before the maid in the mornings and mess up the beds. It's a weak alibi, but if we need an alibi, it's better than nothing."

"What about your sister? If the CIA gets wind of me and comes sniffing around, she'll talk. She knows I've been staying with you."

Starcher laughed as he hung a few shirts in the closet. "She knows *someone's* been there, but she's too much the lady to ask. Probably thinks I've turned into an old queer. Wear this." He handed Justin a beige linen suit from Harrod's. "And go downstairs and get yourself a haircut and a manicure. I want you to reek of money."

"What for?" Justin asked, fitting the jacket.

"For spending a hundred thousand dollars."

Justin laughed. "What on?"

"A boat," Starcher said.

"I don't know anything about boats."

"You don't have to." He pulled from his jacket pocket a neatly folded photograph from a magazine. It pictured a

38-foot cruiser that looked as if it were flying. "It's an Azimut Electron, Italian made. Pay for it in cash."

"Where are we going to get that much cash?"

Starcher opened a suitcase. It was filled with hundred dollar bills. "Here," he said.

"Are you paying for it yourself?"

Starcher smiled. "You forget. My family's wealthy. And this is the old age I've been saving up for," he said. "Now listen. I want the boat to be painted black and towed thirty miles offshore, directly south of Miami following the Keys, within three days. I'll find someone to drive it by then."

"Painted black? No boat dealer's going to—"

"Pay what you've got to. Europeans have a healthy respect for cash. They'll do it. Just stay with the boat, understand?" He handed Justin the suitcase and sent him out.

Next, he dressed himself in some threadbare clothes and examined the stubble on his chin. Not bad, he thought. It didn't take much to turn a wealthy old man into a derelict. It had been Riesling's favorite technique. No one ever looked too closely at seedy old vagabonds. Besides, he was only going to look for Saarinen. For the actual contact, he would need a foolproof disguise.

It took him nearly forty-eight hours to locate the black hulk of the *Kronen*. Couched among the sleek Posillipos and Magnums and Couache Motor Yachts that dotted Miami's Bel-Air harbor, the salt-encrusted fishing boat was as obvious as a black eye on a Kabuki dancer.

Starcher wandered near the marina, keeping his cap pulled over his eyes, searching for the captain of the *Kronen*. No one seemed to be on board. Starcher moved closer and knocked on the portholes. No one came. Finally, he stepped aboard the boat.

"Hey!" someone called from atop the rigging on a nearby sailboat. "You, Mr. Bum. Get off my boat, okay? Get out of here."

Starcher looked up. It was Saarinen, a little leaner than Starcher remembered him, but no older. So he still owned the *Kronen*.

"Hey, I know you," the Finn said, scrambling down the rigging.

Starcher turned and walked quickly away.

"Wait a minute," Saarinen called, but Starcher was gone.

He could still lose himself in a crowd of five people, Starcher thought with some gratification. There were some students fooling around near the piers, and he moved in among them, then led them all unconsciously near another group, where he was safely out of sight. It had always been something he excelled at—a little thing, the by-product of his work, the way a bank teller can count money with lightning speed, or a librarian can pull out all sorts of trivial information from a lifetime of insignificant research.

The CIA men watching Saarinen were all too easy to spot: A deck hand with eyes too wary, a casual stroller with rings of perspiration on his shirt that could only come from hours in the sun and humidity. They were watchers, little men with little jobs, like the KGB watchers who had stood so patiently below his office window in Moscow. They turned when Saarinen called out to him, but they, too, lost him in the crowd. Watchers were the youngsters, easy to dodge. But if they saw him again, they would report the sighting. The disguise for meeting Saarinen head to head would have to be perfect.

It was nearly dusk by the time Saarinen got off the gleaming sailboat. He whistled on his way back to the *Kronen*, his steps light on the plank pier.

"Good work," he said, clapping one of the CIA-watchers on the back with his big grime-blackened hands. The watcher pulled away from him indignantly, his flushed face betraying his embarrassment. Saarinen laughed. "My guardian angels, eh?"

The agent walked away. Saarinen lumbered into the hold of the *Kronen* and pulled a bottle of vodka from beneath the galley sink. Since his immigration to America, he'd switched from Korskenkova to easily available Finlandia, but the effect was the same—a wild, fiery ride down a gullet followed by the warm, stomach-prickling glow that always preceded the numb blankness of his nights.

Spies. Who needed them? he thought as he straightened out a sweat-stained Gitane and lit it with a new American Bic lighter. He tilted his wooden chair so that it rested on its two back legs and swung his feet up onto the table. In his right hand was the bottle of vodka; in his left, the cigarette. It was

the position he found best for thinking during what little time
he had before the Finlandia shut down his brain for the night.

Spies in Finland. Spies on Gogland Island. In the Soviet
Union, there was at least one spy per family. And now they
were in Miami, too, following him around the Land of the
Free.

He belched. "Fuck your mother," he said reflexively.

If he went back to Finland, he'd be thrown in jail again. Or
worse. The KGB, very much a presence in Helsinki, had a
way of relocating local small-time enemy operatives like
Saarinen to the morgue. And the Americans were no better.
Shit! If he'd known the bones tossed to him by the CIA fat
cats would turn him into a Flying Dutchman, homeless and
running forever, he would have stuck to smuggling. It was an
easier life. Now, with no crew, no home, and no money to
pay for even minor repairs on the *Kronen,* he was as empty-
handed as he had been on the day he was born.

He took a swig of the vodka. Well, not completely empty-
handed, he thought. At least there would be more Finlandia
waiting for him tomorrow. After he was through cleaning Mr.
Cohen's sloop. Mr. Cohen, who wouldn't know a nor'easter
from a fart.

He smelled something acrid, looked down, saw his shirt
was on fire, and slapped it out with a barrage of cursing and a
fountain of spilled vodka.

"Fuck your mother!" he screamed. "Fuck *my* mother!"

There was a knock at the door.

"And fuck you!" He threw a vicious kick at the wooden
door.

The knocking persisted.

He threw open the door. "Goddamn your eyes!" he bellowed before his visitor came into focus. It was a woman,
built like the proverbial American brick outhouse. She was
wearing a nurse's cap and had breasts like melons.

"Excuse me," she said throatily, "but I understand you
offer charter cruises."

Saarinen tore his eyes away from her chest, sputtered, then
took another belt of vodka. "It's dark outside," he managed.

"That's fine with my patient. He can only go out when it's
dark. Will you come with me, please?"

Wobbling slightly, he followed her back up to the deck,

occasionally sliding his hand along the nurse's heart-shaped backside, a gesture the woman didn't seem to notice.

"He's over there," she said, pointing to a dark figure in a wheelchair on the pier. He looked like an old man, although his face was almost completely swathed in gauze bandages. Only the tip of his nose showed beneath large dark glasses and a wide-brimmed fedora.

"It's a man? Are you sure?" Saarinen said. The cigarette burn on his chest was beginning to blister, and he'd left his bottle down in the hold. Even the nurse's heart-shaped rear couldn't make up for the lack of Finlandia.

"We're from the clinic," she said pertly. "The CPS?"

Saarinen stuck out his tongue and vibrated it toward her left breast.

"The Center for Plastic Surgery," she explained, gently pushing him away. "Mr. Steiner's had a face-lift, and he can't be exposed to the sun, but he wants to go out on the ocean for a couple of hours. I'm trying to find an available boat and captain who'll take him out alone. Mr. Steiner's very self-conscious about his appearance just now."

The old man in the wheelchair gestured impatiently toward Saarinen. "Pah," the Finn said. "I can see why. Tell the old turd it's too late. You come downstairs." He grabbed her arm.

"I'm afraid not," she said prettily, unclasping his fingers. "Won't you come and talk to him? He's such a sweet old dear." She put her arm around Saarinen and half led, half walked him over to the man in the wheelchair.

"So?" Saarinen said. "What do you want?"

The bandaged man opened his wallet slowly and took out a hundred dollar bill. He offered it to Saarinen with shaking, arthritic fingers.

Saarinen shook his head. "It's too dark to go out to sea," he shouted, because he assumed the old man was deaf, and also because he enjoyed shouting. "There is nothing to see."

Mr. Steiner proffered another hundred dollar bill.

"I've been working all day. I'm tired. Go home, understand?"

For the third time the clawlike fingers fished into the wallet. This time they came up with three bills, which he added to the other two. The money fluttered in the faceless man's outstretched hand for several seconds before Saarinen snatched it away.

"Steiner, eh? Rich old Jew, yes?"

The mummified head bobbed once, slowly.

"Come on, then," Saarinen said with a sigh. "There's no moon, but maybe your friend will oblige us with a view." He rubbed the nurse's thigh abstractedly. She giggled and kicked up the stop on Mr. Steiner's wheelchair.

"Can you lift him?"

Saarinen made a disgusted sound and spat abundantly on the pier before getting on board. Then he reached down and scooped the old man out of the chair. "Someone your age should not be concerned with a youthful face," Saarinen grumbled. "Even if it gets you what you want, you wouldn't know what to do with it."

He set the old man down and heaved the wheelchair on board. "Okay," he said, panting. "Now you." He held out his hand for the nurse.

"Oh, I have to be back at work. I'll meet you back here in two hours. All right, Mr. Steiner?"

The bandaged man nodded again.

"Fuck your mother," Saarinen muttered.

He left Mr. Steiner on the starboard side of the deck, in utter darkness, as he polished off another half-bottle of Finlandia at the helm while motoring out of the sheltered harbor. After twenty minutes, Saarinen came outside. There was no moon, no stars. "Beautiful night," he said. "Lots to see, eh?"

"What direction are we traveling?" Mr. Steiner asked. It was the first time Saarinen had heard the man speak. For some reason, the voice surprised him. He hadn't expected normal male sounds to issue from the decrepit old body and the bandaged, featureless face.

"North," Saarinen said.

"Change your course. Head due south."

"The view won't be any different." Saarinen smiled, then frowned. "You are sick? You wish to go back to the plastic clinic? Here, I will help you to lie down." He slid his arms around Mr. Steiner. The old man pushed him away.

"Just change your course."

Saarinen rushed to the helm, cursing the melon-breasted nurse for refusing to come on board. "I will return with a

corpse, and then the Americans will execute me for murder."
He poured some vodka down his throat as the *Kronen* turned
dramatically in midocean to face the other direction.

"Damn old Jew," he grumbled, coming back to Mr. Steiner.
"Are you dead yet? We'll be back in Miami in twenty
minutes. Unfortunately, I have no radio, but there will be
police." He added, "There always are."

"We won't be going back to Miami," Mr. Steiner said. He
removed his fedora. A shock of wavy white hair gleamed
beneath it. "Just south." He flexed his fingers. They weren't
crippled, after all.

"A trick," Saarinen raged, lifting the old man out of the
wheelchair by his lapels.

"Put me down, you fool. I'm not going to hurt you."

"No? Then what is this for?" He pulled a Browning .38
from the man's jacket.

"Just take it easy, Saarinen." He held up both his hands,
palms out to show he was harmless, then began slowly to
unwrap the bandages from around his face.

"How did you know my name?" Saarinen seethed.

"All Finnish alcoholics in Miami are named Saarinen.
Didn't you know?" He removed the last strip of gauze.

"CIA," Saarinen whispered. "Bastard. I should have known
from your big nose." He jabbed the automatic into Starcher's
midsection. "What are you and your dogs following me
for?"

"They're not *my* men. I'm retired."

Saarinen snorted. "Retired from what?" he demanded.

"I worked in Moscow. With Frank Riesling. And Corfus."

"Ah, yes. Corfus. Is your fat friend retired, too?"

Starcher hesitated. "I think Corfus is dead," he said quietly.

Saarinen sucked in his breath. "Then the ones watching
me . . ."

"No, they're Americans," Starcher said. "Can we go
inside? It's getting cold out here. I'd like to explain some
things to you."

"Explain your balls," Saarinen said, lumbering down the
steps into the hold. He stuck the automatic inside his belt. "I
have seen nothing but trouble since I had the stupidity to get
involved with you dog fuckers." He reached under the sink
and pulled out another bottle of Finlandia. "What makes you
think Corfus is dead?"

Starcher sat at the small table and told him about the strange disappearance of his assistant in Moscow, and the CIA's suspicions that Corfus had gone over to the Soviets.

"Corfus didn't work for the Russians," Saarinen laughed, tipping the bottle to his lips. "He rescued me from them, for God's sake."

"The CIA is citing his help to you as evidence that he was a double," Starcher said.

The Finn choked on his liquor. "They think *I* . . .? No wonder they are watching me like owls after mice."

"It's all a lot of nonsense, but everyone's frightened. The Company's even accusing Riesling. Just about everyone, in fact, who ever worked for me."

"You, too?" Saarinen's face was a caricature of surprise. "Surely not . . ."

Starcher nodded. "Probably me, too, if they get crazy enough. That's why I'm here. I've got something to do that I don't want them to know about."

Saarinen lit one of his Gitanes, then went up to check on the helm. When he came back down, he was smiling.

"So. Now the grand old man himself has become an outlaw," he said through a cloud of white smoke. "And he comes to the smuggler for help, yes?"

"That's about it," Starcher said.

"Well, I suppose it won't break Mr. Cohen's heart if I don't show up to finish cleaning his boat tomorrow. Where do you want to go?"

Starcher removed his jacket. He tore open a seam in the back, reached inside the lining, and extracted a thick wad of bills encircled by a rubber band. He slapped the roll of money on the table.

Saarinen lifted the pile, whistling low as he began to count.

"Ten thousand," Starcher said.

"A long journey, then. Mexico? Venezuela?"

Starcher took out a cigar, clipped the end, and puffed it to life while the Finn waited. "Cuba," he said softly.

Saarinen lowered himself onto one of the wooden galley chairs, raising the bottle to his lips as he sat down. "Fuck my mother," he whispered. "You *are* with the Russians."

"Don't be ridiculous," Starcher said, annoyed. He thought for a moment, then decided to level with Saarinen. "Listen to me. I think the Russians have something planned in Cuba for next week, something big that's going to hurt the United States. I can't convince the CIA about it, and I want to go there and find out for myself.''

"I don't believe this dogshit," Saarinen said. "The CIA's not going to do anything, and an old fool like you is going into Cuba to save the world." He threw the money back on the table. "I've got news for you, Mr. Save-the-World-for-Democracy. I can't get you into Cuba. My boat's not fast enough. The Cubans have more fucking patrol boats than the Spanish Armada."

"Don't forget the Russians," Starcher said with a small grin.

"That's right. They're all over Havana Harbor. At the marina, there is talk of little else. Go find yourself somebody else to commit suicide." He took another hit from the vodka bottle. "Smuggle you into Cuba. Dogshit."

"I don't want you to take me in. I want you to take us out.''

"Us? Who's us?" Saarinen said.

"Me. A friend. Maybe two others."

"The *Kronen* still can't outrun a Communist patrol ship. If they arrest me again, they'll hang my Finnish balls."

"No, not the *Kronen.*" Starcher looked at his watch and climbed the companionway to the deck. The night was so dark that Starcher bumped into his wheelchair. "Do you have searchlights?" he called.

With a shrug, Saarinen switched on the big floods that illuminated strips of stark ocean. "You are perhaps expecting company?" The Finn's eyes narrowed. "Or maybe you have given me this sad story to catch me off guard, to set me up for your CIA dogs. But remember, I still have the gun."

"Oh, stop," Starcher said wearily. "Look, I can get another sailor. Ten thousand can buy most of the ship captains in Miami for the night. I chose you because of old ties, nothing more. Because Riesling always said you weren't afraid of anything. The money would be enough to get you settled wherever you want. And if I can pull anything at all off in Havana, you won't have to worry about being followed for the rest of your life. So if you can't believe me, then just turn the offer down." He looked down at the .38. "Hell, go ahead and pull the trigger, if you're that crazy."

Saarinen took a quick drink, his eyes and the barrel of the

Browning fixed on Starcher. "Where in Cuba?" he asked at last.

Starcher smiled. He held out his hand. Reluctantly, Saarinen dropped the gun into it. "There's a place between Marianao and Guanajay, about thirty miles west of Havana. We'd have to get there at night to meet you."

"Of course," Saarinen said. "You know the area?"

"Somewhat," Starcher said. "I spent a year in Havana during the fifties."

"So long ago." Saarinen made a face.

"This place will be the same. It's a natural deep-water dock, but because of the terrain, there won't be any other ships."

"What about the terrain? Trees can be cut, buildings can be demolished. The place could be crawling."

"Not trees. A cliff. To go ashore, you've got to climb almost straight up for a hundred feet or more."

"I see," Saarinen said. "And you plan to climb down this mountain and swim to meet me?"

"That'll be *our* problem," Starcher said. He looked out to the shafts of light on the water, and pointed westward. "Do you see something out there?"

"Pah, what could be out there? Any ship would have its own lights. What about the Russian cruisers?"

"What?"

"In Havana Harbor. The *Kronen* can't do twenty-five knots. If they find us, they kill us."

"If you're any good, they won't find us."

Saarinen grunted. "Ten thousand is not enough to risk my life."

Starcher grasped his arm absently. "Over there," he whispered, pointing into the darkness.

Saarinen looked. Something dark appeared to be bobbing on the surface of the water. "You snake, you did trap me." He rushed to the bridge, turned the *Kronen* around by ninety degrees, and grabbed a pair of binoculars. The forward foodlights of the *Kronen* rested on a sleek, powerful-looking pleasure boat floating silently in the sea. It was painted a dull matte black, and would have been all but invisible without the *Kronen*'s floods trained on it. The deck was deserted.

"Mother of God," Saarinen whispered, moving his boat closer to the elegant black cruiser. "What's that?"

"That's how we're going to get out of Cuba." He reached behind Saarinen and flashed the *Kronen*'s floodlights once. Immediately the other boat burst into light, its hull gleaming. Then a solitary figure emerged from the bridge onto the deck.

"Who's that?"

"His name's Justin Gilead."

"He's going to Cuba, too?"

Starcher nodded.

"And the boat? She's yours?"

"For the moment."

They pulled up directly alongside the magnificent new boat, tied up, and climbed aboard. "What a beauty," Saarinen said, running his hands along the rails. "How fast is she?"

"She'll average thirty-five knots," Justin said.

Saarinen looked up. "Your friend?" he asked.

Starcher nodded.

"A face like a movie star," the Finn said with some disdain.

He squinted, moving closer to the younger man. "The necklace," he said, his voice hushed. "It's the same."

Justin inhaled sharply. "The same as what?" Starcher asked.

"The drop of gold at the bottom . . . It must be the same." Tentatively, the Finn extended an index finger toward the medallion. He gasped when he touched it, drawing away. "It is! It is the one Riesling stole from me."

"Riesling stole it?"

Saarinen shrugged. "He paid a pittance. But he held me at gunpoint during the transaction."

"And where did you get it?" Justin demanded.

Saarinen stared at him for a long time, then averted his eyes, throwing up one hand with a shrug. "It was so long ago . . ."

"Where?" Justin rasped, grabbing the man by his shoulders.

"Justin, stop," Starcher said.

The Finn eyed Justin curiously. "The medallion, it has perhaps more value than I thought. Riesling asked the same questions." He saw Justin's ice blue eyes staring at him and said quickly, "I bought it in Poland. The man I got it from said it belonged to the Undead One. He said it carries the curse of death with it. Are you the Undead One?" he asked.

Justin turned and went below.

"What's wrong with him?" Saarinen asked.

"Bad memories," Starcher said. "Now, how about my offer?"

Saarinen's expression immediately changed as he looked over the sleek new boat. "Ten thousand plus her?"

"That's the deal."

"What about the *Kronen?* The authorities will look for her when 'Mr. Steiner' and the infamous Communist ship captain do not return. If they find her abandoned, they will know."

"There are fires on board fishing boats with galleys," Starcher offered. "Especially when the captain is known to drink."

Saarinen's eyes widened in surprise. "Burn the *Kronen?* But she is my child, my woman, my lover. I would sooner burn the flesh off my arm."

"Then give me back the ten thousand," Starcher said levelly.

"What?"

"I have the gun now. Don't make me use it."

Saarinen looked longingly at the battered old boat. "I suppose a grease fire would do it," he said with a sigh.

Starcher smiled. "Have you got any matches?"

"Matches, yes," Saarinen mumbled huskily, turning to board the *Kronen*. "But it will be the soul of my soul that I burn."

He was gone for several minutes. When he returned, he carried under his arm a clutch of bottles filled with clear liquid, and a faint orange glow appeared sporadically in the entranceway to the *Kronen*'s hold. Saarinen took the bottles to the bridge. "Open one, please," he said to Starcher. "I'm afraid I will need it."

He started the engine. "When will we have this glorious Cuban holiday?"

Starcher handed him the bottle. "Next week."

As the Azimut sped northward, the *Kronen* burst into tongues of high flame.

"Fuck all our mothers. Sometimes one must change to live, yes?" Saarinen said brokenly.

"Spoken like a true philosopher."

"And there is nothing to keep me from calling this new beauty the *Kronen* also, yes?"

"Nothing whatever."

Saarinen unscrewed the lid on a bottle of Finlandia. When the fire reached the old boat's fuel tank, the *Kronen* exploded in a blazing roar that tossed the newer craft like flotsam on the churning waves.

Saarinen, his eyes moist, let loose with a howling whoop of merriment. "That's how to go, girl!" he shouted, hoisting the bottle high above his head in salute. "To tomorrow." He leveled the bottle to his lips and drank a deep and long toast to the destroyed boat.

Starcher, too, felt a vague elation at the destruction of the craft. Death always provided the best cover. With the wheelchair on board, if anything was ever found, investigators would assume that the captain and his passenger had perished in the fire. But more than that, Saarinen had been right about the way to go. Off in a blaze of glory, that was how to do it. In his youth, part of his attraction to the dangerous and unpredictable line of work he had chosen had been that he had a good chance of dying well. As things turned out, he would most likely be far removed from any semblance of glory when his own time came: His destiny was to die ignobly beneath the electric shocks of a cardiac team's defibrillators after his leaky valve finally gave out; of that he was close to certain. But his old fantasies came to life again in the light of the burning ship. With the wind in his face, he felt the heroics of the old fishing boat's death throes. Maybe Cuba. Maybe he would die worthily there. It was not the worst of ends.

On deck, Justin, too, watched the flames.

Always by fire, he thought. All I have ever loved has perished in fire.

Come back, Justin, the voices in his head called. *Come back to your demons, your fears. We wait for you, Justin. We wait . . .*

The wind blew the hot tears from his cheeks. He couldn't go back. He had promised Tagore to follow the man who had led him this far, and who would take him to the end.

Perhaps in the end, he himself would die by fire.

It didn't matter anymore. As long as it happened soon.

_____CHAPTER THIRTY-FIVE

Starcher and Justin Gilead sat at a small tile-topped table in one of the cocktail lounges at Mexico City's sprawling airport, with an hour to wait before boarding their flight to Cuba.

Starcher ordered a Bloody Mary, but the potion was so hotly spiced as to be undrinkable. Justin had no drink. He looked out the window at the airport's crisscrossing of landing strips, watching planes setting down every ninety seconds. His quiet contemplation annoyed the old CIA man.

Gilead was an impossible human being. Waiting for a plane was any gentleman's lifelong excuse to have a drink; for Justin, it just meant waiting. If the waiter had put a glass of water before him, unbidden, Justin might have sipped it, but more likely he would just have let it sit there while he stared at planes. He made no attempt at conversation. It was as if there were only one thing allowed in his life at any given time and anything else was an intrusion on that.

A totally impossible human being. Then Starcher thought about Justin staying underwater for thirty minutes and crushing stones to powder in his hands and coming back from a Nichevo grave. An impossible human being. *If* he was a human being.

For weeks now, Starcher had been thinking about Justin Gilead, about just who and what the Grandmaster was. He believed that he had spent his childhood raised by a group of mystics in the Himalayas, and he believed that the golden snake medallion Justin always wore around his neck was the sacred amulet of Rashimpur. But what else did he know? What else did he believe? What was the truth?

Justin would tell him nothing. Starcher finally did what a lifetime in government had taught him to do with insoluble problems: He ignored it and tried to forget it.

The change that six weeks had wrought in Justin had been almost miraculous. He had been a withered, dying wraith, but now he looked again like the Justin Gilead whom Starcher had known in Europe during the seventies. His body was filled out with muscular flesh. The time spent exercising and sleeping outdoors had tanned Justin's skin and suffused him with the glow of health. He had been virtually a corpse when Starcher had found him on the houseboat; now he looked like what he was, an unusually handsome forty-one-year-old man who moved with the sensitive grace of a large cat.

The eyes had not changed. They never changed. They were what they had always been: large, clear, as blue as mountain ice in sunlight—and as cold. Sometimes they, too, seemed inhuman in their lack of expression, inhuman in their capacity to fix on a person and make it impossible for him to turn his glance away, as inhuman as if they were the only magnets in a world of metal people. Maybe not human, Starcher thought. Maybe God himself had eyes like that.

Starcher stirred the Bloody Mary in the hope that the bartender had put most of the spices on top and stirring would weaken the fire, but he knew there was no chance when he saw black pepper grains swirl up from the bottom of the drink as he stirred. Best to let the sediment settle. If their plane was a week late, the drink might finally be bearable.

And Justin Gilead didn't care. Starcher could sit there drinking a Polynesian spectacular made of equal parts of rum, arsenic, and prussic acid, and he could die writhing on the table, and Gilead would care only if Starcher's dying might somehow affect his plans for the trip to Havana.

Starcher cleared his throat. Justin looked out at the planes.

Starcher cleared his throat again, and Justin turned to him, smiled vaguely, noncommittally, and looked back toward the planes.

Starcher said softly, "I think I'm going to join the Communist party."

Gilead stared straight ahead.

"Then I'll become a go-go dancer. I've always liked to dance."

No response.

"Sky-diving might be a good hobby for me to take up. I'll find out where you're living and crash through the roof. Land right on your chessboard. Mix up the pieces so you can't reconstruct the game."

Without looking away from the window, the Grandmaster replied, just as softly, "You're too old and homely to be a go-go dancer; the Communist party won't have you; and I'm never going to tell you where I live because I hate having people drop in unannounced."

"Praised be God," Starcher said. "It lives and it speaks."

"I'm sorry, Starcher," Gilead said, turning to look at the white-haired CIA man with an apologetic grin. "I'm not much of a traveling companion, am I?"

"I get warmer responses from my luggage," Starcher said. "From perfect strangers. Even from the bartender. At least he cared enough to try to poison me." He rocked the red drink from side to side in his hand and said, "I'm sorry, Justin. I guess you just make me feel guilty. I think I should be entertaining you or something, trying to make you happy. *Can* you be happy?"

"You don't understand, Starcher. I *am* happy."

"Because you're finally going to kill Zharkov? That's a strange thing to be happy about."

"Because finally the circle will be complete. Because finally I'll have finished what I was born to do."

"Born to do . . . destiny . . . circle . . . karma," Starcher sputtered. "I've heard enough of that. What the hell is it that you were born to do? What's so damned important?"

"I can't tell you," Justin said honestly, with no embarrassment.

"But you wish you could," Starcher snapped bitterly.

"No." Justin shook his head. "I don't really wish I could."

"All right. But just remember—before you go wandering off on whatever mission of destiny is going to complete your circle and round out your karma and iron your underwear or whatever the hell it is that's driving you—remember: You promised that first we would get Kutsenko out of Havana and try to stop whatever Nichevo is up to."

"I gave you my promise," Gilead said. "You don't have to remind me of it."

Starcher rose from the table. "I'm going to make a phone call," he said. He didn't know if Gilead had even heard him. The Grandmaster was again staring out the large observation windows at the planes landing.

Starcher's sister had told him, unable to keep the irritation from her voice, that someone named Harry Kael had been calling him for the last three days.

"Really, Andrew, he is the rudest person I've ever spoken to. Where did you meet him?"

"We used to work together," Starcher said. "I'll call him."

"Are you all right?" his sister asked.

"I'm feeling fine."

"You're taking your medicine?"

"Yes."

"Well, very good," she said in the somewhat skeptical tone of a teacher whose dumbest student had just turned in a perfect test paper. She waited a few seconds, then hung up.

Wonderful, thought Starcher. My own sister can't make small talk with me. Maybe it's not Gilead. Maybe it's me. Maybe I just lack the capacity to make friends. Maybe I became a spy because I knew that nobody in the real world would ever talk to me.

He tracked Harry Kael down through a string of telephone answerers and secretaries until finally the CIA official's voice crackled through the phone: "Starcher, what the hell's going on?"

"Hello, Harry. Why don't we both start with hello?"

"Can that shit. What's going on around here?"

"What are you talking about?" Starcher asked.

"The goddamned *New York Times*. Wait. I've got it here." Starcher heard rustling sounds in the background, then Kael again. "Yeah. Here it is. Last week." He was reading. " 'Because of illness, International Master Stanley Needham of New York has withdrawn from the American chess team, which is scheduled to play a match against a Soviet national team next week in Havana. The U.S. Chess Federation said that Needham's place on the team will be taken by Justin Gilead, an international grandmaster who has been in retirement and not active in competition for the last five years.' What the hell's that all about?''

"Seems pretty clear to me," Starcher said.

"I thought Gilead was dead."

"Guess he's not."

"That's it? You guess he's not? You saw the goddamned pictures of him in some Polack grave, and you've been screaming like a psychotic fruitcake about big problems in Cuba and now suddenly Gilead shows up and he's going to Cuba and you say that's it? You've got your hand in this, Starcher. What the hell are you up to? And while you're at it, where the hell is Saarinen? That goddamned Scandinavian pirate has disappeared. You wouldn't know anything about that, would you?''

"It's easy, Harry," Starcher said. "You see, you were right all along. Gilead, Saarinen, me . . . we're all Communists. We've been planning the glorious revolution for years, and now our day is coming. We're all fleeing the United States. We're going to annex Virginia to the U.S.S.R. We're putting Langley up for sale. Your new office will be behind a tailor shop. See? You were right all the time, Harry.''

"Forget the sarcasm. Just tell me what's going on."

"Harry, I'd love to stay and chat, but my plane is leaving soon.''

"Plane? Where are you? Where are you going? This connection sucks.''

"I'm going to Cuba."

There was a long silence before Kael said, "Andy, are you really going there?''

"Yes."

"You're going with Gilead?"

"Yes."

"You think something's going to happen down there?"

"Yes, I do," Starcher said.

"Your being there might make it worse," Kael said sourly.

"If you had sent somebody else, I wouldn't be going," Starcher said. "Remember? I'm a senile old man."

"And now you're proving that I was right," Kael said. "I could stop you, you know."

"You could if I were in the United States," Starcher said. "I have to go now."

"Andy, wait."

"What?"

"I shouldn't do this," Kael said.

"Don't," advised Starcher.

"Is this line clear?" Kael asked.

"Yeah. A pay phone at an airport."

"Okay. A man named Pablo Olivares. If he looks you up, you might listen to him."

"Thanks, Harry. I know that was hard for you to do."

"Be careful," Kael said.

"I will."

"Don't embarrass the Company."

"I never have," Starcher said.

The sprawling José Martí Hotel, like all the beautiful buildings that remained in Havana since the graying of the sixties, was a relic of Batista's regime. Opulent and grand, with its high archways and ceilings, its baroque splendor reeked of privilege and the hint of banished decadence that gave it the appeal of a royal palace, despite the omnipresent portraits of Fidel Castro in uniform, the cheap new light fixtures that had replaced the crystal art deco wall sconces, and the ugly, thick industrial ropes corralling the long lines waiting for service at the reception desk.

Alexander Zharkov, too, waited in line. Like the women in the markets, he thought, waving their government-issued numbers in front of Havana's heavily guarded stores. Number A-1 was permitted to shop on Tuesday. The A-2s had to wait until Wednesday, by which time most of the goods were already gone.

Zharkov lit one of his few cigarettes of the day, prompting a woman in front of him to start complaining loudly in Spanish. But she stopped when a hotel executive came from an office behind the desk and greeted Zharkov.

"Senor Zharkov, you were pre-registered," he said. "There is no need for you to wait."

"Thank you," Zharkov said as he accepted a key from the man.

"You are in room three-seventeen. If you will point out your bags, I will have them sent up."

Zharkov nodded toward two leather bags near the bellhop's stand, and the hotel official trotted over toward them. Zharkov stepped over the heavy rope that held the lines in order. As he did, the woman in front of him met his eyes, then lowered hers automatically. "Sorry, senor," she mumbled.

Another wonderful classless society, Zharkov mused as he walked toward the lobby's only working elevator. Another nation of people terrified at the thought that they might have offended someone who had real power. And still, on Sunday nights, they would go to their village squares for the regular indoctrination sessions and chant "All power to the people" and somehow convince themselves that they believed it.

The elevator was so slow in coming that the bellhop with Zharkov's bags arrived alongside him. Zharkov took the two valises from him and rode up in the elevator alone.

When he opened the door to room 317, a tall man with Hispanic features rose from the bed. He was deeply tanned, muscular, and balding. Although he would have looked at home anywhere in Cuba, his name was Yuri Durganiv.

He was Nichevo's best marksman and a special favorite of Zharkov, who had sent him to Cuba secretly two years before just to have him in place when he was needed. Durganiv was from Leningrad. He had studied ballet at the Kirov School before growing too tall to be accepted into the company. Even now, at six feet four and two hundred twenty pounds, he moved fluidly, smoothly, giving a sense of restrained power ready to be released at any moment.

After the door closed behind Zharkov and he dropped his bags, the other man stepped forward and gripped him in a powerful bear hug. "Alyosha, how good to see you. And how good to speak Russian again."

There was no shortage of Russians in Havana, or anywhere in Cuba, for that matter. But Zharkov had sent Durganiv to Havana in preparation for this assignment with orders to speak only Spanish, to become Cuban, to take advantage of his unusual skin coloration, and to vanish into the native population. He knew that Durganiv had obeyed his orders. As he would always.

When Fidel Castro died, in four more nights, Durganiv would be the man behind the gun.

When the taller man released him, Zharkov stepped back and looked into Durganiv's eyes. Before he could speak, the swarthy Russian smiled and said, "She's all right. She's waiting for you."

"Thank you," Zharkov said simply.

Five minutes later, after hanging up his clothes in the plain room's unpainted closet, he left with Durganiv. As they walked through a side door of the hotel toward the parking lot, Justin Gilead and Andrew Starcher came through the main entrance doors to the José Martí.

It was late afternoon, and the muted sun shone dully through the dirt-streaked windows of the small apartment in the Old Havana section. A sharp triangle of light slashed across the naked belly of Katarina Velanova as she lay in bed next to Zharkov, smoking, staring at the ceiling.

"I'm sorry you haven't liked it here," Zharkov said. "But I'm glad you're well."

"Yuri sees to all my needs," Katarina said. "And he has gotten me all the necessary papers, but . . ." She hesitated and blew a long plume of smoke toward the ceiling. "I haven't anyone to talk to. I don't speak Spanish. Half the Russians here are KGB, and the other half want to be. A chance word, an unfortunate remark from me, and someone might know that Galina Panova is really Katarina Velanova. I am afraid I may meet someone who might have seen me before. So I stay in my room and watch television. They have no Russian programs here, so I am reduced to watching cartoons. At least they have foreign bookstores in Havana."

"It won't be for too much longer," Zharkov said. "When I go back, I'm going to get rid of Ostrakov. With him gone, there's no reason you won't be able to come back."

"No?" she raised an eyebrow. "What about the *vozhd?*"

"When this mission is done, I will own him," Zharkov said. "He will last in power only so long as I wish him to. And when he goes, I will succeed him."

"When this mission is done," she echoed. There was a faint tremble in her voice. Zharkov knew she was worried about the danger of this assignment. He took the cigarette from her hand and took a long puff before handing it back. Then he placed his hand on her bare breast, still looking at the ceiling.

During the few months she had been away, he had missed her deeply. He had even wondered, at times, if he had fallen in love with her. Was love possible for one such as he was? He believed that she loved him, but was he able to return love?

Lying here by her side, he realized that it might even be more than love. It was life. Katarina Velanova was his confidante, the only person to whom he could speak without concealing his meanings. The only one who knew his plans and his dreams and his secret lusts. She was a lover, yes. But more important, she was his friend. His only friend.

"Don't worry," he said. "This will go smoothly." And with no change in his soft, bedroom-conversation tone, he said, "Justin Gilead arrives today."

Katarina sat up in the bed. The ashtray slid from her belly and overturned, fouling the sheet with ashes and cigarette butts.

"Where is he?" she asked.

"He'll be at the José Martí, where I'm staying."

She stared at the ceiling, biting her lip, deliberating. Then she spoke. "Let me kill Justin Gilead for you."

Zharkov chuckled, surprised. "Why? You don't even know him."

"I know what he means to you, to us. And I can do it."

"He is not easily killed," Zharkov said.

"Perhaps. Perhaps not by you or by other men. Perhaps he is too wary, too much on his guard. But I am a woman. I could move close to him in a receiving line somewhere and quietly put a knife into his heart. I'd be gone before anyone found out. Give me the knife, Alyosha. I want to do it."

"Patience, little tigress," the Russian said.

"I will do it," Katarina said. "I will do it now." Her lips were a tight line across the milky smoothness of her face.

"I'm afraid not," Zharkov said. "He has to live until Friday night, anyway. And then I have other plans."

"Oh?" Her anxious face flicked into a smile. "What plans?"

"First, poor Justin Gilead, the deranged American spy, will be the one who kills that great people's leader, Fidel Castro. He will try to escape but, alas, a Russian bullet will stop him." He smiled. "A simple plan."

Katarina was silent. She brushed the ashes and cigarette butts from the bed into the cupped palm of one hand, put them all back in the ashtray, lit another cigarette, and lay back down.

"An audacious plan," she said softly. "But if it fails, I am going to kill the Grandmaster for you. I hate Justin Gilead."

*   *   *

Justin Gilead turned to look at Starcher, who was lying on the bed in a pair of oversized boxer shorts. His long socks were held up by black garters. His undershirt was of thin ribbed cotton.

The room seemed to vibrate with the heavy periodic thud of Latin music. The room had lacked both television and radio, but Starcher had carried a radio in his luggage. The two men played it to foil the listening devices they knew would be concealed in the room.

Starcher rolled a cigar between his fingers, eyeing it as lovingly as if he were a satyr and it a lifetime supply of the world's most beautiful women.

Justin sat on the edge of the bed and said softly, "Sure you won't go, Starcher?"

"No. I don't want to let our friend know I'm here yet. He might recognize me. And don't call me that anymore. Try Andrew." Harry Andrew was the name on the old forged CIA passport Starcher had used to enter Cuba.

"All right, Andrew." Gilead was smiling.

"You're looking forward to this, aren't you?" Starcher asked.

"Yes."

"Remember our deal. You won't—"

"You don't have to remind me. And tonight, if I get the chance, I'll talk to Kutsenko."

Starcher lighted the cigar. He nodded through the heavy smoke, which seemed to settle around him instead of rising to the ceiling.

After Justin left, Starcher turned off the radio and lay back on the bed. Some of what he had told Justin was true. He did not want to make an appearance just yet, for fear of being recognized. But he also wanted to stay in the room, just in case Zharkov or his Nichevo henchmen had any idea of planting a bomb in Justin's suitcase or poisoning his after-shave lotion. He didn't know the cause of the hatred that Gilead felt for Zharkov, but if it was reciprocal, then Zharkov would unhesitatingly take the first chance to remove Gilead. The Russians had attempted to kill the Grandmaster in the past; Starcher did not want them to succeed now.

He smoked and thought and waited.

*   *   *

The pre-tournament cocktail party was held where the games would be played, in the towering main ballroom of the José Martí Hotel. A wide balcony ringed the room along its second-floor level. When Justin arrived, the room held a hundred persons but still looked as deserted as a Kansas wheat field in winter.

There were only a handful of women, most of them wives of competitors. The rest were chess players, their seconds, local Cuban officials, and members of the world press.

Justin stopped inside the doorway and scanned the room, but did not see the face he was looking for. When he spied Richard Carey, captain of the United States team, he walked over to join his group.

"Justin, good to see you again," Carey said gruffly. "You in shape to tangle with these Russian bears?"

Justin smiled and nodded as Carey pumped his hand vigorously.

The popular impression was that chess players were slim, effete intellectuals who lived at the chessboard because they were afraid of the real world. But Carey was a bluff and hearty man with the build and physical presence of a teamster boss.

He had big, strong hands, hardened by years of exposure to the weather on the Vermont farm where he lived. His robust frame seemed to belie the quiet, subtle nature of his chess game. He was the highest ranked of all active American chess players, his rating just a few points below that of Kutsenko. Many felt that he would be the next challenger for the world championship. Justin did not share that view. In his mind, Carey would not show well in match play—one player meeting another over a long series of games—because of a basic flaw in his game.

Carey spent too much time poring over positions, looking into them for subtleties that they just did not contain. Occasionally, a position was clear and simple, and the way to exploit it was merely to play routine, basic chess grounded firmly in sound general principles. But Carey overestimated his opponents and played as if every position were a mine field and each move a life-and-death decision.

All too often, this forced him into time trouble. Without enough time left on his clock, he sometimes had to make his final crucial moves without fully examining positions that did require careful analysis.

In chess, the clock was merciless, the player's greatest enemy. The American Bobby Fischer, the one-time world champion and great chess genius, was once asked how he managed never to get into time trouble in a game. He responded, "When you're in time trouble, then it just isn't chess anymore."

Justin did not think Carey would be able to beat Kutsenko and the clock, too.

The big American introduced Justin to the other members of the American team and some of their seconds. Gilead had seen the two other members at tournaments before, but had never spoken to them.

"We were just saying how glad we were that Washington didn't put the kibosh on this trip and stop us from coming," Carey told Gilead. "So where have you been, anyway? You kind of vanished there for a while."

"I was burned out," Gilead said. "I just needed some time off and some rest."

"You're feeling all right now?"

Gilead nodded, his eyes still searching the room, "I'm sorry about Needham getting ill, but it's good to be here. I'm looking forward to playing again."

"You up to date on your theory?" Carey asked.

"A little rusty, maybe."

"There've been a lot of changes," he said, and he began to describe two new variations in the Caro-Kann defense, which had been an opening Justin frequently used. Carey's interpretation immediately led to a dissent from another member of the U.S. team, a tall, gangly midwestern youngster named John Shinnick. His viewpoint was in turn challenged by the team's third member, a brooding and intense Syrian-American named Yassir Gousen. Justin took the opportunity to disengage himself and walk away.

He saw Ivan Kutsenko across the room, surrounded by a large group of people, and wandered casually in that direction. Justin recognized Victor Keverin, one of the members of the Russian team. At sixty, Keverin was still a brilliant and dangerous player, although he now lacked the physical stamina to be a serious contender for the world championship. Alongside Kutsenko was a young man with brilliant, sad eyes. Justin guessed that he was the youngest member of the Soviet team, Vyacheslav Ribitnov. Justin had studied the analyses of some of his games in *Shakmatni*, the Russian chess journal. He was a sparkling young player of the kind Russia seemed to produce year after year. They would have meteoric careers for a few years, and then, just as rapidly as their light had flared, it would sputter and die. The contradictions inherent in playing a game that required total intellectual freedom in a regime that crushed intellectual freedom simply became too much for most of them. It was hard to be free at a chessboard and then, moments after leaving the board, become just another faceless number who was told where to go and what to do and where to live and what to think and say.

Most of them wound up either defecting or allowing their chess skills to deteriorate. The kind of Russian who usually became world champion did not have the eyes that Ribitnov had. Russian chess champions were generally stolid, middle-of-the-road types with a large sense of humor who had made all the emotional adjustments that were necessary and counted themselves lucky to have some measure of freedom, even if only at the chessboard.

The burnouts were those who thought they should be free all the time. Ribitnov was clearly one of those. But so, too, from his appearance, was Ivan Kutsenko. His face had the haunted look of a captured animal, and his eyes burned with the glazed, darting confusion of a mouse dropped into the cage of a boa constrictor. No wonder he was trying to defect. Given time, Russia would crush his spirit and destroy his genius.

Justin guessed that the woman at his side, a tiny but strong-looking brunette with severe upswept hair, was his wife, the physician, Lena Kutsenko. She nodded appreciatively as Kutsenko spoke to several men holding pads and pencils. Behind the Russian champion was a wall of men who were large, sullen, and not particularly bright looking.

Many chess players did not look like chess players. These men did not look like chess players because they weren't. They were, Justin knew, KGB—the inevitable traveling companions of any Russian artists or athletes who were allowed out of their own country to compete. They were there both as bodyguards and as jailers. Justin wondered how a Russian ever managed to win a game, knowing that these grim-faced bears with guns in their armpits were standing around watching every gesture, trying to overhear every word.

As Justin walked forward, Kutsenko saw him and stepped away from the crowd to greet him. They had never met before, although Justin had seen the young man's photographs. His career was just beginning to soar when Justin went on his ill-fated trip to Poland, and they had never played each other. But Justin had studied the Russian champion's games carefully in the last few weeks. Kutsenko was a player without a weakness; his strategies were subtle and far-reaching; his tactics were precise and powerful, and his concentration was impressive. Justin looked forward to playing him. He had not realized until he saw Kutsenko's face how much he had missed the game of chess, that solitary companion that had been with him as a child and as a man.

"You are Justin Gilead," Kutsenko said, extending his hand.

"Yes. It is a pleasure to meet you."

"The chess world has missed you very much," Kutsenko said. "I have studied your games."

"And I yours," Justin said. As he spoke, Kutsenko, with surprising poise for a man who appeared so reclusively shy, took his elbow and moved back with him toward the group of Russians.

He nodded to his companions, pointedly ignoring the KGB men standing near, and said, "This is Justin Gilead, the most brilliant American player ever."

"Thank you," Justin said. "Perhaps Fischer might have something to say about that."

"Ooof, Fischer. A patzer. You could give him pawn and move," Kutsenko said, and he and Justin shared a smile over the joke. Fischer's reputation as the greatest chess player the world had ever produced was so solid and stable as to be invulnerable. It could be joked about because it was beyond argument.

"It is one of the losses of my life that I never played Fischer," Justin said. "And yours too, I suppose."

Justin knew that the KGB men behind Kutsenko were straining to catch the conversation. He mentioned casually that he had just seen Kutsenko's latest proposals in the Semi-Slav defense in *Shakmatni*.

As he expected, it touched off a spate of comments and

observations by the chess players and their seconds, each with an opinion, each willing to express it loudly and at any length. And because chess players used an algebraic notation to describe the 64 squares on a chessboard, each square being designated by a letter and number from A-1 in the lower left corner of the board to H-8 at the upper right corner, the conversation must have sounded like computer-generated madness to non–chess players.

"The correct move to maintain pressure on the center," Kutsenko said, "was bishop B-seven. It was all lost with F-five because then knight G-five, H-six, rook E-four and wins."

"Unless," said Ribitnov, the youngest Russian, "D-six. D-six will hold the middle and force the exchange, and black stands better."

"No," Victor Keverin interjected. "D-six loses to D-four, preparing E-five."

The conversation raged back and forth, and, as Justin had expected it would, it soon bored the KGB men, who stepped back from the little cluster of chess players and began talking among themselves. Lena Kutsenko took her husband's glass and walked over to a waiter to exchange it for a fresh glass of bottled water.

Justin took a few steps away from the group. Kutsenko stepped forward to speak to him.

"What do you think, Justin?" he asked.

"I think that in Havana, the sun is hot," the Grandmaster said softly. He studied Kutsenko's face. He was about to finish the identifying password when the Russian chess master's face seemed to drain of color and his eyes became frightened. He looked up at Justin imploringly, then away again. Justin followed Kutsenko's gaze toward the ballroom's main entrance.

There stood Alexander Zharkov.

Justin felt his heart leap. His hands clenched into fists at his sides. Zharkov had not changed. There might have been a little more gray in his hair, but he was still husky and muscular, his face still young and unlined, the lizard-lidded eyes still cold and murderous. The Russian's own face paled when he saw Justin Gilead staring at him. Their eyes locked for a frozen moment. Then Zharkov looked away and started across the room.

Justin felt Kutsenko move back slightly from him, as if to

be nearer the other Russian players and seconds. Perhaps only a handful of people in Russia knew what Zharkov did, but that he was a powerful man was evident. The KGB body-guards abruptly halted their bored conversation and moved back up among the members of the Russian team. One positioned himself between Gilead and Kutsenko. The Russian champion withdrew another half-step. Justin wondered if Kutsenko had understood Justin's message to him. Did he know that Justin was the man who would arrange his defection to the United States? He looked at Kutsenko, but the man was so obviously frightened by Zharkov that no emotion but fear could be seen on his face. Then Kutsenko turned back to his wife and spoke to her, and Justin remembered what Starcher had told him about Riesling's death and Corfus's final conversation in the Moscow hospital. It was only a guess that the statement about Havana's weather and sugar crop was a password to identify himself to a potential defector. Riesling had been dying when he said it. It could have been nothing but the delirious babbling of a dying man, meaning nothing. And Corfus's analysis might also have meant less than nothing. The fact was that no one knew for sure whether Kutsenko was a potential defector or not.

It was like so much of field intelligence work. Guesses, wishes, hopes. No evidence. No realities. Only suppositions and maybes and let's-give-it-a-tries.

As Zharkov walked toward the group, Justin's heart still pounded. At last, after all these years of waiting, his soul had been freed. He was allowed to kill this man who had killed so much of Justin's life. The images flashed, unbidden, unwanted, into his mind: the once peaceful temple at Rashimpur; the great tree charred and dead; Tagore bound to it by wires, dead; the other monks dead. He saw himself bayoneted and thrown into the cold lake, dead. He saw Yva, the Polish girl, her face blown away, her village burning. He saw himself in a Polish grave, the earth suffocating him, clawing his way through the cold damp soil like a mindless animal of the night.

Zharkov always walked with death. He was the Prince of Death, and even though, in his deepest heart, Justin did not believe it, he accepted Tagore's word: that somehow Zharkov had been born to inflict evil on the world and that Justin had been born to fight back.

But he had lost his faith. Perhaps once he had believed that he was special, a man chosen by the gods, but not any longer. Now he was just a tired man, tired beyond his years, who still remembered a few tricks of his childhood and hoped that they would be enough to allow him to kill this lifelong enemy and then to die himself.

For a moment, as Zharkov approached, Justin thought of waiting until the man came into reach, and then stretching out his long, powerful fingers and tearing out Zharkov's throat. It would be easy. And then he could die. He could complete the circle, and he could join Tagore and the others of Rashimpur in death.

They would know their mistake; they would not greet him any longer as Patanjali, as the Wearer of the Blue Hat, but they might greet him as a good man who had tried to do his duty, and perhaps they could make room for him in that far-off place in which their spirits dwelt.

But there was duty. Duty, as Andrew Starcher would have it, with a capital letter, absolute and inviolate. He had given his word to Starcher. He would keep it.

There would be time to kill Zharkov. There would be time because Justin had now been freed, and the earth was too small a place for one such as Zharkov to hide from him and the vengeance he would exact.

Zharkov passed him without a glance and stopped in front of Kutsenko.

The Russian champion said, "Good to see you, Colonel. We are pleased that you will be playing with us." Zharkov grunted, and Kutsenko looked past him, toward Justin, and said, "There is someone you should meet."

Zharkov turned and faced Gilead. Even though Kutsenko had taken his arm and was starting to move toward Justin, Zharkov stood planted as firmly as an oak tree.

"We have met already," he said coldly.

"Yes," Justin said. "Many times." His soft voice was chilling. "The colonel and I are old friends."

There was a long silence. When Kutsenko saw that neither man would step forward to offer the other his hand, he released his grip on Zharkov's elbow. "Have you two played before?" he asked timidly, speaking to a space between the two of them.

"Yes," said Gilead.

"No," said Zharkov.

Justin smiled. "Never a real game. Until now. This will be the first, won't it, Colonel?"

"The first and the last," Zharkov said.

Then he walked away to find a cocktail waiter, and Justin returned to the American contingent.

Later, Justin found himself standing next to Lena Kutsenko near a small podium from which the chairman of the Cuban chess federation was reading the schedule of games for the next four days. Dr. Kutsenko's husband was on the other side of the room, surrounded by KGB men. Zharkov had already left.

Justin learned that he would play Ribitnov, the young Russian, the next day. On Thursday, it would be Victor Keverin, and on Friday, Zharkov. On Saturday, the final day of the match, Justin would play Kutsenko

When Dr. Kutsenko heard the pairings, she said to Gilead with a warm smile, "They've obviously saved the best for last. My husband is a great admirer of yours."

"Thank you," Justin responded in Russian. "Is this your first trip to Havana?"

"Yes."

"How do you like it?" Justin asked.

"Sunshine in January is delightful," she said. "But I suppose it is very hot in Havana in the summertime."

Justin leaned closer and responded, "But it's good for the sugar crop."

They had been standing side by side, politely watching the bald sweating Cuban read from a long congratulatory message on the match from various chess dignitaries. Lena Kutsenko turned quickly to look at Justin.

"What did you say?" she asked, trying to keep her voice casual.

"I said, in Havana, the sun is hot, but it's good for the sugar crop." Her eyes searched his face, and he nodded slightly to her. He saw one of the KGB men approaching them and Kutsenko looking anxiously in their direction.

"I'm your man," Justin said quickly and softly. "We will talk later."

She nodded and left a moment later with the KGB man who steered her back to her husband and the rest of the Russian contingent.

After the announcements, Justin spent some time with the

other American team members, then walked up the stairs to his second-floor room. His first game was scheduled for 1:00 P.M. the next day.

Zharkov answered the soft knock on his door. One of the Russians from the ballroom stood there. He was a gorilla-shouldered man with no discernible waistline. In his light tan suit, he had the configuration of a cardboard box. He stepped inside the room.

"He has gone up to his room, Comrade Colonel."

"Whom did he talk to?"

"To Kutsenko earlier. To Dr. Kutsenko later tonight."

"Did you overhear what was said?"

"No. I could not get close enough. But he said something that seemed to surprise her. I could tell by her face."

"Very good. Tell your men to be very careful with the Kutsenkos. Keep a sharp eye on them."

"Yes sir, Colonel."

"Gilead's second. This Harry Andrew. Was there any sign of him?"

"No, sir," the KGB man said. "Should we do anything special with Gilead?"

"No. I will take care of him."

When the man left, Zharkov returned to the small desk in the room where he had been jotting notes. It had not been necessary for him to be in the ballroom to hear the pairings, because he already knew them. He had arranged to play Gilead on Friday, the match's third day. That was the night Castro would come to welcome the players officially, and Zharkov knew that the Grandmaster, no matter what arrangements were made with the Kutsenkos, would not leave before he had met Zharkov across the chessboard. And until Castro came, Zharkov would make sure that the Kutsenkos were guarded at all times so that Gilead could not attempt to spirit them out of Cuba. Then he would deal with Gilead.

A good plan, he told himself. It was neat, and it was economical. It would work.

But who the hell was Harry Andrew?

"The place is crawling with KGB people," Justin said as he turned on the radio loudly. As he spoke, he removed his tuxedo jacket, went to the writing table in the corner of the room, and scrawled on a piece of letter paper, "I made contact with Lena Kutsenko."

Starcher read the noted, nodded, and handed it back. "What did you say?" he whispered.

Justin wrote, "Gave password. Said we'll talk later. Kutsenkos under close watch all evening."

Starcher took an ashtray from an end table and tore Justin's note into confetti-size pieces. When he was done, he rose, went to the bathroom, and flushed the pieces of paper away. He came out and said, "You'd better get some rest. You're playing tomorrow?"

"Yes. One o'clock."

"Who?"

"Ribitnov. He's a very good young Russian. I get Zharkov on Friday and Kutsenko on Saturday."

"Maybe, Justin, we're going to win all our games," Starcher said.

"Only one of them matters to me," the Grandmaster said.

Later, Starcher asked, "Did you see Zharkov tonight?"

"Yes."

"And?"

"I didn't kill him," Justin said.

Justin sensed that someone was watching him when he left the second-floor room to go downstairs for a late breakfast.

He let the stairwell door close behind him, then stopped and waited. A few seconds later, he heard a faint knocking and opened the door carefully.

A small, dark-haired man in a flowered shirt and jeans was standing in front of the door to his room. His hands were folded in front of him in the manner of someone praying in church.

The door opened, and the man said, *"Dónde está Luis?"*

Justin heard Starcher say, "Sorry, you've got the wrong room." The door closed, and the man came down the hallway as Justin stepped into the hall. The man was buttoning his shirt.

When he saw Justin, he seemed to hesitate for a split second, then smiled casually in the manner of one stranger passing another in a strange place.

Justin smiled back, but when he drew abreast of the man, he reached out his right hand and grabbed the clump of muscles between the man's neck and shoulder. The man groaned as Justin squeezed. His knees buckled. Justin reached his other hand around and tore the man's shirt open. A small camera was attached to the man's chest with strips of adhesive tape. Justin ripped the camera loose and pocketed it.

"Tell your boss no pictures," he said coldly in Spanish. "Now, go."

The man ran off without argument and vanished into the

323

stairwell. When Justin let himself into the room with a key, Starcher was at the window, shaving while looking out over Havana's broad boulevards. He turned at the sound of Justin's entrance.

The Grandmaster tossed the camera onto the bed. "Zharkov's apparently interested in you," he said.

"Where'd you get that?"

"The man who just came to the door had it. I'm sure your picture's on the film."

"Russians are nothing if not curious," Starcher said. He put down the razor and stepped outside into the hall with Justin. "I'll keep an eye out," he whispered, "but I'll be gone most of the day."

"Where will you be?"

"I'm going to talk to Kael's man, see if he's heard anything."

"All right. Just be careful," Gilead said.

"You just win," Starcher said.

Walking downstairs, Justin thought that he had merely delayed Zharkov's identification of Starcher. The Russians could easily get into their room, take fingerprints, and run them through the KGB computers against the files of all known Western spies. It would be only a matter of a few hours.

Justin hoped that Starcher would be able to come up with something fast, find out what Zharkov, Nichevo, and the other Russians were up to in Cuba. He was worried about the old man's health, and he wanted to get him and the Kutsenkos aboard Saarinen's boat as soon as he could.

Because, right now, they were only distractions, keeping him away from his main mission. The killing of Alexander Zharkov.

The mission of his life.

The meaning of his life.

Justin arrived in the grand ballroom at 12:45 P.M. Ribitnov, the young Soviet expert whom he would play that day, greeted him warmly in halting English and seemed relieved when Justin responded in fluent Russian.

For the purposes of the chess match, the giant ballroom had been divided into two halves. In one half, folding chairs for some five hundred spectators had been set up, and high on the side walls were positioned giant diagrams of chessboards with large magnetic chessmen. Underneath were display boards for writing each player's moves, so the spectators could follow the games.

The other half of the ballroom had a chess table and chairs set up in each corner for the four games that would take place at once. In the center of that area, coffee and refreshments were set up for the players and for the tournament officials.

Justin saw Zharkov standing near the game table in the far corner of the hall, but the Russian did not even glance in Gilead's direction.

With one of the Cuban chess officials on hand, Justin picked up a black pawn and a white one, shuffled them around while holding his hands behind his back, then clasped one pawn in each closed hand and held his hands in front of him.

Ribitnov pointed to Justin's closed left hand. Justin opened it to show a white pawn. Ribitnov had won the right to play white, which always moved first in a chess game.

Just before one o'clock, the two men took seats across from each other at the square, cloth-covered table. The chessboard in front of them was made of alternating inlaid squares of walnut and ash, and the pieces were the classic Staunton design, always used in serious play. The chessmen were weighted with lead slugs for better balance, and their bottoms were covered with felt so they would not scratch the highly polished board.

The official adjusted the chess clock and placed it on the side of the table between the two men. It was a clock with two faces, and registered individually the time each player took to move. Players were required to make a minimum of forty moves in two and a half hours, and if any player failed to make his fortieth move before his 150 minutes had elapsed, a red flag would drop on the face of his clock, and he would lose the game by forfeit. Each player also had a score sheet to keep track of the moves of the games, but often, in time pressure, a player would either forget or not have time to record the game's moves, so the tournament officials assigned to their game kept an extra score sheet, which would serve as the official record of the game.

At exactly 1:00 P.M., the tournament official asked both men if they were ready. Both nodded, and the official pressed down the button on Justin's side of the chess clock. Pressing that button started the clock ticking on Ribitnov's side.

The Russian instantly moved the center pawn in front of his king forward two squares and pressed the button on his side of the clock. Justin responded immediately with an identical move, hit the button on Ribitnov's clock. The game had begun.

King knight to king bishop three. Clock.

Justin responded with queen knight to queen bishop three square. Clock.

Bishop to knight five. Ribitnov set the piece down and instantly slapped the clock. Often chess players, to save fractions of a second that might be worth gold in the final moves of a complicated game, will move the piece with the right hand, holding the left hand above the clock. As soon as they have placed the piece and released it, the left hand will slap down and start the opponent's clock immediately. Justin did not do this because he rarely found himself in time trouble.

Ribitnov had chosen the Ruy Lopez opening for the game. It was a fighting game that yielded white a small advantage coming out of the opening. The main lines of the game were well known to all veteran chess players, but required constant study because no chess opening was static. Openings were continuously being analyzed, and current thinking about the strongest continuations was always being revised. Sometimes low-quality players—patzers, as they were termed—accidentally stumbled on an interesting move that might come to the attention of a master who would analyze it and discover a playing line that had eluded the attention and wits of thousands of chess masters for generations.

The great American attacking genius, Frank Marshall, once developed a variation in the opening and, according to legend, saved it for five years so he could spring it on an unsuspecting Jose Capablanca, the Cuban world champion. But when he finally got his opportunity, Capablanca calmly crushed Marshall's new variation as if Marshall were a child.

It proved that chess was the most difficult of games. Playing it well required an encyclopedic memory, the ability to process vast amounts of new material and relate it to other material already in memory storage, and the judgment to know when to veer away from the traditional lines and strike off alone in a new direction.

But there was another aspect of chess that had nothing to do with brilliance or knowledge or judgment. It was what differentiated chess from any other game on earth. It was the factor that elevated it into the sphere of high art, and its best players to the realm of genius.

It was a mental condition that those of the West called "flow"—an inexplicable release in the mind of the player, when the game seemed to work itself out automatically, without conscious thought. It was a mental laser beam directed exclusively at the chessboard, compressing the entire universe into sixty-four squares.

There was a story, allegedly true, that a fire once broke out during a game between two grandmasters. When the critical positions had been reached and played through and the game's outcome was no longer in doubt, the two chess players both eased out of "flow" to see the puddles of water from the firemen's hoses, the overturned furniture and scorched walls. Annoyed, one of the grandmasters complained, "Why is this room so messy? How is somebody supposed to play chess in a place that looks like this?"

At Rashimpur, Justin had developed the power to focus his energy and concentration, blotting out all distractions and interruptions, but "flow" was more than mere mental discipline. It came unbidden, and its dizzying flight was always unexpected.

He did not yet feel comfortable at the chessboard. It was the first time he had sat at a chess table across from a human opponent in five years. He forced himself to concentrate, keeping his mind off Zharkov, thinking only of the chess pieces, but he was not at ease.

The players finished their twenty-fourth move. Justin, while not comfortable, had been playing very well, and the small advantage that Ribitnov had carried through the opening had disappeared. Justin's pieces now controlled the main lines that led to the young Russian's king. For the moment, the king was safe behind a wall of pawns, but constant pressure could break even the strongest of walls.

Justin was calculating his options, playing methodically,

when he felt it, light and perfect, as if a weight had been suddenly lifted from him.

It was the feeling he had first experienced as a child in the chess match in Paris, when he met and conquered Zharkov and the Russian chess masters who helped him. Now, as then, he accepted the surge of power that directed his moves.

For Justin Gilead, the rest of the world ceased to exist. All that mattered now were the chessboard in front of him and the lines of force that connected the pieces to one another with dazzling clarity.

There was nothing else. Nothing intruded as he rested his gray-streaked head on his left hand and studied the board. The position of the game exuded a kind of force field of its own, and now his mind ranged freely into that web of energy, feeling it, understanding the inherent logic and economy in the movement of the game, the pressure of the moves, the ebb and flow of the strategy.

The "book" moves—those played by centuries of great chess players—no longer counted. The game with Ribitnov had taken on its own dynamic. As they played, Justin and the Russian blazed new ground, carrying the game into directions where not a single game in history had ever been before.

Eight moves later, Justin advanced his queen until it stood directly in front of the pawn wall that sealed Ribitnov's king off from the rest of the battle going on before him.

The queen, the most powerful fighting piece on the board, could now be captured by a pawn, the lowliest piece. As his clock ticked away, Ribitnov stared at the position. Was it possible that Justin Gilead had blundered? Had he sacrificed his queen for nothing? Was it possible that there was no checkmate in sight for Gilead? Was the move a colossal mistake?

The Russian studied the position, reached out to take the queen with a pawn, withdrew his hand, then reached out again. But before he could touch the pawn, the red flag on his clock dropped.

"Time," the tournament official called. "The game to Mr. Gilead."

It took Justin a moment to remember where he was and what had just happened. He rose to his feet.

Ribitnov still stared at the position, then remembered his

manners and stood to shake Justin's hand. But he did not remove his gaze from the chessboard.

"I still don't see it," he said. "Is it there?"

Justin nodded and answered him in Russian. "The rooks double and the bishop at A-six. Another rook sacrifice and it's over. Thank you, Vyacheslav. You played a wonderful game."

"Not wonderful enough," the young Russian responded ruefully, then grinned. "I think I liked you better when you were in retirement. No wonder Ivan has been singing your praises to everyone."

It was just after five o'clock. Together, Justin and Ribitnov went to the refreshment table in the middle of the floor to look at the games of the other players. Kutsenko had already won by forcing a resignation on the twenty-third move of his game with the young American, John Shinnick. Keverin, the aged Russian genius, and Gousen, the fiery New Yorker on the American team, had seen their game settle quickly into a well-established situation in which neither side had an advantage, and after only nineteen moves, both players had agreed on a draw. This allowed them both to conserve their energy for games and positions from which they might be able to extract a win, and spared them the rigors of spending what often seemed like an eternity in a dull, empty position.

The only game left was in the far corner of the room where Zharkov and Carey, the American champion, were locked in a complicated endgame. Each had a king, a bishop, and three pawns, but glancing at the board, Justin felt that Carey stood better because of placement of his pawns. He mentioned this to Ribitnov, who agreed. "Unless Zharkov can get his king in front," he said.

A writer for a British chess magazine asked Justin in English for an interview. "We'd like to know where you've been, Mr. Gilead. What you've been doing."

"I'm sorry," Justin said. "I haven't played in a very long while, and I'm really quite tired. Perhaps before the match is over, we'll get a chance to talk."

The reporter nodded politely and drifted away. Justin again looked toward Zharkov's table. He saw the Russian's thick shoulders and bull neck hunched forward. How easy, he thought. How easy to go forward and break that big neck. Kill him and be done with it.

But his word was his word.

He turned away from the temptation, which was almost too strong to resist, thanked Ribitnov again, and left the hall to return to his room.

Tomorrow was another game.

In his room, Justin carefully touched his fingertips to the Formica shelf next to the sink and felt a slight trace of stickiness. Fingerprint tape had been used to try to lift prints from there. And probably, he decided, throughout the rest of the room, too. By now, Zharkov would have copies of Starcher's prints. He would have to tell Starcher to be careful.

Justin went down to the main dining room at eight o'clock, hoping to meet Ivan or Lena Kutsenko, but apparently all the members of the Russian chess team and their entourage were eating in their rooms. Justin sat with the three other American players.

Zharkov had lost his game with Carey. He had tried to block the American's pawn advance with his king, but had failed to protect his own pawns. One of them had fallen, and, faced with a clear pawn deficit and no way to prevent its being promoted into a queen, Zharkov had resigned.

The score stood in favor of the Americans: two wins, one loss, one draw. Five points for the United States, three points for Russia.

Justin waited late in the dining room, but the Kutsenkos did not appear. The Americans talked mainly about chess. Carey said he had figured out why all those Russian warships were in the harbor.

"If we win, they're going to blast the hotel," he said.

Just after ten o'clock, Justin went back to his room. Starcher had not returned by eleven, and Justin felt a stab of anxiety for the old man. The number of KGB men traveling with the Russian team had surprised Gilead. He thought fleetingly that if something had happened to Starcher, he would be free of his promise. Nothing would stop him from going after Zharkov right now.

CHAPTER THIRTY-SEVEN

Starcher returned before breakfast the following morning and listened quietly as Justin told him of the traces of fingerprint tape that he'd found in the bathroom. Starcher turned the radio on loudly before answering. "Zharkov'll know who I am, then," he said. "If he doesn't already."

Justin did not like Starcher's attitude. He had expected Starcher to be concerned about his cover being blown so thoroughly, so quickly, but instead, the veteran CIA man seemed jaunty, almost happy.

"You don't seem very worried," the Grandmaster said.

"In this business, you worry only about the things you can do something about. Leave the worrying to me. I'm good at it."

"*Now* you tell me," Justin said. "I worried half the night when you didn't come back."

"I met Kael's man."

"Who is he?"

"His name is Pablo Olivares. He owns a bar called the Purple Shell on the waterfront. I spent the night there talking to him."

"What'd you find out?"

"Nothing," Starcher said. "He's got one of the cleaner waterfront bars, and a lot of the Russian sailors from those warships go in there. But they don't even know what they're doing here. Who tells enlisted men anything?"

Justin waited, and Starcher said, "The ships have been there now for a couple of months, and all the while, there've been Russian threats about interventions in Cuba. But Olivares hasn't heard a word.''

"Is it possible that the Americans have something planned here that you don't know anything about?" Justin asked.

"No." Starcher hesitated, then said again, more surely, "No, I don't think so. When I was in Moscow, I would have heard something. And since then . . . well, I just don't think Harry Kael is smart enough to lie to me and get away with it. He said we don't have anything going for us here, and I believe it.''

Justin shrugged, went to the mirror, and knotted a tie around his neck. Many chess players showed up at matches looking as if they had just walked out of a service station where they were pumping gas. But the Russians always dressed like gentlemen, and Justin liked the tradition, so he always dressed for a game, too.

Starcher perched on the edge of the dresser, talking in a whisper. "Anyway," he said, "Olivares doesn't know anything. And his girlfriend—she works for the director of Castro's national police—she doesn't know anything either.''

"This Olivares must be under deep cover to be able to work for you and romance a secret police official, too," Justin said.

"He's a native. Been here all his life and is just sour on Castro. I'm glad, by the way, that we set up that other pickup point with Saarinen. The waterfront is crawling with Cuban cops and agents. We'd have our hands full trying to get out of Havana by sea. Did you talk to our friends again?''

"No. There's a guard on their door, and I think they're taking meals in their room. I'll try today.''

"Tell them they'll have to be ready to leave with no notice at all. Saarinen's going to be in the pickup position between eleven and one o'clock for the next three nights. It'll be one of those times.''

"Suppose we don't find out what Zharkov's planning?" Justin asked. "Suppose he has nothing planned?''

"He didn't come here just to play chess," Starcher said. "Not the head of Nichevo. He's up to something.''

"All right. Still, suppose we don't find out what?''

"You'll still take the Kutsenkos out," Starcher said.

"I noticed that 'you.' What about you?''

Starcher shrugged. "I don't know. We'll cross that bridge when we come to it."

"Start thinking about crossing the bridge," Justin said. "I want to know what and when. Remember, I have business here, too," he said.

"I won't forget," Starcher said.

"And from now on, if you're going to be out, call me in the evening between six-thirty and seven. Let me know you're alive."

"All right," Starcher agreed with uncharacteristic meekness.

Zharkov walked impatiently to the telephone, dialed the number of another room, and snapped quickly, "Any report yet?"

His face illustrated the negative reply. "As soon as you get something, bring it to me . . . Yes, that's right . . . even during the game."

He hung up the telephone wondering who Harry Andrew was. Who was the Grandmaster's traveling companion?

Starcher decided that this day he would do something very important: He would find a store and buy a box of Cuban cigars.

Justin had been right. Starcher was not at all worried that Zharkov might by now know who he was. He welcomed the possibility because he regarded it as his only chance of finding out what Nichevo was up to. He was sure there was something, and if it took making himself vulnerable to capture to find out what it was, then that was what he had decided to do.

He was glad that Justin knew the pickup points and the schedule for Saarinen's boat. If anything went wrong, the Grandmaster would be able to get the Kutsenkos out of Cuba.

If anything went wrong. In this business, something almost always did.

Justin's second-round opponent was Victor Keverin. The aging Russian had twice played for the world championship, twice losing, both times to other Russians. There were rumors that in the second match, Keverin, who was Jewish, had been ordered to lose. Justin was inclined to believe the rumors, because Keverin's play in that second match had been spotty and erratic, totally out of character for a man whose games for almost forty years had been characterized by precise, careful, methodical play.

Not for Keverin was the bold attacking stroke, the decisive sacrifice, the sparkling combination that left an opponent battered and reeling, and spectators applauding. Instead, he won chess games the way oysters create pearls—one small layer after another, each layer apparently of no value in itself—and then, late in the game, an opponent would take stock and realize that the infinitesimal advantages, all added together, had given Keverin an overwhelming positional superiority. Justin had played him twice before. He had drawn one game and lost the other when the old master had refuted Justin's proposed bishop sacrifice by ignoring it and, instead, continuing to push pawns down the board. It was the way Keverin won games.

Justin had no illusions about the quality of his own game. He had played well yesterday, but the young Russian he had beaten had not been sharp. And for this own part, Justin was simply not tournament tough. It took a lot of play at the highest levels, plus ongoing practice and analysis, to keep one's game sharp, to save oneself from a suicidal lapse at the table, to have one's mind so tuned to chess that one could instantly disregard time-wasting possibilities on the board and move into the flow of potential moves that bore with them some hope of gaining an advantage. Justin simply was not there yet. He made too many errors at the board.

There was a truism in chess that the winner of the game was the player who made the next-to-last mistake. Justin was still quite capable of making the last error and losing.

He had the white pieces today. He decided to move the game away early from the established, carefully analyzed lines in which Keverin was just too well read for Justin to compete, opting instead for a tricky, trappy kind of contest where, with good play and some luck, Justin might find some kind of game-winning resource.

So he moved the pawn in front of his king bishop ahead two squares. It was Bird's opening, popular at the end of the nineteenth century, but rarely seen in serious chess anymore. Keverin glanced at the bishop pawn for only a few seconds, then smiled and played his own queen pawn forward two squares.

Justin glanced away from the board and saw Zharkov's burly back at the chess table and felt a wave of hatred wash over him.

Why am I playing chess? he asked himself. *Why is that man still alive?* Justin longed to end it all now, once and for all, but he struggled to remind himself that he could not give his attention to Zharkov and have any chance of winning against Keverin. As he started to look back down toward the board, he saw one of the KGB men, the big one in the light tan suit, walk up to Zharkov and gesture to him.

The Russian left the table, and the KGB man whispered something in his ear. Zharkov nodded. His face was turned in profile to the Grandmaster, and Gilead saw it crease into a small but real smile. Something had just pleased Zharkov. What was it?

Zharkov whispered something to the KGB agent, and the man nodded and walked away. Zharkov returned to his seat at the chess table and a moment later was leaning forward over the board again, his concentration totally on the pieces and the position.

Justin clenched his jaw. He understood what the exchange between the two Russians had been about. *He knows about Starcher,* Justin thought. *He knows who Harry Andrew is.*

Starcher knew the tail was on him only a few minutes after leaving the coffee shop of the José Martí.

He had not told Justin Gilead, because he hadn't wanted to worry him, but he had picked up a weapon the night before from Pablo Olivares. It was a four-shot .22-caliber revolver, as small as a derringer. Starcher now had it taped to the back of his left ankle, under his sock.

He whistled as he strolled slowly toward the park. He didn't want to lose the tail.

The game was virtually over.

Justin Gilead had come out of the opening with good development and a toehold in the center of the board. He had tried three different attacks on Keverin's position, but the Russian chess master had repelled all of them, each time gaining another slight edge in position over Justin.

As his small advantages grew into a large advantage, Keverin had begun trading off pieces. Now the game had turned into

Justin's king, rook, and three pawns against equal manpower on Keverin's side. But Keverin's pawns were placed better, and it seemed to Justin inevitable that eventually the Russian would move one of his pawns to the opposite end of the board where it could be promoted to a queen. That overwhelming material superiority would guarantee Keverin the win.

Justin glanced at the clock. As usual he had played quickly. Keverin had just completed his thirty-second move and had about eighteen minutes left on his clock. It was Justin's move. There were forty minutes left on his clock, but it was ticking.

He concentrated on the board, trying to find something in the position, some hidden resource that could give him an edge, or at least stop Keverin's inexorable pawn march down the board.

As he often did, he looked up from the board, the position fixed and clearly visualized in his mind, and gazed off into the distance. He found it a comfortable way to concentrate, away from the disruptions and distractions of the real world. But no voice came as it had yesterday. There was no magical sense of entering into the world of the chess pieces, feeling their power, and letting them direct the flow of the game.

His eyes drifted casually around the room. He saw Ivan Kutsenko move a piece, hit his clock to start his American opponent's time running, and then walk toward the door that led to the rest rooms.

Justin noticed that for the first time Kutsenko had no KGB guard trailing him. He glanced around and saw no Russian agents in the room at all. When Zharkov whispered to the KGB man, he must have sent them all on assignment. Zharkov was still across the room, bent over the chessboard.

Justin rose from his seat and walked to the men's room.

He and Kutsenko were alone.

The Russian looked nervously about, then came close to Justin and whispered.

"My wife said you spoke to her."

"Yes. I was a friend of Riesling's, the man you met in Moscow. I'm to help you get to the United States. We have a boat. It'll be tonight, tomorrow, or the next night."

"What should we do?"

"Just be ready at a moment's notice. If I can find out in advance, I'll let you know. If not, I'll probably just come to your room to get you, and we'll leave. Be ready at all times.''

"There's always a guard on our room," Kutsenko said.

"Don't worry about the guard," Justin said.

"Do we have a chance?" Kutsenko asked nervously.

Justin put his strong hand on the frail man's shoulder. "More than a chance," he said. "We'll get you out of here. That's a promise."

"I have so many questions to ask you," Kutsenko said.

"On the boat going back," Justin said.

"Have you done this before? I have to know."

"Many times," Justin said. "Don't worry, Ivan. You and your wife will be all right."

The Russian searched Justin's eyes for reassurance beyond his words, then nodded his agreement. "I believe you, Justin."

"Now get back to your game. I'll follow in a few minutes."

Alexander Zharkov pushed his chair back from the chessboard, took a deep breath, and relaxed for the first time since the game had started.

Andrew Starcher.

The old CIA chief from Moscow. The Americans could not have played into his hands more totally if they had all been on Nichevo's payroll.

What more perfect scapegoat to blame for the Castro assassination than an American ex-spymaster? The murder would have all the trappings of a CIA enterprise. Starcher, their chief of staff in Moscow, suddenly "retires." Then just as suddenly, he surfaces in Cuba with an American chess team just before Castro is assassinated. A CIA plot, pure and simple, the kind of thing they did so often and usually bungled so badly.

He smiled as he thought of another benefit that came with Starcher's presence.

It had rendered Justin Gilead expendable.

As soon as he was sure that his men had captured Starcher, Zharkov would send out the word: Kill the Grandmaster.

Kill him.

Put bullets in his eyes and knives in his heart. Kill him.

For once and for all.

Kill him.

Burn the body.

Kill him.

Zharkov looked back at the chessboard. His opponent, the young American, had not yet moved, but the position was hopeless. With precise play, Zharkov knew that he would force a resignation before the fortieth move so that the game would not have to be recessed and concluded tomorrow. He had other plans for tomorrow.

Maybe.

The Grandmaster saw a glimmer of hope in his game position, but it was a tricky maneuver, and he had to calculate the consequences exactly.

He was disappointed. Yesterday, in his game against Ribitnov, he had felt the power come on him, even if only briefly. When that happened, the moves came almost automatically, but today that power had deserted him. He had played this game one move after another, logically and coldly, with never a sense that he was becoming absorbed in the game. Yesterday, for a few minutes, he had soared into the mathematical meanings of life and the universe; today, he was adding up large columns of figures. It was the difference between art and craft, between creation and caretaking.

He closed his eyes and pictured the chessboard and the position of the pieces.

If he moved his king up behind his row of pawns, Keverin would surely move his king up to meet him, to prevent Justin from moving ahead of his pawns. It would be a very basic defensive move by Keverin, one that required no analysis or thought.

But then, if Justin sacrificed a pawn to Keverin's king, and then another pawn to one of Keverin's pawns, then . . .

Maybe.

He glanced at Keverin's clock. The Russian had only six minutes left for six more moves. With time pressure, he might not see through Justin's maneuver.

Justin moved his king forward a square. Keverin thought for a few seconds and did the same.

Justin immediately pushed a pawn forward. He wanted to play quickly now so that Keverin would have no chance to analyze the position on Justin's time. The Russian would have to study for a while his own clock was running, remorselessly ticking away the precious seconds that remained before his red flag dropped and he lost to Justin on time.

The old Russian was far too crafty, in this winning position, to let a game slip away because of the clock. Justin counted on that.

Keverin made his decision. With his right hand, he picked up his king and moved it forward to capture Justin's pawn. Then he immediately slapped down his clock with his left hand, starting Justin's time. Almost two full minutes gone. Four minutes left.

The Grandmaster did not hesitate. He pushed another pawn forward a single square and said, "Check."

Keverin's face clearly showed his annoyance. Gilead should have resigned. In chess at this level, each player assumed that his opponent, given a winning edge, would carry that edge through into a victory. It was almost insulting to insist on playing out a game that was clearly lost.

This time, Keverin pondered for only a half-minute before taking Justin's pawn with his own.

Justin immediately moved his rook forward and checked Keverin's king. The Russian saw what had happened.

Done. Too late. It was over.

On the one hand, if he took the rook with his king, Justin would be in a position where he could not move without moving his king into a check, onto a square where he could be captured. That would be an illegal move. But because he was safe on the square where his king now stood, the game would be a draw. It was a position called stalemate, and neither side won.

On the other hand, if the Russian refused to take the rook, Justin could use it to capture one of Keverin's pawns and open a path for Justin's remaining pawn to move down the board to its queening square. He would be one move ahead of Keverin's pawns, would have his queen first, and with it, a clear win.

Keverin looked at the board for two full minutes while his clock ticked silently away. Justin could see the Russian's face reddening in anger at himself for blundering away a win.

He nodded in resignation, then sighed, looked up, and smiled at Justin.

"A draw?" he said.

Justin nodded. "I'll be happy to take one against you."

Keverin pushed the button on his side of the clock down halfway. This stopped both clocks, and the two men rose and shook hands.

"Beautifully done," Keverin said.

"A swindle," Justin responded. "It was all I had left since you chopped my position up so badly."

"The older I get, the more I learn that the hardest thing to do in chess is to win a won game," Keverin said graciously. "Especially against a player like you. I had forgotten how good you are."

"And I still have never beaten you," Gilead responded.

"Go back into retirement before you have the chance again," Keverin said.

Justin knew that the Russian was speaking with real warmth. A player who had lost or been swindled out of a win first felt anger and annoyance at himself, but then usually only admiration for the player who had done it to him. Great players all viewed chess as a life-or-death struggle, but it was a wonderful kind of death because you sprang back to life as soon as the pieces were again set up on the board for the next game.

Keverin clapped Gilead around the shoulders, and the two men walked off to the tournament director to sign the official score sheets. As he walked away, Justin felt Zharkov's eyes burning into his back.

Three of them.

Starcher had spotted them while he was walking toward the giant statue of José Martí, which loomed over the Plaza de la Revolución. They were dressed like Western businessmen on their way to lunch, but their faces were either pale or blotchy red, the faces of people not used to the sun. And they had been too regular in changing their positions. One followed him; another was amidships of him; the third was in front of Starcher. But they rotated positions precisely every five minutes, and while the rotation was the correct maneuver, the rigid schedule was not.

Starcher was surprised that they had not made a move against him yet. It was late afternoon now. Were they waiting for further word from Zharkov? Justin had told him that the chess games must end no later than six o'clock each evening. Would he have to wait until dark before these men picked him up?

Starcher strolled right, down an uncrowded concrete path bordered by bushes, toward the Avenida Ayestara. The park had been emptying for the last hour. It had been filled mostly with women, many with babies, but now they had left, probably on their way home to prepare dinner.

He couldn't help feeling that it was good to be on the street again, good to be an agent again. He had spent more than three hours on the streets of Havana, most of it walking, and his heart felt fine. Maybe there was still room in the CIA for someone like him. He could be a courier, anything, just something to do that didn't involve sitting behind a desk and feeling miserable when young agents went out on missions and never reported back. So he was old, but what was age when you were good? And he *was* good.

He paused to light a cigar and noticed the three men had come together and were walking toward him. He cautioned himself not to make it too easy for them. He took a puff on his cigar, then walked briskly toward the street. He half expected to hear the sound of running feet as the Russians closed on him, but he didn't. He paused just before reaching the sidewalk and glanced back again. The three men had gone, but as he turned back, confused, a black car pulled up to the curb.

The rear door opened, and a dark-skinned man snapped in English, "Get in." He held a gun aimed at Starcher's belly.

Should he run? Would it make his capture look more real?

Before he could decide, the three men who had been following him emerged from the bushes on either side of the concrete walkway, grabbed his arms, and pushed him easily into the back seat of the car.

"What's going on here?" he snapped to the man holding the gun on him. He was a big man, much bigger than the usual Hispanic.

"This is your welcome to Havana, Mr. Starcher," the man answered. "Please put your hands in your lap and do not move them."

Wordlessly, Starcher did as he was told. He was glad they had finally captured him.

Just before six o'clock, the young American resigned from his clearly lost game with Zharkov. After a perfunctory handshake, Zharkov went immediately to his room and dialed a telephone number.

"Do you have him?"

"Yes," said Yuri Durganiv.

"Is he giving you any trouble?"

"None at all. He's too old for trouble," Durganiv said.

"Fine. Be careful of him. He's got a bad heart, and I wouldn't want anything to disturb him. He's valuable."

"I understand," Durganiv said as Zharkov hung up.

Success. He had the CIA man, the man on whom he could hang the blame for Castro's murder.

And Justin Gilead was a dead man.

The telephone was mounted on the bulkhead of a small cabin cruiser anchored out in Havana harbor. Yuri Durganiv, while talking to Zharkov, had stood in the doorway, aiming a snub-nosed .38 revolver at Starcher, who sat on a cot on the other side of the cabin.

Durganiv had made a mistake. He thought that Starcher could not speak Russian. The American was too old to cause trouble, Durganiv had said, and Starcher thought grimly, *I might just teach the son of a bitch he's wrong.*

The Russian had made another mistake, too. When he searched Starcher he had done the cursory police search most people used, patting down the inside and outside of both legs, but ignoring the back of the legs. With a little sense of comfort, Starcher felt the weight of the small revolver still taped to the back of his left ankle.

Too old? Starcher thought. This Russian who looked like a Cuban might learn otherwise.

After Starcher found out what Zharkov was up to.

The day's four chess games had been completed. The Russians had duplicated the American performance of the day before: two wins, a loss, and a draw. The score at the end of two days was the United States, eight points; the Soviet Union, eight points.

The players were advised that the next day's game would start at ten o'clock instead of one. The match chairman announced that Fidel Castro would be at tomorrow night's dinner to speak and to welcome the players, and the committee needed the extra time to prepare the ballroom for his appearance.

CHAPTER THIRTY-EIGHT

When he had received no message by eight o'clock, Justin knew that Starcher was in trouble.

The Grandmaster pushed aside the remnants of the salad plate he had ordered from room service and closed the book of chess openings he had been studying.

He dressed in jeans and a sweat shirt and walked down the steps from his room to the ornate gilded lobby of the sprawling old hotel.

The telephone rang in Zharkov's room.

"Yes?" he said.

"He is leaving now," a voice said.

"Make sure he does not return," Zharkov said.

Starcher looked through the small window of the ship's cabin in which he was locked. Just a few yards away, he saw a sloping gray wall, but as the cabin cruiser rocked backward and he was able to glance up, he saw it was not a wall at all but the hull of a giant Soviet cruiser. From the other side of the cabin, the view was much the same, but the Soviet destroyer there was a hundred yards away and he could see its outline clearly.

Floating nearby were two small patrol craft, machine guns mounted in their sterns.

He paused for a moment to consider his predicament. He was being held captive on a boat, surrounded by warships of the Soviet navy. He might be able to use his gun to escape, to shoot his captor, but then what? He knew nothing about boats. If he could get this one started, what then? Would he even be able to get it to shore? Or would those Soviet patrol boats overtake him and gun him down before he got a hundred yards away?

By now, he knew Justin Gilead would be worried about him because he had not called. But Justin had no idea of where he was, and unless he forced the information from Zharkov, he would not be able to find him. And Starcher still had no idea what Nichevo's plans were.

He finished the last of the large mug of coffee that Durganiv had brought in to him, then lay down to rest on the narrow wood-framed cot. He would just have to wait. He had allowed himself to be captured to find out what Zharkov had planned, and it was pointless to do anything now until he had found that out.

He would wait, and he would rest. He would not act but react.

His eyes felt very heavy, and he realized how tired he was, and as he fell asleep, he thought, Starcher, you're sixty-six years old, and right now you feel every minute of it.

He touched the pistol taped to the back of his ankle. For a moment, it made him feel secure, but then he passed into a deep sleep in which he felt nothing.

From the outside, the Purple Shell looked seedy; the building needed painting, and the windows were dirty and flyspecked. But inside, the barroom was clean and neat, the floor spread with sawdust. At the end of the long bar was a small dining room with four square tables.

The bar was half filled by six men sitting on stools. They had the look of seamen, wearing rough sweaters and baseball caps, and their clothes emitted the smell of fish.

They talked jovially with the bartender, a tall, cadaverous man with sad, droopy eyes. He wore a white shirt and black trousers, covered by a white apron. His sleeves were rolled halfway up his forearms, and on the back of his left wrist was tattooed a purple seashell.

The bar's customers turned to look at Justin as he entered and walked to the stool at the corner of the bar, away from the main group of men. When the bartender came, he ordered a glass of red wine.

Justin put a five dollar bill on the bar, and asked softly in Spanish, "American money good?"

"Americans are running dogs, capitalistic imperialist war-mongers who would enslave the minds of all freedom-loving peoples everywhere," the bartender said. "But in the interests of international harmony, I will take American money. As much as you have." He grinned a crooked smile. "You are American?"

Justin nodded. The bartender said, "This is not a usual stop for Americans visiting the Caribbean."

"I'm a chess player," Justin said. "Are you Pablo Olivares?"

At the term "chess player," the bartender stiffened momentarily. *"Si,"* he said.

"We have a mutual friend," Justin said. "Harry Andrew?"

The bartender looked blank, and Justin leaned forward and said, "Maybe you know his name as Starcher."

The bartender quickly shook his head. "I know no one of that name, senor."

He reached for the five dollar bill, but Justin took the man's arm.

"Amigo," he said, "I mean you no harm. Starcher came with me. I also know Harry Kael, who is somebody else in the United States that you know. I'm looking now for Starcher. Do you know where he is?"

"I know no Starcher," Olivares insisted. He pulled away from Justin and made change at the register, then brought back a few Cuban bills and put them on the bar. Justin said, "Stay and listen." When he noticed that the men at the end of the bar were looking toward him, trying to overhear their conversation, he stood and leaned close to Olivares.

"Senor Olivares, you mean nothing to me. Starcher is my friend, but I have no reservations about calling the Cuban secret police and telling them that you work for Harry Kael in the CIA. I won't mind telling them that your girlfriend is involved, even if she isn't. I won't mind telling them that you were Andrew Starcher's contact when the CIA sent him to Havana. Senor, it doesn't mean anything to me, and if you do not speak to me, with honesty in your heart and in your words, I will do all those things."

The bartender's sad eyes grew sadder as he seemed to

weigh his alternatives. Then he said, "Let us talk in the back. There are too many open ears here." He turned away.

"Luis," he called out. "Watch the bar. My friend and I have to speak privately."

He led Justin through the empty dining room to a small office in the rear of the low one-story building.

"What is your name?" Olivares asked when he had closed the door tightly behind them.

"Justin Gilead."

"You have identification?"

Gilead showed him his passport, and Olivares said, "You look older."

"I feel older," Justin said.

The Cuban had reached a decision, and he said, "Starcher told me about you."

"Then you know I'm his friend and you can trust me. He was supposed to call me tonight, but he didn't. I'm worried about him. He's old and not too well. Do you know where he is?"

"I'm sorry, senor. He was here, and we talked much of the night. He is very tenacious, your Mr. Starcher. But I know of nothing the Soviets have planned here. I have heard nothing from their sailors, even though many of them come here to drink on shore leave, but I hear nothing. My woman knows nothing of what I do, nothing. Mr. Starcher—how do you say it?—he picked at my brain all night but we found nothing there. He left, telling me to notify him if I hear anything. But I have heard nothing."

"Did he say anything to you of his suspicions?" Justin asked. "Did he tell you where he might go or who else he might speak to?"

"No." Olivares shook his head sadly. He looked like a basset hound who'd missed a meal. "Apparently he told you nothing, and he told me the same."

"Did he say he would come back here?" Justin asked.

"He wished me well, senor, and said that he would speak highly of me to some friends of his. I'm sorry I cannot be more help."

"Thank you, then. I appreciate your kindness in talking to me."

"One thing, Senor Gilead. I gave Mr. Starcher a gun that I once took from a sailor. He is not unarmed."

"Good," Justin said. He walked toward the door. "Do taxicabs pass here?" he asked.

"Taxicabs pass almost nowhere in Havana," Olivares said. "But if you walk two blocks away from the harbor, that is Avenida de la Revolución. Sometimes one can find a taxicab there." Justin nodded, and Olivares said, "I would be careful wearing that golden medal around your neck so openly. This is not a peaceable area of the city."

"I am not a peaceable man," Justin said.

When he walked out through the bar again, the stools were all filled. Justin left his change on the bar and went out into the cool evening air.

"Shouldn't you study for tomorrow's game?" Katarina spooned a large serving of steamed fish and rice onto his plate in the single room of her apartment.

"No. Studying is not necessary," he said.

"Aren't you the cocky one? Win one game and now you're ready to conquer the world."

"Do you know who I play tomorrow?" Zharkov asked.

"Who?"

"The Grandmaster."

"Gilead," she said softly. "Tell me about him. I've only seen old pictures of him. What does he look like now?" She sat across the narrow table from him, her eyes intent.

"He looks much older," Zharkov said. "I don't know where he's been the last four years, but wherever it was, it was hard on him. He is thinner and moves more stiffly. Once he moved like quicksilver. He does not move like that now."

"Good," she snapped. "I hope his every joint bleeds."

Zharkov smiled. "Why do you hate him so?"

She looked at the floor for a moment, her face bewildered. "I . . . just do. I feel sometimes that I was born hating him." She laughed nervously. "Of course, that's ridiculous, since I can't . . ." Her voice trailed off in embarrassment.

Suddenly Zharkov was filled with pity for her. "You don't remember being young at all, do you? No childhood friends, no first experiences."

She smiled, too brightly. The tip of her nose was red. "You were my first experience," she said, and kissed him. "The rest doesn't matter. If I was meant to forget, it was for a reason."

He stroked her hair. For a moment, he felt an aching tenderness for the woman with no past, the dead girl he had brought to life with his passion.

"And if I was meant to hate Justin Gilead, that was for a reason, too," she said.

There was no sentimentality to her, and he could not permit any in himself. She was a gift, a gift he would one day have to destroy. Those were the terms.

Zharkov withdrew his hand, bringing himself back under control. "You will not need to hate him much longer," he said. "I'm playing him at chess tomorrow."

"And?"

"He will not appear. He dies tonight."

She looked disappointed. "I wanted to kill him for you," she said. "It would have been my gift to you."

He wanted to touch her again, feel her trusting warmth. Would she love me so if she'd had a choice? he wondered.

He would never know. Katarina, in her way, was no more human than a robot, a manufactured person created for his use. It would be foolish to think she was something more. But, oh, so easy.

"*You* are your gift to me," he said softly, and turned away.

Ahead of him, Justin could see the broad palm-lined Avenida de la Revolución, but before he reached the corner, a taxi came down the side street along which he was walking. It stopped for traffic, and Justin whistled and waved to the cabbie, who leaned out his window, looked nervously down the block, then motioned for Justin to get into the cab.

Justin had decided. He would go back to the hotel and squeeze out of Zharkov the whereabouts of Andrew Starcher.

He closed the cab door behind him. Another man, crouching in the front seat, rose and aimed a pistol at Justin. "You'll sit very still," he said in halting English, then told the driver to move on.

Justin recognized the man with the gun as one of the KGB guards he had seen at the chess match. Headlights glared through the rear window of the cab. Justin guessed there were more KGB men in a trailing car, just to make sure that he didn't try to escape.

"Where are we going?" he asked.

"For the ride, as you Americans say," the Russian said. "Sit back and enjoy."

The locks on the back doors clicked automatically as the driver engaged them from the front of the cab. He jerked forward to move into traffic and sped down the highway away from the heart of Havana. The headlights stayed in position behind them.

With luck, Justin thought, they were taking him to where Starcher was.

Yuri Durganiv pushed open the door to the cabin, saw Starcher lying still on the cot, and stepped inside. He held his revolver in his hand as he sat on a chair at the small table, waiting for the American to waken from his sleep.

Starcher had been awake before he heard the key at the door. He had slept soundly, but he opened his eyes with a long, loud display of groaning and waking up, then looked around as if he were frightened.

"Where am I? What is this place?" He wondered who this man was. He spoke Russian fluently, but he looked Hispanic. Any ideas Starcher had about overpowering him vanished when Yuri Durganiv stood to his full six-feet-four-inch height.

"I came to see if you were hungry," Yuri said.

"Yes. I'm starved. Why am I here?"

"All things in due time," Yuri said.

"I heard you on the phone before. Was that Russian you were speaking?"

"Yes."

"You don't look like a Russian," Starcher said.

"And you don't look like an assassin. Or even like a big spy for the CIA," Yuri said. He was smiling.

"An assassin? You've got the wrong man."

"No, Andrew Starcher, I've got the right man."

"Why am I here?"

"You will only be here for a while," Durganiv said. "Then you have other places to go."

"Where is Zharkov?" Starcher asked.

"He is back in the city."

"Am I going to see him?"

"If he wishes. Perhaps. Perhaps not. He will let us know."

"You work for him?"

"Yes. There is food here. Sit at this table and eat."

He locked the door, then changed places as Starcher sat at the table before the platter of food. Durganiv sat on the edge of the cot, the gun still at the ready in his hand, watching carefully.

Starcher picked at a few mouthfuls, then asked, "Why did you say I was an assassin?"

"Aren't you?"

"No."

"I don't think the world will believe that, Mr. Starcher. Eat."

Starcher ate. Things were going all right. Durganiv was still underestimating him. If it became necessary, Starcher had no doubt that he'd be able to get the gun from behind his left ankle and put a bullet into the big man's eyes before he knew what killed him.

If he had to. But first he would wait and see what happened.

He ate.

A half-hour out of Havana, the cab pulled to the side of the wide highway. Justin was hustled at gunpoint into the trailing car. Two more of the KGB men he had seen at the José Martí were in the car. He was pushed into the back seat and covered by guns from front and back. The car sped off down the highway, moving east away from Havana. None of the men spoke to Justin.

Twenty miles farther down the road, the car turned off the highway and through an opening in a long row of white fence posts that stretched for miles in either direction.

A hundred yards inside the fence posts, there was a tall chain-link fence with barbed wire atop. It bore the words "Electric Fence. Keep Out," in Spanish.

The driver opened the gate with a key, drove through, and then went back to relock the fence. Neither of the other two men moved to help; neither of them took his gun off Justin.

"What is this place?" he asked in English.

"A slaughterhouse," the man in the front seat answered. The man next to Justin said something in Russian, and all three men laughed.

Justin realized that the men did not know he spoke Russian.

The man had said, "Yes. A slaughterhouse for this one."

They planned to kill him. "What kind of slaughterhouse?" Justin asked innocently, again in English.

"This is the Agrupación Genetica de la Habana," the driver said.

"What is that?"

"A state-owned dairy and cattle farm. They do animal experiments here to improve meat and milk production. Now stop talking; you are talking too much."

"Why am I here?"

"Perhaps because you talk too much to the wrong people," the man next to Justin said.

"I don't understand what's going on. I'm a chess player. Why are you holding guns on me? What are you doing?"

"We're chess lovers. We don't want you to play Zharkov tomorrow. You might win."

"Will Zharkov be here?" Justin asked.

"No."

They were riding deeper into the country now, along a narrow, well-paved road. The driver turned sharply right. His tires spat gravel as he skidded.

"Slow down. We don't *all* want to die," the man in the front seat snapped in Russian.

They drove toward the woods now, and the narrow road became not much more than a path. There was no light ahead of them, only the funnel of light from the car's headlights.

The car moved into a blacktopped clearing. Justin could see a connected series of low buildings in front of the car's headlights.

"You're very privileged, Mr. Gilead," one of the Russians said.

"Oh?"

"You're going to be permitted to see one of the most secret installations in the world."

"I don't know what I've done to deserve the honor," Justin said.

"This is a Soviet testing center for bacteriological warfare," the man alongside him said. He was obviously the senior KGB agent; the others deferred to him.

"I thought you said this was a dairy farm, a cattle ranch," Justin said.

"It is. And there is a lot of livestock here, and a large sealed area, and here, in these buildings are tested new poisons and gases on those dairy animals. And sometimes other animals. Far out of sight of people, and with no danger to the peace-loving population of Free Democratic Cuba.''

One of the other men said in Russian, ''And even if there was an accident, what would we lose? Only Cubans,'' and all three laughed. Justin pretended he did not understand.

They parked the car. As Justin got out, he felt the barrel of the KGB's man's pistol pressed against the base of his spine.

''What am I doing here?'' Justin asked in English.

''You're a spy, Gilead,'' the elder KGB man said. ''We thought it would be instructive to give you a tour of this secret installation.''

''Is this where you brought Starcher?'' Gilead said suddenly.

''Starcher? We don't know any Starcher.''

''My second,'' Justin said. ''Where is he?''

''You ask far too many questions.''

''Is Zharkov here?''

''No.''

''Will he be?''

''We'll wait and see,'' the man said. Then the man behind Justin pushed him forward with the barrel of his gun toward a door that the driver had just opened.

A single light went on inside the low building, and when he entered, Justin saw that a long corridor ran the length of the building. One side was flanked by offices, the other by a series of doors with inset windows. The doors were heavy, wooden, and reminded him of a butcher shop's freezer locker.

The men pushed Justin at gunpoint down the hallway. Was Starcher here? Justin doubted it now. At first, he had thought they would take him wherever they had taken Starcher, if they had him.

At the end of the corridor, Justin saw a large computer panel that covered an area five feet square. It was filled with gauges and dials, and as they came closer, he saw that the dials were calibrated to measure blood pressure and pulse rate. Probably it was hooked up to all these small chambers for whatever kind of animal tests they ran there to test poisons and gases.

The man who had been driving was standing before the last cubicle. As the other three men approached, he opened the door, and the two men on either side of him jabbed Justin with their guns and pushed him inside. The heavy door slammed behind him.

He looked around quickly, trying to accustom his eyes to the darkness, as an overhead light came on.

Justin was in a room nine feet long by six feet wide. The walls and floor and ceiling were of thin sheet metal. There were microphones placed where the front wall met the ceiling, and overhead was a small grate that covered an exhaust fan. Set into the metal wall was the heavy wooden door. The inside of the door was covered with metal, except for the glass viewing window into the chamber. There was no handle to open the door, and the hinges were recessed into the wood, inaccessible to his hands.

He went to the viewing window and saw the senior Russian at the control panel.

The Russian turned, and Justin heard his voice.

"You wondered what you're doing here," the man said in English. His voice crackled from a loudspeaker overhead in the small chamber. "You've come here to die."

"I want to see Zharkov," Justin yelled.

"No need to yell. I can hear you very well. Colonel Zharkov will not be coming tonight."

"Where is my friend? You're going to kill me anyway. Where is my friend?"

"I'm sorry. I don't know. That is Colonel Zharkov's business. You are ours."

"You can't do this to me. I'm an American citizen," Justin said.

"This has been done to many American citizens," the Russian said. "To many spies. Human research, after all, is the best kind."

For the first time, Justin noticed that there was a little slot, almost like a mail slot, in the metal over the doorway.

"Do you have a preference?" the Russian said. Justin looked through the window again. The agent had opened a cabinet and was looking at vials holding various-colored capsules.

"Something esoteric perhaps," the Russian continued. "Something that paralyzes the nervous system. You'll still be able to see and to think, but you won't be able to move. And then, finally, your eyes and brain will close down, too. Or perhaps something painful. This one causes agonizing spasms. I'm told that some people jerk around so violently that they dislocate their own arms and legs." He looked over at Gilead's face, visible through the window, and smiled. "No, I suppose we'll stick to the proven methods. Cyanide should do it quite nicely."

Justin was testing the window. The glass was a half-inch thick, and there were two layers of it, separated by a quarter-inch of space, which was filled with a heavy steel grate.

The grate did not appear to be fastened just under the edges of the window, but deep inside the door frame instead.

He watched the Russian pour some liquid into a thin glass test tube and then drop in a dark-colored capsule. He quickly put a stopper in the test tube, then walked toward the door. His body covered the viewing window as he reached overhead. Justin moved away from the door, and then saw the slot over the door open and the test tube thrown through it into the small chamber.

It shattered as soon as it hit the metal floor. Instantly the small room was filled with the bitter nutty smell of cyanide. A visible cloud of gas rose from the floor and began to fill the chamber.

Justin moved to the far corner of the cell and sat down, facing the wall. He wrapped his arms around his knees and huddled forward.

The three Russians crowded together to look through the window. The gas was filling the chamber now, clouding it, and Justin's body was growing harder to see.

Then, as they watched, Justin's hands came free from his legs, and he pitched backward, lying still on the floor, face up. The three Russians looked at one another and nodded.

"We'll wait a few minutes and then call Zharkov," their leader said.

Justin remembered. He was back in Rashimpur, twelve years old again, and Tagore had not been happy.

The old man had reached into the water near the shore of the sacred lake, grabbed Justin's neck, and yanked him, sputtering and gagging, ashore.

"Breathing is all," Tagore said. "If you breathe not, you live not."

"It's hard to think about breathing right when you're drowning," Justin had complained, and Tagore had mumbled something to the effect that some boys were untrainable.

That night, Justin slept in the small grotto that had been carved for him out of the rock of the mountain.

He woke when an unfamiliar smell curled into his nostrils. He sat bolt upright on the thin fiber mat that covered the hard stone floor. Smoke. His sleeping chamber was filling with smoke. He looked around. A large stone had been rolled in front of the chamber entrance, and the smoke was pouring in from under one side of it.

The young Justin jumped to his feet and ran to the stone. He began shouting: "Fire. Help me. Fire. Help. Help." But no help came. He tried to roll the stone away, but his strength was not enough to move it. The smoke poured in.

He moved to a far corner and watched as the smoke slowly filled his sleeping chamber. It was wood smoke, bitter and acrid, and it filled his lungs and made him cough.

A wood fire. There was no loose wood inside Rashimpur. Someone had brought wood and set that fire outside his chamber, then had rolled the rock into place. Someone was trying to kill him.

And that someone was going to succeed. He coughed again. Tears streamed down his face as his eyes flooded with water.

He was going to die. He could not get out.

There was no escape.

He remembered Tagore's words of another day: "Escape into yourself. There is always room there for you. Escape into yourself."

The young Justin lay down on the floor. For the first time, he knew that his life depended on the skills that Tagore had been teaching him, and he curled up in a fetal position, closed his eyes, and concentrated on a black spot somewhere inside his mind. The spot grew nearer, growing larger, and when it filled his mind, he created a white spot in the center of it. And then the white spot moved closer until it, too, filled his mind. And in the center of the white spot, he created a dark spot.

He did not think about the smoke. He thought of nothing except his breathing. An inch at a time he felt his body slowing down. His mind still worked; his senses still functioned; but the body was drifting away from him. Was this death?

Or was it what Tagore had been teaching?

He sensed that he was out of his own body, floating in the

air above it, looking down on the strange, frightened young boy. His body was safe there, he knew. And above it all soared his mind, watching, realizing that there was only smoke, but no fire; if he did not breathe in poisons, he would live. Justin would survive.

His mind had separated from his body and willed the body now to go into deep rest. Justin let it go wherever it chose.

And then he felt no more. He breathed no more.

Yet in the morning he woke. There was no smoke in the cell. The large rock that covered the entrance had been moved away.

Tagore appeared in the entranceway.

"How did you sleep, young Patanjali?" he asked.

Justin thought for a moment, then said, "Very well, Tagore."

He thought he saw the old man smile before he turned away to lead Justin to breakfast and then the day's lessons.

The spirit floats and the body rests. Breathing is all. Escape into yourself.

Justin lay still in the small chamber. As still as death as the poison swirled about him.

Zharkov slept.

He had made love to Katarina many times before, but never had it been so wild, so impassioned, so careeningly breathtaking as it had been tonight. It was as if the impending death of the Grandmaster had caused her body to celebrate, to break loose from some bond, however fragile it had been, and open herself to him fully for the very first time.

Zharkov woke as soon as the telephone rang.

"*Ola,*" he said softly.

"He is dead," the KGB agent said.

"Are you sure?"

"He has been there breathing cyanide fumes for three hours. He is dead."

Zharkov hunched over the telephone, shielding his voice from Katarina. "Make sure. I want you to put bullets in his brain. In his heart. Then take the body out into the woods and bury it. And bring me the medal he wears."

"As you wish, Comrade Colonel."

Zharkov replaced the telephone, took a cigarette from the end table, and lit it. He lay smoking in the dark. Over, he thought. It was all over.

*   *   *

The KGB agent hung up the telephone and said to the two other men, "Zharkov must think this one is superman."

"Why?"

"He wants us to put bullets in his brain and heart. To make sure he's dead, he says. Dead! Lenin couldn't live through that."

The small agent who had been driving the car shrugged. "If that's what Zharkov wants, I don't think it's wise to disobey him. What should we do with the body?"

"He says take it out and bury it in the woods."

"Digging. I hate digging."

"Stop complaining. Dig here or dig in Siberia on the railway."

The chief agent looked at the control panel, and found a string of twelve toggle switches in the upper right corner. He pressed the one for number twelve, and the faint whirring of a fan sounded.

"We'll have to clean the gas out first," he said. "Then we'll get rid of this superman, once and for all."

Starcher woke. He could see the sky. It would soon be dawn.

He had hoped that a night's rest would help him to think more clearly, but he could still see no solution to his predicament. Zharkov had not come, and there was just no way Starcher could get out of his floating prison. Even if he killed the tall Russian who looked like a Cuban, what would he do then? He was surrounded by Russian navy boats, and there were two small patrol vessels anchored near the cabin cruiser. If he tried to escape, he would be overtaken by the Russian patrols, and if he tried to shoot his way out, they'd probably blow him out of the water. He was outnumbered and outgunned. There wasn't anything to do but wait for a chance.

Breathing is all.

Oxygen was returning to his system. The poison that had surrounded him like a mist had gone. His mind was alert, his body ready.

But he did not move. He lay deathly silent, still curled in the same fetal position. He waited.

He heard the door to the chamber open.

"Well, I might as well shoot him now," a voice said in Russian.

"Your ass," another Russian voice answered. "Get blood all over my suit? You put holes in him and he leaks. Forget it. First we carry him to the woods. *Then* we shoot him."

"All right. That makes sense."

"Of course, it does. That is why the great Zharkov of the great Socialist Republic has put me in charge of you two idiots."

"It doesn't make that much sense."

The three men came into the room.

"This smells awful. You sure I'm not going to die in here?"

"Only from the neck down. You've been dead from the neck up ever since I've known you."

"I wasn't the one who wanted to start the body leaking."

"Shut up and carry."

Two men hoisted Justin Gilead by his legs and under his shoulders.

"He's light," one said.

"Not so light that just us two are carrying him. What the hell are *you* doing?"

"Somebody has to hold the doors for you," the KGB leader said.

"From each according to his abilities . . ." the first man said.

Breathing is all. He heard the words again.

He felt himself being lifted and then carried from the room. He had never lost consciousness.

He had closed down his body's internal systems without eliminating his awareness of his surroundings. Science said that the brain needed oxygen to live, to think, to work, but Tagore had shown him that the brain was the most efficient cannibal. Close down the rest of the body's systems. Muscles that did not move needed no oxygen; stomachs that did not digest could stay, suspended, for hours or days, without oxygen. And from all those unused body organs, the brain sucked away every last molecule of oxygen to keep itself alive. Because without his brain, man was less than man, and might as well be dead.

This Tagore had taught him, and he had taught him the

way to return from trance, without a telltale twitch or jerk of
the muscles, without a giveaway groan, without the languor-
ous stretching of a cat. One moment he seemed unconscious;
the next he was fully alert, but to an observer, no difference
was detectable, until the Grandmaster chose to move.

He kept his eyes closed. He sensed that the men were tiring
because he felt their arms lowering. They were holding him
so low now that his buttocks almost grazed the grass. He
smelled the fresh nighttime air. Oxygen washed through his
body.

"Up ahead," the leader called. His voice was fifty feet
away. "Just a little more. I see a spot."

Justin opened his eyes the narrowest crack. It was a dark
night; the moon was hidden behind a heavy cover of clouds.

"Damn, he's heavy," the man at his feet said. "I thought
you said he was light."

"All right, so he's heavy. We'll dump him and then put
some lead in him to make him heavier. At least we won't
have to carry him back. He still smells of that poison."

"Where the hell'd our brilliant leader go?" the man at
Justin's feet said. "I can't see a thing."

"I think he's behind those trees. Let's hope he found a
hole to dump this one in. I don't want to dig tonight."

The man holding his ankles juggled him for a moment,
trying to adjust his grip, and in that moment, Justin Gilead
lowered his leg, then bent his knee, and extended his leg
upward, with accelerating speed, like the snap of a whip, and
buried the toes of his shoe in the man's Adam's apple. The
man dropped to the ground without a sound.

Even before he did, Justin's feet were on the ground. The
man behind him growled, "What—?" But before he could
move, Justin had wrenched his wrists loose from the man's
hands.

He spun. The Russian reached for his jacket pocket, but
before his fingers touched fabric, the Grandmaster was behind
him. His arms were locked around the man's neck, the heel
of his right hand pressing against the right side of the man's
skull.

Justin could feel vibrations under his left bicep as the man
struggled to call out, but the force of his hold had cut off his
air supply, and the man could only softly hiss. His arms

flayed in front of him; forgotten was his gun in his pocket. And then there was a snap as the neck broke.

The man's hands froze in midair for a moment, then slowly dropped in front of him. Justin gently lowered him to the ground.

He turned toward the small stand of trees where the third man, the head agent, had gone. Even in the total darkness, Justin could see better than normal men, and he saw a movement. He dropped to the ground as the Russian walked out from behind the trees.

"Come on, you two," the head agent called, then stopped. "Hey, where the hell are you? Come on. This is no time to be playing games. I've found a hole up here. Good for a grave. Anatoly? Josef? Where are you?" He stopped and listened, but heard nothing except the sound of insects in the Cuban night.

Justin heard him walk back toward the spot where he and the two other men lay on the ground.

He was only ten feet away when he saw them. "What the hell is going on?" the man grumbled in annoyance. Justin, his eyes open only a small slit, saw him walking toward them, taking his gun from a hip holster as he did.

He was standing at Justin's feet, and then kneeling down next to the man whose neck the Grandmaster had broken. He felt for a pulse, but there was none. The man stood up and looked around in confusion, seeking whoever had waylaid his two men. There was no one to see. He finished a full turn, a complete revolution with his body, and when he did, the Grandmaster stood in front of him.

The man recoiled in shock. He remembered the gun in his right hand and raised it toward Justin, but as he did, the Grandmaster's left hand closed over the KGB man's right hand. The Russian's thumb was pressed down into the spot between the hammer and the chamber. When the hammer dropped, it did not hit the back of one of the cartridges, but instead slammed down into the fat part of the Russian's thumb. He howled from the pain. Justin squeezed harder. The Russian could feel the bones of his right hand snapping under the pressure. They sounded like dry twigs breaking under the heavy tread of a careless hunter.

The man screamed as the metacarpals across the back of

his hand separated. Then Justin Gilead had the gun and was pointing it at the Russian.

"You . . . you should be dead," the man said stupidly, his jaw slack.

"I'm hard to kill. Where is Andrew Starcher?"

"Starcher?" The Russian's eyes evaded Justin's.

"That's mistake number one. You're from Moscow. You know that Starcher was the CIA head in Russia. Now he's traveling with me. Where is he?"

"I don't know."

"Number two. You're lying," Justin said.

He cocked the hammer on the revolver.

The Russian agent said quickly, "It's true. We followed him yesterday, but one of Zharkov's men picked him up. Where he is I don't know."

"All right," Gilead said. "What is Zharkov doing here in Cuba?"

"I don't know the answer to that," the man said. He nodded toward the two men on the ground behind Justin. "None of us did. He told us nothing. We were assigned as guards and told to obey his instructions. That's all."

"I believe you," Gilead said.

The Russian raised his broken hand, palm out, to his face. "Don't kill me," he said. His nose was running.

"I killed them," Gilead said coldly.

"I'm not fighting you. It would be an execution. Don't do this, please. I have a family . . ."

Justin lowered the pistol almost imperceptibly. It was what the Russian was waiting for.

He stepped forward, past the pistol in Justin's left hand. His other hand had slipped into his pocket and emerged with a long switchblade, which he snapped open even as he drove it toward Justin's exposed belly.

The knife stopped as if it had been pushed against a brick wall. The Russian looked down and saw with horror that Gilead's bare hand was wrapped around the blade of the knife. And the hand was not bleeding. The Russian tried to free the knife from Gilead's grasp but could not. He looked up with bewildered eyes at the taller American, then twisted the knife loose and pulled it back.

"That's three," Justin said, and fired the pistol into the

man's heart. He felt no remorse as the man fell, and he realized, sadly, that killing had become commonplace in his tarnished, pitted life.

He dragged the bodies off into the woods and put them into a natural declivity in the earth, which he covered with branches and leaves. While he worked, the sky grew noticeably brighter. Dawn was breaking, quickly as it always did in the Caribbean, and the first sliver of sun was appearing on the horizon when he finished.

He went to the parking lot but could not find the keys for the car. Instead of going back and searching through the dead men's pockets for them, he turned and trotted off toward the main road of the agricultural center several miles away.

So many deaths, he thought.

But only one more.

CHAPTER THIRTY-NINE

At precisely 10:00 A.M., the referee nodded to Alexander Zharkov and pressed down the button atop Justin Gilead's chess clock.

Zharkov played pawn to king 4, pressed the button on his own side of the timer, and started Gilead's clock running.

Gilead was not at the table. Zharkov walked away to watch the start of the day's other three games.

The spectator section was only half filled because of the early hour. Many chess fans had found a way to take half a day off from their jobs for the matches starting at one o'clock, but getting off at ten required too much of an investment in time.

One hour. When Justin Gilead did not show up by eleven to make his first move, the referee would turn the clock off and award the game to Zharkov by default.

Zharkov repressed a smile. Default. Death was a very good reason for defaulting.

The American champion, Carey, was playing the old Russian master, Keverin. Tomorrow, Zharkov would play Carey.

He caught himself. But of course he would not. The match would of course be canceled out of deference to the Cuban people's great loss of their wonderful and charismatic leader, Fidel Castro.

What a loss, Zharkov thought. Socialist peoples around the world would mourn the martyr. A martyr for freedom. Gunned down at the peak of his brilliance by a CIA operative who had been cleared for the mission by a fake retirement a few

363

months ago after a heart attack in Russia. Zharkov reminded himself to tell Moscow to change Starcher's medical records. Let the official hospital records show that there was no evidence of Starcher having suffered a heart attack. In fact, Soviet doctors thought that he had feigned the heart attack to obtain some kind of pension or medical insurance fraud, but were too diplomatic to say so.

Poor Starcher. Poor Fidel Castro. Poor United States.

The two youngest players, the American Shinnick and the Russian Ribitnov, had just begun their game. One would do well to watch this young man, Zharkov told himself as he looked at Ribitnov. He is brilliant and unstable; his is the kind of mind made for defection. But Zharkov would make sure he never had that opportunity. It was odd, though, that Ivan Kutsenko would take the chance. Zharkov had always thought of him as a mouse, afraid to come out of his hole even for a world of cheese.

He moved over to another corner of the room and stood watching Kutsenko playing the Syrian-American, Gousen. Their opening was a rather stodgy variation of the queen's gambit declined, and they were still moving through the book lines, moving as rapidly as they could. Each had moved eight times, and neither had yet consumed a minute on his clock.

Kutsenko met Zharkov's eyes, then looked down at the board.

Feeling guilty, friend? Zharkov thought. Don't worry; you have served your purpose. You brought Justin Gilead here, and he has died. You did even better. Somehow you managed to entice Andrew Starcher here. For that, when you are declared a nonperson after we return home to Russia, you might get certain benefits that most nonpersons do not have. We might let you have a chess set. Perhaps your wife, the eminent physician, can get a job cleaning bedpans in a hospital. We always look after our own, Kutsenko.

Zharkov glanced back. The referee was still standing near his table. The Cuban looked at his watch, and Zharkov followed suit. Fifteen minutes more. Then Justin Gilead would be disqualified.

Zharkov would have won.

Won the game.

Won the world.

The Grandmaster was dead.

Zharkov stayed near Kutsenko's game because he knew his presence made the world champion nervous. He wants to please me with his game, Zharkov thought. Kutsenko was playing well; he had a good chance of scoring highest in the match. Only the match would never be concluded. Fidel Castro's death tonight would see to that.

He glanced at the large tournament clock on the wall behind the speaker's podium. Only a few minutes till eleven. He began to stroll back to his table to acknowledge the referee's announcement of Gilead's disqualification.

Ten feet from his table, he stopped cold, as if he had walked into a wall.

He could see only the back of the chess clock, but the button was depressed on Gilead's side. Zharkov's own clock was running.

How? But . . .

He walked to the table and saw that black's king pawn had been moved two spaces forward until it faced Zharkov's in the center of the board.

His heart was beating like a pneumatic drill. It burned him to breathe. He looked around, his eyes wild in his confusion.

And there, leaning against a far wall, watching him, stood the Grandmaster.

Zharkov stared at Justin Gilead in disbelief. Justin Gilead smiled back at him and pointed to the chessboard.

Numbly, Zharkov moved into the chair behind the pieces on his side. He glanced at the clock. Gilead's clock had fifty-five minutes spent. He had gotten to the table at only five minutes to eleven, with only a few minutes to spare before he would have lost the game.

Zharkov moved his knight to the king bishop three square, hit the clock, and looked up to see Justin Gilead staring at him from across the table.

"Your men are dead," Gilead said quietly.

Zharkov could not respond. Words froze in his throat. All he could see was the golden coiled snake around the Grandmaster's neck. Gilead's hair was mussed and his hands dirty, and his clothing was splattered with dirt and mud. He moved his queen knight to the bishop three square, and hit the clock to start Zharkov's time running.

Zharkov responded instantly with bishop to the queen knight five square, gladly accepting the opportunity to slip easily into the prescribed moves of the Ruy Lopez opening, glad for a few moments in which he did not have to think or react.

"Where is Starcher?" Gilead asked as he moved the pawn in front of his queen rook forward one square, forcing Zharkov to retreat his attacking bishop.

"Play the game. You'll find out soon enough," Zharkov snapped.

"Maybe sooner than that, Zharkov."

He looked down at the handsome wooden chessboard and realized, as they moved swiftly through their opening moves, that they were playing exactly the same game they had played when the two had first met each other thirty-one years before. He glanced up at Zharkov. He could see from the Russian's eyes that Zharkov, too, recognized the game.

Time, Zharkov thought. Time was the key. By arriving late, Justin Gilead had given away fifty-five minutes of his playing time. And on a chess clock, time, once lost, was never regained. Zharkov would hoard his time, he would save it, he would toss complications at Gilead that would force him to study and ponder alternatives, and keep eating up the time on his clock. Gilead had been away from the chessboard for too long; he would not know the different variations that had been studied since then; he would probably not know the new recommendations for moves, the new traps that had been found. Equally important as brilliance in chess was memory. The ability to see a position on the board and to remember having played it or seen it or read about it before, and to remember not just that position but also the positions and the threats that had grown out of it. That was how grandmaster chess was won.

Zharkov remembered reading an account of an interview with Bobby Fischer. The reporter had finally enticed Fischer into playing a game against him. The reporter's moves took two hours; Fischer's took two minutes. The reporter resigned after twenty-five moves, and Fischer, who had little social grace, did not even bother to compliment him on a surprisingly strong game. Instead, with his one-track mind, he launched into a critique of the game. The reporter was doing fine, Fischer said, until his twentieth move. Fischer swept the pieces off the board with his arm and then immediately set them back up in the position they had obtained at the nineteenth move. "Now here," Fischer said, "you moved this way, and I remembered that in 1901, Mieses versus Mason at Monte Carlo, Mieses made this on move twenty. Your move lost,'' Fischer said. ''From then on in, the game was just technique.''

''You remembered?'' the reporter asked Fischer. ''You remembered a game from 1901?'' And Fischer had replied, ''Of course. It was a good game.''

Memory was a key, but memory required working and constant study. Unless Zharkov was very wrong, Gilead had not had that kind of study or work available to him. He would, in a sense, be reinventing the wheel at every move he made, while Zharkov had spent untold hours at the chessboard studying. He would make Gilead use his time. The clock would destroy the Grandmaster.

The Grandmaster's head was bowed over the chessboard now, studying the position while the clock silently ticked on. Gilead moved a pawn. Zharkov saw that the move had gained Gilead equality. Whenever the player of the black pieces emerged from the opening with an equal position, it was a plus for black. A victory. A small victory, like the victory Gilead had gained over him in the children's chess game so many years ago.

But, no, he told himself. Gilead had not beaten him then. Zharkov had not been allowed to play the game himself, and while the disgrace of losing to the young American genius had fallen on the young Zharkov, the responsibility was not his. Instead, the onus should have fallen on the five Russian masters who were seated in the back of the room, analyzing the game and then signaling to Zharkov what moves he should play. The loss was theirs, not his.

He had never lost to Gilead. Never. Rashimpur was destroyed. The Polish woman had died. Yes, Gilead had survived death, but *how* had he survived? What had he been doing while Zharkov was marching onward, steadily consolidating his power in the Soviet Union, regularly bringing new people to his side should there ever be a power struggle? Gilead had been lost to the world for four years. The victory there was Zharkov's. Gilead had never beaten him in anything.

And he would not now. Not at this board. Not in this country.

The Kutsenkos would never see America. Fidel Castro would not see another sunrise. The United States would never recover from its role in his assassination, a role that would be proven when Andrew Starcher was thrust into the role of killer.

And Justin Gilead would die. He would entrust that death no longer to underlings. He would kill Gilead himself.

The Grandmaster would lose, once and for all.

Just as he would lose this game.

Zharkov contemplated the board for only a few minutes and then leaped one of his knights forward deep into Gilead's territory.

The Grandmaster looked at the move and immediately conceded its strength. Gilead had come out of the opening with equality, but Zharkov was now preparing to mass his attacking men on the side of the board in front of Gilead's king preparatory to launching a killer attack. It was a bold stroke, and it would take elaborate planning on Justin's part to refute it.

Planning. There was an old chess rule that even a bad plan was better than no plan at all. In this case, however, a bad plan from Justin would have been as fatal as no plan at all. He needed a plan good enough to repel the coming attack and to leave his own pieces coordinated enough to move forward into an attack position of their own.

Planning. It had always been the key to Zharkov's life, Justin thought. Zharkov had planned on getting the defenders of Rashimpur away from the mountain monastery by sending that lone patrol of soldiers up the slopes. And Justin had fallen into the trap. While he was down at the base of the mountain, dealing with that patrol, Zharkov had moved his main body of men into the monastery and slaughtered the priests of the temple. It had been Justin's fault. He had not planned, and he had not considered the plan of another.

He could not afford that mistake now. Not in this game; not in this life. He would have to find Andrew Starcher. There were the Kutsenkos to consider as well. And there was whatever scheme Nichevo had planned in Havana. Those plans had to be dealt with.

And Justin had his own plans.

First Zharkov's death.

And then his own. It was time to complete the circle, to end the life he had not wanted to live. His karma was hopelessly ruined; there were too many deaths on his hands, too much blood on his fingers. It was time to die and hope that someday a real Patanjali might live, one who would not soil the honor of the name and the worth of the office of the Wearer of the Blue Hat.

But first the game. He glanced surreptitiously at his clock and knew that he would be in time trouble before this game ended. He had already used up too much time. He studied the position one more time, and thought with a sinking feeling of apprehension that he was not familiar with it. If there was a trap in there that Zharkov knew, he did not see it, and so he could only play on general principles, could only make the move that nine out of ten times would be a correct defensive move, and hope that this game was not an example of the tenth case when such a move was doomed to fail.

He pushed forward the pawn in front of his king rook square one space and lightly tapped the clock to start Zharkov's time running.

Time. He hoped he had time. Time for this game. Time to find Starcher. Time for all the things he had to do.

Then time to kill Zharkov. And himself.

The defense was feeble. Justin Gilead's attempts at defense against him had always been feeble. Zharkov looked at the unnatural pawn structure in front of Gilead's king. They were men to be sacrificed, those pawns, Zharkov thought. Just as sacrifices had always saved Gilead. The monks, the people in that Polish village, the woman Zharkov had killed. All had been pawns; all sacrificed so that Gilead could escape. Until now.

Zharkov glanced at the clock. He had over eighty minutes left on his clock; Gilead had only fifteen. The Grandmaster had been playing quickly to try to conserve his time, but the rapidity of his moves and Zharkov's greater knowledge of these new lines had led Gilead to a position that was growing steadily more precarious.

Almost casually, Zharkov moved a knight forward and captured one of Gilead's pawns, breaking the barrier that had separated the Grandmaster's king from the full fury of Zharkov's attack.

Now the knight was vulnerable to recapture. Gilead's pawn would take it, and Zharkov would have sacrificed a knight for only a pawn, because in the process he would be able to launch an irresistible attack. He casually pressed down the button atop the chess clock, and as he did, he thought of Maria Lozovan. She had been sacrificed, too. It had been a game of pawns, after all.

He looked up, hoping to meet Gilead's eyes, hoping to mock him now in the final moments of his losing struggle. But Gilead's head was bent down over the chessboard, and all Zharkov could see was the hair so black it seemed almost blue. It was the way he had first seen Justin Gilead, as a young boy, bent over, his concentration focused totally on the board.

He had no time. His plan had not worked. He had neglected chess for five years, and his knowledge of recent developments was too spotty.

There was nothing left for him, Justin Gilead thought. He was going to lose.

And then he realized that he was wrong. The greatest thing of all still remained, and it was still on his side. He heard the voice inside him and it said: *You are the game.*

When time was short, when strategies proved valueless, when tactics had failed, when rote learning and memory had been exceeded, there was always one thing left. There was life. There was an innate sense of power and force and lines that rendered all the other factors in a chess game meaningless. There was the genius of survival, and there was the power of life, and even as he thought that, Justin Gilead felt a warm glow come over his body. The short hair on his forearms bristled, standing up with energy and excitement, and he stared at the board and let himself drift into the game, he let himself be merged with the pieces, become a part of the board, and suddenly he was no longer a chess player looking down from a safe distance at the war of two wooden armies; he was *in* the armies and *of* them, and their struggle was his, and their victory would be his. Because he would live.

You are the game.

As if it were a flash of light, the sequence came now to Justin Gilead. His queen still lived. Many smaller, less powerful pieces had been traded, but his queen—the most powerful piece on the board—still lived, and she would not let her king die. It is not a game of pawns, he thought. It is never a game of pawns.

He no longer calculated; he no longer planned what response he would make to whatever move Zharkov showed him. He was the game, and he would move the game where he wanted it to move; he would make of it what he wanted it to be.

He moved his queen across the board in a long line to protect his king. He was the game. His hand reached out and touched the clock.

Zharkov responded immediately. The Russian thought that the queen move was a blunder and that Gilead now must surely lose a piece to Zharkov's marauding advanced knight. He moved that knight, attacking two pieces simultaneously.

He touched his clock, but his hand had barely moved away from the clock control when Justin moved and turned on Zharkov's clock again. So quick was Justin's motion that their fingers almost touched above the clock.

Zharkov looked across at Gilead. The Grandmaster no longer had his head down; he was looking up, but he was looking past Zharkov at a point in space far beyond the Russian. If it had been another man, Zharkov would have said he was daydreaming, but he knew that Justin Gilead was not doing that.

Justin had moved his queen again, and Zharkov now could pick off Justin's rook.

His hand reached out to make the capture, and then he stopped. He had plenty of time left; he should analyze the position carefully, in case Gilead had some kind of trap planned.

He lowered his head over the chessboard and began to calculate.

You are the game.

Justin felt it now; the power had come on him, and this time it was real and full. He was floating freely in a real world of the mind where he did not struggle, did not try to persevere. Instead, he just drifted. He would go where the pieces took him; he would move them where they chose. There were invisible lines of power radiating out across the board from his king, and he would trust the pieces to find those lines and to march his army of men along them, and he would go where the game took him. Because he was the game.

Zharkov moved.

Justin responded immediately.

Zharkov pondered and moved again.

Justin's answering move was done with but a second passing on the clock.

Justin now looked at the board only to see where Zharkov had moved. He spent the rest of his time staring out into space, seeing the position in his mind, letting the pieces move along their chosen paths.

He had now lost a pawn and a rook. In a different game against a different player he would have resigned. The difference in material was too great to make up in an ordinary game. But this was no ordinary game. This was life.

The queen, the pieces of the board whispered to Justin. Now, we move our queen into his camp.

When Zharkov moved again, Justin immediately responded, slashing forward with his queen, attacking Zharkov's pawn position.

The queen was defenseless. It could be taken by two of Zharkov's pawns. The Russian looked at the move in astonishment. Gilead had blundered away any chance for the game.

Take the queen. Zharkov would be ahead by a rook, a pawn, and a queen. Hardly anyone who knew where the pieces were placed on the board could lose with that kind of advantage.

He reached to capture the queen with his pawn. He hesitated and looked at Gilead. Justin was looking in his direction but did not see him. His eyes were again fixed on something in the distance, and Zharkov knew that if he turned and followed Justin's eyes, he would see nothing there. Because what Justin was looking at was not of the world they occupied. He was seeing into the heart and soul of the game they were playing. Seeing as perhaps no man had ever seen before.

For the first time, Zharkov felt doubt insinuate itself into his mind. He glanced at his clock. He now had only twenty-five minutes left. Justin still had thirteen. The Grandmaster had made his last eight moves in less than two minutes. He no longer thought about the game, about the strategy, about the tactics or the complications. He only moved, move after inexorable move, counting on the game to play itself.

Zharkov cursed under his breath and took the queen. Mysticism was fine, but this was chess, the real world. Let Justin Gilead play the game without queen or rook or pawn. Let him try to find a win in that. Triumphantly he took the queen and savagely hit the button atop the clock.

The queen had done its job. It had protected Justin Gilead's king from Zharkov's attack, refusing to let the king fall before the Russian onslaught.

And now the rook, the voice said within him. Without thought, without calculation, Justin moved the rook over in front of Zharkov's king and checked it. The rook could not be taken because it was protected by Justin's remaining bishop. There was only one move for Zharkov, to put his king into the corner.

He made the move immediately because there was no need to waste time studying moves when there was only one move to make.

As soon as he did, Justin moved his rook across the board, capturing one of Zharkov's pieces. As he moved the rook, it exposed the long diagonal across the board and again checked Zharkov's king, which was in line with Justin's bishop. Zharkov again had only one move, to return the king to the square it had just fled.

As soon as he did, Justin brought his rook back in front of the queen and checked it again. Again, Zharkov could not take it because it was protected by the bishop, and again, he had only one move. Into the corner.

Once more, Justin slid his rook along the length of the board, uncovering a check by the bishop. He brought the rook down on the square occupied by Zharkov's own rook. Another Russian piece had fallen.

Too late, Zharkov saw what had happened. Justin Gilead's pieces were so placed that his rook could swing back and forth across the board, move after move, first checking Zharkov's king, then capturing a piece, then checking the king and capturing a piece, until Zharkov was so far behind in material that there was nothing left for him.

The game was over. He had lost. Zharkov sat at the table,

staring at the position in helpless rage. Then he rose without looking at Gilead and walked away from the table.

He left quickly. Rather than move and lose the game with his moves, he chose instead to let his clock run out. When the red flag dropped on his clock, Zharkov would have lost on time. But he would not have to be there to see it. He walked out of the room without looking back.

Justin Gilead did not see him. He was still looking off into a space beyond space. He fingered the coiled golden snake around his neck and thought only one thought.

You are the game.

And the game is almost over.

There were no messages from Starcher at the front desk. Justin asked for Zharkov's room number, walked up to the third floor, and pounded on the door. It was time to find out where Starcher was.

No one answered.

He gripped the doorknob in his hand and twisted. The metal pins in the lock held for a moment, then snapped with a loud crack under the force of Justin's hand. He pushed the door open wide and stepped inside.

The room was empty. Justin searched through Zharkov's night stand and his dresser drawers, looking for an address or telephone number, something that would tell him what he wanted to know.

Zharkov traveled light. There were no papers, no reports or books, no address and phone directories. All Justin found was a pile of chess magazines on a table near the windows, alongside a chess set with the pieces arranged for the start of a game. The sight of the chess set enraged Gilead, and he angrily swept all the black pieces onto the floor with his arm. He picked up the black king and laid it on the board, on its side, in the universal chess gesture that said the game was lost. It meant the king was dead.

When Zharkov returned, he would know what it meant. It meant that the Grandmaster was going to kill him.

"What are you doing here?" The words came from a big man standing in the doorway to the room. Justin had not seen him before, but he had the appearance of a bodyguard and a Russian.

"Looking for Zharkov," Justin said as he walked toward the door.

"He is not here."

"I can see that. Where is he?"

"I do not know. What I do know is that burglars are not welcome in this hotel. Who are you?"

Justin ignored the question. "I guess you don't know where Andrew Starcher is either, do you?" he asked.

"Who?"

The puzzled look on the man's face told Justin that he was telling the truth. He did not know Starcher.

Justin was standing in front of the man now, but the guard said, "You're not leaving quite so quickly. I think we'll call the house detectives first to see exactly who you are."

"Don't make trouble for yourself," Justin said.

"It's no trouble." The guard was big, but his move to his hip holster inside his jacket was practiced and fast. The gun was in his hand. Justin's move was faster, and when the guard's temple bone shattered under the forward thrust of Justin's knuckles, the man dropped heavily to the floor. He had not lived long enough even to groan.

Justin dragged the man into the room, closed the door, and walked away.

Another death. When would it end? Justin thought. How many persons would have to go before the black king fell?

When he opened the door to his own room, he saw a pink slip of memo paper on the floor. It read simply: "Call your friend with the tattoo."

Justin used a pay phone in the lobby to call the Purple Shell. Pablo Olivares answered.

"This is Justin Gilead. We met last night. I received a message to call you."

"*Si.* Wait. I will take this call in my office."

Justin heard the phone being set down. A few moments later, another line was picked up. Then he heard the click as the first telephone was replaced on the receiver base.

"Senor Gilead, you are there?"

"Yes."

"I don't know if this means anything, but maybe—"

"What is it?" Justin snapped.

"There was a Russian sailor in here this morning. The Russians drink vodka well, but they cannot drink rum. This sailor was no different. He drank too much, and he talked too much. He said that there is a small cabin cruiser out in the harbor. It is anchored in the middle of three big Russian ships, and there are small patrol boats cruising around it day and night. I wondered if that might mean anything."

"He doesn't know what the boat is doing there?" Justin asked.

"No, senor. I tried, but he said it had been there since yesterday, just anchored there, and no one knows anything about it. But he thought it was important because the small patrol boats are around it. Could it be important?"

"It might be," Justin said.

"Good. I thought about our friend who is missing."

"Perhaps. Thank you, Senor Olivares," Justin said.

"One more thing, Senor Gilead. The men riding in those patrol boats. They are heavily armed, this drunken Russian said."

"Thank you."

"Are you going out there?" Olivares asked.

"Yes."

"You will probably be shot before your boat gets there."

"I'm not taking a boat," Justin said. "Thank you, senor."

Yuri Durganiv opened a bottle of Los Hermanos beer and glanced at Starcher, offering him one, but the white-haired American shook his head.

"Suit yourself," Durganiv said. "I find it calms the nerves when I have a busy night planned."

"Maybe it won't be so busy," Starcher said.

"Oh, it will. And for you, too." He drained half the bottle in one long gulp, leaning backward and upending it over his mouth, the bottle almost hidden in his huge hand.

"And what am I supposed to be doing?" Starcher asked, trying to sound casual.

"You can try to fool me into believing you are a nice person," Durganiv said, "But I know you are a paid killer for the reactionary American government and the murderous provocateurs of the Central Intelligence Agency. That you would stoop so low as to . . ." Durganiv shook his head. "I never thought a civilized government would do such a thing."

He thought this very funny and laughed so hard he choked, spewing beer over the tabletop in the boat's small cabin.

What the hell is he talking about? Do what thing? The questions flashed through Starcher's mind, adding themselves to all the other questions he had asked himself. He had been on the boat since yesterday, and he still knew nothing. What was happening to Justin? To the Kutsenkos?

He said, "I think I'll have that beer now, if you don't mind."

"Of course not." Durganiv finished his bottle and took two more from a small foam locker under the table. He tossed one across to Starcher who was sitting on his bunk. "I think I'll have one more, too," Durganiv said. "Did I say it's good for the nerves?"

Starcher twisted off the cap and the shaken beer sprayed into the air.

"Maybe if you're drunk, that'll be an excuse," Durganiv told him. "They might take that into consideration. If the mob lets you live."

The son of a bitch is enjoying this, Starcher thought. He's getting off on taunting me. I should take this gun out now and blow his goddamned face away. But then what do I have? Nothing.

He told himself he had to wait, but how much longer could he wait? Whatever Nichevo had planned, Starcher knew that he was now part of it. Had he fallen into Nichevo's hands like a fool? Was he going to take a Russian scheme and make it worse by his presence in Cuba? Maybe Harry Kael had been right. Maybe Starcher should be home in his blue pajamas, sitting in his rocking chair looking at the stock exchange tables in *The Wall Street Journal* and leaving the spy game to people young enough to play it. People with all their wits.

"Are you a Russian?" Starcher asked.

"Yes. I know, I don't look like a Russian."

"You save me the trouble of saying it."

Durganiv finished that bottle of beer and opened another. "My mother was Spanish," he said. "My father was the direct descendant of a great cossack general. Did you know I was going to be a ballet dancer? But I grew too big."

"If you jumped in the air, you'd go right through the stage when you landed," Starcher said.

"I was a very good dancer. But I was too big. So I became . . . well, what I became."

"What is that?"

Durganiv looked at him, sipped his beer, and winked slyly. "A lifelong enemy of the forces of slave-mongering capitalist oppression. A man who fights the reactionary forces wherever he finds them."

"A spy for Zharkov and Nichevo," Starcher said.

"Nichevo? What's that? And who's Zharkov?"

"Never mind. Are you a killer, too? As well as a frustrated ballet dancer?"

"Only when I have to be. Like tonight. Tonight, for you I will be a killer. A very good killer. Too bad no one else will ever know."

"Why not?" Starcher asked.

"I am sharing credit. When I danced, I would not do that. See? I have mellowed as I have grown older. Now I share credit. Tonight, all the credit for my triumph will go to you. It is a shame. People will not point to me and say, There is Yuri Durganiv, the great killer of dictators. No, they will say, that poor dead body over there, that is Starcher. The CIA man. They sent him here to kill . . ." He stopped and drained the bottle of beer. "Enough talk. There is much to do," he said.

Suddenly, Starcher knew what Nichevo had planned. In a flash, he saw how carefully Zharkov had calculated it and what a fool Starcher had been to wind up their captive. He had made it easier for them, easier to destroy the image of the United States around the rest of the world.

It was time for the gun.

He could kill Durganiv. Maybe he couldn't get out of here, but at least Zharkov's plans would be set back.

Starcher reclined on the bunk, his feet away from Durganiv so that his hand could remove the .22-caliber pistol without the Russian's seeing it.

Then he heard the sound of a small powerboat pulling alongside the cabin cruiser, and he quickly replaced the gun. The motors kept running. Durganiv smiled, drained the last drop from the beer bottle, and rose to his feet.

"We're having company."

Maybe Zharkov, Starcher thought. Good. It would be worth his own death to get Durganiv and Zharkov together. Ruin the plan and destroy the head of Nichevo, both at once. His own life would be a small price to pay for that. He had devoted that life to the service of his country; why not his death, too?

But it wasn't Zharkov who came through the door to the small cabin. It was a thin, short Russian with dark hair, wearing a blue serge suit. Starcher could still hear the putting of the motorboat engine outside.

Durganiv rose and nodded to the new arrival. He spoke to him in Russian. "This is Starcher. You guard him until I call. The radiophone is on the bulkhead outside the door. Bring him when I tell you to. I have to go now to do some work."

The man nodded, not taking his eyes off the American. Starcher wondered if he should shoot Durganiv now. At least stop that part of the plan. His left hand moved toward his leg.

Durganiv switched to English. "Oh, another thing. Starcher has a gun strapped to the back of his leg. But it has no bullets in it, so don't be alarmed."

Starcher felt his heart stop for a beat. He looked at the swarthy Russian, who smiled and shrugged.

"The coffee was drugged last night," he said. "That is why you slept so well. I found the gun and took the bullets."

"Why?" Starcher asked weakly.

"I figured you would cooperate better if you thought that escape was possible. Otherwise, I'd have to be watching you all the time. Behave yourself now, old man. Georgi has not my patience or my winning ways. Don't hurt him, Georgi," he said. "But tie him up if you have to. And don't let him drink any more. I think he has a drinking problem."

The dark-haired guard nodded, and as Durganiv left the cabin, he was laughing. A few moments later, Starcher heard the small powerboat accelerate into life, and then its sound moved away from the boat.

He was trapped with no way to escape.

The Grandmaster sat on the edge of the long string pier that jutted out into Havana Harbor. He had stashed his shoes under a garbage pail, and he dangled his bare feet down toward the water. Behind him, fishermen unloaded the day's catch. Justin had been sitting there for five minutes, and now no one noticed him. He glanced back to be sure no one was watching, then slid off the end of the pier and into the water without a sound. In the water, he again sighted out to where the Russian naval vessels were at anchor, a thousand yards from the shore. He lined himself up with those ships, dropped under the water, and swam toward them.

Water had always seemed to bring him strength rather than drain him of it. He moved powerfully under the water, not like a human, flailing with arms and legs, sapping the body of energy, but like a fish, with a sinuous motion of his trunk. His arms were extended in front of him, primarily to control his direction, but his movement through the water looked as if a creature with the body of a man had been bred to swim with the technique of a fish.

He remembered the patient lessons of Tagore, sitting on the lakeshore near Rashimpur, nodding as Justin crawled ashore, and telling him, "Again."

And Justin would swim the lake again underwater, emerge triumphant, cold, dripping wet, and Tagore would nod and smile once more. And say, "Again."

A small powerboat passed over his head, moving toward shore. Justin looked up and saw its V-shaped wake. The boat was not the cabin cruiser he sought; its wake was too small for that. It was just a little runabout.

He swam on. He did not think of the time he had been in the water or the distance he had traveled. His body worked independently of his mind. Finally he saw a heavy mass in the water ahead of him. As he drew nearer, it loomed over him as if he were a fish and had suddenly swum to the base of Hoover Dam.

He recognized it as the hull of the one of the Russian warships, and he swam toward it, then moved upward to the water line. He broke water alongside the boat and saw the small cabin cruiser fifty yards away. Patrol boats lay on either side of it, drifting casually around, gently circling. The larger Russian warships made a big, broken, irregular ring around the small vessels. The cabin cruiser looked like a lone calf in a large corral, being watched by two lazy sheepdogs. On each of the patrol boats, Justin could see a couple of sailors. Each boat had a machine gun mounted on the stern. But the sailors were bored with their duty. On one boat, the two seamen were arguing with each other; on the other, they played matching coins.

There were no signs of life from the cruiser. Starcher, if

he was there, was probably in the cabin amidships, Justin thought.

He let himself down under the water and moved carefully away from the side of the big Russian warship.

The Russian agent Georgi would not talk to Starcher. He seemed content to sit at the table, his pistol near his hand, staring at the American.

Starcher considered rushing him, but he knew it would serve no purpose. Even if he was successful, which he doubted, what would he do? He was an ex–CIA man, stuck on a boat, surrounded by Russian warships in the middle of Havana Harbor in Fidel Castro's Cuba.

And the Russians were going to kill Castro.

He knew it. Durganiv had teased and taunted him, but he had finally said just too much. There were many people who did that, who felt they had to say something, who had to demonstrate their superiority and their greater knowledge. And if you let them alone long enough, they would eventually tell you more than they should.

So Castro was going to die at Russian hands, and Zharkov's plan was to pin the killing on Starcher. But how had Zharkov known that Starcher would be in Havana?

Starcher suddenly realized that Zharkov hadn't known. Zharkov had learned that the Grandmaster was alive, and he was planning to use Gilead as his scapegoat. And now that Starcher had neatly and foolishly arranged his own capture by the Nichevo men, that must have made Gilead expendable. Was Justin still alive? Or had Zharkov already killed him?

If he was dead, Starcher would have no help. He'd have to get free of Zharkov by himself, and he'd have to try to get the Kutsenkos out of Havana by himself. A large assignment. His own best chance to escape was probably on the boat. Once back ashore, he would not know how many people might be guarding him, how many guns might be pointed at him. He studied the Russian agent. He was thirty years younger than Starcher, no doubt in better physical condition, and he was armed. Hell, maybe he had just had a heart attack, too, Starcher thought bitterly. An even fight. First one to have cardiac arrest loses.

He cast about for other possibilities. When the radiophonecall came, the agent would have to go outside the cabin to answer it. The phone was on the bulkhead a few feet outside the door. If the agent closed the door, Starcher could hide behind it and hit the Russian when he came back into the cabin. As his weapon, he had already chosen a long piece of iron pipe that was stuffed into a basket in the corner.

Suppose he did knock the agent out? What then? Swimming to shore was out of the question. He couldn't swim well, and the exertion alone would kill him.

But he spoke Russian. Perhaps he could start this boat and just wave to the Russian patrol boats and shout something innocuous. "I'm leaving now. Have another vodka, men."

His white hair was a problem. The Russian agent had dark hair. Starcher could put on the agent's suit jacket. Find some oil and rub it into his white hair. Oil. Or gravy or shoe polish, anything he could find.

He had to try it. It was his only chance. Maybe he even had one small advantage. He had heard Durganiv tell the agent not to hurt Starcher. They wanted him tonight alive and well. It might give him a small edge in a quick surprise attack.

As if on cue, there was a metallic buzzing from the radio-phone outside the door.

The agent got up quickly, snatched up his gun, and waved it at Starcher. "You stay there," he ordered gruffly in English. His voice was raspy. He went outside and pulled the door shut behind him.

Starcher ran to the metal can filled with bits of bamboo and metal, apparently used for repairing fishing rods. He took out the piece of pipe, heavy iron water pipe eighteen inches long. It felt reassuringly meaty in Starcher's hand.

For the first time, he had a small hope that his plan might succeed. He walked quietly across the floor to stand behind the door, and strained to hear the agent say in Russian, "All right. Room three-nineteen. Right away."

Starcher felt the thunk through the thin cabin bulkhead as the radiophone was replaced on its wall mount. He pressed himself back against the wall. The doorknob turned. He raised the pipe over his head.

The agent entered, and Starcher pushed the door away and leaped forward, already swinging the heavy pipe down toward the agent's head. But the Russian spun, ducked, and tossed up his left arm for protection. The pipe crunched into the fat part of the man's forearm, and Starcher could tell by the sound and feel that he had broken no bones. Then the Russian was rolling across the cabin floor. He came up in a crouched position, with his pistol aimed at Starcher's belly.

"You American son of a bitch," he snarled in Russian. "The only thing keeping you alive is my orders."

Starcher lowered the pipe, just as low as his hopes of escape. "I was counting on that," he answered in Russian.

"Don't count on it anymore. Or on my good nature," the agent said. "The next time, I'll put a bullet between your eyes. I don't care who'll be disappointed. Now, drop it."

Starcher let the pipe fall to the floor and walked back to the cot.

Too old. But at least he got one lick in, he consoled himself, as he watched the Russian rubbing his arm. "God damn it," the agent snarled.

"I'm sorry I didn't bash your thick Russian skull in," Starcher said.

"And I'm sorry I didn't blow your brains out. You're making the trip to shore tied up."

As the agent lashed Starcher's wrists behind him with a length of rope he pulled from one of the cabin's lockers, Starcher asked, "Are you Nichevo too?"

"What's Nichevo?" the man answered much too casually.

Starcher's last hope withered. If Georgi hadn't been a Nichevo man, perhaps Starcher might have been able to shock him with the realization that Castro was going to be assassinated by Russians; perhaps it could have confused him enough to prompt him to speak to his superiors; perhaps the result might have been countermanded orders or a delay. Any of those things might have worked in Starcher's favor. But those possibilities were gone now.

The Russian roughly yanked Starcher's feet up behind him, to tie his ankles to his wrists. A voice spoke in Russian.

"Not too tight. I'm just going to have to untie him again."

Starcher snapped his head around, even as the Russian wheeled away from him.

It was the Grandmaster. He stood only a few feet from the Russian, his clothes pouring water onto the floor, his eyes burning with the intensity of blue ice.

The Russian snatched for the gun he had laid on the small

of Starcher's back, but as he raised the muzzle, the Grandmaster attacked.

The Russian's body shielded Gilead from Starcher's view, but he saw Justin's right arm move. He heard a snap and then another snap, and then Justin backed away and the Russian sank to the deck of the cabin into a kneeling position, his body twisted around so that Starcher could see his eyes. They were open wide, staring, but they expressed nothing, not even shock. They were dead man's eyes. The agent pitched forward onto the floor.

Gilead stepped over him to undo the ropes around Starcher's wrists.

"How'd you do that?" Starcher asked.

"It's not important. Are you all right?"

"I'm okay. They're going to kill Fidel Castro," Starcher said.

"That's their plan?" The knots were tight on his wrists. Starcher heard Justin sigh, and then felt the ropes snap.

"Yeah," Starcher said.

"Why not let them? Castro's no friend of the United States."

Starcher rolled over and removed the remnants of rope from his wrists. The knots were intact. The heavy line had just been pulled apart. "How'd you do that?" Starcher asked, holding up the ends of the rope.

"Never mind," Gilead said. "Why not let Castro die?"

"Because they're planning to blame the killing on the United States. That's why they've been holding me. I was their prize exhibit. Crazed CIA assassin."

Gilead said, "They didn't even know you were coming. They didn't know who you were."

Starcher rubbed his wrists. The tight knots had stopped the circulation to his fingers.

"I thought about that," he said. "Zharkov must have been planning to use you first. When I came, he decided that I was a better scapegoat."

The Grandmaster nodded. Soaking wet, his clothes stuck tightly to his body, and Starcher was surprised to see how much wiry muscle had grown on his thin frame. He looked nothing like the wreckage of a human being Starcher had salvaged from the *Rook's Tour* . . . was it only two months ago?

"That explains why they tried to kill me last night," Justin said. "They didn't need me anymore."

"I'm sorry, Justin. I wish I could have let you know."

"Nothing to worry about," Justin said.

"How'd you find me, anyway?"

"Your friend at the waterfront bar heard about this boat. He told me. It's one you people owe him. Now, what's next?" Justin asked.

"We could just leave. Without you or me, the plan would probably be canceled."

Gilead shook his head. "There are three other American chess players and their seconds. Zharkov would probably just grab one of them. I'm sure he's got dossiers, and he'd be able to phony something up. When he was done, you'd think our whole chess team was riddled with superspies."

Starcher was thinking. "Besides," Gilead said, "I can't just go. I promised the Kutsenkos we'd get them out. And I've got my business with Zharkov."

"This agent was on the phone. I heard him say, 'Room three-nineteen. Right away.' I imagine he was supposed to take me there. Probably at the José Martí. I guess they were going to set it up then."

"I think one of us should keep that appointment," Justin said.

"Sure," Starcher answered. "But how do we get out of here? We're surrounded by the whole Russian navy. How'd you get here, anyway, with those patrol boats?"

"I swam. You want to swim to shore?" Gilead asked with a smile.

"I wouldn't make it fifty feet," Starcher said.

"Then I guess we'll have to try something else."

Hair darkened by brown shoe polish and wearing the KGB agent's blue suit jacket, Starcher stood at the boat's controls on the stern deck, hitting the electric starter.

The patrol boat to port was closest. He waved to the men and shouted in Russian, "Leaving now."

"Wait," one of the two men on the small boat yelled.

"All right," Gilead said softly from inside the small passageway that led to the cabin. "Wave them over. Since they're coming anyway, let them think you want them to."

"I hope you know what you're doing."

"Just before they get here, go below. Keep out of sight."

Starcher nodded, and Gilead, keeping his body low, out of sight of the patrol boats, slithered to the stern of the boat and slipped over the transom into the water.

The patrol boat moved slowly toward the cruiser. Starcher turned his back as if concentrating on a malfunction with the controls.

When the boat was only ten feet away, Starcher, without turning his head, ducked down into the small passageway. He stayed there, checking the dead agent's pistol, making sure the safety was off and it was fully loaded.

Then he heard two thumps and a voice calling softly, "Starcher, hurry up."

The two Russian sailors had been tossed onto the deck like beanbags. Gilead was at the controls of the small outboard patrol boat.

"Come on aboard," he said.

"What about these two?"

"They're not going anywhere," Justin said. "Let's get out of here."

He reached up to help Starcher into the patrol boat, but the CIA man slapped his hand away in annoyance and, grunting from the exertion, climbed down into the open boat.

The sun was setting, and the big Russian warships cast long shadows over the water. As soon as Starcher was seated, Gilead pulled away from the cabin cruiser, keeping the cruiser between himself and the other patrol boat. Then he gave the small craft an open throttle and sped toward shore.

"Sit at that machine gun and let me know if they're following us," Gilead said.

Starcher watched, but the two men on the other boat obviously thought there was nothing peculiar about their partners making a small run in to shore, and made no attempt to follow them.

"We're okay," Starcher called over the lawnmower clanging of the small engine.

"Good."

They tied up five minutes later at one of the small piers, after Justin expertly nosed the boat in between two fishing vessels whose crews had gone for the day. He retrieved his shoes from under the trash basket, then walked with Starcher away from the harbor toward the streets of the city.

Behind them, the sun set dull and rusty over the Russian ships anchored offshore. The two Americans walked through a parking lot filled with old, battered American-made cars. Justin looked inside each vehicle.

"You can forget finding a cab in this workers' paradise," he said. "Come on. Here's a car with a key in it. You drive."

A few moments later, he and Starcher were on the main road, heading back to the heart of the city and the José Martí Hotel.

CHAPTER FORTY-ONE

"You understand what to do?"

"Of course I do. I'm not stupid," Starcher snapped. "I still don't like it. I want to be there."

" 'They also serve who only stand and wait.' It'll be better this way. We'll have fewer people to get out of the hotel, and you'll be able to shepherd the Kutsenkos."

"I'll be waiting," Starcher said glumly. "But I won't be happy."

"That's odd, Starcher," said Justin. "I've always regarded you as a man consumed with joy."

Starcher grumbled and stopped the ratty old car in front of the José Martí, then drove off as Justin trotted up the steps toward the group of uniformed Cuban soldiers who stood security at the door.

Justin did not like the way Starcher looked. He seemed to be showing the strain of the last few days, and while Justin would have welcomed help, he didn't want it from someone who might collapse at any moment.

Two soldiers moved to block his way into the hotel.

"I'm Justin Gilead of the American chess team. I've got to change for dinner. Has the premier arrived yet?"

One soldier said, "You have some identification?"

Justin took the water-soaked passport from his rear pocket and held it out casually. "Sorry. I was fishing, and I fell overboard."

The guard looked at the picture on the passport, then at Justin and then checked his name on a list. Finally he returned the small blue passport folder. "Go ahead, Senor Gilead. But hurry. Fidel will be here within the hour."

Justin put a handkerchief over the mouthpiece of the telephone in his room and dialed room 319. Starcher had told him that the Russian agent talked with a deep, raspy voice, and when the telephone was picked up, Justin spoke in a gravelly whisper. "Yuri?"

"Da."

"I'm bringing him up."

"Hurry."

Justin walked the flight of steps up to the third floor. Next to the stairwell was an unmarked door to a utility room. Next to it was room 319.

Justin knocked hard on the door, once, then held on to the doorknob gently. When he felt it turn and the lock release, he slammed forward against the door with his shoulder.

Durganiv, taken by surprise, was hammered back against the wall. Justin leaped into the room and slammed the door shut behind him.

The giant Russian recovered immediately and was on him, wrapping his arms around Justin's chest and upper body. Gilead twisted his body partly to the side, then drove the side of his right foot up into Durganiv's kneecap. The bigger man screamed as his kneecap broke. He released his hold and sank toward the floor. Justin lunged behind him and wrapped his arms around Durganiv's throat.

"What is the plan?" he barked in the Russian's ear.

Durganiv did not speak, and Gilead applied more pressure. Durganiv could feel his neck stretching.

"Who are you?" Durganiv managed to sputter.

"Justin Gilead. The plan." He squeezed again, and Durganiv gasped, "The washroom next door. I've cut into the wall to get to the air-conditioning system. There's a vent that looks over the dining room. I shoot from there."

"Not anymore," Gilead said. He yanked Yuri's head backward until the bones in his neck cracked. The Russian's head lolled forward onto his chest.

Gilead dropped him and saw a high-powered rifle on the bed.

The utility room was locked, but Justin found the key in the Russian's trousers. He opened the door and then, moving quickly while no one was in the corridor, carried Durganiv and the rifle into the washroom and closed the door tightly behind himself. It was a small room. To make space, he pushed Durganiv's body into the big utility sink.

Overhead, a piece of Masonite had been mounted on the wall. Justin drove his fingers through a corner of it and peeled it away. The plaster behind it had been cut away. Justin saw a large opening that led into a metal ventilator shaft. He felt the cold flow of air conditioning pouring through the hole and into the small utility room.

He hopped up onto the sink and hoisted himself through the hole. The ventilator shaft stretched out straight in front of him, and he crawled along it to where the shaft ended at a metal grate, two feet square. Careful not to get too close, Justin peered through.

He had a view from over the balcony that encompassed the giant banquet hall. Most of the guests had already been seated for dinner, and Justin could see them clearly at their tables. A dais had been erected at the far end of the room, along with a lectern evidently set up for Castro. Shooting him from this distance would be child's play, Justin realized.

Durganiv had planned to shoot Castro, then slide back out of the shaft, stuff Starcher into it along with the gun, and then make sure the American "assassin" was killed, either by security troops or perhaps even by Durganiv's own gun.

"Good plan," Justin mumbled to himself as he slipped back into the washroom. He hoisted Durganiv's heavy body up into the opening, then climbed in after it, carrying the rifle with him. Quietly, he pushed the Russian's body until his head was just a foot away from the air-conditioning grate, then carefully placed the rifle in the dead man's hands.

He backed out of the shaft and dropped lightly to the floor of the washroom. Before leaving, he jammed the Masonite panel back into the hole over the sink, then reached up and removed the overhead light bulb. Anyone looking into the utility room by chance would not be likely in the darkness to see the broken Masonite panel covering the hole in the wall.

Then the Grandmaster locked the door behind him and walked down to his room to change for dinner.

Yuri was in place.

Alexander Zharkov sat in the front of the ballroom at one

of the small dinner tables reserved for players, their seconds, their families, and their special guests.

The rest of the room was packed with almost a thousand guests, many of them members of the Cuban Chess Federation, and a lot of them political social climbers who wanted to see and be seen by Fidel Castro.

Zharkov glanced at his watch. Twenty minutes before Castro arrived; no more than thirty-five minutes to go before the Cuban premier was dead.

He had been watching the vent over the balcony that ringed the hall. Only a few minutes ago he had seen a shadow moving inside it. Now there was a dark clump barely visible behind the ventilator grate, but it would take eyes that knew what they were looking for to realize that it was a man hiding in that shaft and not just an errant shadow.

It was wonderful. The balcony was packed with Cuban soldiers, all carrying automatic weapons. One of them was stationed no more than five feet from the air-conditioning grate. The death shot would be fired past his head, so close that his ears would ring for a week.

Zharkov looked around at the four other tables in the front line. The Kutsenkos were sitting with the young American player, Shinnick, and two American seconds at the table nearest the ballroom's main entrance. The tables were set in a straight line, and at the other end of the line, farthest from the main door, sat Keverin, Ribitnov, one of their seconds, and two empty seats. Those would be for Gilead and his second, "Harry Andrew."

Zharkov thought that Gilead might show up, if he wasn't wandering all over Havana looking for Starcher. But Starcher was a dinner no-show. By now he was already here, dead in that ventilator shaft, a bullet in his brain, waiting in death for his body to be shoved forward to take over the role of assassin.

Not too long to wait now.

And if the Grandmaster did show up, Zharkov would deal with Justin Gilead when Castro was killed and Cuban troops started firing into that ventilator shaft, ripping apart the already-dead Starcher's body. Unconsciously, his hand strayed to his jacket, and he made a show of removing his breast pocket handkerchief and wiping his forehead. But the heel of his hand had felt the reassuring bulge of the Tokarev in the shoulder holster under his jacket.

He replaced his handkerchief and looked at his watch again. Only a few more minutes. He glanced up casually toward the air-conditioning grate above the balcony. He imagined that he could see Yuri Durganiv lying there, the rifle cradled in his arm, his sharp killer's eyes watching the room below and waiting for the appearance of his target.

First, Castro.

Then, back to Russia for Kadar. Zharkov would own him.

And after Kadar . . .

After Kadar, anything Zharkov wanted.

Anything.

A Cuban chess official standing with the guards at the ballroom door greeted Justin Gilead warmly. "You're at table five on the other side of the room," he said with a practiced, gracious smile.

"Thank you," Justin said. He saw Zharkov sitting three tables away with his back to him, and walked directly to the first table where the Kutsenkos sat.

He leaned over and spoke softly into the Russian champion's ear.

"Later, when you see me stand up, I want you and your wife to leave the room. Go out the back exit. Across the street, you'll see an old brown Plymouth parked. The driver will recognize you. Get in and wait for me."

Without waiting for a response, he straightened up and shook hands with Kutsenko and all the others at the table.

"Good to see you all again," Justin said. "I hope we can talk later."

"A very good game today, Justin," Kutsenko said with a smile and a slight nod.

"Thank you, but the best is yet to come," Gilead said.

"I hope not. You're playing me tomorrow," Kutsenko said.

Justin smiled back and walked past Zharkov's table, ignoring the Russian and nodding to its other occupants, and sat in one of the empty seats at table five.

Keverin greeted him and introduced him to the Russian second. The old Russian chess master nodded toward the empty chair. "Will your second be coming tonight?"

Justin shook his head. "I think he's off sight-seeing in Havana," he said. "I haven't been able to find him. Maybe too much rum."

"It's a curse, all right," Keverin said. He sat back down as Justin did.

Gilead felt Zharkov staring at him from three tables away but chose not to look in his direction.

"A glorious win today," Keverin said. "I have not seen that exact attack since Alekhine in 1939."

"It was 1938," the Russian second said.

"It was '39," Keverin insisted. "I was there. I know. He played Euwe."

"You may have been there," the man insisted, "but it was 1938. And it wasn't Euwe, it was Kashdan. The game opened with a king's Indian . . ."

"Fantasy land," Keverin snapped. "No wonder you don't know the year, because you don't know the game. It was the dragon variation of the Sicilian and . . ."

Ribitnov joined in the argument at this point, and Justin let the conversation flow around him. Russians were contentious chess players, arguing about dates and places and openings, precisely because they were good chess players. The essence of chess was accuracy and perfection, and in a Russian chess argument, everything had to be accurate and perfect. One incorrect point would demolish an otherwise perfectly sound arguing position, just as one element wrong in a plan at the chessboard could turn victory into defeat.

His eyes drifted around the room and met Zharkov's intense stare. The Russian's heavy-lidded eyes glared at him malevolently, but there was a peculiar expression on his mouth. It took Justin a moment to identify it as self-satisfaction. Mischievously, Justin wanted to glance up at the ventilator shaft from which the assassin's bullet was to be fired, but he held the impulse in check. Zharov's smile would be gone soon enough.

Soon enough.

Justin heard sirens through the open doors of the ballroom. A few minutes later Fidel Castro, wearing his ever-present combat fatigues, strode through the doorway as the small band in the rear of the room played the Cuban national anthem.

Everyone rose as Castro walked to the front of the room. The Cuban premier was flanked by four uniformed guards and trailed by another four men in business suits. He smartly saluted the Cuban flag and held the salute until the band had finished.

Ignoring his bodyguards, Castro pushed away from the dais and walked over to the tables where the chess players sat. Like politicians everywhere, he began shaking hands while flashbulbs popped.

When he got to Gilead's table, all the men at the table rose, and Castro greeted each warmly. Gilead had never seen him before and was surprised to see how tall the Cuban leader was. His uniform was sharply pressed and starched, but there was a hint of a middle-aged belly protruding above his belt. His handshake was firm, but his fingers were sweaty and damp.

"Buena suerte mañana," Castro wished them all, after shaking hands around the table. Gilead noticed that he had politician's eyes: Even while he was shaking hands, they were looking elsewhere. It was common among politicians, but with Castro, it showed something else, too. Politicians were looking for the next hand to shake, but Castro seemed nervous, perhaps looking around to make sure he was among friends. Maybe they were the eyes of a dictator out among the people, Gilead thought.

Castro waved to the crowd, who applauded him again, and walked to the speakers' table at the front of the room.

The four men in suits sat down alongside the Cuban leader on the raised platform. One of them went to the microphone. Gilead recognized him as the president of the Cuban Chess Federation. The man introduced himself and the other men in suits who were also federation officers.

He said that chess was not only a great international game, but an international language as well. All two men needed, no matter what their nationalities or their politics, was a board and thirty-two pieces. They did not need language to communicate, except perhaps to say "check" and "checkmate." "And sometimes, 'I lose.'" The crowd chuckled, and the speaker seemed about to go on when Gilead saw Castro reach over surreptitiously and tug at the man's jacket.

Without pausing for breath, the man launched into his prepared speech, explaining that it was an honor for him to introduce the premier of the host country for this great match, a premier who was a chess player himself. "Ladies and gentlemen," he finished, "I give you Fidel Castro."

The crowd rose in a standing ovation. Gilead glanced over toward Zharkov who was on his feet with the rest, applauding enthusiastically.

Obviously, there were still a few minutes to go before the assassination.

Castro rose and spoke without notes. He was a practiced and fluid speaker who knew how to pause and draw laughter from a line and how to emphasize a point dramatically by the pitch of his voice.

His remarks were well thought out and gracious. He welcomed, both by nation and by name, all the players and said how proud he was that Cuba, home of Jose Capablanca, perhaps the greatest chess player who ever lived, could host such an important match.

He went on to say that it was wonderful that men representing nations of conflicting ideologies and beliefs could meet in peace in friendly competition, and he hoped that someday the nations of the world could take a lesson from the world of chess and meet openly in the intellectual field of battle to let the better man and the better vision win.

Justin thought the speech was fine but that it might have rung more true if Castro had not spent the last decade sending Cuban guerrillas to stir up trouble in Central and South America and in Africa. And as for the free exchange of ideas, a free Cuban press might be a start in that direction. The man was a politician, after all; he said one thing, but practiced another.

Justin noticed Zharkov glance at his watch; then, under the guise of turning in his chair to get a sip of water from the glass behind him, he looked up toward the air-conditioning vent at the back of the large ballroom.

Now, Justin thought.

He rose quietly and walked toward the far door where an army contingent of a half-dozen men stood behind a security captain in full dress uniform.

As he drew near the captain, Justin turned and saw Zharkov's eyes trained on him. That was just what Justin had wanted. Two tables behind Zharkov, the places of Ivan Kutsenko and his wife were now empty. The world chess champion and his wife had left the room already, and Zharkov had not noticed.

"Captain," Justin said to the security guard, "I think there's trouble."

"Trouble, senor? What is that?"

Justin drew closer to the captain. "In the balcony at the back of the room, there is a large air-conditioning vent. There's a grate in front of it. I just saw a man climb into that vent. He has a rifle in his hand."

The captain backed away from Justin and searched the American's eyes for a moment.

"Es verdad," Justin said. "It is the truth. Look for yourself."

The captain looked back toward the vent, saw the shadow inside it, and instantly stepped forward into the room. While he snapped a walkie-talkie from his belt, he barked at the guards behind Castro: "Protect the premier. Protect the premier." The uniformed soldiers jumped forward, pulled Castro from the lectern, and shielded him with their bodies.

The captain barked orders into the walkie-talkie. As Justin watched, two of the soldiers on the balcony ran over to the air-conditioning vent. They raised their weapons and began blasting bullets through the grate.

The crowd in the auditorium had been confused and hushed when the captain had stepped forward into the room, shouting. Now, as the shots sounded, some screamed. Most turned to look for the source of the sound; many ducked under tables.

Justin Gilead looked across the room. Zharkov was standing. From under his jacket, he pulled his Tokarev pistol and aimed it at Justin.

The Grandmaster lightly saluted Zharkov with the tips of his fingers, then moved behind the captain, through the door, and out into the service hallway.

He ran back toward the rear exit of the building. Outside, he walked slowly past the soldiers down the steps.

Across the street he saw Starcher waiting in the car. The Kutsenkos were in the back seat.

Night had fallen on Havana.

Despite Starcher's map and directions received at three different service stations, they got lost twice before Justin found the small dirt road that led from the smooth two-lane blacktop highway off through a stand of scrub pine toward the ocean.

It was 10:45 P.M.

The road ended abruptly at a wall of trees. All four of them got out of the car.

There were no houses in sight, and the night was clear and dark, illuminated by a brilliant white moon. Starcher was grumbling. He had hoped for rain, fog, an overcast night, anything that would reduce visibility. In spite of his black-painted boat, Saarinen would be as obvious out in the water as a Roman candle in a coal mine.

If he even showed up. It had all come down to this, Starcher thought ruefully. A lifelong career of service to the United States, and now he was reduced to trying to flee Cuba with his life in the hands of a renegade Finnish pirate who would drink antifreeze if he had to and would do anything for a dollar.

He hoped that Riesling had been right in his assessment of the Finn. The dead agent had once said that Saarinen was fearless and that his promise could be put in the bank and it would draw interest.

At one of the service stations, they had purchased five fifty-foot lengths of clothesline. They took them from the car and plodded through the thick trees and brush toward the cliff they hoped would be waiting beyond.

398

The Kutsenkos were silent. They had spoken little on the flight from Havana, and Justin Gilead knew they were frightened to the point of panic. If their escape attempt was not successful, their lives were ruined, even if they lived. Prison, or worse, awaited them if they were returned to Russia.

The chess champion and his wife had simply huddled together in the back seat of the car, listening with Justin and Starcher to the news bulletins on the Cuban station that the automobile radio picked up.

The reports were sketchy but said that an unidentified gunman had been shot and killed at the José Martí Hotel where Premier Castro was delivering a speech to the players in an international chess match. The gunman was shot by the quick action of Cuban security guards. While he had not been identified, the announcer left no doubt of who he thought was responsible for the attack by stressing pointedly that one of the teams playing in the match was from the United States.

Starcher cursed when he heard the announcer. Justin clapped him on the knee. "Calm down," he said. "They'll get it all sorted out soon enough."

Although the moon was bright, the path through the trees where they moved was as dark as if they were underground. It was a relief to break through the brush onto a flat shelf of rock overlooking the smooth waters of the Caribbean. The table of rock was ringed in a semicircle by tall trees.

Looking seaward, Starcher glanced at his watch. "Ten minutes," he said.

Justin went to the edge of the cliff and looked down. The rock wall dropped straight to a sandy beach a hundred feet below.

He lowered himself to his haunches on the cliff and lashed three of the fifty-foot lengths of rope together. Then he tied large, lumpy knots in the rope every five feet.

"What's that for?" Starcher asked.

"Just easier to hold on to. You can hang on to these knots a lot more easily than on to a thin, smooth rope. Your feet can even get a purchase on them if you have to."

"All right. I guess you know what you're doing," Starcher said. He looked to the dark waves of the sea and then hissed, "He's there."

Justin turned to see a yellow light flashing from about 150 yards off shore.

Starcher counted the flashes. "Three . . . four . . . five. Wait. One, two, three, four, five. That's him." He held up a cigarette lighter, lit it, then used his hand to cover and uncover it, to give the impression of four answering signals. A rapid series of flashes came from the boat. "Okay," Starcher said. "Let's get this show on the road."

Justin pulled one end of the rope back to one of the largest trees and wrapped it around the trunk twice before knotting it tightly at the base of the tree.

He came back and tossed the rope over the cliff. It just touched the sand below.

He tied the two remaining sections of rope into one long line, then knotted a large loop into one end of it.

"Saarinen'll bring an inflatable boat in," Starcher said.

The Kutsenkos had been watching from off to the side, holding each other as if they were cold on this warm night.

"All right, Ivan," Justin said. "You'll go first. Hook this rope under your arms." He helped Kutsenko slip the large looped rope over his head and pulled it up tight under his arms.

"Climb down the rope to the sand. I'll be up here holding this other rope so I'll have most of your weight. You won't fall. When you get to the bottom, slip out of this harness, and I'll pull it back up and send your wife down."

"Can she manage to climb down?" Kutsenko asked. There was doubt in his voice.

"She'll have this harness around her just as you. Don't worry," Justin said.

The world chess champion took a deep, nervous breath. "All right," he said. "Fine. Okay. I'm ready."

He took a firm grip on the long vertical rope, smiled wanly at his wife, and started down the side of the cliff. Justin sat atop the cliff, his legs braced against a large outcrop of rock. He held the harness rope around his back, feeding it out a few feet at a time. Starcher watched from the edge of the cliff.

"As smooth as glass," he called out approvingly. "He's almost at the bottom."

Justin felt the weight release on the rope across his shoulders.

"He's there," Starcher said. "Bring the rope back up."

Justin quickly pulled the rope up and adjusted the chest loop around the smaller Lena Kutsenko.

"Now don't be afraid," he told her. "You won't fall because I've got your weight."

"Mr. Gilead," she said with a smile that shone brightly in the moonlight, "before I decided to go to medical school, I was a member of the Russian gymnastics team. If Ivan can get down this cliff, I can do it with one hand."

"Use two hands and do it twice as fast," Justin said.

Dr. Kutsenko leaned forward and kissed him quickly on the lips. "Thank you," she said. Then without hesitation she grasped the lifeline and scrambled over the edge of the cliff.

There was not much difference between her weight and her husband's, Justin thought, as he fed out the safety line. But she was obviously more agile; she was pulling on the safety line, and he had to feed it out faster to keep up with her descent down the rock face.

He heard Starcher say, "Saarinen's coming. I see him."

The woman reached the sand at the bottom of the cliff, waved up to him that she was all right, then slipped out of the harness. As Justin hauled the rope in through the dark, he could see the faint outline of an inflatable boat moving toward the shore. The crafty Finn had outfitted the boat with a small electric trolling motor which, while not powerful, ran almost silently, emitting only the faint whirring sound of its propeller.

Justin stood up for a moment to stretch his legs, then said, "Okay, Starcher, you're next."

But there was another answering voice, a voice that chilled Justin's soul.

It said, "No one's next."

Twenty feet away, standing with his back to the wall of trees, was Alexander Zharkov, pointing a pistol at the two men.

A cloud crossed the moon, and the night went dark.

Starcher has a gun, too, Justin thought, the one he took from the Russian agent on the cabin cruiser. He remembered it as he found Starcher moving slowly away from him, separating the two men to give Zharkov two more difficult targets. It would be harder for the Russian to cover both men. If Justin could get Zharkov's attention solely on him, Starcher might be able to get to his gun and use it.

Starcher was talking to Zharkov while he continued to edge slowly away from Justin. He was not moving smoothly because Zharkov would immediately have noticed that. Instead, he was talking and taking steps, as if to punctuate his conversation.

"Now, don't do anything rash, Zharkov," said Starcher. "There isn't any need." Step.

"Shut up. What do you know about my need?"

"So your plan didn't work." Starcher held his hand out in front of him. Another step. "A lot of plans don't work. They won't blame you. Try again some other day." Another step.

"I told you, shut up. And stop moving."

The clouds grew thicker over the moon, and the night was becoming steadily darker. It was hard now for Justin to see Zharkov's face, although the Russian was no more than twenty feet away.

Justin moved a step to his left, away from Starcher, and dropped the rope he was holding. At that moment, Starcher reached behind him into his belt, pulled out the pistol and dropped to the ground.

A shot rang out.

Justin lunged forward, covering the distance to Zharkov in three long strides. With one swipe of his hand, he knocked the gun away into the heavy brush behind the Russian. With his left hand, he grabbed Zharkov's throat in a grip of steel.

He squeezed. He could feel the muscles tighten in the Russian's throat.

He heard a groan and looked back. Starcher lay on the ground, on his back, his gun lying useless at his side. The old man's body twitched in pain. He had been shot.

With a cry of rage, Justin swung his right fist into Zharkov's face and felled the Russian, then ran to Starcher's side. Behind him, Zharkov dropped like a wet cloth onto the rock table of the cliff.

Even in the darkness, Justin could see the red stain of blood spreading over Starcher's shirt. He had been shot in the right side.

"It's all right, Justin," said Starcher, his breathing labored. "Take care of yourself. This is a good way for me to die."

Suddenly Justin heard Zharkov's voice, choking on his own blood. "Katarina. Shoot him! Shoot him!"

The Grandmaster looked up as a woman holding a gun stepped from the other side of the semicircle of trees and walked deliberately toward him. She moved stiffly, zombielike, holding the gun low in front of her.

She walked up to him. Only a few feet separated them, and she began to raise the gun toward Justin.

The moon slipped out from behind the cloud. Suddenly, the rock plateau was flooded with light again as Justin looked up at her face, and his heart skipped as he recognized her.

Duma.

The girl of his boyhood at Rashimpur. The young girl who had died at Varja's hands.

She had the pistol pointed at Gilead's face, and then her face contorted, first with doubt, then confusion, then in blind pain. Two tears squeezed from the corners of her eyes and trickled down her cheeks.

Zharkov was scrambling to his feet. "Shoot him, Katarina," he shouted. His mouth sprayed blood. "Shoot him."

"Patanjali," Katarina Velanova whispered, "it is you."

"Shoot him," Zharkov screamed. "He is the Grandmaster. Kill him!"

Katarina didn't move. The pistol, shaking violently in her hands, was still aimed at Justin.

Justin felt tears welling in his eyes. *Duma.*

She was alive. The girl Varja had torn out of his heart had never died, after all. Now, after a lifetime of longing for her, he saw that she was alive.

And she belonged to Zharkov.

Fate had tricked him before, but this final cheat was more than he could bear.

"He was the one you were saved for," he said bitterly.

A sob escaped from her, as sudden as the snap of a thread. "I was made to hate you." She flung the gun away with distaste. "Patanjali, I was not saved," she cried. "I was dead. I am dead still."

Zharkov ran across the plateau and picked up the pistol where Katarina had thrown it.

"No!" she screamed, and an instant before Zharkov pulled the trigger, she leaped at Justin, enveloping his body with her own.

The bullet took her in the back. Her body muffled the sound of the shot, but bits of flesh and a fine spray of blood spattered into the air, as visible in the bright moonlight as warm breath on a cold night. Katarina's widespread hands

slid down Justin's legs as she slipped bonelessly to the ground.
She landed huddled at his feet, the gaping red hole in her shirt
widening with bright blood.

Justin and Zharkov both stared at the crumpled figure for a
moment, stunned. Then, with an animal roar from deep inside
his throat, Justin sprang at Zharkov, knocking the gun from
the Russian's hand. He turned to flee, but Justin grabbed him
by the shoulder.

As if Zharkov were a child, the Grandmaster lifted him
over his head, walked to the edge of the cliff, and hurled him
over.

Zharkov screamed as he fell. The scream ended in a heavy,
wet thud as his body hit the hard-packed damp sand a hundred feet below.

Justin ran back to Katarina and knelt beside her. Gently he
lifted her to cradle her in his arms. Her eyes were open, but
not yet glazed with death. She coughed, and a spurt of blood
dribbled from the corner of her mouth. A drop of water fell
and mingled with the blood. Justin wiped it away, realizing
only then that he was touching his own tears.

She struggled to speak, but her breathing was raspy and
choking. ". . . always loved you," she said softly. Her eyes
melting into Justin's, she smiled. "But they made me forget."

It was the apology of a small girl, the little girl Varja and
Zharkov had not permitted her to remember, the young girl
Justin had loved.

"I always loved you, too, Duma," Justin answered. "And
I never forgot."

He lifted her in his arms to hold her against his chest. She
coughed again, spraying him with her blood. Then she sighed,
long and ragged, and her head dropped forward as if she were
trying to hide from the world inside Justin's arms, and he knew
she was dead.

Starcher groaned again.

With a start, Justin laid Katarina's body aside and went to
him. He had nearly forgotten the old man. Starcher's shirt
was soaked with blood. Without medical attention, he would
die, too.

Justin looked over the cliff edge and saw the Kutsenkos
sitting in the inflatable rubber boat with Saarinen. The Finn
was moving back and forth, parallel with the shoreline twenty
yards away, obviously deliberating whether to flee or stay.

Duma was dead. Nothing could change that now. But Starcher was alive. And he could live. One death Zharkov could not claim.

Justin called down, "We're coming. Starcher's hurt."

Easily, he lifted the CIA man and placed him across his shoulders, then started down the knotted rope, moving as swiftly and smoothly as if he were walking down a stairway.

When his feet touched sand, he ran toward the water. Saarinen had pulled the boat in close to shore and was wading ashore to help Justin. Together, they put Starcher into the small boat.

The CIA man looked up and saw Justin next to him.

"Stay with me," he said weakly.

"I will, Starcher. I will."

The Grandmaster jumped onto the bow of the rubber boat as Saarinen turned up the throttle on the electric motor and aimed it out to his waiting boat. The new *Kronen* was just a black speck far out in the water.

Justin looked back toward shore. On the sand, he saw the crumpled lump that was Zharkov's body.

The Black King had fallen at last. As he turned back to look toward Saarinen's boat his eyes caught something else, perhaps fifty yards away. But the moon again moved behind a cloud and the night darkened, and though he strained to see, the vision was gone. He was not sure what it had been. Birds, perhaps, coming to pick at Zharkov's eyes.

Five minutes later, they were on Saarinen's boat, running without lights, full speed toward Miami. Starcher was on the cot in the cabin. Justin knelt by his side as Dr. Kutsenko cleaned his wound.

"He's going to be all right," she said. "The bullet passed right through."

"His heart?" Justin asked softly.

"It seems to be all right," she said.

Saarinen had put the boat on automatic pilot and entered the cabin.

"I should charge you bastards double for this," he roared. He had a bottle of Finlandia vodka in his hand. "Shooting, fooling around, making me wait. Are you trying to make an old man of me? Making me crazy. I'm steaming toward Cuba and what am I hearing on the radio? That somebody tried to kill Fidel Castro, and it's probably the work of the crazy

imperialist Yankees. Is that what I have on my boat now?
Assassins?''

"We saved Castro's life," Justin said simply.

Saarinen paused, then roared again. "Well, aren't you the
idiot? They're blaming it on you people anyway."

Justin saw Starcher's eyes open. The CIA man was smiling
faintly.

"It's all right," Starcher said softly.

"So what'd we accomplish?" Justin said.

Starcher spoke softly. "Sure, they can blame it on us. But
they'll figure out the truth, Justin. And when they do . . . you
watch. Castro will start being a lot nicer to the United States.
Maybe we made a friend for America, Justin."

"Be quiet and rest," Dr. Kutsenko said. "Is there anything
you want?"

Starcher grinned. "Yes. A cigar."

Justin stood on the rear deck of the boat. Cuba was far
astern now, out of sight, but he kept looking in that direction.

He thought of Duma lying dead on the top of the cliff.

Hers was the most crushing death of all. Everything he had
ever loved had died at Zharkov's hands. She had thought him
Patanjali, but he was not Patanjali. Justin Gilead was a fake,
a fraud who had learned some physical tricks, enough to keep
him alive while others died.

But no more.

Zharkov was dead; the Prince of Death was no more. And
Justin would soon join him in death.

But he wished he had had time to go over to Zharkov's
body and wring its neck. He wanted to feel the last pulse of
Zharkov's life under his fingers and to feel it vanish through
his hands.

But enough. Zharkov was dead. The game was over.

He remembered the dark lump that had been Zharkov,
lying on the sand as their little boat moved away from the
shore. And he remembered the other thing he had seen. He
tried to focus his concentration and his memory, to try to
make the picture come clear in his mind. It was like a chess
position; if he allowed himself to flow into his memory, to
become his memory, the picture would come clear, unbidden,
into his mind.

He stared up blankly toward the bright moon and let his

eyes drift out of focus. Slowly, fuzzily, the thing he had seen in the water began to take shape, to form, to become visible.

And then the full picture burst into his mind like a skyrocket, going off, flaring into color, forcing him to blink and turn away.

In that brief glimpse under the moonlight, he had seen not birds, but men.

Four men, dark, crouched, running, their faces painted black.

Varja's men.

Coming for the Prince of Death.

Was it over? Would it ever be over?

He lowered his face to his arms.

The Grandmaster wept.

Book Six
___

THE RESIGNATION

CHAPTER FORTY-THREE

Time to die.

Justin huddled in the hollow of snow he had dug for himself. It was night in the mountains near Amne Xachim, and so cold that his spittle froze and cracked in midair.

He had been waiting for death most of his life. From his youth, when he lost Duma, to the massacre of the monks at Rashimpur, to the razing of the Polish village where a woman who had cared for him had died in his place, he had longed for the final release of death.

There had been times when he could actually feel its proximity, roaring and mighty, its bloody jaws agape. At other times, death taunted him from a distance, smiling slyly at his fear. But it was always present, always waiting, always offering up its cold, irresistible promise to him.

But each time he had reached out to embrace it, death had skittered away like a coy girl. He had died for the first time at Rashimpur. It had been death's first joke. It had taken him through the pain of dying only to send him back to suffer the pain of living. And he had died again, in Poland. That, too, had been a trick.

But now was the third time, the third death. And this death would be the true one, because he would inflict it himself.

First Zharkov, then Justin Gilead. When the Prince of Death was finally, truly destroyed, the Grandmaster would at last be free.

It was time.

He lifted himself out of the sheltering womb of snow and continued walking. By dawn he was making his way over the ice-blown steppes with their hidden caves. He stopped short as he passed the cave where long ago, before he had grown to need the sweet, sick lust of death, he had once loved a girl.

Why did it have to be this way? The freezing air burned his lungs. Why? Why were Varja's women murdered? Why did Rashimpur have to burn? Why had Yva Pradziad been killed in the burned village in Poland? Why had he found Duma again, after a lifetime of longing for her, only to lose her a second time?

He had no answers. Perhaps his life had been no more than a monumental game of chess that he had played badly. Perhaps things would have been quite different if he had not been born Patanjali, reincarnation of the spirit of Brahma—or, more accurately, if Tagore and the other monks at Rashimpur had not believed him to be Patanjali.

That was the most bitter aspect of Justin's whole terrible existence; it had been based on a lie. He was not Patanjali; of that he was certain. Brahma would not have permitted his spirit to live in a man who had failed so often, and so miserably.

But the monks had been innocents. They believed in magic. Now they were dead. Nearly everyone who had ever befriended Justin Gilead had been destroyed. And Rashimpur, created by the hand of Brahma the Creator himself in the beginning of the world, was burned to ash.

He would visit Rashimpur—the rubble that remained of it—one last time. After he found Zharkov and killed him. After the Prince of Death and the evil legacy that spawned him were eliminated forever, he would go back. To the ashes of the Tree of the Thousand Wisdoms, to the spirits of his dead brothers, to the place where Tagore's precious blood had spilled. He would go back and join them all one last time.

His spirit would not rest with theirs, because the monks of Rashimpur were holy men, and Justin, in his way, had become as wicked as the man he sought to kill. But he could die where the holy men had died. Perhaps he would find peace in the final moments of his life. If he did, he would go gladly to damnation.

In the distance he could see the shimmering copper dome of Varja's palace. In the cold morning light, it shone like fire.

Everything I have ever loved has been destroyed by fire, he thought.

And so he knew what he would do to Varja's palace when he reached it.

He went no closer. Instead, he combed the area for scrub grass laid beneath the snow and for the brittle little bushes that had grown in summer and now lay brown and dry in the cold. When he had gathered enough, he bound the tinder with rope woven from the grass and dragged the bundle in a large circle toward the garden entrance to the palace.

The garden was bare and snow-covered now. Inside it, Justin stood for a moment and swallowed back the tears of remembrance for the girl who had seen herself for the first time in his eyes. But there was no time for tears anymore. Duma was gone. Tagore, Yva, the holy men of Rashimpur . . . all gone. He would have to put his regret aside, because it was his last day on earth, and it was going to end, not in tears, but in fire.

From his pocket he took two pieces of stone—one flint, one iron pyrite. They were firestones that he carried to warm him on his journey, but now they would serve a much greater function. He knelt down with the stones and a handful of kindling and struck the stones together.

A small spark flew. He struck again, trying to shelter the stones and kindling from the wind, but the kindling would not catch. Even in the freezing cold, sweat poured down Justin's face. Why wouldn't they work? Throughout his long journey to the mountains, the firestones had never failed.

Then he heard it. A deep, soft laugh, neither masculine nor feminine. He looked up and gasped. A small, bald, gnomelike creature stood in front of him in a place where a moment ago had been only air.

Justin clutched the firestones tightly. The little person who had walked so silently that he'd seemed to materialize out of nowhere pulled a long leather thong from out of his robe.

Justin threw the firestones. He aimed for the gnome's head, but the creature's movements were so fast they were almost a blur. Before Justin's eyes could follow the gnome's changing positions, the strip of leather cracked through the air, winding with a slap around Justin's chest and arms.

As he landed, Justin heard a snap and knew that one of his

ribs was broken. In his pain, his only thought was of the strange little being who had bested him so easily. How could he move so fast? Justin hadn't seen speed like that since his early days at Rashimpur.

A monk, Justin realized with sudden certainty. The little man had once been a holy man, as well trained as he himself had been.

The monk drew nearer. "You are from Rashimpur," he said, his face expressionless.

Justin struggled to keep the pain of the cracked bone in his chest from his voice. "As are you."

The monk nodded. "My training was at Rashimpur. But I have always belonged to Varja."

"Belonged?" Justin asked, trying to stall for time as he worked the leather knots behind his back.

"Our tie is deeper than this life," the monk said. "My ancestors were of the sect of the Black Hats. You know of them, perhaps?"

Justin didn't respond.

A faint twitch of amusement played at the corners of the monk's mouth. "The most powerful beings on earth."

"The Black Hats no longer exist."

The monk's eyes flashed. "Only because of a fool and his tricks. Patanjali was an old man who believed that the spirit of life was stronger than the magic of death. Through trickery, he destroyed our people, but he could not destroy the magic of the Black Hats forever."

A note of passion had crept into the monk's voice. "The magic remained, unharnessed and wild, through centuries. While the Black Hats faded into oblivion, there were many new incarnations of Patanjali, but none powerful enough to evoke the sleeping spirits of the Black Hats."

"Then why do you bother to serve Varja?" Justin asked.

"A generation ago, Sadika, the sage of Rashimpur, predicted that the true Patanjali would be born once again. That was when the spirits of the Black Hats awoke again in anger. I left Rashimpur then to follow the living goddess of evil, who has waited through ages of oblivion to exact her revenge."

Justin tried to struggle out of his bonds, but the knots were perfect. The monk watched him, smiling.

"Take me to Varja!" Justin cried.

"You have no need to see the goddess. You cannot even

fight me, and my power is mortal. Varja reserves herself for the great, not the weak and unworthy of the world.'' He spoke near Justin's face, enjoying his captive's humiliation.

It was the moment Justin had been waiting for. Spinning where he lay, Justin retracted his legs and then kicked with all his strength. The monk crashed against the wall of the palace.

The monk cried out in anger. In one bound he was up and grasping the thong that held Justin, lifting him into the air and whirling Justin's much heavier body as if it were a toy attached to a string.

The monk let go. His aim was flawless. Justin fell in a heap inside the doorway, in the empty room that had once been the living quarters of the palace women. As he tried to right himself, he felt a vicious kick to the side of his head, smashing it against the floor. He passed out.

He came to in another room he remembered, a stark white room devoid of furniture except for a high, square platform. Duma once lay there, he thought. For how long? Years? She still looked young when Justin saw her for the last time. She had been robbed of her life while she still lived, just as Justin had.

He felt for the knots on the thong. The monk's exertions had stretched the leather. In time, he would be able to loosen them enough to free himself. He worked frantically, trying hard to focus with his still fuzzy vision on the little man.

The monk was straining at a corner of the bare white wall. His fingers made a hollow sound on it. It's made of metal, Justin thought. But what is he doing? Then, surprisingly, the wall itself slid open, and the monk threw Justin through the opening.

His broken rib throbbed, but Justin forced himself to think while he continued to manipulate the leather thong. Was he outside? It took a moment for his eyes to adjust to the darkness. There was no ceiling that he could see, but he was still indoors, in some sort of cavernous corridor. Flickers of light shone dimly from an area some distance away, along with the faint, smoky fragrance of incense. Another chamber?

Varja's quarters, Justin realized. Of course. He was in another section of the palace. During his visit, he had not seen the goddess until his final day in the Sacred Chamber. The women who served her did not normally see her, either. If Varja was anywhere in the palace, it would be here.

One hand slipped free. A flood of relief washed through him, but he could not give himself away too quickly. Grasping the loose ends of the thong tightly to hide them from view, he allowed the monk to drag him down the dark corridor.

At the far end, where the open doorway let out the scent of incense, some flickering light danced on the polished wood floor. But the monk was taking Justin in the opposite direction, toward deeper darkness.

He heard men's voices somewhere, muffled and distant. Men? He remembered the black-painted faces of the men who had executed the young women of the harem while Justin looked on helplessly. The same ones who had come for Zharkov. But where were they?

They stopped before an expanse of darkness that caught the distant light in a sheet. Iron, Justin thought. Another metal door. Like the wall in the Sacred Chamber, the black iron door slid open at the monk's touch. Immediately the sound of voices grew louder and more distinct. Now Justin knew where they were coming from. Below, in the cellar of the great palace, lived a teeming mob of Varja's laborers.

"I must see Varja," Justin demanded. "This is my warning to you."

The monk turned to him. There was hatred in his eyes. "Do you think I do not know who you are . . . what you are?" He kicked Justin around to face him. "Patanjali," he sneered, "Varja will never see you. I will spare her the odor of your presence."

He spat. Then, preparing to kick Justin into the dark human-filled hole, the monk took a step backward.

It was the moment to strike. Justin threw his arms open in a wide arc, knocking the monk off balance. As the leather thong flew away from him, he spun and struck the monk in the face. With a high scream, the monk fell head first into the stinking pit. There was a sudden silence broken only by the little man's frightened wail as he fell with a thud and the crack of small bones.

Justin looked into the pit. It was so deep that the black-painted men, lit by the flames from a huge fire pit, seemed to swarm like rodents far below. There were no stairs leading to the metal door from the depths of the cellar, only a worn rope ladder rolled into a scroll at its top.

The pit was at one end of the corridor. Justin reasoned that the room on the other end, where the faint light glowed, must be the one in which Varja waited. He walked slowly toward the light.

As he neared, the light grew brighter. With an unseen evil force that made the hair on his neck stand on end, the dim flickering light pulsated and brightened until it spilled out of the incense-filled room like a vague, shapeless entity.

Justin stopped, frozen. The light expanded, seeming to take on a life of its own, as it moved from the room into the corridor. The area where Justin stood, once nearly black with darkness, was now awash with a blinding cold light that moved, slowly and inexorably, toward him.

In the center of the light was a vision. A dream, Justin thought, a trick of the eyes. But he knew it was no dream. It was Varja herself, iridescent, shimmering with pure, violent light, more beautiful than any mortal woman.

She was painted, as she had been on the night of Justin's rite of manhood, with a third eye in the center of her forehead. But where he had once viewed her as disgusting, he now found her irresistible. The third eye was the focus of the light. It was blackness, the beginning. It was the center of Varja's death-nurtured spirit.

"You sought to burn me with your pitiful fire," she said mockingly.

Justin could not speak. He tried to turn away, but the light that burned from her compelled him to look. Her beauty was terrifying, hypnotic. It carried the eternal fascination of death.

"You cannot burn me, fool." Her face, with its three eyes, seemed to look into his very soul and judge it to be contemptible. "You know that you are weak. You have failed in every poor attempt you have made against me. The force behind me is too strong for you, nameless, spineless man. I am too strong, and my prince is too strong. He was strong enough to kill the woman he loved. She was the same woman you loved, coward. But you could not save her. Or the others. You had to let them all die. In the end, it was your weakness that killed them." She pointed a finger at Justin. He sank, groaning, to his knees.

"Would you like to see fire?" She smiled, and the smile grew into a loud, sadistic laugh. "Here is your fire."

She held out her hand. A spark flew from the tips of her

fingers and gathered into a ball, growing as it rolled at tremendous speed toward Justin. It filled the corridor. There was no place for him to hide from it.

His clothes ignited instantly when the fire touched him, burning his skin like a bucketful of boiling oil. Screaming, he fell back into the pit. He landed atop the lifeless body of the monk.

"Kill him," she breathed, so softly that it was less a spoken command than a thought. Then she said the words again, shrilly: "Kill him!"

She raised her arms, and a wall of flame rose up in the pit, encircling the terrified men. "Kill him or die in the flames of my anger!"

As the men watched, still unable to comprehend the powerful magic they had just witnessed, the luminous vision of Varja the goddess disappeared. In its place was blackness and emptiness—a closed metal door. She had never been. Yet the flames were real.

The men shouted, running wildly to put out the fire, but it surrounded them. One of them approached Justin, pulling a long-bladed knife out of his waist wrap. He spoke a bastard version of Hindi. "You have done this to us."

Another followed him, also unsheathing his knife. "Kill him," he said. "The goddess will put out the fire when he is dead."

"She cares nothing for you," Justin said. "You are merely a horde of murdering beasts, and death by fire is too good for you."

"Kill him!"

"You will not kill me as easily as you killed the helpless women on the steppes. You." He pointed at the leader. "Fight me."

The man's dirty face broke into a grin. "I'll fight you. And I'll kill you, too."

"Try," Justin said.

The leader jabbed, long and quick. Just before the knife touched Justin, he kicked the blade out of the man's hand, caught it, and in the same motion slit open the man's throat.

"For the women you butchered," he said.

He took the second man by the arm, broke it behind the man's back, and threw him into the flames.

A third bludgeoned him from behind. Justin felt the club a moment before it struck, and flattened himself on the floor to escape the blow. It was a mistake. In his prone position, the men were on him in a swarm. A dirty heel ground into his hand, tearing off the burned skin. Beneath it, Justin's raw flesh lay exposed and bleeding.

As he tried to get up, another of the black-painted men kicked him. A third doubled his fists together and slammed Justin on the side of the head. Two strong arms grabbed him from behind and lifted him to his feet. As Justin opened his eyes, he saw the tallest of the mob, a giant more than seven feet in height, come at him with a knife glistening in his sweat-shiny hand.

He lunged for Justin's heart. Justin wriggled free, but not in time to miss the sharp point of the blade. It struck deep in his side, ripping open his flesh in a spurt of blood. Justin moaned. He slumped in the first man's arms as the tall man stood back, watching.

Justin lay still. His breathing ebbed and finally stopped. The old voices called to him again in the darkening recesses of his consciousness. *Come back, Justin. Come back, hide with your fears and weakness . . .*

The tall man, gasping for breath in the airless pit, raised his arms and shouted above the din of the men: "Varja! Our goddess and protectress, we have done your bidding. The one you call your enemy is dead. Stop your fire of wrath. Permit your servants to live."

There was no answer. The black metal door remained closed.

The man holding Justin threw his limp body to the dirt floor. "Cut him to pieces," he hissed. "Let nothing of him remain. Then will the goddess be satisfied."

Come back to us, the voices called, *where it is safe and warm and forgetting. This life is too hard. Come back now, and when you die, there will be no more pain, no more suffering. Allow yourself to find some comfort, some peace, some rest . . .*

But then another voice spoke, jarring and uncomfortable. It was Tagore's voice, as clear as if the old man were himself present. Whereas Varja manifested her power in resplendent light, Tagore's voice came from a pure void. But Varja's light was centered around the bottomless darkness of her third eye. The darkness of Tagore's presence was focused around a pinpoint of shimmering light. Justin's mind followed the light in the darkness, willing himself nearer Tagore.

"I hear you, teacher," he whispered.

Who are you?

"I am no one. I am nothing."

Do you fear death?

"No, master. I welcome it."

But you fear life.

"I . . . I cannot live. Varja's magic is too strong."

Then you believe in magic?

"I believe in all things now, my teacher. All is possible."

What is karma?

"A circle, master."

Past and present . . .

"The same."

Yin and yang, good and evil, light and darkness . . .

"The same."

Life and death?

The light was very close now.

"The same, my teacher."

Justin was bathed in light. But it was not Varja's blinding, fearful light of destruction. It was, instead, the light of the sun reflected on a rippling lake, and the cloudless sky of summer, and the sparkle in the eyes of an infant. And into this light came Tagore, again living and whole, his arms outstretched to Justin.

Come to me now, Patanjali, and embrace life. For now are you truly the Wearer of the Blue Hat, the bearer of light in the darkness. If you do not fear death, then you cannot fear life. Go forth and do what you must. For life.

Justin walked into Tagore's arms. The old man's spirit suffused him with a calm power, pure and perfect. For a moment, Justin felt as if he were not made of flesh at all, but solid energy. He opened his eyes.

His own blood was everywhere. The tall man was withdrawing his dagger from Justin's chest.

"He's still alive!" one of the men cried.

"Surely this is no mortal."

"Try again. You have missed his heart."

The tall man lunged.

If you do not fear death, then you cannot fear life.

Uncoiling, Justin sprang upward, knocking the knife out

of the man's hand. He saw his own blood spatter on the faces
of his astonished attackers and sizzle on the hot stone floor.
With a slap, he sent the tall man sprawling to the ground. He
kicked out instinctively behind him. One of the men fell,
doubled over. Justin made his way through the mob like a
spirit, unfeeling, mindless of the airless heat, smashing whatever was in his way.

One of the men ran toward him, crouching. Justin leaped,
spinning, to land on the man's back. From there, he cata-
pulted himself onto the stone wall, now dry from the tongues
of flame that licked up its sides, and clung to it. The stone
was blisteringly hot, and there was no air to breathe except
the sooty black film that rose from the licking flames, but
Justin felt nothing anymore. He had chosen life, with its pain
and suffering and defeat. He was not afraid.

Those who were still conscious watched with amazement
as the dying man inched his way upward over the rough, hot
stone. He was surrounded by flames, and the trail of his
blood flowed beneath him, drying from the heat before it
reached the floor.

"He, too, is a god," someone whispered.

He was answered by a deafening roar as the flames burst in
an explosion of fire. The screams of the burning, suffocating
men filled the pit with a horrible din as they scratched at the
stone walls. The body of the monk had been consumed by
flames, and the smell of burning flesh was acrid and nauseating.
Justin felt his own legs burning, but he continued to climb,
one hand, one foot after the other.

He reached the top. Swinging his legs to the ledge at the
base of the iron door, he pulled himself erect, and with his
blistered, skinless hands, opened the door.

The rush of incoming air gave new life to the fire below.
The bodies of the men were completely engulfed in fire.
Only their dying moans could be heard now, and the sight
was a vision of the disembodied spirits of a Christian
hell.

For a moment, he wondered if his own afterlife would
resemble the scene in the fire pit. It was no less than he
deserved. Varja has destroyed by fire everything I have ever
loved, he thought. It was the way of the Black Hats, consuming,
complete. She and her kind could never see the magic of
water that melts rock, or of running sap in spring, or of the

sweet sky at morning. The magic of the Blue Hat is small compared with hers. Will my soul, with its broken karma, be made to burn also?

He walked back into the corridor. Although the flames were already licking at the opening, it felt cool to him. He walked toward the dim, flickering light in the room at the end of the hallway. As he approached, he could hear the faint tinkling of a bell. It seemed to call to him, beckoning him with its shrill, mocking beauty.

He was tired, so tired. The effort in the fire pit had exhausted him. His wounds hurt. His head slumped with weakness. Inside the room, he knew, Varja and Zharkov would be waiting for him. He had nothing left to fight them with. Zharkov was a strong man, and Varja's magic was the magic of the Black Hats. Justin had no weapon but the peace Tagore had finally placed in his heart. The effort of a lifetime, he thought sadly, had been for nothing. But he was not afraid.

This is where it will end.

The thought did not anger him. There was no more hatred in his heart. *Tagore and the others have died, just as I myself shall soon die. Zharkov, too, will be ashes in a blink of Brahma's eye and, in time, even Varja herself will fade into oblivion.* He remembered a prayer he had recited as a boy at Rashimpur:

> *All winds, all seas,*
> *all the heavens and earth will grow*
> *and die and pass away to nothing.*
> *I give myself up to the eternal sands.*

He walked into the high, vaulted room. The sound of the bell solidified into a pinpoint of black in the center of the room. Around the darkness grew the cold, unearthly light Justin had seen before. Out of the light grew the magnificent image of Varja the goddess, triumphant in her victory. And beside her stood Zharkov, the Prince of Death, his hooded eyes gleaming with malicious strength, his body clothed in silver.

"Where is your magic, Wearer of the Blue Hat?" Varja teased.

"I have no magic," Justin answered.

The goddess smiled. "You are dying. You cannot even heal yourself."

"If it is my destiny to die, then I will die."

Varja laughed. "Very well. My prince will help your destiny."

She looked at Zharkov, and the Prince of Death raised his right hand high. In it, out of the darkness, appeared a gleaming silver sword.

"Now," Varja commanded. "The world is yours. The Wearer of the Blue Hat can fight you no more."

Zharkov brought the blade singing downward. Justin did not resist. The sword struck him on his right wrist, severing his hand. Justin looked at the bloody stump of his arm. The pain was excruciating, but he did not cry out. If he was not afraid to die, he would not be afraid to live the moments before his death.

The goddess's eyes were furious. "His hand?" she shrieked. "Why did you not strike his head, his chest . . . ?"

"I tried," Zharkov said, bewildered. "The blade moved itself."

"But his *hand* . . ." She stared at the severed appendage, her body trembling with loathing. Then, as the hand on the floor began to glow, she whispered frantic incantations, backing away until she was pressed against the wall. The words spewed out of her mouth in a torrent.

No power came from her. The light that had surrounded her and Zharkov dimmed and vanished.

But the hand, invisible beneath its golden light, began to hiss.

"Patanjali," Varja sobbed. "Hail to thee . . . Hail to thee, Wearer of the Blue Hat . . ."

The hand had been replaced by a coiled golden snake.

"Spare me," she whispered.

"As you spared Tagore?" Justin asked. "As you spared Duma and the monks of Rashimpur? As your prince spared everyone who had ever shown me kindness?"

"Then take him," Varja pleaded. "He is your enemy. The man you call Zharkov was born in the same hour of the same day of the same year as you. As you live, he shall live as your opposite. Take him now to end the suffering of your own life. I beg you . . ."

But Justin no longer heard her. Another voice was speaking

to him now, the same voice he had heard a lifetime before, when a strange man had cornered a child in an alley in Paris. It was Tagore's voice, asking the same question it had then.

Is it your will?

Justin looked at the coiled snake, understanding nothing and everything. There was magic, but it was not his. It belonged to the Wearer of the Blue Hat.

"It is my will," he said.

The snake uncoiled. Darting swiftly as a lightning bolt, it wrapped itself once around Varja's neck and struck in the black center of her third eye.

Varja shuddered. A drop of bright blood appeared in the middle of her forehead. She closed her eyes and seemed to shrink before him. The smooth skin of her face began to wrinkle and crack. Knotted veins stood out on the backs of her hands. Her black hair turned white and fell out in matted clumps. Her cheeks hollowed; her red-painted lips opened, and she spat out the brown stubs of her teeth. Then she sank slowly, her brittle bones unable to support her, as her flesh dried on her skull and the skull itself rolled onto the folds of the sumptuous gown that lay rumpled on the floor, covered by the ashes of a hundred thousand years.

And resting on her garment was a small snake the color of pure gold.

When there was nothing left of her, the snake uncoiled itself and slithered up Justin's body to his wrist, where it wound itself around the stump tightly. It glowed for a moment, then was gone. In its place was Justin's restored hand.

Horrified, Zharkov turned panic-filled eyes toward Justin. He brought the sword up high overhead and slashed downward with all his strength. Justin reached up and shattered the blade. Silver shards sprayed around the chamber, tinkling like a thousand bells.

Zharkov ran frantically from one end of the room to the other. The fire had reached the main floor of the palace, and the doorway of the vaulted chamber was filled with flames licking at the inner walls. There was no escape except through the wall of flame.

Screaming, Zharkov rushed headlong into the fire.

Justin followed him, feeling the flames burning him, but indifferent to the pain. Zharkov was straining at the door to the white Sacred Chamber, but it had been sealed closed by